STEALTH

STEALTH

Guy Durham_____

G. P. PUTNAM'S SONS   *New York*

G. P. Putnam's Sons
Publishers Since 1838
200 Madison Avenue
New York, NY 10016

Library of Congress Cataloging-in-Publication Data

Durham, Guy.
    Stealth: a novel/by Guy Durham.—1st American ed.

    p. cm
    I. Title.
PS3554.U683S74   1989   89-3993 CIP
813′.54—dc20
ISBN 0-399-13503-0

Printed in the United States of America
1 2 3 4 5 6 7 8 9 10

ACKNOWLEDGMENTS

To the dean of literary agents, Sterling Lord;
my surgically gifted senior editor, George Coleman;
Don Rumbelow, of the City of London Police;
Manny Kapelsohn, who taught me Front Sight;
and, most of all, my family—
more thanks than I can ever express.

"*Cruelty has a human heart,*
And Jealousy a human face;
Terror the human form divine,
And Secrecy the human dress."

—WILLIAM BLAKE
A Divine Image

1
ROUTE 58,
THE MOJAVE DESERT,
CALIFORNIA

It was nearing nightfall, and the sunset threw reddish glints off the big car's metal as it moved east. The driver's eyes scanned the highway ahead for the abandoned gas station coming up on the left.

At this time of day, a lone California Highway Patrol cruiser was known to inhabit the weed-strewn area just behind and to one side of the gas station, lying in wait for speeders tempted by this long and lonely, ruler-straight stretch.

The driver, a man of lean, dark appearance, saw the cruiser in its customary position and began pressing the accelerator. He watched the needle creep slowly past seventy. Then eighty. Then ninety.

There was a searing screech of tires, and dust swirled and billowed as the cruiser hurled itself forward. Its prey continued along the highway, keeping its course seemingly without concern. Inside the civilian car, the driver flexed his fingers on the steering wheel.

The cruiser's flashing lights suddenly came alive in the rearview mirror. The driver backed off the accelerator, flicking the signal lever up, easing the big car onto the shoulder of the road.

Waiting for the trooper to exit his cruiser and come alongside, the dark man placed his hands high on the steering wheel where they could be seen.

The sky was darkening. Off somewhere to the west, thunder-clouds were building and, for a change, the wind off the Mojave felt cool, almost damp. No other vehicles were visible on the roadway.

The tall officer walked alongside the big car and halted just before coming up to the driver's door. He took care to be in a textbook position where the door couldn't be swung suddenly into his body, and where the driver, if armed, would have to swivel awkwardly to bring the trooper within his cone of fire.

"Step out of the vehicle, please," the trooper instructed, the heel of his hand resting on the butt of his duty weapon.

The driver, nodding slightly, kept one hand on the wheel and used the other to press the door lever. As the door opened, the trooper's final flickering thought was that the driver was dressed in a uniform shirt somewhat like his own.

At that moment, the driver gave an almost imperceptible pull on a wire next to the door lever, and the barrel of the 12-gauge shotgun mechanism concealed within the doorframe roared, and flame shot from the ugly twin holes in the door's edge.

The trooper took a massive discharge of double-O buckshot in his lower torso, which immediately severed the spinal column and right hand.

The dark man removed his keys from the ignition, stepped out over the trooper's body, walked around to his own vehicle's trunk, and opened it. He returned to the trooper's corpse and, pulling it behind him by the one remaining hand, moved slowly around to the yawning trunk and lifted the body inside, taking care to avoid the blood and fluids.

A small ANFO-type explosive device, its nitromethane and ammonium hydrate components separated by a magnesium foil membrane, was already held in place by a magnet inside the trunk.

After carefully arming it, the driver cleansed his hands with a solution from a small bottle, then used paper toweling to wipe off fingerprints from the steering wheel, keys, door handle, and the door apparatus. The device would detonate within three minutes, incinerating the car and its contents, but the man never left anything to chance.

Pausing only to scoop up the trooper's fallen citation book from the roadside gravel, he moved swiftly to the highway patrol cruiser, switched on the ignition, and pulled out onto the highway.

2
DARTMOUTH, DEVONSHIRE

A lone English oak commanded the hilltop, a tree which—owing to its great size and age—surveyed the valley with no little dignity.

Against one side of its trunk leaned a 496 cc. Norton International motorcycle, circa 1935, its original deep green finish polished within an inch of its life.

On the opposite side of the tree, his back against its trunk, sat the Norton's seventh and current owner, Michael Pretorius.

The rough bark felt good against his back, and every so often Pretorius adjusted his position for the pleasure of feeling it rub against his sweatshirt and his back underneath.

A scar—in places an inch wide—crossed his back in a diagonal line. Along its course, the skin was somewhat puckered and stretched, and the scratching of the bark felt soothing, almost sensual.

His feet were bare, and the thick green grass felt good between his toes. He tapped one foot as he played the tattered remnants of a Bessie Smith blues on his harmonica.

He came here often in the early evenings, gathering tranquility about him like a cloak as he played, looking over the rolling green patchwork quilt of the Devon landscape.

His only audience was a group of three silent Hereford cows who regularly came to listen, and to stare.

His playing seemed to awaken some long-forgotten bovine interest in the blues, and they would gaze at Pretorius until he would finish his music, and then they would amble away, satisfied and lowing.

As he played, he watched the blue-gray mist settle over the hills, floating downward like a silk veil. The birds slowly hushed, and his harmonica was now the only sound in the landscape.

Pretorius was not an especially good harmonica player, but that had never bothered him. The important thing was to have a good time.

His muscles felt good and limber, more relaxed than they'd been in years. Lately he'd been spending afternoons out sailing on the River Dart, and his tanned skin, contrasting with his sun-bleached hair, gave him a healthy, attractive look— although nobody would ever think of Pretorius as handsome. His blue eyes turned down a little too much at the corners, giving him, no matter what his mood, a slightly melancholy expression.

His jaw, though good and strong, was a little too wide; his nose was slightly offset, a souvenir of some long-forgotten fight. And Pretorius' blondish hair, perpetually in need of cutting, fell over his forehead in an untamable lock.

He stopped his harmonica playing in mid-phrase. His eyes narrowed for better focus. Again he'd seen the glint of glass flashing in the sun, down in the tall grass near the road. Binoculars, more than likely.

He was, he realized, under surveillance. For about a week he'd begun to notice small things. Heard rumors of people asking about him, apparently for the most innocent of reasons. And had even detected several drops in the line volume on his telephone.

He'd gotten a curious phone call from his friend Donald Catchpole, up in London with Special Branch. Catchpole hadn't identified himself, but had uncharacteristically asked Pretorius to call him from a booth, leaving a number which Pretorius didn't recognize. Catchpole said some people from the States, senior spook types, had been asking questions about Pretorius. Questions that sounded as if they already knew the answers.

Pretorius knew those questions. Once upon a time, he'd asked them himself for a living. Someone was very interested in him, someone official and in the intelligence community.

Pretorius sighed and began pulling on his boots. Paying no more attention to the silent watcher below, he leaned the Norton away from the tree, mounted, and kicked it into life.

As usual, the old bike responded to the first kick and opened up with a throaty purr like a cat in a creamery. Pretorius drifted the bike downhill, away from the silent observer, toward the split in the woods that led to an old portion of Roman road.

The road, like most of those crisscrossing this part of Devon, ran about twelve feet below the surface of the fields on either side of it, its limestone walls rimed with vegetation.

As the Norton sped down the road, Pretorius enjoyed the cool wind in his face and thought of how much he genuinely loved this part of the world.

He flexed the long muscles in his shoulders and thighs as he rode, feeling glad to be alive. It was cooler and darker down in the road now, and he switched on his headlamp to light the way.

Pretorius' cottage was made of fieldstone, built about the time of Waterloo by a farmer who'd been a devout believer in durability. The walls were almost two feet thick and would easily last for centuries past Pretorius' own lifetime. It was joined to a similarly built but even more ancient barn, the possessor of some admirable hammer beams.

Pretorius lived simply here in southern Devon. His income came partly from a monthly disability check mailed from a U.S. Treasury accounting center in Austin, Texas, and partly from a small inheritance from his family. The amount was not enormous, but in Devon it gave him the ability to live well. It was peaceful here; the precise opposite of the life he'd lived for eight years in considerably different parts of the world.

His neighbors thought him eccentric. But then, to most of them, Americans were an odd lot anyway.

He twisted the throttle down and let the bike drift downhill the last few hundred feet to the front of his cottage. Swinging off while it was still in motion, he wheeled the old Norton into his forecourt and then through the great open doorway of the old barn.

After covering the bike for the night with an ancient horse blanket to shield it from the dust, Pretorius came inside the cottage and lit a few lamps. Rubbing his hands, he walked over to the fireplace and built a small fire of paper and twigs, blowing to breathe life into it.

The dry kindling crackled as the fire suddenly caught the chimney's draft. Kneeling on the hearth, Pretorius placed some lumps of coal in the fire. Most evenings at home, he preferred a coal fire for its soft, blue glow and its steady warmth. And, of course, the fact that he didn't have to be forever poking at it.

Tonight he had some thinking to do. Somebody, somewhere, was too interested in him. And that was never a good thing.

He'd spent a little over twelve years as a working spook, most of it with DIA (Defense Intelligence Agency, intelligence arm of the U.S. Department of Defense). And then one fine spring day, he'd been dumped with a medical discharge after an incident along the East German border.

In many ways, he'd been glad to end it. If you're at all good in the trade, there comes a time when they either take what you do too much for granted—because most section heads eventually lose their touch for the field—or they simply keep pulling you out of the hat for last-ditch stuff, knowing some day you'll either fuck up or go up against somebody better, but they don't really care because at those times there's just no alternative. You try to say to yourself it doesn't matter that nobody cares much, but it still eats at you. You lose sleep, and your nerves get shot, and still you keep on, knowing all the while you're losing your edge, bit by bit.

Before they finally canceled his ticket, Pretorius had been constantly working the borders, never knowing when his particular cover would disintegrate, or when someone would roll up his small, carefully built network: a first-rate source of troop and materials movements of Warsaw Pact members. Pretorius had lined up a half dozen field-grade operatives, including an electronics technician in the DDR's armored corps.

The technician had tossed up a list of Soviet tank corps radio frequencies, together with formulas for their periodic change-overs.

Pretorius' bosses, of course, rated this as prime meat, as it could gain critical extra hours spotting armored movements as a prelude to any cross-border invasion. Pretorius had several commendations added to his file, now beginning to be thick with promise. Still, despite his successes, Pretorius' work began to bother him. Not because he didn't appreciate its value, but because it didn't permit a personal life that involved such simple, impossible things as trust or freedom. Things which most people were able to enjoy so often that they took them for granted.

But then, most people weren't spooks.

Settling back in the cradling comfort of his leather wingchair, looking deeply into the flames, Pretorius saw it all again: One night near Nordhausen, as he was crossing the border back into West Germany, a moonless sky exploded into day with flares and *Maschinenpistole* fire.

He zigzagged through the minefield with one of his operatives, a woman who—as her price for years of sending information west—had only asked for freedom. The woman was literally blown into oblivion as she panicked, ran, and stepped directly on a mine. Pretorius ran after her and was close—very close—to her just as the mine exploded.

Lifted by the force of the blast, Pretorius was flung six to eight meters, finding himself sprawled on the churned earth, stunned and temporarily blinded. He raised himself slowly on all fours, a red mist whirling, spiraling in slow motion before his eyes. He heard the dogs and soldiers running toward him, and he began crawling in the opposite direction.

More fire erupted and Pretorius got to his feet, unable to see, and simply ran from the terrible sounds toward what he hoped was the West. Machine pistol fire spurted again and creased his back, but he couldn't feel it. Faster and faster his knees pumped, moving his bleeding legs against all odds, propelling his body in a thrashing windmill-like parody of running, running, running through the rain until finally arms caught him and he smelled the rank dampness of wool uniforms as he sank into the utter peace of unconsciousness.

He awoke three days later in an unknown place, much of his face and body covered with bandages. Raising his mind through the mists of drug-dampened pain, he forced his lips to move and his diaphragm to push the breath that would make the sounds, but only an unintelligible murmur emerged. Exhausted, drained by the effort, he sank back into the mists of unconsciousness.

Much later, he came to and found three smiling men standing by his bed: one obviously a doctor, and the other two in military uniforms. Squinting the one eye that wasn't covered by gauze and tape, he forced the image into focus, and saw two United States Army officers in full uniform, each with the brass lapel device of I Corps.

"Hi there, fella," Number One said, grinning broadly. Number Two smiled just as broadly and said, "You're one shot-up cowboy. How're you feeling, ace?"

Pretorius' eye lost its focus. He forced the words out, *"Bitte? Ich kann Sie nicht verstehen. Wo ist meine Weibel? Wo bin ich denn?"* The two officers exchanged sharp glances. "Your old lady lost it back in the minefield, buddy. You're goddamn lucky to be alive. Now what's your name? How can we get you back to your unit?"

The fake hospital scene would have worked if only they had

chosen a room with windows. But Pretorius, having seen the West's own whitewashed windowless rooms of this sort before, had known at once he was still in East Germany, and not in the hands of friends.

Pretorius grimaced with the effort of speaking. *"Ich kann Sie doch nicht verstehen. Sind Sie Englisch? Bitte, haben Sie eine Zigarette?"*

Number One spoke quietly and authoritatively to the physician, and a hypodermic syringe was lifted from the tray on the table next to his bed. As it pricked his skin, then slid effortlessly into his vein, Pretorius experienced a flooding warmth and let it overtake him, knowing it must be an Amytal-based solution. He reminded himself firmly that he was Gerhardt Dieter Seedorf, a factory worker trying to escape West with his wife.

The interrogation took over a week.

His room was no longer the one in which he'd awakened to find the two *ersatz* officers. Instead, he found himself in a white-tiled laboratory of sorts, strapped onto a padded table, staring upward into a lamp similar to those seen in the more expensive dentists' offices, but brighter. Pretorius' head was immobilized by a device used by eye surgeons. His angle of vision was greatly restricted, and the intensity of the lamp made the contrast of the sides of the room too dark to penetrate. The light seemed to bore itself into his brain. Even with his eyes closed against it, the light came through his eyelids, amber-colored, insistent. When his eyes were open, and he moved them to attempt to see the rest of the room and his questioners, the image of the lamp, printed on his retina, moved with his gaze.

There seemed to be at least three interrogators, although he couldn't move his head enough to see them. In what he imagined to be the first few days (although there was no way to have any accurate idea of the passage of time), the first two seemed to take turns going over and over the same routine questions, again and again. He recognized the voice of Number One from the original pair of fake U.S. Army officers, the one with a slight nasal twang. The second had something of an English accent, although overlaid with a trace of something else Pretorius couldn't quite identify.

But it was the third, the one with the soft, almost slurring Eastern European accent, that Pretorius feared most. The voice was so oddly soothing, and yet so insistent, one instinctively wanted to confide in the speaker.

Pretorius thought of him as the Priest, for his voice reminded him of the rhythmic monotone in which the old Lutheran priest used to conduct services in the little church near Random Lake, when he was a boy. This voice, which always came from somewhere to the left of the lamp, and considerably farther away than the first two voices, was strangely lulling, relaxing. Pretorius wondered whether one could be put under deep hypnosis, and even autosuggestion, merely by the sound of a voice.

The Priest began to occupy more and more of the time, almost as if the first two had been used merely to set the stage.

His questions were usually about Pretorius'—or Seedorf's—childhood. Pretorius responded with an amended version of his own childhood, contoured to what he imagined that of a young *Leipziger* would have been.

The Priest trapped Pretorius constantly, catching him up in contradictions, scolding him for not knowing where his school had been, or the street on which his family lived when he was six.

The Priest's attitude was anything but sinister; it was, rather, that of a father coaxing an errant child to tell all, to gain the acceptance which was always just on the edge of being evident.

Soon Pretorius' resistance began to ebb, and he felt his volition slip away, as if pulled by an ethereal yet irresistible undercurrent.

And then they began the drugs in earnest.

Pretorius knew little from that point forward. Only, at one time, when he surfaced for a moment from the miasma of the drugs, he saw—or thought he saw—the head of the Priest for a moment. The man's head was a bald dome, strands of graying hair plastered straight across in a vain effort to conceal the gleaming pate. And then, before Pretorius' eyes could drift down to see the face below, and just as he caught a glimpse of light flashing off steel-rimmed spectacles, the drugs took him down again.

Finally, after an undetermined amount of time, the drugs were reduced, and he was—for the most part—conscious. The first two interrogators resumed, and Pretorius was questioned relentlessly in English and in German. He replied only to the German, and then only in a slang that would place him from somewhere near Leipzig. The CI people were good, very good. But so was Pretorius. Pretorius was subjected to massive injections of many drugs, and the disorientation of having the room lights on constantly, with trays of food brought at infrequent intervals—sometimes with a lunch tray being brought only an hour after his breakfast.

The attendants' watches were, he knew, being constantly reset to alter his perception of time, as his captors knew he would look at their wrists. But he knew the techniques and knew he had only to believe, really believe he was Dieter Seedorf in order to survive. He willed himself not to think of the other life, the other name.

They became fictional, not a part of his life and this place. He *was* Seedorf, alone in this small, glaringly lit room with the *Sicherheitsdienst* or the KGB or GRU or whoever the hell else they were. And, in the end, when they had found a Gerhardt Dieter Seedorf and his wife were missing from a suburb of Leipzig, and that the man's description fitted Seedorf's closely, he was released.

The cover had been put together tightly, and it seemed to hold.

Finally one day, he was moved in a windowless gray ambulance to a civilian hospital, where the staff labored to put him together again. After three months of crutches and bandages and painful physiotherapy, he was finally permitted to go home to Leipzig.

He surfaced in the *Bundesrepublik* three days later and placed a telephone call to his unit. He was picked up, flown into Andrews Air Force Base, and then moved to Bethesda Naval Hospital for plastic surgery, more therapy for his back muscles, and final debriefing.

And that was the end of his career.

The examining physician at Walter Reed declared him unfit for further active physical duty. He was offered the choice of remaining in the Agency at a desk job, or accepting early retirement at age thirty-eight.

He chose the latter and moved to this part of England so removed from the threat and turmoil that had been an integral part of his life. He had never looked back, except in relief—and now, when his tranquility had been disturbed.

The wind, kicking up outside, blew a shutter loose. It slammed hard, again and again, into the wall of the stone cottage, and Pretorius went outside to secure it.

It had turned bone-chillingly cold and damp. The trees—seen dimly now in the darkness—were spread stark and sere against the night sky. He pushed the errant shutter back in place, turned up the shutterdogs that held it in place, and re-entered the enveloping coziness of the cottage.

He drew the curtains over the windows and returned to the capacious leather chair next to the fire. Staring into the softening glow of the coals, Pretorius wondered who his unseen watchers were, and what they wanted.

3
DARTMOUTH, DEVONSHIRE

The next morning at six, Pretorius was—as usual—wakened by the sound of crows from the farm next door. A farm called, aptly enough, the Rookery.

Despite the farm's name, its owner was no fan of the genus *Corvus*. He'd tried everything to rid his fields of the quarrelsome birds, but had succeeded only in stirring them to even greater vocal heights. In the end, the harried farmer surrendered to nature, and let the crows have their way.

Pretorius, on the other hand, always enjoyed the sounds of the crows. To him, it was one of the pleasing eccentricities of Devon.

He lay in his bed a full half hour, listening to the sounds of the wakening outdoors. The early morning crows were now joined by a fairly diverse crowd. Mingling with the meadowlarks, robins, starlings, and curlews, he could hear the keening of a gull, and imagined it soaring in from the sea.

He thought of Susannah and imagined he could still smell her gentle fragrance in the room. He stared at the ceiling and recalled their conversation. Was it just last week?

In a rare fit of impatience, she'd accused him of never really opening up to her. "What are you *thinking?*" she'd ask time and again. "Can't you ever trust me to share your thoughts? Do you ever trust *anyone?*" she'd said, hurt filling those deep blue-green eyes.

He loved her, he knew. But trusting someone—anyone—was, by now, an alien act to him. For years it had been something reserved for other people, something unaffordable to anyone in his line of work. He even wondered if the ability to trust had been surgically removed from his psyche, carved away from him.

The process had begun years ago, at college.

The day before Pretorius was about to leave for Christmas vacation in his senior year, one of his instructors introduced him to a friend who'd known Pretorius's father. The friend was a naval officer stationed in Washington, in the Office of Naval Intelligence (ONI).

Pretorius had been planning on going on to graduate school, to MIT, to study metallurgical physics. He'd shown great promise at Yale: his undergraduate papers had been viewed as brilliant, and his professors saw a great future for him as a research scientist. But money was a problem. It had been hard enough making it through Yale on what little the lawyers sent him from his inheritance, still in trust.

His father's friend, though, offered a solution: Go into the Navy, first going through Officer's Candidate School, put three years in ONI, and the Navy would bankroll his education. Not only through his master's, but straight through to his doctorate. The Navy needed good, bright young men like him. Vietnam had just started to boil, and he'd likely be drafted anyway. Oh, and by the way, it would be better if he didn't mention any of this to anyone. Repeat: anyone.

Pretorius thought it over through the Christmas vacation, took a wistful look at his fast-dwindling financial resources, and called the man on January 7th. "Where do I sign?" he said.

An interview was arranged in New York. But first he had to take his application papers to the police precinct house on Charles Street and get fingerprinted. Later that week at ONI headquarters downtown, he was first given a bland, undemanding interview by a young two-striper, then given a two-hour battery of psychological tests. Afterward, the lieutenant said things looked good, and could he be ready for a review board day after tomorrow? Oh, and don't speak to anyone about this, either. Anyone.

Pretorius said he'd be there, and no he wouldn't speak to anyone. The lieutenant recommended he catch up on current events, as it would make the review go better.

Pretorius thanked him and proceeded to go to the Village and get blasted with a few of his friends. The next morning he found himself recumbent in the Mills Hotel on Bleecker Street, with an attractive though somewhat distraught young lady just pulling on her dress.

After exchanging a few pleasantries with the girl (whom he utterly failed to recall ever having met), he said goodbye and began making plans to end the gargantuan hangover which inhabited every atom of his body.

Much later, at a newsstand, he bought copies of *The New Republic*, *Time*, *Newsweek*, *National Review*, and *Foreign Policy*, and spent the evening hitting the books.

The next day, a freshly combed, shaved, and starched Pretorius sat in front of eight naval officers, each of imposing demeanor, each bearing the shoulderboards of full commander or captain.

The interview began easily enough, but then the officers began firing politically oriented questions: Was the Bay of Pigs invasion necessary in light of the communist threat to the Western Hemisphere? Was Castro hell-bent on exporting communism to the rest of the Americas, or was he simply a naive socialist who'd gotten control of a corrupt country, and was instituting the necessary nationalist reforms? Was communism actually a good thing for some countries, at certain stages of their emergence or evolution?

The interview lasted one hour and forty-five minutes, then

Pretorius was dismissed. The young lieutenant met him outside, made him sign a few more papers, and told him he thought he'd done well, that they usually don't spend that much time with candidates, and that he'd let him know the result in a day or two. And would he continue to treat all this in confidence? Pretorius said he would and once again thanked the lieutenant. The call, of course, came the next day, and he was told to report to an office in the old Brooklyn Naval Yard for initial processing.

From that point on, things moved quickly. One week after graduation from college, he was packed off to OCS, and after that to Little Creek, Virginia, for UDT training. He was constantly given all kinds of tests, from the GCT (General Classification Test, roughly similar to the Wechsler-Bellevue test), to tests for particular skills. Two showed up with near record-breaking scores: an uncanny ability in science and mathematics and a superb ear for languages.

Orders were cut sending him to the Naval Postgraduate School at Monterey, where he loped easily through German and Czech.

He was stationed next for nine months at the U.S. Naval Base at Guantánamo Bay, Cuba, until he was called in by his commanding officer one day and handed a peculiar set of orders. It seems he was to be assigned to temporary duty (TDY) in Fairfax, Virginia, with the Pentagon's Defense Intelligence Agency. His CO handed him the sealed orders with raised eyebrows and an oddly speculative look. This kid must have somebody big as his rabbi; ONI doesn't give up its star pupils all that easily.

Pretorius had attracted DIA's attention with his languages and an odd flair for both electronics and firearms, discovered during his early ONI training. At the Agency's school in Fairfax, he was schooled in field intelligence and CI (counterintelligence) techniques, far different than the more straightforward reporting and analysis activities of Naval Intelligence.

Pretorius felt a curious attraction to this kind of work. He soaked up subjects like cryptography and surveillance enthusiastically, and his instructors often included him in their after-hours drinking sessions in a roadside bar near the base, just outside Fairfax.

Somewhere in this period, Pretorius realized he could never tell anyone about his work, that he could never genuinely trust anyone with something that had become so central to his existence. He'd even signed agreements not to reveal anything of his ONI or DIA work after he left the service.

DIA also gave him training runs in D.C., doing surveillance on other agents in the same training program, running message relays with cutouts, setting up blind meetings, bugging hotel rooms, all the rest.

As part of his DIA coming-of-age, he also spent two weeks in Maryland at the National Security Agency at Fort George C. Meade. Known to its intimates as SIGINT (Signals Intelligence) City. There, he studied their impressive technologies, and made occasional forays into Baltimore to sample the crabs at Faidley's and Hausner's. Finally, when the Agency pronounced him ready, Pretorius was assigned to a Defense Intelligence unit working out of Frankfurt near the USAF facilities at Wiesbaden.

Almost single-handedly, he stopped a local honeytrap operation run by the East Germans from a house in Wiesbaden's Idstein Strasse. The trap employed several women who went so far as getting a few U.S. airmen in sensitive jobs to marry them. Pretorius, posing as an Air Force first lieutenant, wrapped up the operation in less than a month. His superiors felt he had a natural aptitude for the work.

Pretorius' term of service was nearing its end, and he was suddenly faced with a choice: go back to school, get his master's and his doctorate, and live the life of a research scientist, either working for a university or one of the big defense contractors—companies like Grumman, Northrop, General Dynamics—or continue in the intelligence trade. But by now he was hooked. No university and no corporation could ever drive his adrenalin

like CI work in the field. So he signed a contract as a full-time
DIA spook and forgot about the Grummans and the Berkeleys.

Now, lying in his own bed this morning, thinking of Susannah, he suddenly frowned, remembering the watcher of the day
before. Pretorius slid his legs over the bedside and stumbled
naked into the bathroom. His shower was an ancient affair suspended over a huge, deep-walled tub, with a brass showerhead
easily two feet wide. A canvas sheet was suspended from brass
tubing forming a four-foot circumference around the showerhead. Pretorius' occasional guests—including Susannah—hated
his shower, which produced a deluge like that in the main dance
sequence of *Singin' in the Rain*. But Pretorius loved the old con-
trivance and considered it one of his most valuable possessions.
The downpour from the enormous brass fount cleared his head
and, after a shave and wrapping a terrycloth robe around him,
Pretorius negotiated his way down the perilous stairs—nearly
vertical, and narrow as a barrister's brain—to make his breakfast. His stove was a large, coal-fired Aga cooker, a four-oven,
blue-enameled behemoth weighing slightly less than the average battleship. A fire was kept going in it at all times. To bank
it, you simply closed up the damper to a crack. To get the Aga
going in the morning, all you had to do was open things up a
bit, give the fire a poke, and you were off and running.

Pretorius held his hand over one of the lids to check its
warmth. He got the cooker up to working heat and began the
quite deadly serious process of making his coffee. Coffee, to Pretorius, was no cavalier matter. He had tried every known means
of making coffee. He despised filtered coffee in any form, by
any technique, as it removed all the vile impurities and poisons
which gave coffee its good flavor.

He felt that anyone who made coffee in such a sterile, pedan-
tic way thoroughly deserved it.

His method was to begin with green coffee beans—a blend of
Mocha and Java, preferably—and roast them lightly in a cast-
iron frying pan, keeping them in a gentle, constant motion over

low heat. Pretorius' grandfather in North Carolina had taught him the method as a small boy, over a wood-burning stove in their farm near Guilford College. Pretorius worshiped his grandfather, a Quaker gentleman of great wit who had only recently died, in his 105th year.

Making coffee in this manner was, in a small way, a means of reminding himself of the wisdom and companionship of the old man.

Always, when making coffee, Pretorius would absentmindedly muse on all the times he spent with his grandfather on the old tobacco farm. After roasting the beans with great care—for Pretorius believed this was the most critical step in making coffee—he would rough grind them and use an enormous plunger pot whose glass had been replaced at least a dozen times in its brief history.

The fact was, Pretorius was uncommonly clumsy. He was known to stumble on curbs, to have an uncanny knack for breaking expensive stemware, and to drop things with alarming frequency. Being accomplished in a great many things made this all the more curious, and one of those things was cooking. He'd added to what Susannah had taught him by buying and studying old cookbooks, trying this and that, whatever sounded intriguing. And through Susannah, he discovered the more unusual forms of English *haute cuisine* which, since its decline in the eighteenth century, was at last beginning to come back.

His favorite restaurant for this sort of cooking was located off the edge of Dartmoor, within sight of the Cornish border. There, always with a good chilled bottle of Hambleton wine, he spent at least one lunch or dinner each week, often with the bearded proprietor, a great bear of a man who doubtless knew more about good food than anyone in the west country.

Pretorius felt such knowledge was precious and often asked the bear for his recipes, to which the bear replied with a smiling silence. No matter. Pretorius either found or invented his own.

Still in all, the bear's famed lettuce and bacon soup and his boned French duck breasts in veal sauce were, despite Pretorius' best efforts in the kitchen, unduplicable. Now, in the dawning of a fine November day, he set himself to making breakfast. He'd found an old Victorian recipe for a baked omelet, which was first to butter a small pie dish, then beat two freshly laid eggs with two dessertspoonsful of milk and a little pepper and salt, add some minced cooked ham and a sprig of parsley, then pour into the dish and bake in a moderate oven until it sets, usually anywhere from ten to twelve minutes.

He worked up the recipe, and when it was fully baked, took it outside to have with his coffee on the old rough-hewn wooden table on the back terrace.

The dawning sun felt warm and calming, as Pretorius perched on the edge of the old table. A wisp of steam spiraled upward from his coffee into the chill morning air. Sipping his coffee before tucking into the omelet, he noticed two large rabbits peering intently across the garden at him.

He grinned. They'd had more of his vegetables this past summer than he'd had himself. "Smug bastards," he said aloud, raising his coffee mug in a salute. The breeze came slowly across the garden, fresh and reviving and scented with lilacs.

He sighed, had another sip of coffee, and tasted the baked omelet. Not bad, he decided. Not bad at all. But possibly better with a bit of anchovy.

The phone rang, and it was Catchpole.

4
NELLIS AIR FORCE RANGE, NEVADA

Sweeping in low over the desert, the aircraft seemed to devour the few remaining miles at a rapacious rate. It was a black and moonless night. Perfect for this kind of op, the pilot thought.

His eyes flicked over the instruments with that swift, all-seeing glance which only years of experience can produce—and which had saved his life and some expensive hardware on a number of occasions. The aircraft, a factory-new Tupolev strategic bomber, codenamed Blackjack A, was capable of an over-target dash of 1380 mph (2220 kph) and a full weapon load of 36,000 pounds.

Some important elements of the United States' new OTH/B (over the horizon backscatter) radar system were not yet in place. The facilities at Mountain Home AFB, Idaho, were still under construction, as were the new installations in Maine, Oregon, and California. The only full operational site which could be a threat—Central, directed south in a 270-degree arc—was under mission orders.

The aircraft's pilot, having the dual advantage of low altitude and a low radar cross-section, felt confident at the controls. He also had the benefit of being escorted by a single United States Air Force E-3A Sentry, whose crew were among the total of twelve individuals cleared for certain levels of the mission.

Beneath its new coat of matte-black paint were the markings of the Soviet Air Force, complete with original identification numbers applied at the Kazan manufacturing facility.

The pilot pressed the PTT button to key the mike and released it without speaking. The HF-128 radio, engineered to withstand strategic nuclear radiation levels, tuned to the special preset channel in just eleven milliseconds. And, unlike standard airborne high-frequency radios, radiated just one watt of power for one second. Its signal reached out and the responding voice came through clearly. "Peyote 27, Pearly Gates. We have you on screen. Maintain 310 heading, reduce speed to 550. ETA 0300 Zulu. Over."

The pilot silently keyed the mike once again, signaling confirmation.

Some 120 miles behind the Tupolev, the big E-3A, its shepherding mission complete, wheeled lazily in a turning arc, and began its lumbering progress back to base. The men at the consoles in the rear of the aircraft leaned back and, except for one duty officer, removed their headsets. It had been a long flight for them as well.

The E-3A had relayed the transmission from the Nellis air traffic controller to the headquarters of the 552nd Airborne Warning and Control Division (TAC) at Tinker Air Force Base, Oklahoma. A specially cleared bird colonel entered it in the "black log" reserved for the most sensitive covert missions. The colonel had been informed the aircraft was a specially modified B-1B, testing a new composite for reduced radar signature.

Below in the Nevada desert, other ears also heard the exchange. A battered Chevrolet van, its bulk concealing an advanced-technology Rohde & Schwarz RDF and a Sunair GSB-900R transceiver modified for mobile use, monitored the transmissions near Tonopah. Soon, a separate antenna would be raised through what appeared to be a roof vent on the van, and high-speed code transmissions would radiate in short bursts.

The bursts, spit out from a specially adapted Magnotech reel-to-reel tapedeck and containing well over 2200 characters per burst, would last only a few seconds each, and the directional antenna would be carefully rotated slightly after each burst. Detection of the transmissions was a certainty, as any high-speed transmissions in this band were suspect, being unusually near frequencies reserved for certain classified Department of Defense transmissions.

But the antenna direction variations, coupled with a technique of converting the bursts into PM (Phase Modulation) made direction finding difficult. In any event, within minutes both antenna and transmitting station would have been moved from the area, leaving only a few tire tracks in the hills.

The matte-black Tupolev sped closer and closer to its destination: a small, ultra-secure landing area within the Nellis Air Force Range. This field, off limits even to most of the top officers of Nellis, served as a holding pen for the most security-sensitive aircraft of the United States Air Force. Controllers at Nellis worked the field's aircraft to within visual distance, where the planes were then turned over to special controllers for talkdown. The secret field, known as Dreamland, took pains to be as invisible as possible, even to the most inquisitive of Air Force personnel, or the most advanced of Soviet intelligence satellites. Most flights into or out of Dreamland took place at night, and there was even one underground hangar, with a sloping approach of some 1500 feet of concrete apron.

At ground level, Dreamland was encircled with fairly ordinary-looking chainlink fencing, which only served to direct any intruders to positions where they could be more easily intercepted. Beyond that perimeter, and past an area covered by the telemetry units of a remote intrusion monitoring (RIM) system, were three additional fenced border sectors.

At night, infrared detectors working on different frequencies produced eerily clear pictures of these sectors, and each detection area between the fences would set off silent alarms if anything larger or warmer than a jackrabbit entered it.

The field's complex of low buildings were camouflaged by

netting and, in some cases, by being enclosed within rusted Quonset shells of what looked like WW II vintage hangars. The main hangar, measuring some 300 feet by 450 feet by over 100 feet tall, was constructed to appear as an obsolete administration building, and even had a glass-roofed control tower above it, all built in the style of a 1940s style military air base. It could have easily passed for a set used in *Command Decision.*

The runway was painted twice a year to simulate, from the air, depressions and large cracks which appeared to be the result of years of disuse.

These were somewhat unsettling to pilots, even though all those landing at the base were briefed on this visual sleight of hand. But touching down with an attack bomber that weighed 260,000 pounds on a runway that looked like an aging actress on a bad morning gave even the coolest pilots second thoughts. The field's controller had the Tupolev on his close-range scope and began to talk him down. In seconds, the Blackjack was within visual range and the field's emergency equipment was in silent position, ready to pull out their bags of tricks in the event of the unexpected.

The aircraft passed once over the field, then circled, hawklike, for its final approach. To the watchers below, the Blackjack had an eerily sinister aspect. Its sleek black profile and oversized wings resembled a raptor of gargantuan proportions.

The field's duty officer did little to dispel the ominous feeling when, after the aircraft touched lightly down and wheeled itself toward the hangar, he ordered all personnel out of the immediate area. Slowly, the towmotor pulled the great black form through the hangar doors, a funereally paced parade of two.

Only when the hangar doors were once again closed and a five-man AP guard positioned in front—armed with fully automatic CAR carbines—did the duty officer order the normal deployment of men and vehicles resumed.

Inside the hangar, the pilot dismounted from the Blackjack, his legs stiff as he backed down the ladder.

The flight had been long. Inflight refueling had been tense

and edged with danger, due to a mismatch between the flying tanker's nozzle and the Soviet-designed fuel intake port. The big Boeing KC-135 tanker, from the 917th Air Refueling Squadron, had lazily snaked out its boom only to find someone had made a serious miscalculation. The bomber's intake port was undersized, yet the fueling couldn't be aborted: They were midway over the Atlantic and fuel was running light. So the tanker commenced pouring fuel into the big Tupolev, even though excess fuel streamed past the intake port and swept over the bomber's fuselage.

Finally, its load discharged, the KC-135 peeled away and slowly vanished into the distance.

The Blackjack's pilot, Buster Wildner, a Navy Lieutenant Commander on TDY to the Defense Intelligence Agency, was glad to be down, although flying the Soviet bomber had been exhilarating. He wondered what would become of it, other than the usual menu of tests at Nellis. He also wondered at the fate of the original Soviet pilot, who had brazenly flown the craft across the border to Hessisch-Oldendorf AS in West Germany.

The hand-off had been a miracle, thought Wildner. The Soviets, of course, had seen the Blackjack going off their screens and had even sent up a fighter wing to intercept and destroy—but a little too late. For the flight between Hessisch-Oldendorf and the USAF base at Mildenhall, a midair collision had been faked to convince the Russians their new bomber had not, after all, fallen in western hands. Pre-recorded pilot tapes, synchronized with the destruction of two radio-controlled seventeen-foot drones (one of which was carrying damaged Soviet structural material) had simulated the collision. The drones appeared on radar far larger than they actually were: They'd been built to one-half wavelength size (5.3 meters), which resonated to produce a much stronger radar return.

Special defensive avionics installed aboard the Tupolev were activated just as the fireball blossomed three miles away, and the big aircraft seemed to disappear at the moment of the collision.

But to Widner, this was now ancient history. It was over, he was down, and the first order of business was to report back to McLean by a secure landline. In a few hours, he'd be driven to a less security-sensitive part of Nellis and catch a MATS ride back East.

By now it was nearly five, and the sun began rising over the hardened Nevada desert. Small desert creatures—scorpions, rodents, reptiles, and small mammals—began scuttling for shelter until the next darkness, when they would emerge again.

A few hundred miles away, on a remote farm near Barstow, California, a recently stolen California Highway Patrol cruiser and two civilian sedans would soon begin rehearsing a scene that appeared as if it might be for a television series or a movie.

But there were no cameras, no equipment, no crew.

5
DEVON, SOMERSET, AND LONDON

Pretorius knew his friend in Special Branch was being controlled.

The message was clear: Meet me in London for dinner, but know that someone else is arranging this and monitoring the call.

No words, nor even coded references, had been used. Everything had been in the tone of voice. Anybody in the trade who'd ever worked as part of a team could detect the slight difference in tone, the ever-so-slight shift undetectable to anyone other than the working partner. It was one of the things, one of the curious little bits and pieces of sensitivity, that one picked up.

But why would anybody want to drag him back into it all? He was a relic, a burnt-out case, something to enter into a minor ledger book of the clandestine services. But nothing to consider at all useful, not any more. In the first few weeks in the hospital, he'd kept everyone up at night with his screaming nightmares. Even now, five years later, he'd sometimes awake bolt upright in bed, shivering in fright from he knew not what, the sweat suddenly chilling his skin.

No, it would have to be somebody digging into something in his past. Some long-forgotten, minor op that might have come up in a committee meeting. But why all the bullshit, why the surveillance? Probably some minor functionary just over-fulfilling his brief, trying to get in a little covert experience. Pretorius sighed, looking up at the morning sun just breaking through the damp gray pall of the low-clinging clouds. Devon mornings were seldom promising, he reflected. Still, more often than not, they surprised you with perfect days.

But whether today turned out to be perfect or not, Pretorius was due in London before nightfall. He slid open the barndoor on its well-oiled rollers and pulled the polythene tarp off his old Jaguar, a rehabilitated and crisply shining black Mark VII.

Pretorius had found the car in a nearby farmer's yard, where it had been perilously near becoming permanent statuary. The car hadn't run in ten years, the farmer said. But the body was sound, with negligible rust beneath. Pretorius offered the man a hundred pounds for the hulk, and the farmer had taken the money gladly, wishing him the best of good luck.

Over the next year, Pretorius sweated over the Mark VII, replacing the seized-up engine with one that seemed fresh from the factory, though it had been part of a recently pranged show car. Piece by piece, he replaced all the rubber seals, most of the upholstery and dashboard, and its legendarily fiendish electrical system—wrought by Joseph Lucas, the man who generations of Jaguar owners referred to as The Prince of Darkness. The car's suspension system was still in remarkable shape, as were its brakes.

Pretorius loved working on the car and put much of himself into it. He'd never been a real mechanic, but between reading the workshop manual as if it were a major piece of western philosophy, and gathering the odd bit of advice from a local veterinarian (something of a mechanical genius who'd spent part of his feckless youth in a racing pit crew), he came by quite a bit of knowledge in putting the old car back together again.

Pretorius inhaled the heady aroma of leather as he swung open the driver's door and eased himself inside. He inserted the key in the ignition, and the old engine fired up instantly, the needles wheeling over to their marks.

Framed by the burl walnut dashboard, the round dials were as obsolete as Pretorius himself, replaced in newer cars by digitally dazzling spectra of colored lights which managed to be far less accurate and informative than their analog ancestors. *Score another round for progress,* thought Pretorius.

Pretorius was, at heart, a thoroughgoing traditionalist. He believed painting stopped with Turner, and piano with Thelonius Monk.

Pretorius put the Jaguar on the A380, then got to the M5 shortly after. Once on the great wide motorway, he pressed the accelerator flat to the floor, and the Mark VII shot out like a sliver of wet soap.

The day was magnificent. White clouds hung motionless, perfectly defined against a cornflower blue sky. The car seemed almost soundless inside as it swept past the somnolent Somerset landscape.

Pretorius was conscious of his great good luck, a feeling of well-being only lightly tinged with irritation at his unknown watchers, and at whoever or whatever was behind Catchpole's summons.

But he'd been through too much for too long to waste time worrying. He felt through the cassettes on the seat beside him, found one he'd bought years ago, and slid it into the player he'd concealed under the dash.

June Christy's voice, light and perfect as a frosted vodka collins, filled the car's interior. The song was Lionel Hampton's *Midnight Sun,* built on the changes of *How High the Moon,* and set with the diamonds of Johnny Mercer's words.

Jazz had been one of the things that had drawn Pretorius close to Susannah: She loved it nearly as much as he, and had a sizable collection of records herself. As Pretorius drove, he realized he was now very near where he'd first met her, at Ston Easton Park.

In his first month after leaving the hospital and being handed his medical discharge, he'd decided to take a vacation in England. Renting a car at Heathrow, he drove aimlessly for days, pulling up at a pub or inn at dusk, trying to get a full night's sleep without the persistent nightmares.

On the fourth or fifth night, he found himself near Bath, in Somerset. His Egon Ronay book had recommended a place called Ston Easton Park, which had a broad sweep of grounds landscaped by Humphry Repton in 1793, two generations after the house had been built. As the car nestled itself into a parking space in the graveled forecourt, he noticed with a wry grin that the place looked as institutional as the hospital he'd just left. The cars parked were different, though. In addition to the usual group of Fords, Vauxhalls, Volvos, and such, there was also a covey of BMWs, Mercedes, Jaguars, and even one Rolls-Royce Corniche convertible sitting apart in solitary splendor.

Well, thought Pretorius. There's more to this mausoleum than meets the eye.

He'd gone in and registered, and was assigned a lovely room with a few eighteenth-century antiques, including a canopied bed (mattress fortunately late twentieth century). His room overlooked a croquet court of billiard table flatness. It was as tranquil a place as he could imagine.

His bathtub was one of those deep, long affairs the English are so justifiably fond of. He ran the water nearly up to the rim, scalding hot, then—with great trepidation and no little wincing and grimacing—slowly lowered himself in.

Pretorius soaked a full hour in the Roman-sized tub, finally emerging relaxed and pinkish. It was what he so badly needed—something to relax him utterly, to lower his defense mechanisms without drugs or chemicals. The doctors had taken him off all his medications and prescribed a diet which, they assured him, would slowly purge his body of everything the East Germans had pumped him full of in the long, destructive weeks of his interrogation.

He knew, though, that something about the nightmares wasn't totally related to the drugs they'd fed into him. They were from something in the interrogation itself, something his mind refused to remember or accept, but which still lurked in the farthest, darkest recesses of his mind.

Dressing in a double-breasted blue blazer, cavalry twill trousers, a Cutlass & Moore cotton dress shirt, and a smartly knotted four-in-hand striped tie, he went down to dinner.

As is the British custom, Pretorius was first seated in the lounge for drinks before dinner while he studied the menu. In this case, the lounge happened to be a huge salon which was breathtaking. An ornate plaster ceiling presided over the grandeur of the room. In front of the beautiful Adam fireplace was a four-square upholstered bench. And on it, staring into the fire intensely, was the most astonishingly beautiful woman Pretorius had ever seen.

Her hair was blonde and shining, cut in a longish, almost old-fashioned pageboy that seemed of an ineffable softness. Pretorius found himself, incredibly, wanting to breathe the fragrance of her hair, this woman he'd only glimpsed in these few split seconds. He couldn't recall ever feeling both so curiously and profoundly moved and, at the same moment, so confoundedly foolish.

The woman's shoulders, against the black velvet cocktail dress she wore, were alabaster white. The effect was glowing—from the shining helmet of hair, which swayed softly as she gracefully shifted her position on the bench, to the incredible whiteness of those shoulders.

She was, to Pretorius, achingly beautiful. But there were none of the conventional configurations of beauty.

Her eyes, in fact, seemed almost upside down, like those of the British actress Glynis Johns. They were a vivid, virtually electric blue-green. Still, for all their intensity of color, her eyes seemed curiously tranquil. There was, as well, something elusive about her that made her seem older than she looked, although Pretorius was not quite sure what it was.

As he stared at her across the room, she slowly turned, then rose, as if she'd somehow felt his attention—and suddenly, soundlessly left the room.

He felt as if he'd been caught doing something he shouldn't, felt curiously elated and disappointed at the same time. He shook his head, to rid it of the giddiness which inexplicably engulfed him, and went in to dinner. Dinner was, to the best of his recollection, one of the most wonderfully conceived and executed he'd ever known, although he ate but a mouthful or two of each serving. He put his behavior down to having gotten dizzy from the heat of his bath. But he grudgingly suspected this wasn't, after all, really the case.

After dinner, he returned to the salon for his coffee, hoping to see her, hoping against all reason that she would return to the room and resume her concentration on the fire, forgiving him for his rudeness in staring at her. But no, not a sight, not even throughout the next day, though he walked restlessly through all the grounds. Not until that night.

Looking out through his window as he buttoned his shirt for dinner, he heard the crunch of gravel as the big Rolls-Royce drew up, its convertible top down. There she was, with the shimmering blonde hair, the careless, effortless grace that had fascinated and shamed him so last night. He went down and entered the salon, determined not to look at her, if she were there. She was not. He was hugely disappointed. He made his selections from the menu, and was, in the fullness of time, brought in to his table by the maitre d'.

It was directly across, although separated by some thirty feet, from another lone table, that of the mysterious woman of the night before.

Pretorius made a courageous attempt to never, not even once, look in her direction. He plunged into his hors d'oeuvres with a focused, fervent concentration, probably not unlike that with which Oppenheimer observed the first firing of the atomic bomb near Los Alamos.

She was (he observed despite himself) wearing a loose, open-throated cream silk blouse, twin strands of pearls descending to the gentle swell of her breasts. Her hair was up this evening. But just as shiningly, maddeningly beautiful. No, even more beautiful. He thought he would lose his mind.

"Are you quite through, sir?"

"What?" Pretorius snapped out of his reverie. The young waiter was regarding him with concern. Pretorius realized he'd finished his hors d'oeuvres and had been simply making eating motions with an empty fork. He colored deeply. "Oh, yes. Very, I mean, thank you."

"Shall I bring the soup now?"

"Yes, by all means. The soup. Yes. Thank you."

"Very good, sir." He felt foolish. He swiveled in his chair to see the view better through the dining room window, and take his attention off Her. In this awkward, sideways position he managed to have his soup (cream of leek with truffle), and most of his entree (Aylesbury duck in wine sauce) before he finally returned to a more conventional and anatomically probable position.

He stared at the ceiling. He looked at an elderly couple who smiled back at him. He looked up at the busboy clearing away his plate and utensils. He looked at the waiter now rolling up a trolley of desserts for his inspection. He looked anywhere, and everywhere, except at Her.

It was precisely then that he felt her eyes on him. He glanced quickly, then away. He still felt she was looking in his direction. He felt he'd once again made her feel uncomfortable by his idiotic staring. He looked again. She was *definitely* looking at him. *O God*, he thought. *I've really blown it. She's got to think I'm the worst kind of creep . . .*

Finally, despite himself, unable to resist looking back into those unbelievable upside-down eyes, he shot a look in her direction—and was locked into staring back, unmindful and suddenly careless of the consequences. Her face was totally expressionless for a few interminably long, long moments.

And then, with a maddening slowness, she did it:

Her eyes slowly crossed, and the most beautiful pink tongue in all the world slowly stuck itself out at him from between her glorious red lips.

Explosively, wonderfully, he laughed. And so did she.

Diners all around them looked curiously at the strange man and woman laughing at each other across the room.

He signaled the waiter and whispered to him. The waiter shot a glance across at Her and then disappeared.

To reappear moments later with a bottle of champagne which he presented to the lady. The lady appeared to accept, then whispered to the waiter, who once again disappeared.

To once again reappear, this time at Pretorius' table, with a similar bottle of champagne, and the lady's compliments.

The days that followed seemed bathed in a luminous haze, and Pretorius experienced an unthinking joy he'd never known.

Her name was Susannah Kenney. She lived not far from Ston Easton, in a microscopic village with the improbable name of Ripping Beck. Her well-to-do parents had died within months of each other five years ago, and she'd been nearly devastated by the loss. Besides being her parents, they'd also been her best friends.

Her father had ensured her security, leaving her a formidable inheritance which included a handsome Elizabethan house (Grade II listed) on the outskirts of the village, as well as the enormous car.

She'd used part of her inheritance to open a small restaurant in nearby Bath which specialized in that rarest of all things, British *haute cuisine*.

Pretorius, upon being informed there was such a thing, laughed. Susannah momentarily darkened, then stormily informed him that in the eighteenth century, English cooking was considered quite as good as—and often better than—the best

French, but had lapsed into unfashionability for over two centuries. What most people now thought of as English cooking was merely plain home cooking, predicated on the theory that all food had to be boiled, baked, broiled, or grilled as much as possible to ensure it was, indeed, demised. But now there was a strong resurgence in great British cooking, especially game dishes, and Susannah rightfully considered herself one of its champions.

Even the most humble of dishes became ennobled in Susannah's supple hands. It was said, in fact, that Susannah Kenney knew more than twenty-four different methods of translating Brussels sprouts into edible objects, and it was probably true.

She was also emphatic in her feelings about current fads in cuisine and voiced them frankly. On their last evening, walking in the dewy darkness of the croquet court, she expressed displeasure at the passion of Beauchamp Place eateries for *la nouvelle cuisine*.

Wrinkling up her nose in disdain, she pronounced in a voice of throaty disapproval, "The only thing in the slightest *nouvelle* about it is that it's the same stuff we got when we were all ourselves rather *nouvelle* in the world, fed to us by Mum, straight from little jars. Only now, a waiter plops it down in dollops, in little pools of oozing drool, in the middle of cheap white plates, calls it *nouvelle cuisine*, and charges us twenty quid."

Pretorius grinned at her indignation. He was beginning to learn and love all her many moods. He could listen to her talk about food, or, indeed, anything, for hours. He found her intelligent, funny, and altogether the most desirable woman in all the world.

For the first time in years, Pretorius allowed himself to open up. Trusting someone, though—that was something else again. The idea of trust had been surgically removed from him; the business didn't allow it.

But he was out of it now, and just beginning to enjoy a few

of the luxuries the rest of the world has always enjoyed un-
questioningly. And Susannah? He was in love with her, that
much he knew. But the distance between them—kept by his
defenses—formed a fragile barrier, tempting and yet seemingly
impenetrable.

Susannah's previous relationships had been mostly unsatisfy-
ing, and she had never married. She wanted something more
than what most available men in London seemed to want to
offer, something more romantic, and more permanent.

Many of the men she went out with were at first fascinated
by her beauty and wit, but seemed to regard her as a sort of
potential ornament to carry the title Missus, and to accomplish
the tasks of a stewardess with good cheer and little pay. She
was too independent for that and didn't want to marry merely
for the sake of being married. Too many of her girl friends had
chosen that unfortunate course, suddenly finding themselves
saddled with nappies and boring, bland husbands who com-
plained endlessly about the drudgery they'd knowingly selected
for themselves.

In meeting Michael Pretorius, though, she'd fallen quite head
over heels. Yet she didn't want to be merely a convenient cure
for loneliness and shock. She wanted a great deal more from a
relationship and suspected Pretorius could—if she ever let him
and if he could ever learn to lower his defenses—become an
important part of her life.

On the afternoon of their second day together, she'd invited
him to come see her little restaurant in Bath. Walking along
the High Street, she found to her surprise Pretorius had suddenly become transfixed by a puppy in a pet shop window. It
was a tiny bullterrier puppy, as ugly as one could imagine, its
overlarge head staring up at them balefully, sad eyes placed too
high on its head for any pretense at doggy attractiveness.

Pretorius, to her amusement, was speaking softly to the dog,
although the comical-looking beast couldn't possibly hear
through the glass, let alone understand. She took Pretorius' el-

bow and, breaking his reverie, guided him into the shop. "How much is that wretched-looking animal?" she asked. The shopkeeper, a gray-haired woman, was cheerfully feeding a quartet of kittens something from a spoon.

"Oh, he's not for sale, dearie," replied the woman mischievously. "We're keeping him around for decoration, great handsome thing that he is."

"Don't be daft," persisted Susannah, "of course he's for sale and you'll be well rid of him. People must be afraid to enter the shop, with a beast like that lurking about."

"Quite the contrary, he draws them in like flies. People queue up outside for the privilege of meeting such a well-bred, attractive animal." Susannah and Pretorius both laughed. "We'll give you thirty pounds to take it off your hands, and not a penny more," Susannah said.

"Och, it'd break his heart, if he could hear you talking about him that way," rejoined the woman. "Fifty pounds."

"Thirty-two."

The woman grasped her head in both hands, in mock agony. "You'll be our ruination. Why, he's worth that much seven times over. Forty, and I won't hear a word more."

Susannah leaned across the counter and slowly counted out thirty-five pounds. "Here is all the money the horrible thing is worth. You should be paying us to haul it away."

"Thirty-five will do nicely, ducks," replied the woman in a dazzlingly swift change of mood. "I can see he's going to a fine home, and that's all that's important. Now, would you like a fitting collar and lead for the handsome divil? Nothing tatty, now; it'd upset his fine temperament."

Susannah and Pretorius (who by now was quite bewildered by the exchange) selected a stout leather lead and a collar several sizes too large, which they had the shopkeeper perforate to accommodate the dog's neck.

"We need one for him to grow into," explained Susannah. "Besides, I couldn't have a dog like that around my house if he weren't adequately attired. Right?"

And they both laughed and they walked on in their happiness: Susannah, Pretorius, and their four-legged adoptee.

The dog, which Susannah promptly dubbed David Lloyd George, gravitated to Pretorius, who, in the next few months, was to form a strong attachment to the unfortunate-looking animal. David Lloyd George seemed the one being on earth Pretorius was able to be completely open with, and Susannah thought it a good sign. She would sit bemused while Pretorius would have a one-sided conversation with the dog, who seemed to pay close and exacting attention to every word.

David Lloyd George, however, had one curious facet. As Pretorius spoke softly to him, the dog seemed to grin, more and more, which had the effect of causing Pretorius to double over in helpless laughter, which caused the dog to grin even more, until Pretorius would ache from laughter.

Despite the salutary effects of David Lloyd George and his first days with Susannah, Pretorius continued to have the dark, lonely moments that had haunted him even after his release from the hospital. Susannah would catch him staring into the distance for long moments, his long, tanned face creased in thought. And yet, when she would ask his thoughts, he could remember nothing of what he'd actually been thinking, only a cold feeling of alienation, inexplicable and seemingly ineradicable.

After four days spent on long walks together, quiet candlelit dinners together, and a single long, lingering last night together, Susannah announced she had to return, had to get back to the restaurant—which she'd kept closed for the few days at Ston Easton. And Pretorius had to get on with his life, although he suspected this woman was about to change it forever.

And now, months later, driving to his meeting with Catchpole in London, Pretorius knew she had. She was what few men ever have and seldom ever hope for—a lifelong love. He flicked a sudden glance in his rearview mirror, realizing his awareness had been lowered as he'd been daydreaming about the time at Ston Easton.

A black Rover detached itself from the traffic behind him, braked as the driver apparently realized he was in view, and then tucked itself back in place several cars behind Pretorius.

They were still with him.

He arrived in London three hours later and checked into Duke's Hotel, a small accommodation tucked into a gaslit *cul-de-sac* called St. James's Place. He was happy to be in London again, although distinctly displeased at the purpose of his visit. After settling in, he perched on the edge of his bed and dialed one of his old contacts: Dick Coldwell. Coldwell, a former career officer with the DIA, had been lured away to the Central Intelligence Agency in the past year, with the offer of one of the Company's plums: London Station Head. If anyone knew anything about the Special Branch putting the arm on him, it would be Coldwell. Conversely, if it were genuinely a large affair, Coldwell would have the lid on tight.

He dialed both Coldwell's office in Grosvenor Square and his home around the corner in Lee's Place. An irascible late-working assistant answered the former, a machine the latter.

It was as Pretorius guessed. Coldwell wouldn't—or couldn't—answer his phone. Whatever was up would have to be played out the way they wanted it. But at least he knew somebody was really serious, somebody with enough muscle to put the squeeze on even the Head of Station.

Pretorius looked at his watch. Time to meet Catchpole.

Walking over to Pall Mall, Pretorius felt happy to be in London once more. He'd always loved the city, and agreed with Dr. Johnson's observation: "When a man is tired of London, he is tired of life."

There was a light fog this evening—not the dense, often yellowish fog of years past—and walking past St. James's Square, Pretorius could almost imagine he was in Victoria's London, the London of Sherlock Holmes and Jack the Ripper.

The iron torch-snuffers leaning out from one of the houses

were relics of an even earlier time. In the eighteenth century, they'd been a practical device for extinguishing one's torch before entering a dwelling. Pretorius' odd feeling of venturing into the past was heightened when, as he turned left into Pall Mall, he could see the tall flames of gas lanterns burning just past his destination.

Indeed, the only thing missing was the heavy scent of coal smoke, which had vanished from London in the 1960s after more than four centuries. Pretorius had always liked the smell and on a night like this almost wished it were still in the air.

In just a few steps, he arrived at Catchpole's club, the Reform, one of London's great Victorian institutions. Its presence was subtly proclaimed by a small, well-polished brass plaque just to the left of its entrance.

The Reform had been founded in 1836 by Parliament's Liberal whip, Edward Ellice, and it was claimed (not wholly without justification) that its excellent food caused many of its members to turn conservative, having tasted too much of the good life.

Its architecture was impressive and lavish, based, it was said, on the Farnese Palace in Rome. Pretorius had enjoyed many excellent dinners under its roof with his friend Catchpole and often wondered that a policeman should be a member of such a patrician club.

But then Catchpole was no ordinary policeman.

A towering fellow with unfailing good humor, he was an accomplished historian and had, indeed, published several excellent books on the Georgian era. One of his books, on the eighteenth-century architect George Dance, was reckoned to be among the best in its field, surpassed only by Dorothy Stroud's own work on the same subject.

He had been born into what was known as a good family, and went as expected, up to Merton, as had his brothers. Upon graduating with honors, Catchpole then plunged his family into an uproar by announcing his intention to pursue a career in law enforcement. It was his contention, vastly unpopular with his parents, that the police are, on many occasions, one of society's most effective means of not merely containing or curtailing crime, but of doing social good in a most direct way.

His father, the grandson of a man who'd made his fortune in the wool trade, thought the notion nonsense. He urged his errant son Donald to give up this crime business and follow in his own, more respectable footsteps, trading securities in the City. Catchpole, however, had other ideas.

He began as a constable on patrol (c.o.p.), and spent a great deal of time taking night courses, studying police science. He was sent to the police staff college at Bramshill, where he deeply impressed the faculty, and, in later years, was regularly invited to lecture there.

His keen mind, coupled with a somewhat broader viewpoint than his fellow officers, soon earned him the attention of the higher-ups.

Within five years of entering the Metropolitan Police Force, Catchpole was invited into the presence of several senior officers, and grilled rigorously. Ten days later, his orders came: assignment to Special Branch. At first, Catchpole felt he was being removed from the mainstream of police work. But as he entered into his work, he realized much of what he did had vastly more impact than his former duties. And certainly, a great deal more than trading gilts in the City. The Branch considered Catchpole an unusually good investigator, with something approaching mystical skills in interrogation.

But then he'd been specially trained by the legendary Jim Skardon, to whom he'd been seconded for a special assignment with Mil 5. Skardon was a former policeman, and his relaxed, pipe-smoking demeanor made him Catchpole's model for years.

Until Catchpole joined the Reform Club, few members had been in anything like law enforcement or intelligence work. One such exception was Guy Francis DeMoncy Burgess, who had been quite active in the intelligence trade, though few of his fellow members had been aware of it. Burgess (part of a small circle formed in Cambridge in the late 30s which later earned the notorious sobriquet "The Ring of Five"), had held the rank of Executive Officer in the Foreign Office.

Burgess had, in fact, been working for years with Harold A. R. ("Kim") Philby: a likable chap, and singularly industrious, for Philby was simultaneously employed as a Foreign Office diplomat, a serving officer in the British Secret Intelligence Service (still known by its old military designation of MI6) and—which later surprised a good many of his friends—a colonel in the KGB.

Both the Reform Club and the Foreign Office lost the pleasure of Burgess' company at 11:45 on the evening of the twenty-fifth of May, 1951. At that precise moment, he and Donald Mclean took the boat train to France and proceeded thence to their masters in Moscow Center.

Pretorius was told Mr. Catchpole (he avoided using his Chief Superintendent's title in off-duty life) was waiting in the Smoking Room.

He found Donald slouched in one of the big creased leather chairs, his long frame arranged lankily, his furrowed forehead wrinkled deep in thought.

Catchpole's brow lent him the appearance of being Most Gravely Concerned even on the most innocent of occasions, such as when deciding whether or not to order a scone off the afternoon tea trolley at the office. His subordinates at SB referred to him (out of range of his hearing, of course) as Inspector Hound. The sobriquet had a double meaning, referring not only to his furrowed brow, but to his unswerving tenacity when pursuing a case to its ultimate conclusion.

"Say nothing to alarm the others, but rejoin your regiment at once," whispered Pretorius.

Catchpole chortled and waved Pretorius over to a chair opposite. "Sorry to be so preoccupied, Michael. God's trousers, but you're looking tanned. And slim. Why don't you ever put on a belly like the rest of us?"

"That's easy," replied Pretorius. "I've got to eat my own cooking, and there's not a lot of temptation there."

"Well," mused Catchpole, "I should have thought Susannah would've had you rivaling Brillat-Savarin by now . . ."

Pretorius laughed. "I'm not exactly a great student, you know."

"Not from what I've heard. My sources tell me you wield a wicked saucepan. They also tell me—" and here Catchpole raised two bristling quizzical eyebrows—"the lady's in love with you. Or didn't you know?"

Pretorius was surprised Catchpole knew. They'd been circumspect in showing their love to anyone and had certainly never discussed it with others. He decided to ignore the comment, and asked the age-old question between policemen, "How goes the Job?"

Catchpole grinned. "You know the Job. Always lots of business. Always somebody someplace getting twisted up in their knickers, and always somebody like you or I getting the midnight call."

Pretorius stretched himself in the deep leather chair. "God, I'm glad I'm well out of it. Nowadays my only bad guys are rabbits down at the other end of my garden. But we've arranged a sort of peace—I just plant three times as much as I should."

"Well," Catchpole reflected, smiling, "if the rabbits have been on the winning end lately, we can easily remedy it with our dinner tonight. By the way, we have a surprise guest. Think you'll be pleased. At any rate, you'll certainly be surprised."

"Was the guest the reason for the invitation?" said Pretorius. "You know I'm the suspicious type."

Catchpole scratched his ear. "Well, I wouldn't say no. You'll get the whole story at dinner. Which is more than I've gotten to date."

"A wink is as good as a nod," said Pretorius, rising. "Don't tell me this is our mystery guest."

The man approaching was tall, in his late forties, impeccably dressed in a well-tailored pinstripe suit. His lean, almost hawk-like face was creased with a grin the width of Will Rogers', and he extended an enormous hand to Catchpole as he approached. "Good to see you, Donald. And the redoubtable Mr. Pretorius. Country living has been good to you."

Pretorius was surprised and more than a little pleased. "Well, well—the distinguished Mr. Coldwell, larger than life. How goes the civil servant business? Heard you'd been made Head of Station. Knowing you, you must have gotten a crib sheet for the exams."

Coldwell rocked back on his heels and laughed, his hands in his pockets. "No, just waited for all the others to either die off from sheer boredom or get a medical boondoggle, like you. How goes the rural life?"

"Pretty well. At least the only people shooting at me are hunters down from London, and they never quite get the knack of hitting things. Must come from soft living."

Catchpole gestured toward the door and said, "I believe our table's ready. Gentlemen?"

The three men walked into the great dining room to find their table set some distance apart from the others. The dining room was nearly always well populated, due to the quality of its food.

The Reform, unlike many of London's other clubs, has a tradition of superb food, stemming from its early chef, the legendary Alexis Soyer. Even today, members mention his name with reverence, though no one who dined during his reign is around today to confirm the legends.

Pretorius, Catchpole, and Coldwell all chose the Club's Reform Cutlets, served with an unusual sauce based on red currant jelly. Catchpole ordered a '66 Palmer which married nicely with the meat.

They made small talk through dinner, Pretorius catching up on who had been posted where, and the three of them telling some of the more humorous stories of the trade. Then, after dessert was served, Catchpole nodded to the waiter who then restricted his attentions to other tables some distance away.

Catchpole said, "I suppose you thought I had the wind put up me, Michael, from the way I invited you here. And at that point, I must admit, I was a bit put off. But Coldwell here has filled me in with one or two details, and I think he might have something interesting for you."

Curiously, Pretorius felt a cold chill along his spine and the old scar tissue seemed suddenly tight.

"My God, Michael, what's the matter? Catchpole said with concern. "You look as if you'd just seen old Marley . . ."

"No, no . . . it's nothing. Just something I forgot. I'm all right, really." Pretorius frowned. "I think you both know my sentiments about the business. I'm out of it, well out of it, and fortunately I enjoy my life now."

"Michael, Michael," interjected Coldwell. "Please don't think we're trying to dragoon you back into being a serving officer. There's just—something that's come up, something that's very important.

"The net result of it is that we want you to join us as a freelance operative, only for a few months. The pay's enormous. You could pay off the farm, invest the rest, and live off the interest. But the main thing is, it *is* important. Not just another job."

"No good, Dick," replied Pretorius, who was beginning to feel a prickly sensation along the base of his neck he'd felt years ago, a feeling he thought he'd forgotten. "I'm out. Retired. *Finished.*"

"Nonsense," retorted Coldwell. "We know your disability's only minor. You're just as good as you always were. And for what we've got in mind, there's no one—absolutely no one—better."

Catchpole sat looking speculatively at Pretorius through this exchange. "I know Dick better than you do, Michael," he said. "You might as well give in now. He's got the bone in his teeth and he'll not let go. At least let him tell you what he's got, for God's sake."

"Donald, with respect," Pretorius said slowly, "I don't want to hear it. It's not my world anymore. At least his part of it isn't my world."

Coldwell drew his chair closer and looked intently at Pretorius. "Michael, believe me, it is very much your world. You've been on easy street. But some of us still go on and give up really quite a lot to keep you and other people happy on your farms or in your apartments or whatever.

"Spare me the violins, Dick," interrupted Pretorius. "You're in it because you love it, same as I did. But my love affair's over."

Coldwell bristled. "It isn't just a fascination, and you damn well know it. It's less boring than the average insurance actuary's job, but only on those days when it gets to be dangerous as hell. You fuck up, and you're gone, and there's nobody who can even say you did one hell of a good job to your widow—if you've been crazy enough at some point in your career to have married. We're paid to do it, but not nearly enough. The reason we do it is because somebody who's got the training has damn well *got* to do it, or the whole thing begins to tumble. You know that." Pretorius made patterns with the tines of his dessert fork on the white tablecloth as he listened.

Coldwell, leaning closer, continued, his voice subdued, but gathering in intensity. "We appreciate what you've done and what you went through. And God knows you deserve to be left in peace. But sometimes—sometimes there's something particular, something no one else can really do. It's that kind of assignment, Michael. I wouldn't ask you if it weren't absolutely vital. At least let me lay it out."

Pretorius settled himself back in the chair. "Let's hear it."

Coldwell looked at Catchpole. "Donald, I appreciate your help in arranging our meeting . . ."

"Right, then, I know. I'll see you two in the library later.

Good luck, Michael. I've a feeling you're going to need it."
Coldwell watched Catchpole until he'd left the room, then interlaced his fingers and stared down at them. "Okay, it's like
this: We've got a new aircraft, Michael. Something very, very
good. A strategic bomber with greater stealth capability than
anything anybody knows we've got. Far better than anything
the Soviets are likely to have for at least a decade. The edge is
tremendous."

"The thing is," Coldwell continued, pushing back the black
cowlick which always seemed to tumble down over his forehead, "certain things have happened which lead us to think the
Soviets already know about it, though it's far from operational.
We don't know through who, or how much they really know.
Very simply, we've got to find out. We do know they've somehow penetrated the Agency. We don't know to what degree, or
at which levels. Therefore, we can't use anybody who's ever
been on the CIA lists. That's where you come in. You've never
been recorded as part of any operation in which the Company
has had a stake. We also need someone with your technical
background, as well as someone with your field experience. The
difference is, this time, you'll be using it against both the opposition—and a few of our own people."

Pretorius asked, "Dick, what happens if I turn this down?"

Coldwell considered this, then said, "A lot of very good people get killed, some other people have several decades of their
work wasted, the bad guys win another round, and, oh yes, you
lose your right to live in the UK. The Brits owe us a few favors
these days."

"No more Mr. Nice Guy, then. Jesus, you guys are really
unbelievable . . ." Pretorius said.

"No more Mr. Nice Guy. Michael, we've got to get it done.
It really requires you, and no one . . . absolutely no one else
. . . could be better. It's only three or four months, and the fee
is more than most people earn in a lifetime. Ready to hear my
side of it?" Coldwell grinned his lopsided, engaging grin.

"Well," said Pretorius, smiling ruefully, "now I know why you're Head of Station. Go ahead, I'm listening. But I'm not buying."

Coldwell stared for a long time down the length of the impressive room, gathering his thoughts. When he spoke, it was in a curious monotone. Pretorius recognized it as a habit which certain case officers would lapse into when briefing their people, a technique to give their words a certain analytical detachment. Or so they thought. "In addition to the penetration problem, there are a number of people within the Agency who have set new records for indiscretion.

"Most of them have no idea of the damage they do, but as a result of their well-meaning leaks to the media and to certain congressmen and senators, we've been severely compromised in a number of cases." Coldwell paused for a moment as a member passed their table on his way out, obviously carrying a fair load of brandy as ballast. Pretorius thought he recognized something about him, but couldn't quite place it.

When the man was out of earshot, Coldwell continued in the same monotone. "Dick Helms was good with the press; he courted them constantly, taking them to lunch, giving them choice bits which weren't harmful—things that, in fact, were really helpful explaining what our job is really all about—and they seemed for a while to be less antagonistic. But these days, our public relations activities are pretty poor, and the only Agency people the press seems to be talking with are . . . less than concerned over the Company's well-being. And it's fairly obvious that whatever doubles the KGB have inside the Agency are accelerating the process by feeding them just the right morsels to discredit the Agency and our operations. But so far, what remains of our so-called CI staff hasn't been able to find them.

"Between these two groups of people, CIA is anything but secure, and so by this operation we hope to do several things at once: First, plug the leaks—as many as we can—for the immediate future. This is especially important, considering the future of our strategic bomber program. And second, equally important, we've got to lay a tracer to find the doubles inside the Agency. It's got to be real and it's got to be tempting enough to smoke them out.

"We're going to arrange a leak to them. Something irresistible but believable. Something that will draw them right to the source, and there you'll be. We need your talents. You've got no CIA dossier, and that will be vital in this. With what you know about electronics and aerodynamics, plus what we'll be able to bring you up to speed on, you'll be perfect. Perfect. First, you had plenty of physics in school, especially material sciences as they apply to aerodynamics. You can soak up a great deal of information quickly. Plus, of course, you've got your background in CI.

"You've got the training, you've got the skills, you've got the ability to handle yourself well, to get yourself out of a tight spot. And that's precisely what you'll have to be in. A very tight spot. But one that's critical to your country."

Pretorius smoothed out the patterns on the table and put his head in both hands, staring down. A vein in his temple throbbed.

"You people never let us alone, do you? Well, I'll tell you. This is one spook who's out of it for good. You say a lot of good people will get killed if I don't do your bidding. Too bad. A lot of good people get killed in this business *anyway*—it's that kind of job. DIA bounced me out on a medical, and it should've been a couple of years earlier. I'm burnt out. Burnt *out*, damn it."

Coldwell said nothing. A few members at nearby tables gave Coldwell and Pretorius glances. Richard Coldwell looked down at his plate and spoke quietly. "You've got every right to feel the way you do, Michael. You've given everything anybody, any country, could ever ask from a man. We just want you to do this one thing, just this one thing only you could do, and then it's quits. Really."

Pretorius stared down at the swirling indentations he'd made on the white cloth. "Have I a real choice, Coldwell? I don't mean to just listen, I mean—do I have a choice in not doing the job?"

Coldwell stared at him for a few seconds, thinking hard. "You want it straight, no tact, no bullshit?"

Pretorius nodded.

"Well then," Coldwell said, "you don't have much of a choice, because *we* don't. This job comes straight from the Man, Michael. It's big, very big. And we need your particular talents. Period."

Pretorius looked at Coldwell with cold, incurious eyes. Then, rising, he shoved back his chair—and, as it toppled over backwards onto the oaken floor, strode out of the huge dining room.

Richard Coldwell watched Pretorius until he passed from sight. An observer would have been surprised to see a small smile materialize on Coldwell's lips, if only for a moment. Coldwell finished his coffee alone, in silence.

6
NEAR DARTMOUTH, DEVON

Pretorius had spent the afternoon sailing on the River Dart, lazily tacking back and forth, the sun and the wind and the salt against his face, feeling the occasional moment when his body and the boat seemed to blend into one instrument. The long muscles along his back flexed with the wood of the hull, and with the filling and billowing of the sails.

Pretorius was an economical sailor, always preferring to use the minimum possible sail. He knew you could get into trouble faster with too much sail, and that if trouble suddenly happened, just knowing how to handle a small patch of sail would serve you better.

His boat had been built back in the 1940s, by a local zealot who believed in wooden boats and canvas sail. And although Pretorius could've easily switched his canvas sails for Terylene, he loved the tradition of sailing with materials that hadn't changed since Drake's time, nor, indeed, for thousands of years before. Slower, certainly. But then Pretorius didn't sail to race. He sailed to think.

And this day, despite perfect sailing conditions, Pretorius' mind was ranging far afield, still fixed on the conversation in London with Coldwell, and the few days since his return to Dartmouth.

Knowing people like Coldwell, Pretorius had expected some pressure, and it had come quickly:

The Inland Revenue people had been polite, almost cheerful. Two of them had come calling on Pretorius without notice, and had asked for all his records for the past five years. Just a formality, they said, just routine.

Pretorius' finances had always been extremely simple. He had a few investments which yielded only a modest portion to supplement his medical pension. Some of his dividends, though, had been banked directly in the United States, and not reported to the Inland Revenue. And they, through some sudden miracle of international cooperation, had been furnished with records of all his bank accounts, on both sides of the Atlantic.

"Not very nice to not report this as income to us, Mr. Pretorius," they said. "Not very nice at all. You are, after all, a guest in our country, Mr. Pretorius. A resident alien, as it were. Most irregular for someone in your position to fail to report income. Well. We'll naturally have to take this up with our superiors, Mr. Pretorius. Here is our card. Please call us if, um, there's something more you'd like to tell us. Best to be forthcoming in matters such as this. Well. Cheery-bye."

Pretorius came close to slamming the door through its frame after the pair left. It was Coldwell, he knew. Turning the screws. Nothing too overt, nothing too threatening, just enough to let him know who's boss.

A call to Catchpole produced no answers. Catchpole sounded even more guarded than his first conversation at the start of this business a few weeks ago, and wouldn't even call him back from a pay phone. Considerable muscle was being applied on this one, Pretorius realized.

The wind shifted suddenly on the Dart, moving quickly down the slopes of the hills that surround Dartmouth Harbour, catching Pretorius unawares. He shifted his weight and hauled in a sheet, gritting his teeth against the sudden strain, and managed to get the small mahogany-hulled boat under firm control again.

Tacking in to his customary slip, Pretorius dropped the sail and caught the edge of the dock with his hand, keeping it from scraping the varnish. Old Shaw had come down to give him a hand—Shaw, who had taught endless midshipmen the rigors of sailing at the Royal Naval Academy up the river, and who could still handle anything with sails.

"Feller bane askin' atter ye," Shaw said, trying off the lines that held Pretorius' boat fast. "Sort of a Yank, like yersel', but oddlike, mindful of a university bodger. Knowin' yer like fer privacy, I kept ignorin' him, like. But the more I kept ignorin' him, the more he kept atter me."

"Oh?" replied Pretorius. "And what did he want?"

"Just wantin' to know when you'd be back off the river," drawled the laconic Shaw.

Pretorius' eyes scanned the dockside and the parking lot beyond. Nothing unusual, no one there watching. He shrugged and thanked Shaw, clapping him on the shoulder as he left. Shaw actually touched his forelock, to the old sailor an action as automatic as shrugging one's shoulders.

The venerable Norton motorcycle sped him back to the cottage in quick time, and the wind cooled the sting of his now slightly sun-burnt face.

There was a Humber parked in the road directly in front of the cottage, big and black, ominously official, the sort the Special Branch often used on formal calls. Catchpole, Pretorius thought.

But the man waiting on the bench in the front garden wasn't Catchpole, and, indeed, looked less like a policeman than even Catchpole himself. He was a large man, carrying considerable weight, wearing, despite the warm weather, a thick three-piece tweed suit with a neatly knotted bow tie. He also wore a handkerchief which almost matched it, and which threatened to fall out of his jacket's upper pocket.

As he rose, Pretorius had an impression of considerable strength, despite the man's girth. He radiated an aura of power unlike anything in Pretorius' experience. "Mr. Pretorius?" the man asked. But Pretorius knew he really had no need to ask; he knew precisely who Pretorius was and had doubtless digested his entire dossier.

Pretorius nodded and shook the other man's outstretched hand. A powerful grip, quickly released. The eyes, a piercing, icelike pale blue. "Arthur Hornbill," the man offered. "I work with Dick Coldwell now and again, although I'm somewhat retired, I suppose you'd call it. May we talk inside?"

The two men went inside the unlocked cottage and Pretorius offered him a drink. "Ah, the very thing," Hornbill replied with obvious pleasure. "A single malt, please, if you have it. Just as it comes, no ice, thanks."

Pretorius busied himself pouring Hornbill's drink and his own. "Always glad to meet a friend of Dick's," said Pretorius warily. "Now do you have any identification?"

"Oh my, yes, yes indeed. How rude of me," replied Hornbill, who opened a small leather case to reveal a Defense Intelligence Agency plastic badge, replete with an unsmiling portrait of its portly bearer in the upper right hand corner.

"Are you here on business, Mr. Hornbill?" inquired Pretorius wryly. "Or just down here on holiday?"

"Would that it were only a holiday, Mr. Pretorius, that would be the thing. Would that it were." Hornbill chuckled as he took the large drink offered him. "But I'm afraid it's rather different. Good malt, this. Very good."

"Would you like to share with me the purpose of this—visit, then?" prodded Pretorius impatiently.

"Ah. A man after my own heart; straight to the point. Well, then, Michael—if I may call you Michael—the point is, you're a man who's rather badly needed. A man with special talents, and a special background. And a one-of-a-kind job waiting to be done."

Pretorius tried to place the man's oddly twanging New England accent. Not Massachusetts. Possibly New Hampshire, or

Vermont. Somewhere farther north, likely along the Canadian border.

"So I've heard, Mr. Hornbill. But as you yourself might've heard, I'm also retired. Not somewhat retired, completely retired. Your people settled all that a couple of years ago."

Hornbill sighed and moved forward to the edge of his chair, warming the whisky by rolling the glass between his two large palms. "Yes, I know all that. A sad business, and you've already been put through a lot. But this, this is rather different."

"It's always rather different," Pretorius said dryly.

"Point well taken, sir. I know you feel that way. But let me—if I may—take a few seconds just to explain. We've gone to some lengths to prepare a certain operation, and it appears your participation is, um, vital to its success."

"With respect, Mr. Hornbill, I've been through all this with Coldwell. It's beginning to get boring and I'm not buying. And all the Inland Revenue numbers-crunchers in the world aren't going to make me go back out there again. I'd rather go to Leavenworth."

Hornbill looked directly into the younger man's eyes. "Mr. Pretorius," he said evenly, "I can't send you to Leavenworth, nor would I. But I would like to tell you a brief story, one which you may not know, but one in which you already play a certain part."

There was a stillness in the small room and Pretorius stared back into Hornbill's pale blue eyes. He nodded at Hornbill, who settled back into his chair, swirling the golden liquid in his glass, speaking in a quiet tone.

"Once upon a time, as all stories begin, there were several young men who went to college together, in a different age, in a very different world. I was one. Your father was another." Hornbill looked at Pretorius, and received the expected reaction. "Yes, your father. John Pretorius and I knew each other quite well, shared many of the same dreams, the same goals.

"We both went off to war together, with a number of other

like-minded fellows. We were out to show that right could conquer might, and, surprise of surprises, we did precisely that. And when the war was over, we all came home. Your father entered private law practice, while I and a few others stayed on to fight a rather different battle which was only then beginning to be apparent, and then only apparent to a few."

Pretorius began to interrupt, but Hornbill waved his hand, "No, please be patient. There's much to tell, much to explain. And I must get it all right, in the proper sequence. Now then— from time to time I called on your father to give us counsel, not in his legal capacity, but as one of the finest minds ever to grace the intelligence community. And I must say, John Pretorius never failed us. Not once. Not even when he was struggling to get his own practice built up, and trying to raise a family, John was instrumental in shaping much of our intelligence policy and invaluable in helping us analyze and understand what was beginning to happen to us."

Pretorius got up and poured Hornbill another drink, then began pacing the floor as he watched the nattily dressed DIA officer spin out his tale.

"Now your father was one of the very few who could see the threat of the Soviets' post-war intelligence apparatus. He knew, better than any of us, that intelligence work was not simply spying. In fact, that it was—or could be—something far larger, more powerful in the scheme of settling things. Ideas, whether good or evil, could be far more powerful than bombs or bullets or bayonets.

"John Pretorius had been among the group handling our Soviet desk in the war. Those people knew from firsthand evidence that once World War II was over, World War III—a war which would not be a simple military matter, but rather a war of economies, ideologies, and intelligence capabilities— would begin with a vengeance.

"Now there are those who say Europe has not been at war in forty years, but they're wrong, quite wrong. Our current war began officially at Potsdam, when Stalin, Churchill, and Roosevelt carved up Europe, and entire nations—in terms of nations governing themselves as sovereign states—were dissolved at the stroke of a pen."

Hornbill looked across at Pretorius and smiled. "Your father grasped the genius of what was happening and realized that a few of us would have to begin to orchestrate countermeasures which would avoid a nuclear holocaust, countermeasures which would use our best minds—and hearts—to keep us all sane, free, and alive. It was, he realized, a race between ourselves and the Soviets, each of us trying to disarm the other through either propaganda or technological superiority, before one of us lost rationality and pressed the nuclear trigger.

"Another man at the Agency, Sherman Kent, was like your father. He'd gone to school with us, had gone on into the OSS with us, then after the war went back to Yale, to teach. But he became so concerned for our survival that he ultimately came back full-time into the business, like your dad. Kent lived to a fine old age, writing children's books, lecturing, and enjoying life to its fullest. But your father didn't."

Hornbill looked down into his glass and swirled the liquid as if to divine some hidden truth from it. Then, abruptly, he stopped—and once again looked directly into Pretorius' eyes. "Your father," he began painfully, "didn't die in any accident. He was quite deliberately executed."

Pretorius stood up suddenly, an icy chill rippling down his spine, and the old scar seemed to twinge with a sudden memory of pain. "What do you mean, 'executed'?" he asked in a low, almost threatening voice. *"What the hell are you saying?"*

Hornbill held up his palm, and continued. "He'd gotten too close to something very big, something within the CIA that had, even in those days, begun to gnaw at its vitals like a cancer. We never knew what it was, only that he'd called Sherman Kent the night before and alluded to it in somewhat elliptical terms, because the phone wasn't known to be secure.

"The next day, we collected your father's body on the Baltimore Washington Expressway, his car crashed, his skull shattered by a large-caliber bullet which was never to be found, despite an army of forensic people covering the scene."

At this, Hornbill emptied his drink. Pretorius had slumped back in his seat, gone quite pale. "Why . . ." he began unsteadily, "why wasn't I told of this? Why was I told it was an accident?"

"Because, Michael, it would have done you absolutely no good at the time and could have done us a considerable amount of harm. I only tell you now, because what we want you to do . . . may be somewhat linked to your father's death."

"God, you people are incredible. You always know how to get at somebody . . ." Pretorius got up and stared out the window at his garden, which suddenly seemed far away.

"No, it's not merely a matter of pressing the right button, as you imply," said Hornbill. "It's a matter of telling you truthfully what's going on, so you can make up your own mind."

Pretorius drained his glass and held it out to the grim-faced Hornbill. "Would you . . . do the honors this time?" he asked. "This looks like it's going to be a long evening."

7

OXON HILL, MARYLAND

The record player, a glistening, mahogany-sheathed Zenith with a hinged top, had been lovingly polished for decades.

Having survived into the electronic eighties, it was something of a predigital dinosaur. Strictly 78 rpm, with a full, warm tone which had never known high sizzling cymbals, nor fat, booming bass hits, it had long been made obsolete by a thousand technologies. But the Fisherman loved it, and took great care of it and the frail records neatly stored near it, records with names like Bluebird and Decca and Aeolian.

In the long winter evenings, especially after dinner when he would retire to his library with a large glass of brandy, one record in particular was his favorite.

And on this evening, slowly sipping the golden liquid in its crystal cylinder, he listened, recalling a life long since lost.

> Once you warned me
> That if you scorned me
> That I'd be playing solitaire again
> Uneasy in my easy chair again
> It never entered my mind
> Once you told me I was mistaken
> That I'd awaken with the sun
> And order orange juice for one

It never entered my mind
You have what I lack myself
Now I even have to scratch my back myself
Once you warned me
That if you scorned me
I'd say a lonely prayer again
And wish that you were there again
To get into my hair again
It never entered my mind

They'd more or less stumbled into each other in Washington in the early war years: She'd been a young WAC lieutenant attached to the War Department, and he, a tall, gaunt young captain in the OSS. It had been at yet another of D.C.'s interminable cocktail receptions welcoming yet another ambassador from yet another country.

The party had been even more of a paralyzing bore than expected, and she'd selected the saturnine young officer as her challenge for the evening. He'd been taking the proceedings all too seriously, she decided, and was in great need of cheering up.

"*You're* a gloomy gus," she'd said, looking up at him from beneath long dark lashes.

He peered down through his glasses to discover a petite brunette in the trim, tailored uniform of a WAC lieutenant. "It's difficult to find anything funny about these folks," he'd responded in his laconic way.

"Nonsense, Captain. They're actors in a comic opera, all waiting for their cues. For example," she said, her small dimpled chin indicating the new ambassador, "he's just about to go into his speech about our common interest in preserving liberty being our greatest strength, and the necessity for sacrifice rather than rhetoric . . ."

And, indeed, to the young captain's amazement, the ambassador promptly proceeded to do precisely that.

"Do you read palms as well?" he asked the pert little WAC.

"And tea leaves, when I can get enough ration stamps," she replied impishly. "They *all* make the same speech at their first D.C. cocktail party and they never bother comparing notes. Almost makes you question the quality of the diplomatic corps, doesn't it?" And together they laughed, drawing not a few frowns from the assembled cast.

They left the party much later, and took a cab to one of the many after-hours clubs on which Washington has always depended for nightlife. They laughed and drank and danced, and the young captain found he'd never held anything quite so precious in his arms. Her name was Beverly. The next day, at his desk, he wrote the name again and again. And encircled it. And underscored it. And resisted the temptation to call her until nearly five, at which time he was informed that the lieutenant would be unreachable for the next three weeks, and no, they weren't permitted to divulge her whereabouts.

The captain was on edge. The captain was, in fact, an exposed nerve for the better part of a month. And when the lieutenant returned—from a vacation with her parents in California, as it happened—the captain was on her front doorstep with an armful of roses within minutes. It was simply one of those wartime romances, they both knew, and they both kept telling each other that. But the passion was so unexpected, so completely disarming—certainly for the captain—and the anticipation of being with each other exquisite.

From the beginning, the captain had thought of her as his Beatrice. Dante had been his obsession in college, and the idealism of Dante's Beatrice had made him feel that such a woman would, for the average man in his lifetime, be utterly unattainable.

But here she was, Beatrice in khaki, with a dimpled chin and mischievous brown eyes and a voice that could melt anything, anyone. And so the captain was hooked. And so, too, was his divine Beatrice.

Their affair was intense, almost painful in its concentration. The young captain had always been in tight rein of his emotions and, as was the case with most such people, he found control difficult once the floodgates were open. She, on the other hand, felt as natural in the relationship as a fish swimming through water. He called on her constantly, and the restaurants in Georgetown knew them now by name. She'd never received quite so many flowers in her life. Together, they would walk long hours in the streets after dinner or a movie, preferring to prolong their goodbyes as long as possible.

His work was now gearing up to a record pitch. He was commuting back and forth regularly to New York, meeting General William ("Wild Bill") Donovan in his Rockefeller Center lair at least once a week. On the train, as the countryside whizzed by, he imagined himself and Beverly on a farm somewhere out there, doing the things normal people do, once the war was over.

Soon the effort of setting up the new organization became an almost Herculean process, and his time with Beverly began to shrink. She wasn't upset, at first—they both knew they were there to fight a war and that anything else had to take a back-seat—but then a certain edge began to creep into their relationship.

"You know we can't just—just take off for the weekend. Donovan has to be able to reach out and contact any of us within minutes. Look, maybe we could go to Eddie's tonight, have some of his fettucini, spill a little more Chianti . . ."

"We've been to Eddie's three times this week so far. Can't we . . . oh, *damn* it!"

But it was the time of many such things, and the damage, after some weeks, began to seem irreparable. Until finally one evening the young captain told the diminutive brunette WAC that he found it almost impossible to concentrate on his work any more, that the strain was too much for him to handle both a demanding relationship and a demanding job. That perhaps, for a little while, they should back off a bit, maybe she should even see someone else when he was away in New York.

She fled the restaurant that evening crying, leaving her cap

72 / GUY DURHAM

on the table. He sat in silence, wearing his guilt like a dank and heavy coat, staring at the door through which she'd run.

He finally realized she'd left her cap there, but by the time he'd run out to the street to find her, she'd vanished.

Repeated calls to her office failed to bring a response. Calling her at home produced only a constant busy signal. He thought about her even more, now, and wished to God he'd been more able to handle it. Yet part of him felt relieved that his life had once more gotten simple and ascetic. For there was something of the monk in the young captain, something which felt a curious satisfaction in self-denial.

After a while he stopped calling her and tried to forget as best he could. But something had changed within him, and he occasionally found himself walking alone late at night on the streets where they had walked together, simply to experience something of those moments, and possibly to scourge himself with his own memory. Finally, he was shipped off to Switzerland to work directly with Dulles, then infiltrated into Nazi-occupied France to set up a network there.

He heard later she'd married a man he'd met once at the War Department, a young congressman very obviously on his way up. Over the years, even long after the war had lurched to its conclusion, he'd read the papers for news of the congressman, hoping for some mention of Beverly, and occasionally finding it. Once, in *Life* magazine, there'd been an article on the congressman's family, showing Beverly and their three children—two boys and a girl—on a beach somewhere in southern California.

> That I'd awaken with the sun
> And order orange juice for one
> It never entered my mind

The fingers of his left hand, long and delicate as a surgeon's, drummed a silent staccato on the top of the telephone. The call would come soon, he knew. Very soon. And so much would depend on this call, as, indeed, would many other elements of the Plan depend on similar small occurrences.

He had known Pretorius' father since they'd both been juniors in Davenport, in the thirties. They'd been separately approached for some secret work for the government—"all very Philips Oppenheim" was the way John Pretorius put it—and found they'd been recruited for intelligence, although they would nominally be working for the Department of State as minor attachés to one consulate, mission, embassy, or another.

Being tapped for intelligence work was, in those days at Yale, like being tapped for "Bones"—although vastly more intriguing, more special. They were not allowed to speak of it to anyone, yet the few young men who had been quietly spoken to soon knew who else the strangers from Washington had contacted.

The Fisherman and John Pretorius, although near-total opposites, were drawn to each other for the keenness of intellect they shared, and, quite possibly, because of their very differences.

The Fisherman was something of a star scholar on Dante and could recite endless stanzas at will. He was a solitary, brooding young man, often seen bicycling off to some quiet bend in a nearby river to fish in the dawn hours, always with two or three books strapped to his handlebars by a tattered leather belt.

John Pretorius, though, was an engaging, almost garrulous youngster, gangling yet handsome. He had many friends, and his only solitude appeared to be in studying.

John Pretorius thought this secret service stuff a bit of a lark, while the Fisherman knew—absolutely knew without question or hesitation—that it would become his life's work. It fitted every line, every nook and cranny of his character, as a seamless and unseen covering.

In accord with the conventional wisdom of undergraduates in those days, neither young man believed war would really come.

This hooligan, Hitler, this upstart Austrian paperhanger,

would shortly get his comeuppance. The rest of Europe was too strong to tolerate his rantings, and, besides, hadn't the German people learned a rather expensive lesson only two decades ago? It all seemed so unlikely, even when the first enthusiastic young men were killed, wearing the uniforms of nations not their own.

In the meantime, the two friends, each in his different way, were looking forward to being part of a privileged part of government work, an elite corps of intellectuals. (It was this same attitude, persisting among many in intelligence work even in the midst of war, that led others to regard the OSS as standing for "Oh So Special.")

The two men would remain in intelligence work the rest of their lives, although in very different ways. The Fisherman would remain a full-time professional, not only throughout the Second World War, but through three decades thereafter. John Pretorius would serve in the OSS, directly under Allen Dulles, but would leave the intelligence community at the war's end to begin his law studies, ultimately joining a prestigious but small firm in Baltimore, and serving the newly formed CIG (Central Intelligence Group, later to become the CIA) on a consulting basis.

The Fisherman would never marry, in part because of his belief that a second Beatrice would, indeed, be forever beyond his grasp, but mainly because he was married—totally, inextricably—to his work. John Pretorius married a softly attractive girl he'd met in Switzerland during his Dulles sojourn, and she'd Anglicized her original name, Lise-Maria, to Mary. They would have one child, Michael, and would share their deep love for years, until John met his death in a sedan on the Baltimore-Washington Expressway.

From time to time, the Fisherman would call on John Pretorius for advice and counsel. Living and working close to Washington, John could easily drive over for a meeting with the Fisherman. By this time, too, he had his own law practice, with a few clients in D.C., so his periodic absences were easily explainable.

Young Michael Pretorius grew up loving his father and mother greatly, and living in a home filled with grace and love. He began to realize something was unusual about his father, because he was so reluctant to talk about his work.

By the time Michael was eight, his father had become once more drawn into the intelligence community, although principally as a policy advisor to both the Central Intelligence Agency and the National Security Council.

His absences became more and more frequent, but Mary never spoke of them, nor attempted to concoct explanations for the boy. Only once, in Michael's memory, did she ever refer directly to his father's other life. It was one summer's afternoon at the family retreat at Random Lake, New York, when the telephone inside the large house had rung, and John had gone inside to answer it. In a few minutes he returned and said he had to go away on business for a long while and they must try not to miss him, and it would be best not to talk about his absence with anyone else. It was simply another business trip, just a bit longer than usual.

Michael's mother had looked at her husband oddly, but the expression soon passed. She turned to her son and said, "We must do as your father says, Michael. He's an important man, and lots of his work shouldn't be discussed with other people. Do you understand? Not even your friends. It's terribly important, Michael. May I have your solemn promise?"

Twelve-year-old Michael Pretorius hugged his mother and then his father. "How long will you be gone, Dad?" he asked.

"In all honesty, I don't know. They haven't told me," replied his father. Michael nodded, trying to understand. He wondered who "they" were, and why they needed his father for so long.

For the next hour, the three of them sat on the lawn looking down toward the lake, watching people lazily drifting their rowboats through the stillness of a soft summer's day, and others swimming in the distance. The idea of "they" having anything to do with this seemed so alien, so at odds with everything in the life he knew.

Young Michael Pretorius was thinking of this, sitting on the grass in front of his father's wooden lawnchair, when he first heard the soft scissoring of the Army helicopter's rotors as it came in low over the hills in back of them. Shielding his eyes from the sun directly in back of the helicopter, he could just make out its black dragonfly silhouette. Soon the helicopter's engines filled the air, and the blast from its rotors flattened the grass on the lawn. Slowly the craft settled down on the lawn, its tail arcing around like a scorpion's as it came to rest.

His father rose and inhaled deeply, almost as if this would be the last breath of clean air he would take. He turned to his wife and held her, not saying a word. Then he held out his hand to his son and shook it. "I'll be back before you know it. Remember your promise."

And he took his small bag—the one he always kept packed in the hall closet—and walked over to where the helicopter was waiting with its impatient roar and climbed up the ladder to disappear inside. Michael and his mother watched the machine rise unsteadily, swaying from side to side, beating the tall grass flat with its breath, and then saw it swing slowly back in the direction from which it had come, and head directly into the sun once again.

Other people measure their loss of innocence in sexual terms, or intellectual levels of realization, but Pretorius remembered that summer day as the beginning of when he had to keep secrets, as the start of his life that must be forever compartmentalized, shielded from others.

It was only a few months later when John Pretorius—after coming home briefly from his mission—had his brains blown out in a government motor pool Chevrolet.

In the years to follow, Michael's mother made sure the boy's life was as full and intellectually nourishing as possible. But no man moved into her life to replace John Pretorius.

Yet the Fisherman, through a variety of means, kept close watch on the boy and his development. It was the Fisherman, in fact, who quietly made certain the boy's application to Yale was accepted—and those to certain other universities diplomatically rejected.

He also made sure, through his considerable influence, that young Pretorius was carefully guided to certain courses of study, certain people who could shape his development.

The Fisherman had been close enough to John Pretorius to know a great deal about his family. In the hours waiting for the results of some mission in the Middle East or Asia, the older Pretorius would tell him about some small thing the boy had done, or something of their last Christmas in the house on Southview Road in Baltimore.

In this way the Fisherman came to know much about Michael Pretorius as the boy grew, came to know his emerging strengths and weaknesses, his abilities and limits. It was odd, the senior Pretorius felt, that the Fisherman never wanted to meet young Michael, and yet always asked about him, always seemed to want to know more and more about the boy.

Suddenly in the stillness the telephone rang, and the Fisherman lifted the receiver.

A voice on the other end spoke briefly. There was no need for identification procedures; both men had known each other for years and would have detected even the slightest irregularity in the timbre of either one's voice.

"He has accepted, then?" the Fisherman asked.

"And on his way to the facility," responded the voice on the other end.

"Any last minute considerations?"

"None. Except, of course, to keep up the pace, to keep the mind just a little too busy to reflect. He's very bright, you know. We could have used him quite a few times before."

"He won't tumble. There are too many levels, too many layers, like peeling an onion," the Fisherman said.

"Sometimes I wonder if you've even let me know all the levels," mused the disembodied voice.

A smile played on the lips of the Fisherman. "There's no appropriate—or even acceptable—answer to that one."

"Any new developments on the bird?"

"No, everyone's working at full tilt, but no surprises, at least so far. All the prep work seems to be integrating nicely."

"Good. The more time it's actually in place, the longer and slower the leak. More plausible. Have the transmissions been going on as scheduled?"

"The receivers in the towers at both Edwards and Nellis have had notch filters built into them during recent overhauls. Our transmissions are just slightly off tower frequency, but bang on the notch. The towers can't hear them, but anyone monitoring can."

There was a brief silence as the other man considered this. "Any covert transmissions in the area since?"

"They're still playing their games—moving the transmitter, changing the direction, going to P.M. But every time we transmit a fake control message, they send out a report. Most of them we unscramble, but frankly, it's not necessary. The other side should be well primed by now, I should think."

"As should our own people," said the other voice.

"As should our own people," concurred the Fisherman.

8

ARIZONA

With the effortless grace of a swallow, the 747 brushed the runway at Phoenix Sky Harbor and Pretorius slid back to consciousness. He glanced at his watch, a tarnished, treasured old
Hamilton, and squinted out the window.

Out past the dazzle of the airport lights, necklaces of street-
lights were strung between the airport and the Superstition
Mountains. Pretorius thought how much clearer the air was
here than in New York, where he'd changed planes from British
Air to American, making the connection with only seconds to
spare.

The flight attendant—a stunning redhead with the bright,
fixed smile of a taxidermist's squirrel—wished everyone a real
pleasant stay here in Phoenix, and hoped they would fly the
airline again real soon.

The big plane tucked itself in next to the terminal, and Pretorius waited for the passengers to filter out before taking his
lone canvas case from the overhead compartment. As he waited,
he thought back over the past few days. He'd told Susannah he
had to go back for some more medical treatment at Walter Reed
hospital and then wanted to do some serious sightseeing across
the country.

Susannah knew he'd been a naval officer and had been injured in some sort of accidental explosion aboard ship, but very little more. He was very close-mouthed about his naval career, as if it pained him in some way to discuss it. He told her he'd be away a few months and scratched David Lloyd George behind the ears. The dog seemed to understand, and followed Pretorius around Susannah's house like a pull-toy, never letting him out his sight, pressing his big head next to Pretorius' leg whenever he paused or sat down. David Lloyd George somehow knew he was leaving, and Pretorius marveled at whatever sixth sense governed the dog.

When he checked in at Heathrow as instructed, using the name Daltrey, a message was waiting at the counter which asked him to proceed to a certain small office nearby, where a mechanic (technical specialist attached to an operations group) in a Customs uniform locked the door and spread out a number of items on the desk.

He was required to write a number of postcards dated over the coming six months and all bearing U.S. postage stamps. They had pictures of various American sightseeing attractions, from Washington D.C., to an alligator farm in an obscure Florida town, to Utah's Monument Valley, even to the La Brea Tar Pits in Los Angeles.

They had been addressed to a number of his friends, and the mechanic instructed him to only write general pleasantries, and not invent any details about the location he was supposed to be visiting.

Pretorius was also given a complete set of travel ID with the Daltrey name, including an American passport, a California driver's license, pictures of someone's family, a dry cleaning receipt, several credit cards, a bank card, two blank checks bearing the name on the passport, and a little over $500 in cash. He was instructed to strip down and change into a set of clothing provided on a hook behind the door, and given the carry-on bag which he now carried off the plane in Phoenix.

Despite himself, he felt an upsurge in his adrenaline at being on the job again. Emerging in the fluorescent harshness of the airport, he blinked and looked around him. A tall, lanky figure separated itself from the crowd and strode toward him with a loping, athletic gait. The stranger was a man of about fifty, wearing a cowboy hat that looked as if it had been stomped on by something mean, and a well-scrubbed, slightly frayed white Western shirt.

The man's face was seamed and bronzed with the look of a life spent outdoors, the kind of face one never sees in cities. Pretorius thought of Randolph Scott, then of Chill Wills. "Well, Daltrey," the stranger boomed, "it's good to see you. We were kinda worried you wouldn't make it, with that New York connection."

Pretorius had never met the man in his life and stopped short. "Sorry, I think you've mistaken me for somebody else . . ." he began.

Quickly, unobtrusively, the tall man flipped out a small black wallet and showed a Defense Department ID. It showed the same face and correlated it with the name Fraker, Maxwell C., LTCOL, USMC.

"Call me Max," he said with a broad grin.

"Glad to meet you, Max," Pretorius returned. "Where to?"

"Well, we've got a little trip north to make. Not too far. Bet you're really ready to hit the sack."

Pretorius shouldered his canvas carryall. "No, I'm fine. Slept from Heathrow to New York, then slept most of the way here. Something about the engines drones me to sleep. Thinking of putting one in at home."

Max chuckled as they crossed the huge parking lot and came up to a battered F-100 Ford pickup, its red paint scarred and peeling to reveal an even earlier coat of dark blue paint beneath. All in all, not a vehicle with which to win motor shows, thought Pretorius. "Just sling that case in back," said Fraker. "It'll be safe enough. Hasn't rained in three weeks. Probably won't rain for another three or four more."

Pretorius looked up at the stars and saw all the great constellations. The air was fresh and only slightly tinged with the smell of Number Two kerosene from the big jets. Still, it was good to be out here.

The old truck sped up I-17 North, and the way it moved told Pretorius that beneath the hood was something more than your average 351 Cleveland. Fraker was obviously a professional, both from the way he drove and the way his eyes kept flicking to the rearview mirror, even when the highway was empty.

When they got far above Phoenix, the highway lights got fewer and fewer. In the headlights Pretorius could see dozens of tall saguaro cactus, standing sentinel duty in the darkness.

Just after they turned off at Cordes Junction and onto Highway 69 toward Prescott, Fraker kept staring in the rearview mirror. "Looks like we've got some fans back yonder."

Pretorius looked around and saw strong headlights rapidly gaining on them. Fraker floored the accelerator, and the Ford snapped forward as if its leash had broken. The speedometer's needle sharply whipped past ninety. The headlights of the other car were not gaining as fast, but were still steadily narrowing the distance.

"Well," Fraker drawled, "if he was a state cop, he'd be flashing by now, and he's definitely not an escort vehicle. So I reckon he's either drunk or up to no good. We just better see what he can do."

He kept up the pressure on the accelerator, and Pretorius unbelievingly saw the speedometer needle move slowly past 120, then 130, and keep going.

The pickup wasn't shaking in the slightest. Whoever had worked this one over really knew his stuff. The headlights of the other car slowly began to fall behind.

Rounding a curve, Fraker suddenly shoved the light switch against the dash, plunging them into darkness, flicked a switch that killed the brake lights, and downshifted to second, then first, as he pulled into a side road leading down to a wash.

Handling the truck expertly in the blackness, almost as if by touch, Fraker brought it to a stop below the level of the highway. Pretorius' heart was pounding; Fraker had brought the pickup down from over 135 mph to a halt in less than fifteen seconds.

They sat there for a minute and saw the other car streak by. Fraker flicked on the two-way radio and called in the vehicle's location, requesting a DWI stop from somebody at the other end.

"Well, that ought to tether that particular cat," Fraker said, lighting up a cigarette in the darkness. "You see anybody at the airport watching you?"

"No, but it's hard to tell in a place that size," Pretorius said.

"Hell, let's not lose any sleep over it. Better hit the bricks; we've got company waitin'," Fraker said, flipping the headlights back on and easing the truck back onto the highway.

They kept the speed at a leisurely sixty-five or so, and in about ten minutes passed a highway patrol cruiser parked by the roadside behind another car, whose two male occupants were spread-eagled against the side for a body search. They wore three-piece business suits and were clean-shaven, well groomed.

"Don't look like anybody from around these parts," Fraker observed with a wry smile, "Look like anybody you know?"

"No. Never saw them before. How much farther to go?"

Fraker leaned back and pressed the accelerator down, swinging the needle up to seventy-five. "Oh, about another hour or so, I guess."

Pretorius relaxed back in his seat as they passed by roadhouses and bars, beer signs beckoning, sounds of Waylon Jennings and David Allan Coe pounding inside, pickups parked in rows outside.

"Sure as hell doesn't look like Kansas, Toto," said Pretorius.

"No," Fraker replied. "And it sure as hell don't look like the East German border, either."

Pretorius turned to look at him. Very few people knew about

that. Even fewer would have the clearance to mention it aloud without signing a flock of forms first. "You're pretty well-informed," Pretorius said.

"Hell, I'm paid to be," laughed Fraker. "Don't you worry. You're in good hands."

Pretorius looked back at the road. They had slowed down to pass through the town of Chino Valley, speed limit 35 mph. There was a homeliness and simplicity about this part of the States that Pretorius liked. Unadorned and unpretentious, it seemed far removed from the conflicts of the world outside.

But this was the country all the cowboy movies were made about, the stuff that made kids from Cambodia to Nicaragua whip out imaginary six-shooters in imaginary High Noon shoot-outs. Long before they had real AK47s or real M16s or real legs and arms blown off.

It was a strange time, and a strange place, Pretorius thought.

He wondered what the next day or the next week would bring, whether he would be alive himself, what he would be put up against.

And then Fraker wheeled the old pickup on a sharp left-hand turn off the highway, jolting and jouncing down a deeply rutted side road.

They passed a small sign which informed them they were on a U.S. Department of the Interior Environmental Studies Center, and that trespassing was strictly forbidden.

Pretorius held one hand to the roof and another hand on the dash to brace himself inside the bucking, bouncing cab. "You guys sure know how to make a guy feel welcome," he managed to get out between clenched teeth.

"Gets this way in winter," replied the laconic Fraker. "Snow and rain turn it to mush, and by the time summer comes and it dries up, it's got ruts three miles deep in places."

The truck jolted its way for another fifteen minutes, jackrabbits scattering back and forth across the road in the high beams, their tall tufted ears standing stiff as cornstalks.

Then they came up to a wide aluminum gate spanning the narrow road, a cattle grid directly beneath it. Fraker pulled something out from under the dash and pointed it at the gate which slowly swung open.

"Handy thing to have," Fraker said. "You don't use it, and try to finagle that gate back yonder, and you get a claymore up your backside from beneath the cattle grid."

"Remind me to borrow that thing when I go into town for a beer," Pretorius said.

Fraker laughed and in a few minutes they slowed down as two Marines in fatigues, each armed with a short-barreled M16 carbine, motioned to the truck to stop.

Fraker showed them his ID. One checked it carefully with his flashlight as the other kept the truck covered with his carbine, finger on the trigger.

Finally, the Marine with the flashlight handed the ID back, saluted smartly, and waved them on.

"This is some picky kind of country club, Fraker. Not sure I can pass the membership requirements," Pretorius said.

"You'll do just fine," Fraker laughed. "You paid all your dues a long time ago, the way I heard it. Here we go."

And they wheeled into a yard where two or three ranch buildings formed part of the perimeter. Quartz halogen floodlights, mounted on forty-foot towers, shone down on the scene, contrasting up every particle of gravel in bright relief. Three other pickup trucks were parked outside, and two plain cars that could only be government issue. Another Marine in fatigues, also armed with the shortened M-16, stood duty in front of the largest building.

They slammed shut the pickup's doors, and from out of the back Pretorius picked up his bag, which had miraculously managed to stay in the pickup's bed despite the bouncing on the way in.

Closed-circuit cameras peered at them from the shadows. As Fraker came up to the main building's door, he showed his ID to the Marine, who registered its acceptance with a flicker of an eyelid. The first room was brightly lit with fluorescents, and at a desk near the door a slight, spare man in civilian clothes and a military crewcut looked them over carefully.

Fraker showed the man his ID, and, indicating Pretorius, said, "He's my property." From one of the desk's drawers, the man produced a temporary ID on a neck chain, the word VISI-TOR in bold black letters across its top, a red border rimming the laminated card.

"Mr. Hornbill's been waiting for you, Colonel," the civilian said.

"Thanks, Andy. Hope we haven't kept him up too long."

"Nossir. But he's just a mite testy tonight," he replied, with a grin.

"We'll keep that in mind," grinned Fraker. "Thanks again."

Swinging open a heavy metal door, they entered a compartment which resembled either a suite-room in a Holiday Inn anywhere in the U.S. or a visitor's lounge at a very good psychiatric center.

After about five minutes, Arthur Hornbill entered the room.

Despite the hot southwestern weather, he wore his usual tweed suit, a neatly tied bow tie, and a blue and white striped shirt with white collar and cuffs.

He spoke. "Well, the good Colonel. Home at last, I see. And Michael. Good to see you again."

Once more, Pretorius experienced a highly concentrated aura of power radiating from Hornbill. It was difficult to guess at who this man really was, or what he had been. But it was obvious Hornbill was someone used to commanding, a man at ease with the exercise of power.

Pretorius chose one of the upholstered chairs and pulled it slightly nearer Hornbill's own. Fraker lounged against a table, regarding Pretorius and Hornbill with an expressionless, even gaze.

Hornbill leaned forward, clear blue eyes staring intently at

Pretorius, his hands clasped in front of him. "Now first, Michael," he began in his curious Yankee accent, "we're delighted to have you join us in our little exercise here. Delighted. Yes.

"You doubtless have a great many questions about your new duties, and I shall, in time, be able to tell you much more about them. In time. But for now, because of the somewhat sensitive nature of things, I'm afraid I shan't be able to tell you much more now than we shall be asking a great deal of you in the weeks ahead.

"I understand from your file that in the past you've been a fairly, um, busy agent in the field, and that your training has been somewhat intensive.

"Nonetheless, I've also been given to understand that your new duties may require considerable exertions on your part, and it is our job here to prepare you adequately for them. You've been out of the field for several years now, and you doubtless need some brushing up.

"It is also possible we may be able to pass along one or two little techniques which have been developed since you've been, um, vacationing.

"So your first few days here may be somewhat in the nature of a refresher course. You may be bored. But the greater part of your training here will be considerably more demanding, more, ah, rigorous than your previous training in either the Navy or with Defense in the old days.

"You may be assured, however, we shall ask you to do nothing beyond your physical, intellectual, or emotional limits. Although, at times, you'll think this not to be the case.

"Being but a small part of a very large, somewhat bureaucratic whole, we are sometimes obliged to pass along some of our superiors' requests for forms and such, and so I must ask that you take a few moments to read and sign these—rather cumbersome—documents." With that, he handed Pretorius a large manila envelope, blank on the outside, except for a Washington, D.C. postal sort number. Pretorius opened a fat twenty-five page contract from the Department of Defense, self-carboning in triplicate, which excused the Pentagon from any liability or damages arising from his performance of the contract, set an open-ended term of contract to be determined by the Secretary of Defense or any of his designated representatives, explained the penalties, and gave reference numbers to obscure federal penal codes for revealing information pertaining to national security, and—finally—set terms of payment upon satisfactory completion of the contract.

Pretorius smiled. Bureaucracy had taken yet another giant step forward. In the old days, actually less than ten years ago, DOD contracts for outside agents were only three pages long, when and if they existed at all.

He signed all copies with a ballpoint and returned them to Hornbill.

"Now," continued Hornbill, "I shall visit you from time to time in order to answer what questions I am able to and to monitor your progress. "If you wish to contact me for any reason, kindly inform the good Colonel here, and I shall either contact you by telephone or appear personally. Although due to the nature of my work, the latter may be extremely difficult.

"Now then, do any questions occur at the moment?" he asked as he raised his tufted white eyebrows quizzically.

Pretorius had the fleeting image of an owl reflecting upon its dinner-to-be.

9
CHINO VALLEY,
ARIZONA

Ten meters away, the gunman clamped the woman's throat with his forearm. His other hand—wrapped around the grips of a large-caliber revolver—stretched toward Pretorius. In that instant, the muzzle of the piece seemed huge, larger than a shotgun bore. It had happened so suddenly, Pretorius' reactions were frozen for a few milliseconds. Too long.

Then, in one swift, fluid stroke, Pretorius whipped up the Smith & Wesson 469 in a two-handed hold and fired two shots into the felon's head, scarcely an inch apart.

Fraker, throwing down his sweatstained Stetson, shouted, "Sweet leaping Jesus, Pretorius! He could of had you for *breakfast!* You were *way* over the two-second mark. You think he's gonna wait forever? He wasted both you *and* the lady before you got your shit together. *Think*, goddamnit, *think!*"

Pretorius bit the inside of his cheek and reholstered, then walked over to the target stand to tape over the two hits on the gunman's cardboard forehead. The target system was electronic. As Pretorius walked through the scenario, Fraker walked behind holding a small radio transmitter with an array of colored buttons like so many M&Ms. Depending on the way the student was reacting, Fraker would press his buttons.

The targets were supported in metal frames and could be

controlled electronically to show either one side or the other to the student: one side friend, the other side foe.

The "friend" side held innocent objects such as groceries or an attaché case, while the "foe" side held lethal weapons. Positions of the targets were always shifted so no student could relay any information to others coming later through the scenario.

People depicted in the targets included a black man holding either a hand grenade or a law enforcement badge, a housewife who greeted you warmly with either a bag of groceries or a sawed-off shotgun, and a well-dressed crewcut type with a choice of revolver or electric drill—which looked at first glimpse to be some exotic type of silenced weapon.

Students who "killed" the housewife with groceries after having once seen her with the shotgun were penalized. Students who did this sort of thing too often were washed out of the course and sent to desk jobs, where their eagerness couldn't endanger the general populace.

Pretorius showed considerable coolness and good fast judgment. But he had to unlearn much of what he'd learned in the past, from his crude early training in ONI and from his days in DIA. Using the new techniques, his speed gradually increased, soon eclipsing some of the best times logged in at this remote facility.

Fraker was pleased. But instead of relaxing, he made things even tougher for Pretorius, pushing him more and more.

Among the scenarios he led Pretorius through was the house-clearing drill, in which the electronic targets were set up in a cinderblock house. Pretorius had to edge through the house in semidarkness, flashlight gripped alongside his pistol, approaching corners from the far side, learning to approach doors the right way, avoiding the cone of possible fire, as well as, in general, avoiding all the techniques Starsky and Hutch promoted on prime time for years. All the while Fraker walked carefully behind, screaming threats and contradictory instructions, piling the pressure on, more and more.

Many of the shooting sessions were held at dusk and, on more than a few occasions, at night. (Both police and federal agencies' statistics showed most gunfights occur after dark, at ranges of seven feet or less. Still, many police training programs continued to concentrate on broad daylight shooting at long ranges, and even emphasized one-handed "bulls-eye" type shooting for periodic qualification.)

By far, most of Pretorius' training was in dim light at five meters or less: Long-range work seldom happened, and most shooters got rattled when confronted by an opponent two or three meters away in semidarkness. Pretorius also trained mostly wearing a jacket, having to sweep it aside with the edge of his palm to get to the weapon. Adding a few loose rounds to his strong-side pocket (and keeping his keys there, too) helped give the jacket some momentum—a habit Pretorius learned from a friend who worked plainclothes in the NYPD.

The jacket slowed his time down some, but he knew most times he'd have to go for a weapon would be while wearing a jacket. Doing without it would give him good speed in training—but would cut his life expectancy down sharply on the street, out in the real world.

To keep up the stress on Pretorius, Fraker worked him hard at the three-meter and five-meter levels, slicing away at his time in tenths-of-a-second slivers.

Like most good firearms instructors, Fraker was a dedicated believer in the KISS principle: Keep It Simple, Stupid. He trained his students in one draw-and-fire technique for all ranges except arm's length, at which range the recommended action was to step quickly backward to get some distance as you drew your weapon and got into a two-handed hold.

Other federal instructors usually taught a variety of firing strokes to be used in varying conditions, at varying distances. Fraker believed—when in a stress situation—the fewer decisions to make, the better. And so a single technique was printed into Pretorius' memory by relentless repetition. Breaking Pretorius of the habit of crouching into the old isosceles position was tough. The isosceles, still taught by many police departments, and until only a few years ago by the Feebies, put the shooter facing the target head-on, using both arms coming together to form a sort of crude triangle—was a tough tactic. Fraker's preferred technique was the Weaver, developed years ago by a western lawman named Jack Weaver, and refined by a number of people into the most accurate, fast, and lethal way of getting a handgun into action.

The Weaver technique uses one shoulder positioned slightly forward of the other, and the elbow of the weak arm slightly bent—pushing with the strong arm against the pistol and pulling back with the weak hand to get better control of the piece under rapid repeat fire.

As Fraker once remarked to Pretorius, "For effective crisis management during close interpersonal confrontations, it beats shit out of dialing 911." Fraker always admonished him to fire no less than twice at any enemy. "Single shots are tactically inadvisable," he would intone. And, God knows, Pretorius didn't want to do anything tactically inadvisable. Except, just possibly, in one of the local bars down in Prescott.

Pretorius' firing stroke picked up quickly: In only a few days he had mastered the new technique. He was able to come from a hands-behind-the-back position to draw, fire, and plant two rounds in the "disable" area in under 1.2 seconds.

He could also draw on and disable multiple targets with practiced ease, adding only a fraction of a second for each additional target. Not satisfied with any level of success, only with the potential of his subject, Fraker kept the pressure up, driving him harder and harder.

He also refused to let Pretorius settle on a favorite pistol, although he'd gotten somewhat used to both the 9mm Smith & Wesson 469 and the newer Austrian Glock 19—a radical pistol made of steel hardened to Rockwell 19C specs, with polymer frame, magazine, trigger, and sights.

Fraker said, "Someday, somewhere, you're gonna be stuck

with a piece that looks like it fell off the battleship *Potemkin*, or that you bought off some asshole in a back alley in Beirut, and guess what? It isn't going to be your nice new Tefloned IPSC special with your Behlert sights and your Barstow barrel and all kinds of weights hanging off it, and then you, my friend, are gonna be up shit's creek. Never get too used to *anything*. Concentrate on just getting used to yourself and getting the job done."

Fraker also gave him sessions with special weapons, burning in the eccentricities of the Uzi, the MAC, the Sterling L2A3, the Soviet AKM, the Heckler & Koch sub guns, various suppressor systems, how to convert almost any current military firearm into full-automatic fire if necessary, and more. Much more.

The training was tough, and—standing out all day in the Arizona desert under an August sun—Pretorius lost more than a few pounds as he refined his abilities.

Pretorius also endured some stiff training in hand-to-hand combat with Henry Koo, a young Korean who'd grown up in Chicago's South Side before joining the Marine Corps and later being assigned to Defense Intelligence. Koo was short, dark complexioned, and had a face like a jack-o'-lantern. His smile reached nearly from ear to ear, and he was never seen without it, even while chewing out the most incompetent student—although, in his current job, Koo had very few students, and none of them incompetent. Henry Koo was a man who found happiness in his work. He taught a different kind of martial arts, one based on a combination of street-fighting techniques and the more surprising of the classic oriental martial arts moves. He threw in the use of everyday articles like rolled-up magazines or newspapers, beer bottles, and ballpoint pens.

Henry Koo didn't fight fair. His form of fighting was a kind of one-on-one terrorism, in which part of the drill was to instantly strike terror into the adversary as part of the disabling process. It was his belief that it was going to be all over within three seconds, so it had better be your best three seconds, and not the other guy's.

Once, in a session on the mats in the gymnasium, Koo and a much-enlightened Pretorius circled warily until Koo suddenly reached into a hidden pocket and threw a plastic bag of red watercolor dye at Pretorius, showering him with the stuff and bewildering him just long enough to get in a sudden disabling kick with the callused edge of his foot at Pretorius' throat. Covered from head to toe with crimson dye, Pretorius sank to the mat, clawing at his throat, unable to breathe for at least thirty seconds, while Koo sat down, grinning, slowly shaking his head at his student's vulnerability.

During Koo's course, Pretorius got stomped on, cut, punched, kicked, thrown out windows and into walls, and generally made to expect anything—and to react with lethal suddenness to any threat. It was a definite improvement on his old training, which leaned heavily on old judo techniques, every one of which had certain well-known countermeasures.

Pretorius got lean and hard and stringy and tough as whipcord, and pressed all thoughts from his mind except for getting faster and better. His hair got lighter than ever from the Arizona sun. His mind worked faster too. His perceptions were sharper, his decisions in split-second situations were better. Almost as if his mind were, itself, a muscle, and responding to his overall physical training like any other.

Pretorius often wondered what Susannah was doing, what she was thinking. He thought of the gentleness of her, of the peals of laughter when he'd said something she thought was funny. He remembered the soft swing of her golden hair, brushing his face as she bent over to kiss him. He knew the postcards he'd filled out in New York were being mailed at appropriate intervals from post offices in different towns and cities. But Pretorius felt cheap at having to lie to her, and to have given her so little reason for leaving her for so long. It was part of being back in the business again, he knew. But it didn't make it any easier. In fact, if anything, he felt even more trapped, more saddled with a destiny created by someone he would never see and never know. A destiny, he knew now, which would in all likelihood never end. Anybody in the business should know that. And he'd been fool enough to think he was an exception.

And then one day a plain gray government Ford LTD with blackwall tires cruised up to the firing range, and Arthur Devlin Hornbill got out wearing a gray three-piece wool suit, glaring up accusingly at the Arizona sun.

It was Graduation Day.

10
MINGUS MOUNTAIN, ARIZONA

The big car streaked up the highway toward Mingus Mountain, passing aluminum windmills and large-wheeled irrigation rigs that looked like axles and rear wheels of abandoned Brobdingnagian tricycles. Pretorius hadn't been off the compound in weeks, and even the sparse scenery of the area seemed fascinating in comparison. Looking out the window, he reflected on the past few weeks—and on the weeks to come.

Freedom's just another word for nothin' left to lose, went the Janis Joplin song. *Bullshit,* thought Pretorius. *You spend enough time either in prison or working for the government, and pretty soon you get a good idea of what freedom means. You're about as caged as anything in a zoo, with about as many options. And even if you get through this thing—whatever it is—in one piece, sooner or later they'll send somebody around for you again, telling me this thing or that thing is absolutely essential, fucking up your life one more time, putting you through their own personal billion-dollar Skinner box. No, freedom is having the bastards off your neck, or having them forget about your file, or you just plain disappearing off the face of the earth forever.*

Finally the land began to show a few trees, some greenery. The highway began a slow, gentle slope upward. Hornbill hummed along as he drove, managing to keep in surprising proximity to the melody of a Bach cantata on the car's tape deck.

As Pretorius watched through the tinted window of the government Ford, the landscape slowly changed from low scrub brush into pines, then into boulders and larger trees, and then the highway slowly tilted up toward Mingus Mountain. Pretorius remembered the town of Jerome, just over the top of the mountain, perched precariously on suicide-steep slopes: a Phelps-Dodge copper mining town that had once supported a tiny population, and then, when the copper gave out, emptied itself of its inhabitants as suddenly as if a trapdoor had suddenly opened beneath each house. He'd been through Jerome years ago, in the sixties, when dropouts discovered the unwanted town and set up craft shops here and there on the dusty streets.

By now, Pretorius supposed, it's probably looking like a lot of California coastal towns, overlaid with the cloying commercial cuteness of pottery shops and ice cream shops and turquoise-and-silver gift shops and real estate offices as far as the eye could see.

Pretorius stretched. His muscles were feeling good; the exercise and the time spent outdoors had given him a lean, lithe look. But he wanted more than anything to be out of all this and back in Devon, maybe out sailing with Susannah and David Lloyd George. He thought of the dog, and smiled. DLG was no sea dog, being unable to keep his footing for more than a minute or two. Nevertheless, the dog loved going sailing and was always first on the boat and last to leave. A day like this would be good sailing on the Dart, thought Pretorius. Plenty of sun, a good stiff breeze.

He snapped out of his reverie as Hornbill turned off the main highway and onto a dirt road that led off to one side deep into the woods. It reminded Pretorius of certain parts of Germany, dark trees arching over the road, shafts of sunlight filtering down through the branches.

Hornbill drove carefully, competently. He was a cautious

man. He had also, many years ago in Europe, had a flat tire tearing along a twisting road at 120 mph, surviving with a sharply-etched memory.

The primitive road led on for a mile or more, as Hornbill slowed down to less than 15 mph. Finally, the road opened on a clearing next to a cliff, set around a large contemporary house. Its architecture resembled something by Frank Lloyd Wright, and Pretorius said so.

"A keen eye, Michael," responded Hornbill. "In point of fact, it was built after Wright's death to his plans. It was a design he'd been putting off building until he'd satisfied several major public commissions. And, of course, the commissions kept coming, and the house kept getting put off.

"I had no difficulty in purchasing the plans from his estate, as I had known him—briefly—in years long gone. It was the despair of two successive building contractors until I found a young man willing to experiment with some radical concepts in both structure and materials. Then, at long last, and with no little difficulty, the house got itself built."

Hornbill showed Pretorius around the house, cantilevered out from the enormous rocky face of the cliff that rimmed the far edge of the clearing, and Pretorius marveled at its feeling of space and light and air.

Besides several tall, fit-looking young men in casual clothes who were obviously security people, there was a single servant, a Filipino Moro of about fifty who was cook, housekeeper, butler, valet, and, from the look of his wiry frame and the way he moved, probably also Hornbill's bodyguard. Pretorius had seen men like this before, men with an impressive economy of movement in hand-to-hand combat, reducing the number and distances of motions to produce dazzling speed.

As he looked around the huge living room, Pretorius realized the furniture had to be designed by Wright. All solid oak, mathematical and Spartan in appearance, but surprisingly comfortable. There was a longish couch of oak, upholstered in fabric patterned in a Hopi Indian design. This remarkable piece also had an oversized arm on one side for magazines, drinks, or odds and ends. He'd once seen a similar couch in New York's Metropolitan Museum, part of an entire Wright room, and had always considered the room one of the city's great treasures. "I hope you like the sundry concoctions we've prepared for dinner," said Hornbill, as the Moro helped him exchange his customary tweed suit jacket and vest for a cardigan. "It's something reasonably special. I know you're fond of game, and venison is one of our strong points here."

Pretorius nodded appreciatively. "I haven't had venison in months. Most people don't know how to deal with it."

"Well, hanging it the proper length of time is a great part of the secret," said Hornbill. "Patience is not only the first requisite of the hunter; it's also the first for the chef. Our marinade, for example, takes a full four days to work its wonders."

The venison was served in the form of steaks, cut two inches thick, seared darkly over hickory wood coals, brushed with a light currant and juniper berry sauce. Hornbill's audience was astonished. He'd never had such venison in his life. "How on earth do you do it?" Pretorius asked.

Hornbill smiled. "You're not the first to ask. The marinade is basically just a half cup of lemon juice plus the grated rind, two dozen toasted-and-crushed juniper berries, a dozen peppercorns, two tablespoons of ground coriander seed, two celery stalks chopped to smithereens, two cloves of garlic, two cups of sesame seed oil, and one cup of malt vinegar.

"Cut your steak two inches thick—yes, it's conspicuous consumption of the worst sort, but it works—and, as I said, let it relax in the marinade four days."

Pretorius shook his head as Hornbill continued in his oddly twanging New England accent. "You get a good hickory fire going with branches about two or two and a half inches in diameter, so your coals will be the right size. Don't even think about substituting mesquite, by the way—contrary to popular legend, hickory beats mesquite all hollow. In about an hour and a half, the coals should be about perfect.

"And did you know," Hornbill digressed, "the Old English word for coal is *glow?* And the Latin word for fireplace is *focus?* Very satisfying, that."

Pretorius smiled at Hornbill's linguistic rambling. Bringing forth another wreath of pipe smoke, the older man pursued his recital. "When you put the steaks on, you cook them no closer than four inches from the coals. Sear each side just short of black. While they're still smoking, give them a good, healthy ladling of a very, very light currant and juniper berry sauce, and there you have it. My modest contribution to Western civilization as we know it."

Later Pretorius, tasting his after-dinner Port (Dow '37) served by the silent Moro, felt contented as a cat. For the first time in weeks he was able to feel part of civilization again and marveled at the sophistication of Hornbill's retreat in what was, by anybody's reckoning, a fairly remote area.

The two men talked at length on cooking, on the genius of Wright, on virtually everything but the subject at hand: Pretorius' mission.

Finally, Hornbill led Pretorius by the elbow to what appeared to be a closet door set in a hallway. He waved a magnetic card in front of a light switch, and a resonating electric whir issued from behind the door. Then, with a smooth and deliberate motion, the entire closet—including the door, doorframe, and the three-foot deep working closet behind it—slowly moved forward, then swung to one side, revealing a large well-lit room with a white tiled floor.

From Pretorius' memory of the outside of the house, this clandestine room must have been tunneled into the rock cliffside the house was built against.

As they stepped into the room, Pretorius recognized both a VAX and a Cray X-MP/14se computer, similiar to those he'd known at the Pentagon. Pretorius knew the machines well: he'd even learned to program in ADA*, cursing his way through array declarations, index constraints, and worse.

Pretorius whistled under his breath. "Be it ever so humble, there's no place like home," he said.

"Well, we do love our toys," chuckled Hornbill. "Then, too, I like to keep track of things. Saves me no end of time at the office."

Hornbill indicated a chair, and Pretorius sat down. Hornbill flicked several switches, enabling some unseen electronic anti-surveillance devices, and then sat opposite Pretorius. He began filling his pipe with that rapt concentration reserved for concert violinists and pipe smokers alike.

"No doubt you've picked up a thing or two since we last took tearful leave of each other?" inquired Hornbill between puffs.

Pretorius grinned. "The hardest part wasn't learning. It was forgetting that once upon a time, not so very long ago, I knew it all—or thought I did. Having Max as an instructor is a humbling experience."

"It is every bit that," replied Hornbill, now enveloped in a haze of smoke which he attempted to disperse with a wave of his hand. "Formidable. We were together in another war, once, a long time ago. He is the most trustworthy person I know. In point of fact, Max is the *only* trustworthy person I know. Although I occasionally have the odd doubt." Hornbill smiled at Pretorius. Then, as if a cloud had passed across the sun, his face took on a serious cast.

"Michael, you know something of the mission we're entrusting to your tender mercies. But there are certain elements which we—which *I*—feel necessary to tell you now."

Pretorius settled himself more deeply in his chair, beginning to get that same prickly feeling around the base of his neck he'd

*ADA: official programming language of Defense. Named after Ada Leigh, daughter of Lord Byron and very likely the first person to "write" a program for a primitive calculator/computer.

had—when was it? When he realized he was being observed on the hill.

Hornbill continued, staring at Pretorius with a curious intensity. "It should now be obvious to anyone that electronic warfare systems play the dominant strategic role in our defense. Not throw-weight of missiles, nor masses of hardware, nor sheer bulk in any form.

"With all our resources as a nation, and from the tone of our disarmament discussions with the Soviets, one would think we were enormously concerned with having lots and lots of stuff to throw at each other. Not so.

"Success and survival are now resolved to a matter of either coming in fast and low without radar detection—or detecting intruders early and knocking them out before they know what hit them, launching your own birds in the process. Put simply, it comes down to electronics and, of course, those designs, materials and budgets which influence and control such technologies. More than half the cost of every United States military aircraft is now in electronics." Hornbill's brow furrowed, and he spread his hands wide as he continued.

"Picture a possible scenario of the future, one not so very unlikely, given the insecurity of our era: Due to some brushfire occurring in an obscure portion of our planet, each of the superpowers takes a position with each of the adversaries. Our President has taken a hard line, because he feels to be returned to office by the electorate, he must be perceived as a strong, decisive chief executive.

"The Soviet leadership, on the other hand, have also taken a hard line, because they feel they must be perceived as the defender of the emerging Third World nations, in order to scoop up more of the same within their network.

"Accusations between the two superpowers escalate. Other nations begin to align themselves on either side. Troop movements are detected along the borders of neighboring nations. Fleet movements of both Soviet and U.S. forces are seen on our screens.

"And then someone, on one side or the other, recognizes we are very, very likely to have a major clash—simply because of the combination of rising emotions and rising numbers of troops and equipment now arrayed against each other.

"And that someone knows—knows without question—that whoever strikes first has a far greater probability of winning. And that the risk incurred by striking first is far, far less than waiting around to see if the other chap will strike first.

"The military mind has been schooled for centuries in this mode of thought. This scenario has been played out endlessly, eternally, on battlefields from Agincourt to the Somme to the Mekong Delta.

"And so, my friend, the decision is made: Strategic bombers carrying cruise missiles or gravity bombs are given the proper codes. Roof shutters of missile silos slide open. Politicians and advisors and generals and admirals gather in large rooms deep beneath our streets and fields, maps of the world displayed in superscale.

"But the result—the determination of who shall win and who shall lose—has been determined years before. Determined in the budgets of the Department of Defense and defense contractors, decided in the caucus rooms of Washington, settled in the halls of Congress by roll-call vote.

"Because the real determinant is the massing of economic power behind the proper technologies. *In other words, wars will be won primarily because of which budgets are allocated to which technologies.* And more and more, that implies technologies devoted to the art and science of surprise.

"In that context, what we now have as our strong suit against any threat is a three-legged stool: One, the most sophisticated threat-detection system ever devised—on land, on sea, in the air, and in space. Two, submarine-based launch capability for nuclear-tipped cruise missiles. And Three, the next generation of strategic bomber—for launching either nuclear cruise missiles or nuclear gravity bombs. It is this last leg of our theoretical stool that gives us something of an awkward time.

"There is no such thing as the perfect plane, as any pilot worth his ticket will tell you—with the possible exception of the DC-3, which has, upon occasion, been able to land itself without benefit of either pilot or electronic guidance.

"Consider the inherent difficulties within each of our current strategic bombers, the B-1B and the Northrop B-2:

"The B-1B is a creature of considerable compromise—a 1960s aircraft onto which we've rather hastily bolted technology of the '70s and early '80s. Its stealth characteristics are primitive, and all too likely to remain so. Then, too, there's the massive problems the B-1B has with its flight controls, its terrain-following radar, and especially its defensive avionics system, the ALQ-161A. They found part of the ALQ actually sends out a beacon—alerting Soviet radar instantly. Lots of Air Force people going gray fast, out at Dyess." Hornbill shook his head and stared meditatively at a point just over Pretorius' head.

"The B-1B is also extremely limited in range. It weighs a whopping 477,000 pounds and can go only 6,500 miles when empty. On the other hand, it can carry eight of the twenty-one-foot-long nuclear-tipped AGM-86Bs—Air-Launched Cruise Missiles—whereas the Northrop product is currently set up to only carry SRAMII missiles and B83 nuclear gravity bombs. Finally, by rounding the original B-1B's engine intakes and getting rid of a rather large, sharpish ridge which ran down the top of the aircraft's fuselage, Rockwell got their radar cross-section down from ten square meters to about one square meter. Not bad, considering the B-1B was originally a product of the sixties, when stealth was still basically a laboratory idea.

"On the other hand, the Northrop B-2 is phenomenally expensive—current estimates are $515.9 million apiece—and won't be deployed at Whiteman AFB in any significant numbers until mid-1993. It's got a fairly short range and has, according to the so-called planners within the Air Force, a curious role: to seek and destroy mobile targets—such as rail and truck launching platforms for ICBMs. In my view, a rather Alice in

Wonderland approach to a so-called strategic role, but then I don't have the distinction of being an Air Force planner.

"Finally, despite its rather elaborate quadruplex digital flight controls, the Northrop plane is about as maneuverable as a hog on ice, due to its all-wing construction. But then, the B-2 has a significantly lower radar signature than the B-1B. Depending on its angle of attack, and a few other variables, it would either appear as a radar signature of nil, or as something very much resembling a small bird.

"However—and all good things are steeped in howevers—the Soviets have been stepping up their radar development efforts to someday be able to counter either bomber. And remember the B-1B and the B-2, unlike cruise missiles or ICBMs, find their targets with crew-manned radar instead of coordinates. Which means those radar pulses are announcing their presence at long stand-off ranges before reaching the target zone, and that may easily be enough warning for the enemy to obliterate the aircraft. In short, the enemy may not see our aircraft, but may instead see its radar emissions. Not an enviable state of affairs, especially when you've paid a half-billion-dollar admission ticket.

"Also, consider the satellite observability of the B-2—which has its four F118-GE-100 engines thoughtfully placed on top of the flying wing. Configuration of the intakes and exhausts will help to some degree, but there will inevitably be some infrared signature." Hornbill paused to regard a perfect wreath of pipe-smoke as it floated toward the ceiling, then leaned forward in his chair, continuing with a more concerned expression.

"It also now seems likely, in fact, that the Soviets' Tall King long-wave-length radar will be evolved into something far more efficient against our technologies, with an ability to sweep through several wavebands simultaneously, running 5 to 28 MHz.

"Finally, there's also a fairly serious effort afoot in their satellite surveillance systems, which have relied on IF signatures to detect aircraft, but which will eventually be able to detect masses of certain shape and speeds vectored on probable mission courses. In other words, their computers will be fed all satellite images and will be programmed to instantly recognize and report patterns within those images which are threat-probable. Full development and deployment will take years, of course. But it will happen.

"Even more foreboding, they are also quite far along in developing a new carrier-free radar which, instead of the usual pulse—which agitates the subatomic structure of radar-absorbent material and is then converted to heat—emits a "square" pulse of radar energy, which can neither be absorbed nor dissipated by either of these two worthy and considerably expensive aircraft. Which means, of course, a prime portion of our much-publicized stealth technology, the ability of the Northrop B-2 to absorb and dissipate radar energy, will, quite shortly, cease to exist. *Quod erat demonstrandum.*" The older man shifted forward in his chair as he summed up:

"Michael, what I'm telling you is this: Our best intelligence indicates both our strategic bombers targeted for the future will be, within five to six years, *next to useless.*"

At this point, Hornbill stood up and stretched himself slowly, almost luxuriously. Pretorius once again gained a fleeting impression of immense strength residing within Hornbill's bulk. Despite the man's girth, there was something of the trained athlete about him, something which spoke of reserve power, confident, concealed.

Hornbill began pacing, punctuating his thoughts with motions of his pipe, alternatively waving it or using it to poke at imaginary illustrations in the air.

"It has become apparent that quite another solution is in order; something fairly radical." Hornbill took another reflective puff, examining the ceiling with bright, inquisitive eyes.

He paused to let this sink in and regarded Pretorius curiously through a cloud of pipesmoke. "We have, in fact, that solution near at hand. Under the strictest possible security cover, a third strategic bomber has been developed within the past year and a half, using the NCAD advanced computer-aided design and manufacturing techniques developed by Northrop in creating the B-2. The entire aircraft has been created by computer algorithms with but one objective: to counter either conventional or square radar pulses.

"In a conventionally stealth-oriented aircraft, with conventional configuration and the usual 1980s variety of radar-absorbent materials, the square radar pulse hits the aircraft and—instead of influencing the molecular structure of those materials so the radar energy is converted into heat and dissipated—is bounced back to the radar receiver and registers as an incoming unfriendly of such and such a size, at such and such a speed.

"But in this new beastie—which we've provisionally named the B(AT)-3—*all radar energy is captured and stored by the surface and structure of the aircraft itself, much as energy is stored in a battery.* Nothing is reflected; not one infinitesimal portion. Oh, there is a limit, of course: The surface and structure of the aircraft can only store so much, and then it has to be discharged. But by then, the aircraft will have done its work—either loosed its gravity bombs, or let fly its cruise missiles. The aircraft is also virtually undetectable by any known or probable satellite surveillance system, due to new technologies which I cannot discuss but which are, I assure you, quite real."

Christ, thought Pretorius. *He's talking about a totally invisible aircraft.* The impact of this, he realized, was incalculable. The thing could literally be in and out before anyone would have the least idea what had hit them.

Hornbill, smoke now all but obscuring his round countenance, continued with a wave of his pipe. "Thanks to some of the advances in Northrop's NCAD technology, we now have a full-scale, proof-of-concept aircraft which is about to fly. Like the Northrop stealth bomber, it has zero RCS from straight ahead. But, virtually the entire surface of the B(AT)-3 is new-generation composites, chiefly two-ply Spectra 3000 over a Hexcel-manufactured honeycomb core, with uni-directional graphite reinforcing straps. All surfaces and structural portions, though, have a sort of controlled conductivity which is governed by a specialized computer.

"It also is a true supersonic aircraft, unlike the B-2, which is not, due to its rather thickish flying wing shape that has to carry both fuel and engines. Also unlike the B-2, it is highly maneuverable, able to execute banks, rolls, and turns in a manner normally unsuitable to an aircraft of this size and designation.

"It can also carry McDonnell Douglas' new ACM 129-A Advanced Cruise Missile and has a range of 12,000 miles—far greater than either of its predecessors. Add the aircraft's inherent range to that of the range of its cruise missiles, and you have *a combined striking range of something over 14,000 miles.*

"So sophisticated is this aircraft that direct piloting is impossible: The digital flight-control computer generates literally thousands of commands per second, using fly-by-light fiber optics to cause the few control surfaces to adjust to terrain, offensive missiles, thermal and wind phenomena, everything.

"The pilot, when using his stick, is actually sending very simple commands to the rest of the aircraft; the computer translates them into the infinitely complex commands needed for flight and mission control. Another of its six on-board computer systems even interfaces with Datalink ground sources which can send a stream of digital signals in milliseconds from far larger, even more sophisticated computers."

Pretorius ran his hand through his thick blond hair, leaning back in his seat and stretching his legs full length. "How've you people been able to keep this thing quiet? Strategic bombers aren't exactly inconspicuous things to have hanging around the garage. You can't do it without lots of people. Don't the Soviets know by now?"

Hornbill smiled and nodded. "Astute, Michael. Of course they know something, but precious little at this stage. We have got their curiosity up, however, and they are racing to find out everything they possibly can. It is only a matter of time, perhaps only months, before they uncover something useful, given the current direction of their pursuits.

"However, if we can redirect their efforts—and we believe we can—we can keep them working for years on dead-end technologies.

"We plan, in a nutshell, to turn their own intelligence *apparat* against them, to send them scurrying off in a direction satisfactory to our own goals, and away from some of the new technologies present in the new aircraft. And this, indeed, is where you come in.

"I mentioned two points before. They are, in fact, two very different tasks for you." Hornbill stopped his pacing and sat down in the chair opposite Pretorius, fixing him with that curiously piercing gaze.

"First, the surface job, which is to be a sort of security task, but undercover. You will be put in place as the Chief Project Engineer, replacing a chap who will shortly be taken ill with an odd breed of influenza, hitherto unknown in this part of the world, and difficult to treat.

"In your new *persona*, you will play a role in a way which would make an Academy Award–winner blush with envy. For we have perfected a method by which you will, for a period of time, actually *be* the individual concerned—on both a conscious and a subconscious level.

"And that is an accomplishment which even the Lawrence Oliviers of this world fall short of, despite their matchless talent and training. But we will detail that in a moment."

Pretorius shifted uneasily in his chair, waiting for the punchline. For he knew enough of people like Hornbill to know they were seldom puzzled for long, and never, ever, expressed their dilemma until well after the solution had been thoroughly thought through.

"We don't know their exact timing, but we do know the KGB's Executive Action Section—Rodin's end of things—with some help from their friends planted deep inside the CIA, will attempt to penetrate our B(AT)-3 program sometime within the next few weeks.

"We also have reason to believe they have identified two targets: the B(AT)-3 itself, to obtain photographs and detailed information on same. And, as the other target, the extremely knowledgeable Chief Project Engineer. Who will turn out to be you.

"They will, in all likelihood, remove you from the premises, in a manner calculated to cause the least disturbance. They will then, at a place we do not yet know, attempt to debrief you for their own purposes.

"They will not be kind." Hornbill stoked up his pipe again, using the action to gather his thoughts, to put them in the best possible form.

"In fact, we anticipate they will use chemical means—augmented with stress techniques—to withdraw from you the information they require.

"They will attempt to peel away your strongest defenses and they will most undoubtedly succeed. And that, Michael, is precisely what we wish. For beneath—immediately beneath—your outermost defenses we shall have prepared a surprise for them.

"For there, lying exposed to their curious gaze, will be the innermost secrets of the B(AT)-3's Chief Project Engineer, one Charles Vojtec, neatly arrayed, carefully compiled, detailed and tidy and awaiting their inspection.

"Fortunately, your university training has provided you with something of a foundation for your cover. We note, from our sources, that while at Yale you studied such subjects as mechanics of deformable solids, materials science—which introduced you to certain aerodynamically attractive alloys and their phase transformations. Yes, Mr. Menzies and Mr. von Bader taught you well."

Pretorius was stunned at Hornbill's intimate knowledge of

even his college studies, and of the career in physics he'd once contemplated. But Hornbill only smiled benignly at Pretorius' reaction, as if reading his thoughts. "My dear boy, it's my *business* to know such things. I'm in the knowledge business, as you are. We differ only in our ages, our methodologies, and our responsibilities."

Pretorius, now leaning far forward in his chair, asked tensely, "All right, then. What sort of thing will you have me give them—what's the package?"

Hornbill beamed at Pretorius, pleased at being able to reveal his trump card at last. "That, indeed, is the remarkable part. For they will find everything they wished, and—in the fullness of time—a bit more than they wished. We shall have, um, programmed you to give them information of a sort which will cost them years of effort, and quite a bit of their budget, to pursue to its ultimate conclusion."

Pretorius sat up, startled. "Programmed, you said?"

Hornbill chuckled and continued, puffing with an intensity that sent up a barrage of flames from the pipebowl. "Our technical people have made some rather startling advances in the last few years. Advances which, for our own reasons, have not yet found their way into the medical journals.

"We are discussing here a fairly radical form of psychological programming. But what, in lay terms, we shall be doing with you is to temporarily displace your own personality and your own immediate memory with those of a fictitious individual, one of our own creation.

"It's roughly equivalent to removing all the furniture from a first floor room, sending it upstairs to be locked in the second and third floors for secure storage, filling the first floor with furniture of our own choosing, and then inviting in a thief to steal it.

"What you will do is to furnish them with formulae, with supposedly new directions in research, with a number of very clever diversionary branches of information.

"You will, under interrogation, reveal information about

vastly different metallurgic technologies, which are now precisely those which the B(AT)-3 boasts. You will give them chapter and verse on certain rather arcane aerodynamic formulae which will take literally years to fully unravel.

"We will give you details which will be imminently plausible, reflecting research we've already left far behind us, having taken years to exhaust them and discover their dead ends."

Hornbill gave a few satisfied puffs and observed the smoke rising into the air, waiting for a reaction from Pretorius.

"They will, of course, subject you to some fairly generous doses of Amytal-related drugs. But they will certainly not be lethal and they should not produce any lasting effects to the central nervous system. We know you have some experience in resisting this sort of treatment, and that, quite candidly, was one of our criteria in recruiting you.

"It will then be your prime responsibility to see they receive the intelligence with which we shall have prepared you—and that should be largely an involuntary action on your part.

"We also know that, should our best efforts in programming fail, and you must then fall upon your own devices to resist your questioners, you have an excellent history of being able to cope with most forms of applied stress."

Hornbill sighed heavily, and stared with that curiously piercing blue gaze at Pretorius. Again, he resembled a predator bird of ancient and dark experience.

"To come to the most unpleasant point of several, Michael, there is every likelihood they will not wish you to leave their, um, hospitality. In fact, I'm sure they would rather, as is predictable, wish you to be counted as simply having disappeared.

"It was precisely for this to eventuality that we've given you the additional training in which you have shown, if I may pass comment, quite remarkable progress.

"But there is another job for you to handle, something which may be equally important. And this is the second reason we have chosen you, and no one else."

At this, Hornbill tapped out the ashes of his now demised pipeload, and began pacing the narrow confines of the room. "You well know the sad state to which the Agency has descended in recent memory. Having never worked for the CIA, you have no idea how disheartening, how gut-churning it is to watch it being torn apart, to see it even used against the nation it was created to protect.

"When a few of us came out of OSS, we had a dream—an idea of building the world's most competent intelligence agency, pooling all the resources at our command into one central, highly efficient intelligence organization.

"It's a very different kind of organization these days. Run by an inflated deepwater sailor whose ideas about intelligence simultaneously contradict both meanings of the word. The amateurism and the zeal for publicity by the hangers-on and the incompetent are only part of a far larger parcel.

"The real threat is that the KGB has taken direct control of certain key portions of the Agency, using both penetration agents as well as a few "turned" officers to do their bidding.

"Ultimately, over the years we were able to trace and identify several of the penetration agents and left them in place—but compartmentalized and fed lesser stuff. We know now the number is actually far larger than we'd ever suspected. We believe, in fact, that as many as forty to fifty CIA officers may be involved. Not agents—*officers*.

"We also know a number of these officers are taking their orders from both sides at once, including some very smart men who have used their direct pipeline to *Ulitsa Dzerzhinskogo 2* to build their careers.

"Their masters at Moscow Center have fed them enough for them to score quite a number of coups, sacrificing the odd agent, even entire small networks, to make their prowess and progress believable.

"And what they've been able to feed back has made it all worthwhile, at least for their control officers. Your father, I believe, had evidence of some sort which was obviously damning to some of these people, and was—in his painstaking attorney's way—attempting to put together a very complete case against them before he showed his hand to anyone, even me. I think it was his carefulness, his unwillingness to share his evidence until he was absolutely sure, that got him killed."

Pretorius took this new information in shocked silence. In the past half hour, he'd been rocked with realizations of a world that exceeded even his own experience. By comparison, his own limited career in intelligence was naive, almost a child's exercise.

Hornbill—in a quieter voice now, sensing Pretorius' mood—continued. "We come now to several problems in dealing with this, if, indeed, it can be dealt with at all:

"One. How can we root out both the amateurs and the opposition professionals in this cancer within the Agency? Two. How can we expect anyone in the White House to believe any of it? Three. Considering the orientation of our current administration, even if they believed it, would they do a damned thing about it?

"Your additional task, then, will be to discover what you can of the Agency connection with these people, gather whatever solid, irrefutable evidence we can use to bring it before the President and the National Security Council, and return to us. You should stand a better-than-average chance, as you've no CIA workfile, no voiceprints, no retinal ID at Langley. Yet you've got all the skills to go in and get out intact.

"Quite a lot is riding on your success in this, Michael, including a great deal of the future of the U.S. intelligence community.

"That, in brief, is the job. The question is simply—are you up to it?"

Pretorius leaned back in his chair and wished devoutly he were back on his hill, playing his harmonica and watching the blue mists of evening gather yet again.

He closed his eyes and slowly let his breath escape. "Is there any choice?" he asked evenly.

Hornbill fixed him with an incurious gaze. "None whatever," he said quietly. "But one needs to check your temperature now and then."

11

NELLIS AIR FORCE RANGE, NEVADA

Inside the enormous hangar, men swarmed like ants over the Tupolev's fuselage, which had been resectioned to reduce its length from 175 feet to 162; still some fifteen feet longer than the B-1B.

The Tupolev's air intakes had been restructured and smoothed, as had several areas of its fuselage surface which were now more rounded, and less likely to print on the Soviet's Tall King radar screens.

Small sharkfinlike ride control canards had also been fitted on either side, below the cabin's side windows. Their angle canted toward the ground.

The tail section had been totally removed and was being worked on in one corner of the building. New elements, prepared months in advance, were replacing the recognizably Soviet configuration with an entirely different profile.

The nose had been reshaped, given a slightly Concordesque contour, then spiked with a trident antenna. Large surface areas of aluminum had been carefully cut away and substituted with sandwichlike sections of a honey-combed composite material, but with a curious difference: a ribbonlike element had been integrated within the material, metallic yet curiously transparent. This material was highly conductive, with virtually no loss of energy throughout its course along the surface of the aircraft.

Certain structural elements in both wings and fuselage had also been removed, then replaced with carbon-carbon castings. These castings, infinitely more expensive than their originals, were capable of withstanding far greater stress, as well as leaving far less of a radar signature.

They gave improved structural integrity to the new wing design, which—especially in its full swing-wing configuration— seemed so disproportionately large it gave the aircraft almost the look of a delta wing.

The weapons bays had been enlarged significantly, with white-painted AiResearch activating motors installed where they could be easily seen with the doors open for inspection.

Up above, a special "glass cockpit" had been prepared, with eight monochromatic amber CRTs and full-color plasma screens to monitor every aspect of flight, weather, possible threats, even to a constantly scrolling map of the projected route and its terrain. A single illuminated green line, projected across the fascia by a laser just over the pilot's left shoulder, would give a constant indication of the aircraft's attitude during difficult terrain-following, terrain-avoidance operations. By using this peripheral vision display, the pilot had one less round dial with which to contend. In fact, the pilot had far fewer dials with which to deal and could concentrate his attentions on actually flying the ship: no mean feat in terrain-following mode at an altitude of only 200 feet.

Most of the electronics had Collins, Litton, and Lockheed parts numbers and identification codes, although few of them existed in any known USAF spec sheet. In fact, with the exception of the quiet radar system (common to both Rockwell's B-1BB and the Northrop B-2), the electronics systems were new and bafflingly unfamiliar to the technicians.

The original Soviet look-down shoot-down unit was carefully removed, and replaced with a U.S.-made unit somewhat re-

lated to that found aboard the F-15. Although differently con-
figured than the original Soviet equipment, the unit dropped
snugly into the locking mechanism without a millimeter to
spare, fitting as if it had always been there.

The Russian yoke-type controls had been replaced by the more
recent USAF-type sticks, each topped with a single white button
centered, a smaller gray button to the left, and an even smaller
red button to the right. All electrical switches and all indicators,
digital or analog, were replaced with U.S.-manufactured units.
Northrop, Rockwell, Boeing, Collins, Bendix, Lockheed, General Dynamics, Garrett, and other contractors were represented
on board, as were a number of other corporations engaged in
classified advanced-technology work for the Air Force.

A few top executives at these corporations from whom elements were purchased by the Air Force were advised that certain highly sensitive, compartmentalized work was being done
in cooperation with the DOD, and that future contracts would
depend on their not discussing it with anyone. Period. On the
sleek aircraft's entire outer surface, a special surface coating
had been applied: an anti-radar finish in dark matte gray, so
thick it added 530 kilos to the aircraft's total weight. Yet this
extra burden was more than compensated for by the reshaped
engine intakes, high-thrust engine modifications, and the aero-
nautical efficiencies gained by the overall reconfiguration of the
aircraft.

New Bendix carbon brakes and wheels were fitted to the
sinister-looking aircraft, duplicates of what were now standard
equipment on every new Air Force release.

Finally, the McDonnell-Douglas Advanced Cruise Missiles
were locked in place on the big bird's underbelly.

It would, at this stage, be extremely difficult for the young
Soviet pilot who defected from his base at Ramenskoye to recognize his original Tupolev.

The civilian team of fifty-four men working on the Tupolev
would continue at least another month. The security surround-

ing them was complex and airtight. Before their arrival at Nellis, they'd been informed their destination would be an Alaskan base for classified work. Soon a rumor circulated that they would be doing last-minute modifications to the new F-19 fighters just rolling off the assembly lines, to counteract recent developments in Soviet defensive avionics.

But instead of arriving in the anticipated Arctic tundra to work on new USAF F-19s, the technicians were set down blinking in the dazzling sunlight of the Nevada desert. They were even more confused when confronted with a full-blown Soviet Blackjack bomber on United States soil.

The project was exacting, and plotted down to the last detail. To complete the schedule on time (with a buffer in case of unforeseen hitches) blueprints for the alterations had been worked out months in advance, with materials tested and prepared for sequential installation beginning the day of the Blackjack's arrival.

No explanation was given the technicians during their work at Nellis, no cover story. None was needed. After completion, they would be quarantined a minimum of six months, completely isolated from outside contact. During that quarantine, each individual would undergo mild drug-assisted hypnotherapy for deprogramming purposes.

In the end, not one would remember significant details of the project.

12

LANGLEY, VIRGINIA

There are a few organisms and a few organizations with behavioral characteristics not only anomalous, but bordering on the bizarre.

A seemingly logical, straightforward animal may, for example, have an inbred desire to hurl itself to destruction: witness the lemming. An educated class of human beings, given the right training, and gathered in a more or less elite group, may still exhibit totally irrational behavior. Witness, for example, our own intelligence community.

The intelligence trade is influenced by a confluence of American traditions, a curious combination of the noble and the comic. These include a belief in the Wild West ethic of action and justice, a healthy distrust of politicians, a dash of avarice, a strong streak of gamesmanship—and, as an extension of a deeply seated national belief, the willingness to assume innocence until proven guilty. Being raised with these beliefs often produces profound disturbances within intelligence practitioners, who must reconcile them daily with a professional suspicion of The Other Side.

For example, most of America looks at *perestroika* (restructuring), and sees tangible evidence of the seeds of ideological union sprouting daily in headlines.

On the other hand, professional Soviet-watchers, both in the gentle groves of academe and along the cement-clad shores of the Potomac, generally take a more pragmatic view. Their assumptions being (a) the Soviet economy has, over the decades, been steadily marching nearer and nearer to collapse, a process assisted by a disproportionately large defense budget, and (b) the Soviet citizenry, deprived of so much for so long, has now become somewhat dangerous to any ruling clique.

Therefore, *perestroika*. Therefore, the illusion and (just possibly) even the eventual reality of *glasnost*.

Their reasoning is that restructuring is necessary to avoid economic collapse, and that the defense budgets can only be pruned by getting the West to reduce in at least as great (if not greater) proportion, cutting down on the types of ICBMs, IRBMs, and other missiles within the Soviet Rocket Forces, Air Force, Army, and Navy, rather than giving up mass ability to deliver a knock-out pre-emptive strike.

Therefore, at the bargaining table, they narrow down the too-wide and too-expensive range of their weaponry, put the money back into more profitable military technologies such as their own strategic defense system (does anyone in the Soviet Union, even under *glasnost*, dare call it *Star Wars?*), and put a little back into the public breadbasket before things get altogether out of hand. And, of course, the coming age of Peace, Plenty, and the New Social-Capitalism is nicely heralded in the bargain.

All of which suits not only our own national mindset comfortably, but serves Soviet political objectives admirably.

As a necessary part of this, the Soviets constantly generate information in a carefully shaped form, much as a capsule is carefully shaped for ingestion and digestion. Indeed, the Soviets' principal and most formidable weapon is neither military, nor economic, nor ideological. It is, quite simply, information carefully reshaped and attractively packaged so as to cause or influence events. This, we call *dis*information. In Russian, *desinformatskaya*.

Even the least curious university student of comparative political systems soon reads, and occasionally even remembers, the words of Lenin on this subject. It is clearly articulated state policy, as much a part of the Soviet Union as the Constitution is a part of the United States.

And yet few members of Congress or our Executive Branch appear to have plumbed even these shallow depths. And so we enter into *détente* willingly, and we seriously engage in Strategic Arms Limitation Talks, and we continue to refuse to believe in the scope—or even the very existence—of the covert disinformation offensive against the West. The cost to us is dear. The cost to the Soviets is minuscule, compared to its enormous effectiveness.

For example, when Oleg Penkovskiy, a Soviet army colonel in the GRU, came to us, it was years later before we discovered we'd welcomed a one-man timebomb. Inexpensive, fascinating, but very much alive and ticking. In 1961, we were desperate to learn the state of advancement in Soviet IRBMs, and whether or not their ICBMs even existed. Francis Gary Powers had been shot down in his high-flying U2 the year before, and our satellite reconnaissance had not yet been fully developed, let alone deployed.

The Soviets were equally desperate to keep us in our radiantly innocent state, to make Kennedy's "missile gap" appear as yet another piece of western paranoia. The object, of course, was to give our Congress a rationale for not voting sufficient funds to close this gap.

To accomplish this, the Soviets did two quite simple but extraordinary things.

First, they knew we were able to monitor through telemetry certain internal devices in the Soviet IRBMs during their tests. So they built in three gyroscopes: two operational, and a third which sent off erratic signals, but which was actually a dummy, and not a working part of the missile. From this, we deduced their missiles were woefully inaccurate and therefore not the threat our doomsayers had been yammering about.

Second, they sent us, neatly wrapped, one Oleg Vladimirovich Penkovskiy, Colonel, Chief Intelligence Directorate (GRU), Soviet General Staff. Who proceeded to inform our intelligence experts that, in fact, the Motherland as yet had no ICBM, and the IRBMs were (surprise) inadequate and inaccurate. He also served us up some fairly detailed information about the GRU and KGB, the bulk of which we knew, but which seemed to confirm his bona fides.

Strangely, Penkovskiy, despite his exalted rank, seemed unable to give us much of anything about Soviet illegals (intelligence agents without diplomatic or consular cover) in the West, or anything about KGB penetration of the U.S. or British intelligence organizations.

Curiouser and curiouser, said Alice. But no matter: Now we could relax a bit, and perhaps spend less on the military, and once more congratulate ourselves on our superior technology. Until, of course, we found the Soviets were well along in ICBMs, and that—contrary to the very best wishful thinking—they were astonishingly accurate. We couldn't, for the life of us, figure what went wrong. Hadn't Colonel Penkovskiy himself told us the contrary?

Even when another defector, Anatoly Golitsin, warned there would be defectors who would have, as their mission from Moscow, the spreading of false information to divert our attentions, our efforts, and our defense budgets, most of us simply refused to accept it. Too labyrinthian; too much of—as the Fisherman himself once put it—a "wilderness of mirrors." The craft and practice of disinformation is alien to our culture, to almost all our traditions. It isn't *right*; it isn't *nice*. But there it is: an essential part of Soviet diplomacy and intelligence work. Part, in fact, of a seamless fabric of continuing confrontation.

There were, to our credit, a few men and women in our intelligence services who knew Soviet capabilities all too well. One such individual was the Fisherman.

But the Fisherman was, even in the late '50s, regarded as

more than a little paranoid about the Soviet threat. MI6's Kim Philby, for example, thought he exaggerated the potential of Soviet penetration greatly. Upon being told this, the Fisherman redoubled his efforts. And, by 1973, when Colby fired him from the Central Intelligence Agency, the Fisherman was regarded by many as something of a lunatic on the subject.

When the Fisherman left, 250,000 KGB externals around the world breathed easier. These operatives, working in embassies, consulates, trade missions, and under foreign employ, constitute history's greatest deployment of intelligence agents. Add to that the external agents of the GRU (Soviet Military Intelligence), as well as the combined intelligence services of the Soviet-orchestrated nations (Cuba's 17,000-man state security being but one example), and the manpower commanded by the head of the KGB is awesome indeed.

William E. Colby, like Richard Helms and the Fisherman, came from the operations side of the OSS. But when Colby became DCI, it was almost as if some alien influence entered him. A few agency hands, rightly or wrongly, felt Colby ultimately caused more damage to the Agency than even Anatoly Golitsin's speculative "supermole" could have.

Colby's collaboration with Senator Frank Church's Committee was remarkable, for a career intelligence officer. The Agency was literally turned inside out. The 100-man Counter-Intelligence Staff was decimated. CI, for any practical purpose, had been neutered.

Senator Church, in his zeal to achieve national status, goaded Colby to reveal more and more.

And Colby seemed only too eager to help. Apart from trying to keep Dick Helms' reputation intact (for Church was now howling for Helms' blood over the Agency's involvement in Chile), Colby continued to carve up many of the Agency's vital organs.

Many thought it an odd way of acting, for an ex-OSS operations man. Almost as if he were imitating the worst sort of business bureaucrat, bumbling his way through a highly sensitive organization. Colby brought in the mental baggage of B-school Babbittry, buying into whatever business management theory was then fashionable.

One such effort was the introduction of MBO (Management By Objective) techniques into the Agency. Under Colby's MBO, subordinates scurried frantically to quantify everything, including that which was not quantifiable.

Colby also created KIQs, or Key Intelligence Questions, a form of knee-jerk response to politicians' inquiries. But although Colby, with his newly surfaced comptroller mentality, could be comic in imitating the lower orders of business academicians, his systematic dismantling of the Agency's defenses could only be viewed as tragic.

But the Fisherman had foreseen much of this. The influence of the Agency had already begun to wane from the day Kennedy fired Dulles for the CIA's ill-planned, ill-executed (partially due to JFK himself) Bay of Pigs invasion.

John McCone, the new DCI after Dulles, was chosen for his detachment from the operations side. And, indeed, McCone's management of the Company during the Cuban missile crisis was exemplary—buying back much of credibility lost at the Bay of Pigs.

McCone, a businessman with zero background in intelligence, was seldom called in for counsel by Kennedy. The Fisherman continued to have JFK's ear, as the young President felt he was one of the few consummate realists in the intelligence community. But then came Kennedy's assassination, and with it, the beginning of the end of direct CIA communication with the presidency.

When Johnson was sworn in as President, the Fisherman knew the Agency would not be welcome in the White House. And, in fact, John McCone finally resigned in 1965 due to the lack of access to the President. Under both Johnson and Nixon, the DCI became a less and less important member of government. Admiral Raeborn—the naval administrator responsible for the Polaris missile program—replaced McCone, and after serving only a year, was in turn replaced by Richard Helms.

Dick Helms was the unanimous recommendation of Washington's intelligence community. A product of almost twenty-five years in the Clandestine Service, Helms was a practical man, and recognized the importance of compromise and public relations in keeping the Company's perimeters defended.

Despite Helms' experience and his best efforts in trying to rebuild the Agency, the White House considered him much like a competent night watchman: necessary to one's sense of well-being, but not the sort to invite in for advice.

The Fisherman, seeing that even so obvious a professional as Helms was continually being ignored by the White House, could also see the damage resulting from disconnecting the intelligence function from foreign policy.

Only a President with a serious appreciation of intelligence could both extend its excellence and protect it from external damage. But neither Johnson nor Nixon had that ability, and the Fisherman watched as the Agency's credibility was eroded on an almost daily basis. By the end of the Nixon regime, Helms was often not even permitted to see the President. The DCI— one of the finest in the Agency's history—was reduced to leaving notes on the President's notepad before National Security Council meetings, to ensure getting his attention on this matter or that.

Helms shared his frustrations with the Fisherman, who, although feeling Helms' plight as deeply as anyone could, could not reveal that long before Colby became DCI, he had begun very carefully to lay his plans, ever the Compleat Angler.

It was suspected by a few that the Fisherman was mounting some sort of major disinformation operation, but no one seemed to know anything specific. Most people dismissed it as yet another aspect of the Fisherman's excessive flair for drama. The Agency was a different place these days, they said; it was at last being run in a solid, businesslike way. The cowboys were gone, or very nearly so.

The Soviet intelligence services, meanwhile, were operating at maximum effort. Penetration of Britain's MI5 and MI6 was at every level; very little of the UK's intelligence operations was hidden from the eyes in Moscow. Penetration of the CIA had been more difficult, but had also been accomplished. However, no one in Washington wanted to hear of even the possibility. The Fisherman continued to search for the enemy within, right up until his firing by Colby. The Washington cocktail circuit spread rumors of the Fisherman's soon-to-come downfall. Rumors were primed and fueled by politicians who wanted no boat rocking; no disturbing revelations such as the British had with Burgess, Maclean, Blunt, and Philby, among others.

And so it was that the Fisherman's firing seemed somewhat anticlimactic. Those who met with him afterward saw his wide, thin mouth curve up at one end and down at the other, almost as if one side were amused and the other dismayed. Which, in light of later events, was very likely the case.

He voiced his pleasure at finally, for the first time since the beginning of the Second World War, having the time to read his beloved Dante, as well as grow his orchids, do some leatherwork, and of course perfect his fishing techniques.

It was an eminently civilized retirement, he confided to his friends, but roughly akin to fiddling while Rome burns.

Like a wise old pike seeking the deep, shady pools undercutting the riverbank, the Fisherman finally sought anonymity— after giving the press a few final barbs about Colby and the KGB.

13
SOMEWHERE
NEAR PHOENIX

The hypodermic needle slipped swiftly into the vein, lifting the white skin up in a tiny ridge as the steel shaft tunneled its way beneath like an evil and metallic burrowing animal, its progress marked by a graying of the ridge.

With an anesthetist's sleight of hand, the man in the green lab coat deftly substituted an IV catheter for the hypodermic, and the colorless liquid began to slip into Pretorius' system.

A flooding warmth spread. Lights. Movements blurred, then focused, then blurred again. Darkness.

I am . . . I am . . .

A greater warmth, an all-pervading, overwhelming silence.

Deep within him, a thing fragile and slipping into helplessness fought against the warmth, against the wholesale invasion of the body through every vein and capillary, through every element of the subconscious. It clawed for survival, scrabbling to hang on the very edge of the self, now slipping, now falling, now propelled ever more deeply into the abyss . . .

"He's under now."

He could hear them discussing him, but was powerless to indicate his consciousness. He could feel a cold, prickly sweat breaking out all over his skin, could feel the very sounds of their voices as they spoke. His scalp itched and tingled where the electrodes were implanted. These were the last things he detected before a great wash of warmth slowly overtook him, numbing his remaining senses, carrying him down, down.

"Signs?"

"All normal, considering the character of the injection."

"How long do we have?"

"He should be responsive by now, but actual length of programming opportunity varies greatly. At the least, you should have two hours."

The electrodes were checked by feeding neutral signals and watching the oscilloscope. All loops gave positive readings, and the subject exhibited no anomalous activity.

The tapes began to roll. As the sounds came over the speaker, the men in the room watched the screens. The pulse rate slowed perceptibly.

A calm and yet insistent voice—at first only at the threshold of hearing, but then increasing to a level of greater strength— began speaking softly against the muted background of the sounds. The pulse became slightly more rapid, although still below normal, then slowed once more.

The men exchanged glances. The voice on the tape was deep and reassuringly resonant.

It spoke of many things, some expressed as mathematical formulae, others in engineering argot, all dealing with phenomena such as singular perturbation problems, thin-wing theory, transonic small-disturbance flow, altering the natural frequencies of torsional vibration, and more.

The men hovering over the tape machines and oscilloscopes monitored the subject's responses minutely. As the pulse rate rose, the tape speed was adjusted in tiny increments, but always increased.

When the pulse rate rose too quickly, the tape speed was held constant until the rate leveled somewhat; then, once again, the speed was increased.

By this curious process, the voice rose in pitch with the speed of the tape, and the amount of information being fed to the subject was increased considerably.

The physicians and psychologists were well satisfied with the first session. It lasted 105 minutes, and the subject seemed to have integrated the information well, at least according to the monitoring devices.

The true test would come after the fifth and final session, and would take the form of what were euphemistically called stress interviews. For now, the men were satisfied, and the subject was wheeled back to his room, still unconscious.

14
LANGLEY, VIRGINIA

The trip from Dulles had taken less than the usual thirty minutes. In front, the driver flicked his eyes between the parkway and the mirror, scanning for any position of advantage, checking the vehicles behind.

A fully automatic Uzi nestled in two rubber-covered retaining clips just under the dash and to the right, giving the driver's knees adequate clearance.

The car itself looked like thousands of other government limousines. But there were important differences.

It had two fuel tanks. One was steel, wrapped in yellow DuPont Kevlar to resist penetration by anything but AP (armor piercing) rounds, and a second tank of rubber occupying a portion of the trunk for long-range use, should the need ever arise. Normally it was kept deflated and empty.

All door panels and most of the roof section were filled with sandwiched panels of Kevlar and Spectra, and the inch-thick tempered glass had a high degree of projectile resistance.

The engine—the largest General Motors produces for four-wheeled passenger vehicles—had special high-output modifications. The oil pan was oversized and specially reinforced; the springs, shocks, and antisway bars built for heavy-duty use; and the wider diameter front brake discs made to California specifications.

An enormous alternator and heavy-duty battery were also installed to support the four two-way radios and their scramblers, and a number of other improvements added for the occupant's general security.

Only the Secret Service limousines assigned to the President were as well-equipped, and even those were not made to move as quickly as this one, for it was the car assigned to the Director of Central Intelligence, Vice Admiral Palmer Wakefield, USN.

Behind the grille were red flashers, and inside the left front fender well was a loudspeaker for the siren. These were provided in case the Director needed to move through traffic quickly, but in fact were rarely used.

A bodyguard sat next to the Director in the rear seat, one of a small cadre of men especially trained for this task. He was never to let the occupant from his sight.

He wore an earpiece connected to a Motorola VHF portable clipped to his belt, working at 166.528 MHz, DPL (Digital Private Line). He also carried a Smith & Wesson Model 13, its cylinder filled with 38 Special Plus-P's—a no-nonsense revolver, secure in its Rogers clamshell holster.

At this moment, the DCI was scanning the countryside. The parkway's verges here were carefully tended, attractive, with trees and shrubbery fertilized and trimmed to standards which somewhat exceeded the Virginia roadside maintenance specifications.

But then, this was a very important stretch of highway, often traveled by Washington's elite.

Once, there had been a large sign just at this point which indicated the turnoff was to the Department of Highways, but which everyone, down to the last taxi driver and tourist guide, knew was the off-ramp to the Central Intelligence Agency's headquarters.

After someone finally realized it was exceedingly hard to keep anything as large as the 219 acres of Langley HQ hidden, the sign had been changed to read simply "CIA" in white letters against a brown background.

The Director felt the car turn off the parkway and glanced up from his papers. The guard at the Dolly Madison gate—one of three gates to the complex—saluted and waved the limousine through, then reached for the telephone after the big vehicle passed.

CIA Headquarters looked, in many ways, like a cross between a college campus and a large corporate research facility—which, in some ways, it was. There were always joggers on the grounds, sweatbands and grimly set lips silently affirming their dedication.

The Admiral smiled. He believed in exercise, and plenty of it. As for himself, the DCI only took a good walk now and then, for he believed his own time was too precious.

He was also a firm believer in visible leadership, not unusual in military men. The limousine pulled up soundlessly under the huge T-shaped portico in front of the building and the Director and his bodyguard exited, walking up the low steps toward the front door. While other DCIs had usually entered through a more secure route via the basement, Wakefield preferred to stride in through the main lobby. He admired its white columns, the expanses of Georgian marble, the forty-six stars for officers killed on duty, and the motto emblazoned on the frieze: "Ye shall know the truth and the truth shall make you free"— John VIII: XXXII.

Entering through the front door was also like entering any large corporation in any of a thousand industrial parks around the U.S. Two guards standing by a desk at the end of the foyer saluted and painstakingly checked his badge, although his face was familiar to virtually everyone here.

Once, at the beginning of the Admiral's reign as DCI, a guard had recognized the Admiral, saluted and waved him on without following procedure and checking the photo badge.

Within the hour, the unfortunate sentry had been transferred to a less-sensitive job ten miles away, on permanent night duty at the Bureau of Weights and Standards.

The Admiral strode into the one elevator exclusively reserved for his use and took it to his seventh floor offices.

As he exited with his usual military stride, he was met and matched in stride by a tall, immaculately groomed man who would appear, to the casual observer, to be either a men's clothing salesman in a large city, or a successful litigation attorney.

Emil Borchner was neither. He held down one of the most powerful yet precarious jobs at Langley: Executive Assistant to the Director of Central Intelligence.

Having been clued over the phone by the guard at the Dolly gate, he'd been waiting by the seventh floor elevator door. "Good morning, Admiral," said the dapper Borchner, handing the DCI a clipboard with the day's agenda. "You've got a full plate today, I'm afraid. How was the flight, sir?"

Wakefield, without breaking his stride, grumbled something unintelligible as he took in the contents of the clipboard, reaching the open door of his office just as the list ended. The DCI's executive secretary, Kathy Alders—a woman in her late fifties who habitually wore no other colors but varying shades of gray—received a curt nod from the Admiral as he swept through the door. Despite her predilection for gray and the fact that her figure had gone slightly plump, Alders was still a highly attractive woman. Like a number of young women who entered the Agency in the '50s, she had given her life to it. Her dedication to the Director was legendary; some said she never left the building, and that she often slept on the seventh floor's reception area couch.

Alders hated Borchner with a soul-withering intensity.

The Admiral looked upset this morning, she decided, settling down at her carefully arranged desk. Something on Borchner's clipboard. Something there had got his wind up. *Damn* that clipboard, anyway.

In practice, a great deal of CIA work never found its way to the DCI's clipboard or his briefing papers. One reason was the normal sifting to keep less-important matters from crowding the Director's schedule. The other was somewhat unique to this particular DCI: Many officers had learned, to their stupefaction, that the Director was apt to blurt out sensitive information at whatever Washington lunch or cocktail party he happened to be attending, as he more or less trusted all U.S. citizens.

Wakefield didn't have the career intelligence officer's suspicion of everyone and everything, nor was he apparently able to control his lifelong habit of trying to impress and command.

And having been a close friend of the President for many years since the Chief Executive had been a decidedly junior congressman on the Hill, he would immediately communicate anything of political advantage, regardless of its impact on the Agency.

All of which was why management-level officers never let anything sensitive reach the DCI's attention if they could at all avoid it.

The items which came to the DCI this morning, like most mornings, were somewhat sanitized. But on this particular occasion, Wakefield's normally baby-smooth forehead became furrowed.

Alarm bells went off in Borchner's brain as he realized the DCI was unpleasantly surprised. Anxiously he scanned the clipboard over the Admiral's shoulder, trying to see where Wakefield's eyes were focused.

Of course. The stealth bomber item. The reports coming out from California had been puzzling to Borchner as well as to the processing officers. Something was going on that failed to add up in any logical way.

Borchner had finally added it to the Admiral's sheet when the reports had become more and more persistent. And, he reasoned, there was likely not to be anything in it that could embarrass the Agency if spilled.

In fact, the remarkable thing about the item was that the CIA had so little knowledge of it.

After standing perfectly still and glaring at the offending item for more than a full minute, the Admiral finally strode around to his desk, plopping his considerable heft into the high-backed leather armchair.

He steepled his carefully manicured fingers. The furrows in his forehead failed to smooth out, Borchner observed. And—another danger signal—the DCI began to stare at a particular point on the ceiling.

Admiral Palmer Wakefield was acutely upset.

The Admiral was not a career intelligence man. He was a deep-water sailor, and proud of it. He was also, in common with one or two of his predecessors, singularly ill-suited to hold the top intelligence job in the western world.

He had been appointed by the President for his exemplary record in the Navy, his devotion to duty, and the fact that the President knew Wakefield would hold no surprises for him.

And, indeed, Wakefield held no surprises for anybody. Least of all the KGB, who—in addition to having been able to penetrate the Agency with consummate ease under Wakefield's benign reign—could confidently predict each of the CIA's reactions in any given situation.

Moscow Center had a psychological profile on Wakefield that was updated weekly. Seldom did the DCI do or say anything even remotely unpredictable.

And what Wakefield did was automatically executed, for he ran a tops-down Agency. No covert action was planned or discussed without his knowledge and consent. No promotion of any case officer was contemplated without the Admiral's direct and personal participation.

When a National Intelligence Estimate was about to be forwarded to the President, the Admiral did the final edit—even, some said, to the extent of rewriting it to make sure it conformed to the President's own estimate of the situation.

His was a tragic regime, with dozens of career officers leaving the Agency, unwilling to sit it out until a change of administration.

For until that time, Palmer Wakefield, VADM, USN, was extremely likely to continue to be the President's ever-faithful dog at the gates.

The Admiral's concentration on the fixed point overhead finally relaxed, and he smoothed his silver-gray hair, looking at his reflection in the glass of his wife's photograph, which occupied the near left side of his desk.

What he saw there reassured him. Since boyhood, he'd been strikingly handsome. His wavy hair, having turned gray prematurely in his late twenties, gave him a leonine appearance, an impression strengthened by his oversized lower jaw.

It was a leader's face, a face of conviction and courage. The sort of face political king-makers search for and seldom find, but which often occur in the military trades.

He turned his attention away from his own face and looked directly at Borchner's, clearing his throat in preparation for a pronouncement.

"Borchner," he began, "here I sit, charged with coordinating the world's second largest intelligence community, and one of the United States' newest and most important strategic weapons is being Chinese-walled on me. Would you—or, if you can't possibly manage it, someone else—mind telling me precisely what's going on?"

Seeing the DCI's ego aroused, and knowing Wakefield would therefore order a full-scale inquiry anyway, Borchner decided to surface more of the problem. "There's something in the wind, Admiral. Nothing tangible, but I've got five separate mentions of a new stealth bomber initiative—something different from Northrop's thing—that seems already pretty far advanced.

"Defense is handling all the CI work and the Feebies are locked out. The whole thing's ultra-tight, and nobody's talking. Even the Air Force is keeping zipped, those of them that know anything. That's unusual. I've been thinking of asking our people to step things up to full project level, with your permission, Admiral."

Borchner, a career CIA officer who had survived at least six different purges, was a careful man. He was also a survivalist in the Washington bureaucracy, and this was due to his enormous network of contacts, both within the government and out.

Few things ever took Borchner by surprise. He'd heard rumors about the new superstealth bomber for months, and had followed up most of them—leading, inevitably, to dead ends.

He'd then redoubled his efforts, and found a slim lead. Something unusual had been tracked by NSA's COINT (Communications Intelligence) slipping inside Nellis Air Force Range, north of Vegas.

Yet nothing was visible by satellite recon, and none of his assets at either Edwards or Nellis reported anything unusual. The whole thing was elusive as hell. It confused Borchner, and he was as uneasy as the DCI. Borchner and the DCI discussed the new stealth apparition for the better part of an hour, punctuating their conversation with occasional phone calls. But nothing came of it. Nothing, that is, until that evening at a cocktail party in Georgetown.

The party was thrown by one of the Foggy Bottom higher-ups, in one of the antiseptically restored clapboard houses which went for prices that would stagger their original builders. Champagne was the order of the evening, and the guests were getting more than a little oiled.

One of them was a young man from INR (Bureau of Intelligence and Research) at State, who—to impress the Director of Central Intelligence with his own knowledge of weighty matters—remarked that the new superstealth bomber was going to cause the Kremlin to rewrite their radar defense plans considerably.

"Oh?" inquired the Admiral evenly. "And what have you heard?"

Put on the spot, the young man sputtered, then recovered. "Well sir, all I've heard was from somebody out at Edwards. They've got something on for next month, but nobody's actually had sight of the prototype. The lid's about as tight as I've ever seen, Admiral."

"Well, we're all working to keep this thing secure, son." The Admiral smiled, a warm, fatherly smile, and put his arm about the Brooks Brothered young man.

"You should keep in touch with us, across the river. I like to meet bright young people, and we can always use friends. Give me a call if you come up with anything on the new plane. We like to check out things, just to keep a line on security. You seem like a man who keeps his eyes and ears open."

As soon as the young man moved on, dazed and pleased at being so addressed by the Director of Central Intelligence, the Admiral maneuvered his way to a phone and got through to Borchner.

"The rollout's next month. I want people out at Edwards *tomorrow*. I want you to pull whoever you know out of bed and get us involved with that rollout. Check the prime defense contractors, put the squeeze on whoever you have to. I want action, Borchner, and I want some answers by noon tomorrow."

At the other end of the line, Borchner gave Wakefield his assurances and replaced the receiver.

He looked thoughtfully at the instrument for a few moments, before picking it up again and dialing the first of several numbers known to very few people in Washington.

15

EDWARDS AIR FORCE BASE, CALIFORNIA

The wind swept across the sun-blasted cement, carrying with it the signature fragrance of Edwards, the slightly sweet smell of carbonized jet fuel. Pretorius looked out from behind his sunglasses at the dignitaries shuffling along behind the barricade rope. Each felt he had been granted a high and unusual privilege to view the rollout of this, the United States' most highly classified piece of military hardware. Each man stretched and squinted, eager to take in as much of the long, low, brooding profile as possible.

There was, Pretorius felt, an almost *reverent* feeling in the air, the sense of being in the presence of something limitlessly, awesomely powerful, which was unquestionably the case with the B(AT)-3. Within its weapons bays, it could nestle more than sixteen advanced cruise missiles with nuclear warheads, releasing them unseen, wheeling lazily back to safety as the holocaust engulfed its targets, snuffing out life measured in the millions, backlighting the aircraft's tail section with a whiteness bright beyond all comprehension.

Pretorius fidgeted, his hands in his pockets. He'd been waiting here at Edwards more than a month now, going through the motions as the bomber's chief project engineer. And patience was not Pretorius' strong suit.

He wondered when and how and where the snatch would take place. Who would the people be? How good? Would he even realize when it was taking place?

Pretorius' training kept him on edge, and his muscles tensed in anticipation. Possibly a man with less conditioning would have found the waiting game easier. But Pretorius at this stage was like a coiled spring, resonating at the slightest vibration. It would be foolish to say fear was not a factor, but it took second place—by far—to an almost eager anticipation for the job to go down.

Pretorius found this feeling unsettling, and thought of the tranquility he had left behind in another world, in Devon.

Was he some kind of freak, to actually be *anticipating* this assignment? Had he been lying to himself longer than he knew? Or had the plunge back into the business rekindled something which would always be there to reckon with?

He shook his head, and returned to the current reality, the one he had to deal with. The desert sky over toward Barstow loomed dark and threatening; a late-afternoon storm might be stirring. He almost welcomed the idea. It would, for example, drive the VIPs indoors, and accelerate the schedule. With any luck, they might be back in the cars by five and on their way.

The rollout ceremony itself had been unusually private. Several officials from the administration and the Department of Defense were on hand, as were three congressmen and a man identified as being an acquisitions accountant from the DOD—actually the project's newly assigned representative of the Central Intelligence Agency.

Five officers of general rank from the Air Force attended, including the new Air Force Chief of Staff, General Nathan Spiesman.

Only a few members of the press were invited—an unusual occurrence at such a ceremony.

The civilians who had worked on the born-again Tupolev had all been sent to a special area on the huge range, a luxuriously fitted out rest and recreational area. They would be kept there in virtual isolation for months.

The only member of their group at the rollout was the B(AT)-3's Chief Project Engineer, Dr. Charles Vojtec, who handled questions with impressive technical expertise. The plane itself was even more impressive, rolling out into the glare of a bright fall desert day. The matte black finish overall only emphasized its sleek lines, strongly reminiscent of the Rockwell B-1B, but with an outsized swing-wing design, which came close to being a true delta wing configuration.

No press kit was available on the B(AT)-3, but it was confided that this new aircraft was capable of continuous automatic altitude adjustment (due to its TF/TA electronics), sharp lateral maneuverability (partially due to its ride-control canards, originally tested on the AFTI/F16), all while flying at treetop-level over uneven terrain, and the capability of speeds in excess of Mach 2.

It was also revealed that a new technology which countered both standard and square-pulse radar energy gave the new B(AT)-3 virtually unbeatable stealth characteristics and showed no radar cross-section whatever, even with the new carrier-free radar currently under development by both the United States and the Soviets.

This made the B(AT)-3 the world's most formidable penetration bomber. And its unveiling explained a great many things: the hesitation of producing the B-1B initially, then Jimmy Carter's decision to kill its production—but not its further development.

It explained the curious decision later to produce limited quantities of the B-1B, basically a creature of the technology of the sixties, with a few new bells and whistles bolted on for the eighties, and a prodigious record of avionics failures.

Not to mention the oddly erratic funding and the government's cavalier treatment of the Northrop B-2.

It was hinted that, in fact, both the B-1B development and

that of the B-2 bomber had been merely testbeds for a quantum jump in stealth technology.

The new B(AT)-3 was, in fact, the prototype of a new generation of aircraft destined to become the mainstay of American air power. Provided, of course, tests at Edwards proved satisfactory.

The already-legendary aircraft was cordoned off behind ropes, with several USAF officers—Ray-Bans reflecting the blue California sky—standing near the edge to dispense information to the congressmen and other VIPs. The B(AT)-3 itself seemed like a sleekly evil, impatient-looking creature, enduring its public exposure only as much as it had to, ready to hurl itself into the sky, there to disappear from the vision of men. For this was its mission: to strike at the enemy from beneath a cloak of utter invisibility.

No photographs were permitted. But no one could fail to remember every detail of this long, low, ominous-appearing aircraft.

16

THE NEW YORK TIMES

"Superstealth" Bomber Unveiled at Edwards Air Force Base

BY CLIVE HARRISON
Special to The New York Times

October 15—Edwards Air Force Base was the setting for yesterday's low-key rollout of the B(AT)-3 Superstealth Bomber, the United States' latest entry in the race for air superiority.

The new aircraft was introduced in a climate of maximum security and minimum publicity. Few members of the press were invited to the highly restricted ceremony in the Mojave Desert facility.

The B(AT)-3 appears to combine the best elements of electronic stealth technology, state-of-the-art configuration and all-composite construction for minimum radar presence, and auto-piloted low-level terrain flying below radar defenses.

A high-ranking government spokesman stated the new B(AT)-3 was "the lynchpin upon which we will hinge our total global strategic structure."

The aircraft's Chief Project Engineer, Dr. Charles Vojtec, has shepherded the B(AT)-3 from its initial design stages to yesterday's rollout. He was quoted as saying, "The B(AT)-3's capabilities will only be fully appreciated in the decades ahead. It embodies the best thinking of government and industry scientists, incorporated in an aircraft that will, quite literally, make mincemeat of Soviet defenses on the ground and in the air. It is virtually undetectable to any known or projected radar defense system and has offensive capabilities which can only be guessed at by opposition planners."

Dr. Vojtec, a contract employee of the Department of Defense, has written extensively on technical aspects of strategic air power.

17

MOSCOW, UNION OF SOVIET SOCIALIST REPUBLICS

COMINTSurvRep 003116/BH/KL (OP:AURORA, SENIOR STRETCH, DSCS-ROFA.)

Location: Ministry of Defense, Office of Minister of Defense Sergei Leonidovich Sokolov, MSU, Ulitsa Kirova 37, Moscow 103160.

Subject Surveillance: S.L. Sokolov, MSU; S. F. Akhromeyev, MASU, V. S. Miroshnikov, COL, KGB.

(Note: Subject V.S. Miroshnikov holds rank of full Colonel in the KGB and until this surveillance report has not surfaced to any of our COMINT or HUMINT sources since November of 1979.)

Login: 1600 GMT, 10/18/90.

Source: Omicron 67.

(Five minutes' transmission after log-in unintelligible due to unknown electromagnetic interference. Computer-assisted restoration ineffective. Following is transcript of first acceptable material.)

SLS: "It is time, then. The Center has completed all preparations?"

VSM: "Yes, Minister, everything is in place. The American will not be missed for at least four days, by which time we shall have learned everything of importance. Deputy Bobkov has the project under his personal supervision."

SLS: "Excellent, Miroshnikov. We shall watch the KGB's progress with interest."

VSM: "We are honored, Minister."

SLS: "You may go now, Comrade. The Ministry is counting on you . . . perhaps even more than you know."

VSM: "Thank you, Minister."

(Sounds of chairs, door opening and closing.)

SFA: "An intelligent man, even for KGB."

SLS: Let us hope so. Also Miroshnikov does know the United States. He circulated in the Russian studies groups of a few New England colleges in the late fifties, and recruited five or six quite acceptable assets. A few are now in the State Department and furnishing good product . . . but what's your assessment of (TRANSMISSION FAULT) . . . reliable?"

SFA: "Our people seem quite optimistic over the possibilities. The indications, from all stations, are consistent. There appear to be no anomalous reports. Our probability estimates are running high, Comrade Minister.

SLS: "Yes. Just so. Still, I am not wholly at ease with this operation. *Ulitsa Dzerzhinskogo** is never completely to be trusted in military matters. I would feel more comfortable with our own Third Directorate running things. And something seems too good, too predictable . . ."

SFA: "With respect, Minister, the Center has excellent professionals in the field. In the event of reversal, they have the necessary resources and training to respond well. There is nothing to lose, and everything to gain."

SLS: "That, my dear Sergei, is exactly it. The balance is too well tipped in our favor. One suspects the butcher more who puts his thumb on the scale in our favor, rather than in his."

SFA: "We can always delay, run further checks . . . if the Minister wishes."

(Silence for eight seconds.)

SLS: "No, Sergei, I think not. As you say, we have good peo-

*Dzerzhinski Square, Moscow Center of the KGB

ple in the field, and time is valuable just now. Defense budgets are being drawn up, and the yield from this could radically effect their deployment. I need support, good solid intelligence support for our position. No, I am just an old man, seeing shadows in the fog."

SFA: "The Minister is hardly an old man."

SLS: "You are kind, Akhromeyev. You are also speaking bullshit. I wake every morning an old man, and I go to sleep older still. I am more aware of the passage of time than of anything else. This gives me an inevitable uneasiness which you will not know, possibly, until you too are old to do anything about it. Go now. Keep me in the picture, as your American friends say."

SFA: "Yes, Comrade Minister. Thank you."

(Logout: 1608 GMT.)

18

EDWARDS AIR FORCE BASE, CALIFORNIA

The abyss stretched to infinity, a limitless chasm of blue, deepening ultimately to purest black. From time to time, tiny aircraft would hurl themselves into it, testing their prowess and that of their occupants. Their progress across its vastness was marked by contrails—streaming parodies of clouds—and by the noises of their engines and the sudden whacking vacuums as they entered supersonic flight.

It was to the mysteries of the abyss that the people here at Edwards were dedicated, and in which they often expended their lives. Even in the days when it was a godforsaken desert blot called Muroc and so hot as to be considered inhospitable even to scorpions, the place had a reverence about it which made men talk of it in bemused, uneasy tones, the way men speak of death, or certain women, or other things which lay beyond their comprehension and inspire the tiny prickling fears of uncertainty.

It was, in brief, a holy place, and the abyss was its altar.

In this place, Pretorius played out his part as Charles Vojtec, Chief Project Engineer of the B(AT)-3, and watched, and waited. It had been two and a half weeks since the rollout. No contact had been allowed between Pretorius and his control. In his briefing, it had been estimated that his abduction—if in fact it was to happen—could occur at any time up to a month past the rollout.

On this Saturday, after a week of going over electrical circuits checking for a supposed malfunction, Pretorius had decided to take his rental car for a drive north to escape the tedium. The car, a big yellow Oldsmobile convertible he christened The Yellow Peril, had a sound system which could, if pressed to its limits, bulge the top and windows outward.

Pretorius turned the big Oldsmobile onto Vandenburg. The street was lined with infinite variations on a theme: righteous rectilinear shoeboxes, each with the requisites for a married Air Force officer's home. Everything in place, from the vegetable sprayer in the kitchen sink to the bar alongside one wall of the living room.

The air on this Saturday morning was soft and pleasant, the sounds of the day predictable: jet engines droning a constant distant sound. Kids playing, lawn mowers, birds, and the thousand lulling sounds of a well-regulated community.

He was glad now to take a long weekend off. The pressure of the rollout and the tension of playing out his cover had kept his nerves taut as catgut. He stopped the car at the main gate, letting the sentry get a good look at the plastic ID. The sentry, a black Airman in white AP helmet, belt, holster, and leggings, waved him through with a snappy salute. Took a good AP to get gate duty at Edwards, thought Pretorius; the brass rolled in and out of here like kids at a Saturday movie.

Turning into the highway, he began to relax. The day was bathed in dazzling sunlight as he pointed the car north. He'd packed camping gear, including a fishing outfit, and was looking forward to a couple of days in the mountains. He wished for a moment he could share this with Susannah. But he also knew at any time the opposition would make their move, and his chances for survival were, at best, slim.

He compressed his lips and punched on the radio to KOIT, Barstow. The system connected with some vintage Otis Redding. It reminded Pretorius of his DIA days near Wiesbaden, where the USAF radio station had played requests. The Doors and Otis Redding always topped the lists. His mind ran free, playing over the memories of those days, before the minefield and his capture.

Until then, he had been engaged in a great game, scarcely thinking about such things as defeat or failure, or even being hurt. He'd been invulnerable. Untouchable. Pretorius smiled wryly; he'd gotten perspective, all right.

The highway stretched far and flat as he drove north. With the top down, the sun felt gentling, reassuring. It would be hours before he got to where the trees would be green, and where the highway would begin to curve. Something tugged at his reverie, and his eyes swept to the overhead rearview mirror and saw the two cars overtaking him.

The Air Force staff car moved gently, smoothly alongside his, the officer inside motioning him to pull over. As if to underscore the gesture, a California Highway Patrol cruiser, flashers revolving, swerved into position directly behind Pretorius.

Pretorius' mind kicked into Condition Orange.

At Fairfax, they'd taught a four-color system of alertness to agents: White, in which you're relaxed, unobservant. A condition no self-respecting field operative should ever find himself in, even on his own time. Yellow, a general alertness to the possibility of danger. Orange, an increased awareness to a specific suspected source of trouble. And Red, when the thing is definitely on and an immediate response is required, and you move into it without any thought of checking it halfway through.

Keeping pace alongside Pretorius' car, the Air Force officer's gestures grew more pronounced, and the CHP driver hit his siren.

Pretorius flicked down his right-hand turn signal. As he moved the Oldsmobile onto the highway's shoulder, the Air Force staff car pulled in front of him and the CHP car edged up behind to within three feet.

Pretorius was boxed in. The move was slickly executed, totally professional.

He knew, at that moment, the snatch was on.

As the Air Force officer emerged from his vehicle and began walking back toward Pretorius, the CHP policeman remained in his car with his door slightly ajar.

Unseen by Pretorius, but pointed directly at him through the gap between the cruiser's door and its pillar, was a tranquilizer gun of the type used to stun large animals for capture by zoos. It was there in case of difficulty.

The cruiser itself, recently given new identification numbers, had been stolen two months previously, at which time its driver—a veteran trooper—had been executed.

The Air Force officer was a captain, tall, almost cadaverously thin. Pretorius could not remember having seen him before at Edwards or any place else. The black rectangle on his shirt gave his name as Kostermann. As the officer spoke, the tones were flat, unaccented, the cadence almost too carefully measured.

"Dr. Vojtec?" he asked. "Excuse me, sir, but there's an emergency back at the base."

"What's the story?" Pretorius asked in an impatient voice. "What's going on?"

"Well, sir, all I'm permitted to say is there's an emergency of some sort with the prototype. An electrical fire started somewhere forward in the aircraft, and they need you back right away to sort things out. Sorry."

Pretorius swore in the manner of an overworked man interrupted on the way to a well-deserved vacation, then relaxed. "Not your fault, Captain. Okay, I'll follow you guys back."

Once again, the officer's flat tones struck Pretorius as oddly mechanical, lifeless. "My orders are for you to leave your vehicle here and to ride in the car with me, sir. The trooper has already radioed for someone to drive your personal car back to base for you."

"Well, I guess you guys know what you're doing. Just make

sure they get it back in one piece; I'm personally responsible to Mr. Hertz for it."

The man in the uniform smiled mirthlessly, his lips a grim curved line. "No problem, Dr. Vojtec."

Pretorius got into the staff car's front passenger seat and eased back. The officer accelerated onto the highway and executed a flawless U-turn at a speed beyond the ability of an average driver.

Pretorius took mental note. The man had been trained in pursuit driving somewhere; his hands now lay on the wheel at 10 and 2 o'clock, fingers flexing lightly, thumbs resting on top.

"By the way, Dr. Vojtec," the Captain said, "we've got to stop and pick up two enlisted men on the way. They're needed at the base commander's office for something else that's hot. Okay?"

"Fine, Captain."

"Thank you, sir" the man in the uniform said, displaying his death's-head smile once more.

They continued driving south for some twenty minutes and finally, at a rusted iron street sign saying "E. Reseda Avenue," they turned off the highway and entered a weed-strewn street, cracks in the cement lying zigzag beneath the shimmer of the heat. The CHP car kept pace behind them.

After a few minutes, the two cars braked to a stop in front of a single-story adobe house painted a faded green. Two Air Force enlisted men came through the screen door almost immediately; both in short-sleeved, pale blue uniform shirts. The taller of the two, a black man with a mustache and a shaved head, was a three-striper. The other man—carrying a brown paper bag— wore one chevron, was white, pudgy, with stringy blond hair, longer than regulation cut. They got into the backseat from either door and settled down behind Pretorius. "Men," intoned the man in the officer's tunic, "this is Dr. Vojtec; Dr. Vojtec, this is Sergeant Quinn, and Private Shessler."

Pretorius swiveled around and nodded to the two. Although

they both smiled broadly, their eyes seemed flat, expressionless. They were, he knew, sizing him up, calculating the difficulty of taking him. Pros. It would come soon now, he knew.

The officer swung the car around and headed back toward the highway. He rolled the windows up and punched on the air conditioner, full force. Pretorius didn't turn around, but assumed the highway patrol vehicle was still behind them.

Two minutes later, at the stop sign just before the highway ramp, one of the men behind suddenly leaned over the front seat, pinning Pretorius' arms in an immovable, viselike grip, while—softly, almost tenderly—an unseen hand pressed the ether-soaked gauze pad to Pretorius' face.

19
WESTCHESTER COUNTY, NEW YORK STATE

The sleek white Mitsubishi jet whined to a halt, the engines reluctantly winding down. Across the cement apron, a near-silent ambulance slipped swiftly forward, lighting up the aircraft in stark relief with quartz-halogen headlights.

The pilot began flicking off his switches in a methodical rhythm, and one of the crew triggered the switch for the hydraulic door, which began to slowly open.

Two of the ambulance attendants received the stretcher, its occupant securely strapped in, as it was lowered from the plane.

The airport tower people watched with interest, although they'd seen several such arrivals for the Van Cortlandt Institute. The hospital specialized in psychiatric as well as general medical care for the wealthy, including a generous share of those addicted to alcohol, cocaine, heroin, and a range of other fashionably debilitating substances.

Their families paid handsomely to give them luxurious surroundings, in most cases hoping for their eventual return.

The tower people supposed the patient in the stretcher was another such casualty. Their curiosity satiated, they returned to their screens.

The ambulance accelerated swiftly down toward the highway, beginning its trip back to the Institute. The Van Cortlandt

Institute was perched imperiously on a hill high above the Hudson, within view of the United States Military Academy at West Point.

Built in the late 1880s, it had once been an inn for wealthy families from New York and Boston who had favored it for languorous summer vacations, which usually included painting the local scenery.

The main building was reminiscent of an Austrian chalet whose designer had gotten carried away, and whose enthusiasm had produced too much of a good thing, grown out of all proportion and Victorianized as an afterthought. A capacious porch wrapped itself around the first floor and, once upon a time, hundreds of rockers kept time to the humming of nature in the gardens nearby.

Adjoining portions of the huge complex were painted a light apple green, and each room facing the lawn leading down to the Hudson displayed its own miniature porch.

The difference, of course, was that now each of the windows was sealed with a network of tempered steel bars, and if an occupant somehow found his way out onto one of the porches, alarms would instantly produce a phalanx of armed guards.

At night, floodlights made the large main building stand out against the blackness of the sky. Few room lights were lit after dark, except in the maximum security wing, where no light was ever allowed to be extinguished.

A long, curving drive snaked its way up the hill, and the ambulance followed its bends effortlessly, finally coming to rest behind the maximum security section.

Within minutes, its principal passenger had been whisked inside and isolated from the rest of the Institute's population.

In case of surprise visits by county or state medical authorities, he was registered as Charles Oliver Dana of Shaker Heights, Ohio, under treatment for advanced alcoholism, complicated by cirrhosis of the liver.

Charts had been prepared in advance, showing the patient

had been under treatment for six weeks and been lately showing some progress, although complete recovery seemed less than likely.

The Van Cortlandt Institute's Director, Dr. Bob True, stopped by to observe the examination of the new arrival.

Dr. True resembled a television minister.

His smile was broad and winning. His hair was a neat crew-cut, a mixture of gray and blond. His glasses were bottle-bottom thick, and through them, merry eyes twinkled: large brown eyes which seemed to radiate warmth and understanding.

The families of his patients trusted Dr. True completely.

Those who bothered to check his credentials found the good doctor had been graduated from the Harvard Medical School with honors, and had gone on to study in Edinburgh, becoming a Fellow of the Royal College of Surgeons before ultimately returning to the United States.

The fact that he had been a *rezident* for three years at Moscow's Serbsky Institute would, of course, never appear on any written record, for his identity there had been somewhat different.

Families of the patients usually felt completely at ease with his cheerful bonhomie, his jolly, reassuring style.

The patients, though, on those rare occasions when they emerged from the narcotic haze in which the staff kept them, often felt distinctly afraid, even chilled, in his presence.

Their instincts were correct.

Dr. True had personally killed no less than seventy patients in ten years of clandestine experiments conducted within the walls of Van Cortlandt.

He considered the loss of these patients no more than a hindrance, a temporary impediment in an inexorable and necessary process.

The victims were usually men and women of families who had not visited them in years, families who would frankly be rather relieved at the termination of the patients' miseries.

Dr. True was conducting a radical form of neurological research, on a scale impossible in a normal hospital under legal restraints.

Much of what he had learned over the years could not be published. After all, the stimuli applied to patients in the experiments would be recognized as inhumane. Then, too, the experiments were obviously dedicated not to saving life, but to surgically altering human behavior.

Looking down at the new patient, Dr. True observed a white male, in his mid-forties, in superb physical condition. The only evidence of trauma was a large scar running diagonally across the back, varying from 1.4 cm to 3 cm in width, a total of 42 cm in length.

Dr. True hoped that after the interrogation he might have this specimen. The superb physical condition might enable the subject to survive some new experiments and yield some interesting results, which the usual patients entering Van Cortlandt—due to their often advanced years or deteriorated alcoholic conditions—had not been able to endure.

Easing open one of the patient's eyelids, Dr. True noted minor dilation. The narcosis was wearing off. A gentle finger on the carotid, and the pulse rate was measured at sixty per minute.

"Get him ready," Dr. True said crisply to the male attendant. "Call Mr. Clovis and tell him we'll be prepared to begin the procedure within the next hour."

Pretorius was connected to an IV drip, and straps with Velcro fasteners were secured across his forehead, chest, hips, and legs.

The video camera focused on his face as the microphones were positioned for maximum clarity.

Patients undergoing this form of interrogation often mumbled and slurred their words, particularly under heavy sedation or physical stress, and their words had to undergo later computer reconstruction. It was important, then, that the microphones be correctly positioned.

As the drugs flowed into Pretorius' veins, the prepared sound-track began to play. The sounds were of clicking, at regular intervals, coupled with very low frequency tones. Research at Serbsky had shown these particular frequencies to be especially helpful in narcotic-assisted interrogations. The regular clicking gave the patient a reassuring element as the low tones reduced both physical and mental resistance.

Simultaneously, in the next room, video and audio tape machines silently began rolling, recording every sound and movement of the patient.

20
RIPPING BECK, SOMERSET, ENGLAND

Susannah walked through the rain-glistened cobblestone streets toward her restaurant, the Dreaded David Lloyd George struggling to keep pace with his stubby legs.

It had been raining for nearly two weeks straight, and even the inhabitants of Ripping Beck who preferred a good damp day were now reconsidering their position. It was enough, as Susannah remarked privately to the equally damp DLG, to make a person sprout gills.

She thought of Michael often and long and wondered at the strange places from which he'd sent her postcards. Most of all, though, she wondered at the curious impersonality of his letters; almost as if he had something written between the lines, something he wanted her to realize without his actually having written it. And it all seemed so everlasting lonely. Almost as if he were marooned somewhere instead of having a holiday tour of the U.S.

She wondered how long it would be before she'd see him again: She missed his wise, funny smile, and his sad eyes. She wanted to hear the rumble of his voice, and the way his laugh seemed to explode from deep somewhere in his chest. She wanted to be held by him in the night, to feel his sinewy, lean muscles.

Damn! she thought, *I'm acting like a love-struck teenager. Best get on with things and not think too much of the missing Mister Pretorius.* Reaching the door of her restaurant, she glanced down at the dog and was met by David Lloyd George's questioning upward gaze. *Well, old thing,* she mused, *it's got to be almost as bad for you as for me. Suppose we'll just wait for His Lordship together.*

And the two of them went inside, never noticing the man looking into the neighboring tobacconist's window, nor his quick glance in their direction.

21
WESTCHESTER COUNTY, NEW YORK

The questioner was perched on a chromium and leather stool very near Dr. True. His voice was quiet, yet oddly insistent; his demeanor kind, almost fatherly.

To judge from his accent and appearance, the questioner was an American. He was, in fact, from Soviet Georgia, a highly regarded specialist who held the rank of Colonel in the KGB.

The Institute referred to him as Mr. Clovis. His name, both respected and feared in the corridors of Moscow Center, was Gvosdilin.

Pretorius soon felt—almost from the beginning—a curious obligation to please the questioner, an obligation born of the euphoria caused by the introduction into the IV of a "cocktail" which included seven milligrams of PCP (phencyclidine). This would be alternated with a sodium amytol mixture, and the subject's will would be whipsawed back and forth between the two.

The PCP had been synthesized at the Institute and was similar to a surgical analgesic and anesthetic once introduced on the American market as Sernyl. The drug had been quickly withdrawn because of patients reporting extreme agitation and disorientation on emerging from the anesthesia. Repackaged as an animal tranquilizer, it soon found its way to street use under various names: rocket fuel, crystal, hog, and angel dust.

Now the solution flooded into his system, and Pretorius experienced a drifting, curiously floating sensation, euphoric and tingling.

His entire body seemed warmed, calmed, utterly taken care of. It seemed to expand, and then to blend, to mingle with air, creating a sensation of nothingness.

His concept of time became more and more elastic. The idea of *now* seemed to have no meaning, no relevance. The past and the future were constantly telescoping, then changing places, then merging into a new feeling of time which Pretorius had never, up to this moment, experienced.

And then the anesthetist switched over to amytol, a few air bubbles rising up to the top of the IV bottle to mark its entry into Pretorius' bloodstream.

Pretorius suddenly felt an almost aching warmth, a feeling of compulsion to move, to *do* something, anything—and yet his body still had the curious sensation of being suspended in air above the operating table, of being disassociated with the being below, his other body.

The anesthetist checked his digital readouts on the machinery stacked just below the table, and nodded to Dr. True.

Within ten or twelve minutes, Pretorius' will to resist was utterly annihilated. Dr. True asked him a few simple questions, and his responses came almost eagerly. Gvosdilin then pulled his stool closer and, referring occasionally to papers on an aluminum clipboard, began his questions.

Pretorius felt a strong kinship with his questioner, almost as if they were long-standing friends, reunited. He wanted the questioner to know everything he alone knew. It was a strangely compulsive feeling, almost as if his very existence depended on pleasing the questioner.

He gave direct answers to every question and felt an almost desperate need to fill the silence that followed his answers.

Pretorius affirmed he was, indeed, Dr. Charles Vojtec, Chief Project Engineer on the B(AT)-3.

He also affirmed his previous employment with two of the

leading defense contractors in New England, that he had also worked for the West German office of an American metals firm, and that his academic background included mathematics and aerospace engineering at MIT, obtaining his doctorate in June of 1973.

Very specific questions of a highly technical nature then followed. The answers came quickly, almost eagerly, many of them expressed in mathematical formulae.

As the subject talked, Gvosdilin slowly became aware of a nagging feeling of familiarity. Something about the tone of the answers, or was it the face of the subject himself? Something . . . something, it seemed, from long ago, possibly in Germany.

The anesthetist switched back to the PCP solution once more, and the patient felt a sense of relief, of a curious tingling numbness, and again a dislocation of his sense of time and space.

Dr. True's eyes flicked over to the readouts. Everything as expected. He nodded his satisfaction.

The interrogation continued. Gvosdilin was obviously pleased with the outflow of information, yet continued to feel the strange sensation of familiarity.

Then suddenly, with the impact of a powerful vehicle bursting through a barrier, Gvosdilin finally knew what had been disturbing him. At a certain angle, he recognized the face: *He'd interrogated this man before. But where—and in what context?*

He looked closer at the face: This man had been a soldier. No, no . . . now it came . . . the man was an agent, an operative of some kind. He'd been a minor western intelligence employee. And then everything fell into place. The affair near Nordhausen, with the minefield. This had been the man who so pitifully had tried to cling to his cover as a German farmer, when it was all too obvious what he was.

Gvosdilin had been on a training and supervision mission in Leipzig, on loan to the East Germans, who were eager to absorb Moscow Center's latest techniques. On Gvosdilin's advice, the interrogation team had put the prisoner under deep sedation and used several experimental drugs to bring his pathetic secrets to the surface.

In the end, he had told them everything, what little of value he knew. And when they slowly brought him back to consciousness, they behaved as if they still believed his story—even to the extent of releasing him, and letting him return to his unit in Wiesbaden.

The HVA (*Hauptverwaltung für Aufklärung;* the East German External Dept.) monitored all his activities from then on, and unwittingly the man had led them to bigger fish. Gvosdilin had been kept informed by the East Germans, who openly appreciated his help and were also anxious to curry favor with someone so highly placed in the apparatus.

And now here he was again. What did it mean? Why was an intelligence agent—or an ex-intelligence agent—serving as an engineer on a super-secret bomber project?

The anesthetist continued to slowly alternate the PCP and amytol, and the layers of the subconscious began to peel away.

As the answers continued, Gvosdilin began to think he had the concept completely in hand, and then the answers began to take a sly, almost playful turn.

Gvosdilin's instincts sensed something deeper, something hidden far below what he was hearing, what they had been recording for the past hour or so. And so his questions changed, ever so subtly, probing lightly, teasingly. And the answers began to sharply alter.

Realizing what was happening—that the initial yield had been only a plant, only decoy information—Gvosdilin began to bristle with excitement. He stood now beside the subject, too agitated to sit on the stool. *Now* he knew why this man had been chosen for his post: an engineer who had been previously an intelligence agent would be best prepared to withstand interrogation, or to implant disinformation if ever abducted.

And it would have worked, had the engineer been placed in the hands of anyone less worthy than he, Gvosdilin.

If what he thought was happening was true, then the Americans had been carefully, and quite uncharacteristically, putting together a disinformation scheme which could have cost the Soviet Union billions upon billions, an operation worthy of the great Ivan Ivanovich Ayants, who had been head of the KGB's Department "D" (Disinformation) in the early sixties. And if he, Gvosdilin, was the one person to unmask it, then his future was unlimited, unparalleled in terms of human power.

This was information beyond any means of valuation. Even Gvosdilin, though easily the *Rodina*'s most highly trained and experienced interrogation expert, found it shocking. The Americans were far, far more devious than had been previously suspected.

The information would have to be transmitted quickly, but would have to be presented in complete form; the intelligence was too sensitive to be presented in pieces without context. Possibly even too sensitive to risk radio transmission in the normal codes.

It was also of sufficient importance to assure generous rewards for those most associated with it. All of which meant an immediate return to Moscow Center by the questioner, the information in his possession alone.

The anesthetist tapped Dr. True on the shoulder and pointed to one readout showing a dramatic increase in systolic blood pressure. True looked at the patient closely. The muscles were beginning to tense in the face and neck, and a slight sheen of perspiration was beginning to show.

"He's very close to an overdose," said Dr. True. "We'll take him down from it and go for the rest tomorrow. Too much more and we'll lose him altogether."

Gvosdilin nodded his assent. The anesthetist unscrewed off the IV from the needle and replaced it with a hypodermic. He depressed the plunger slowly, releasing haloperidol into the vein. He finished, withdrew the needle, and taped a gauze square over the puncture.

And then, as Gvosdilin scurried into the listening booth to replay the tapes, the patient was wheeled along a tunnel-like corridor.

Pretorius, unconscious, his system in a state of near-collapse, was taken into a steel-doored recovery room. The chamber with white-tiled walls, ceiling, and floor. In the door, a $4'' \times 4''$ aperture of thick quartz glass made observation of the patient possible by anyone outside.

A single light bulb overhead, shielded by iron grillwork, provided constant, pitiless light. Directly beneath it, a single drain was centered in the tiled floor.

The room, being two floors below the supposed basement of the Institute, needed no windows. What little ventilation there was came by way of a small ceiling outlet, protected by the same grillwork as that over the light. An attendant remained outside the locked door, a loudspeaker monitoring every sound from within.

In this cell Pretorius spent the next three days, kept in a twilight miasma of drugs, wheeled again and again down the long corridor to the tender mercies of Dr. True and Gvosdilin.

Gvosdilin bent to his task with enthusiasm. A masterpiece of interrogation was in process—perhaps the interrogation of the century, a yield of information which would guarantee his place in history. Not even Chebrikov himself, poised like a venomous spider in the center of the *Komitet*'s* web, could deny its worth.

And so the layers of disinformation were slowly, painstakingly, stripped away, and the meat below exposed to Gvosdilin's pitiless examination.

As the interrogation progressed, the tape reels whirred and ingested the sustenance fed them from the microphones, and the information which lay coiled upon the tapes was remarkable indeed.

At the end of the third day under Gvosdilin's increased activ-

Komitet Gosudarstennoy Besopasnosti (KGB), Committee for State Security ities, the subject was beginning to show dangerous levels of toxicity as well as becoming increasingly repetitive in his answers. Gvosdilin and True conferred and agreed to a hiatus and to a specialized nutrition formula placed in the IV, to build up the subject's strength for further sessions. Besides, as Gvosdilin thought to himself, in the past three days they'd gained years of technical knowledge. He, the great Gvosdilin, also deserved a rest. And so the subject was connected to a new IV, bathed, and sent back to his white-tiled cell on the gurney, restraint straps securing his body to the surface.

After approximately eight hours, Pretorius began to slowly surface from the miasma of the drugs, dimly aware of his surroundings.

As Pretorius opened his eyes, he couldn't judge the distance to the wall, or to the ceiling. Strong feelings of anxiety pervaded his entire being. He was, he felt, very close to death, very close to a nameless, threatening thing.

He closed his eyes and willed himself to clear the thing from his mind, to jettison whatever had invaded his senses. Like a drowning man, deep underwater, he began mentally clawing his way upward, upward through the murk and turbulence, sensing the daylight, the oxygen so very far above. Pretorius summoned every ounce of strength, every particle of energy, forcing his mind into control, squeezing the intruder from his being. And then, with a sudden shimmering reality, his mind seemed to break free, and his body was once more his own.

He rested, there in the white-tiled room, looking up at the ceiling, sweeping his eyes around analytically. With one arm, he tested the strength of whatever was holding him to the gurney. It wouldn't give. His strength, he knew, was at a minimum. There was a threatening numbness in his limbs. Slowly he began to push the arm back and forth. Some movement was permitted in this direction, but only the barest fraction of an inch.

Next, he tested movement of the other arm and his legs. Some small movement available. Possibly, just possibly, enough. Little by little, he realized there were at least two straps wrapped across his upper torso, holding him at the wrists and at the elbows.

He tried rotating his arms. A slight sound told him the straps were very likely Velcroed. Easier to deal with. Better and better, he thought. But Pretorius' system was still affected by the drugs, and he could only concentrate with the greatest effort.

Staring up at the bare light bulb, Pretorius worked at the straps holding his elbows tight to his midsection. By exhaling completely, he found he had considerable latitude of movement. His wrists, too, had marginally more freedom. He was careful not to rub them against the straps too much, for he wanted them moist, not dry from friction.

He concentrated even more, willing his muscles to relax, to become as limp as possible. He slowly increased the depth and frequency of his breathing, artificially elevating his pulse rate, forcing his cardiovascular system to respond to his exaggerated breathing.

Pretorius' pulse began racing, set into a higher and higher rate by his forced breathing.

After a half hour of sustained deep and frequent inhaling and exhaling, he felt the beginning of a prickling, clammy sensation on his skin. It was beginning to work.

He was careful to moderate his breathing slightly now, for there was a distinct danger of losing consciousness. Little by little, the perspiration rose through his pores and formed on his skin. A large droplet ran down his forehead, tracing its way downward.

He judged now was the time. He slowly—very slowly—exhaled all the air in his lungs. And let all his muscles relax, willing them to go limp.

Then, as if in slow motion, Pretorius drew one of his wrists backward—slowly backward—through the straps. Concentrating powerfully, Pretorius felt the sweat ease his wrist's way under the straps.

And then it was free.

He tried to cross his arm over, but it was still restrained at the elbow by the strap crossing his torso, and the buckle was just inches away.

The door clicked and opened. Pretorius remained motionless under the pitiless light. The free wrist strap was obvious.

Pretorius tensed as he heard the guard advance, the footsteps hurrying over to the gurney. He sensed, rather than felt, the guard's hand reach for the Velcro strap to secure it. And then snatched the guard's wrist with his own free hand, with blinding speed. Twisting it, he brought the off-balance guard falling onto the gurney, and it overturned.

The panic-stricken guard thrashed, trying to free his wrist, using his other hand to strike at Pretorius, who slowly and steadily continued twisting the wrist until one of the bones snapped.

The guard howled in pain, writhing on the floor, and Pretorius released his grip, now using his free hand to unsnap the other Velcro straps.

Just as Pretorius got the last one released, the guard struggled to his feet. Pretorius pivoted to one side, suddenly whipping his left foot around in a sweeping full roundhouse kick—the deadly *ushiro mawashi geri*, landing it with shattering force just below his target's ribcage, in the vulnerable solar plexus.

The guard crumpled, then—with surprising swiftness—drove his hand up with four fingers rigid, directly into Pretorius' midsection. All the breath was driven out of Pretorius, and he could scarcely move as he watched the guard rush toward him.

Pretorius—using his last scrap of energy—dodged to one side, and, using his knee as a fulcrum, allowed the guard's forward-falling weight to engineer his own destruction.

The edge of Pretorius' stiffened hand whipped downward to the base of the guard's skull with approximately 700 foot-pounds of energy, instantly shattering two vertebrae.

The guard was still alive but totally paralyzed, his eyes staring with glazed hatred as Pretorius relieved him of his keys.

22
VAN CORTLANDT, NEW YORK

Pretorius flattened himself along the corridor wall, the perspiration on his back beading and prickling against the cold tile, the scar tissue in the broad ridge across his back pulsing with a peculiar sensitivity of its own.

He forced his breathing into silent shallow drafts as he listened intently, his musculature coiled, tensed to act.

But the sounds were the thousand muffled echoes of a hospital after midnight—voices in the distance, doors softly opening and closing, a radio playing.

Frozen in position, Pretorius wondered what this place was, and where he could possibly be. He let his mind pick its way gingerly through the dim, half-lit memories of what he'd just experienced. The drugs were still coursing their way through his system, hostile bodies only now being diminished by his adrenaline. And as the effect began to fade, ever so slowly, strange images tinged with overtones of horror began working their way to the surface . . .

Suddenly the staccato sound of footsteps separated from the overall pattern. At least two men hurrying down the intersecting corridor. Pretorius moved soundlessly to the corner.

As the two guards reached the intersection, his foot snapped forward in a sharp, lightning-quick kick, striking one—a heavy-set, burly Oriental—in the crotch, doubling him over in speechless agony.

The other guard reached for his pistol, nestled in an FBI-style high-ride holster at his waist, and was stopped in mid-motion by Pretorius' hand chopping at the wrist. Pretorius cupped one hand under the guard's elbow, and—striking with his other at the man's exposed forearm—dislocated the elbow.

Now the first guard came at Pretorius, the position and the slow, circular motion of his hands telegraphing professional training.

The danger was real, Pretorius knew. And he was not yet over the numbing, slowing effect of the drugs. He shifted weight on his two feet as he backed away slightly from the man, dropping his hands to his sides. As the disabled Oriental writhed on the tiled floor, the advancing guard cast a swift downward glance to check his companion's position. Mistake. *Now!*

Spinning around, Pretorius struck with the side of his stiffened foot against the guard's throat, crushing the larynx, causing death instantly.

The Oriental rose unsteadily to his knees, in agony from the dislocated elbow, but managing to get his gun out as he scrabbled forward. Pretorius kicked the weapon out of the guard's hand and brought the toughened, callused edge of his palm down on the base of the man's skull.

As the weapon clattered and skidded on the hard tile floor, the guard toppled forward, slowly, oddly, collapsing on the tiled floor like a puppet released from its strings.

Pretorius scooped up the weapon and sped down the corridor to a staircase door, opening it and edging up the staircase in silence.

One flight up, the door opened onto a considerably different hallway. In dignified silence, nineteenth-century oil landscapes and sepia-toned photographs of bewhiskered men peered from their places on papered walls above wooden wainscoting.

A quick glance in either direction showed the hallway was

for the moment empty. Pretorius darted quickly to the doorway across the hallway and silently turned the knob.

A matronly woman in a nurse's uniform, reading a newspaper at her desk, looked up to observe a somewhat anxious-appearing naked man holding a Colt .45 automatic. She had only time to reach toward a hidden switch, then gasp before Pretorius decked her with a blurred downward blow of his weapon.

Pretorius looked around and saw it was the anteroom to an office, obviously belonging to someone important.

Quietly opening the door, he pulled the unconscious woman into a much larger room, lined with books, dominated by a huge walnut desk on which rested only a telephone, a stack of papers, and a silver mounted pen-and-ink set.

No one was in the room. Pretorius moved to the closet and opened the door. Nothing inside. Not a jacket, not a pair of trousers, nothing. A few wire hangers dangling, some old newspapers on the floor. Nothing. He shut the door.

Pretorius scanned the room, looking for another door, another way out. Then he noticed something odd about the bookcases. All the books in one section looked curiously matched, a little too perfect, unlike those in the other sections. Running his fingers around the edges of the shelving, he felt a hair-line break where none should be.

He'd seen an arrangement like this once before, in his grandfather's library. Pretorius looked for a release button on the inside of one of the shelves, but none was there. Then, on the carpet immediately in front of the odd portion of shelves, he saw a slightly raised section—about the diameter of a fifty-cent piece.

Stepping on the raised section, he saw the wall of books swing slowly, silently, toward him, revealing the interior of a large bedroom. With relief, he found a pair of dark woolen trousers draped over a wooden valet near the bed, a wallet on the valet tray with approximately $300 and several credit cards, and a pair of well-polished Loafers gleaming on the lower rails of the stand.

He opened three drawers in a bureau before he found a thick, gray pullover sweater and some thick woolen socks. Pretorius scrambled into the clothing, listening intently for sounds of disturbance from outside the room. But—as yet—his escape was undiscovered. Still, in scant seconds all hell would break loose.

Looking out the window into the darkness, he wondered where he was. He didn't even know what time it was. His body felt plundered from the drugs, almost as if all the arteries, veins, and capillaries had been methodically entered, stripped, turned inside out. His perceptions, he knew, were affected. But there was something else—something sinister, something dark and evil beyond all imagining. His body sensed it almost as much as his mind. And there was an all-pervading sense of loss, of guilt. *Good God, what was happening to him?*

The window seemed to be on the first floor. Only a short drop from this window to the ground.

Pretorius flicked off the window catch and was about to raise it when he saw an intrusion alarm wire running to a switch at one side.

Pulling a lamp out of its wall socket, he sliced the wire with a razor blade from the bathroom. Next, he exposed the copper wires at either end and joined them to the terminals of the alarm contact switch.

Pretorius took a deep breath and slowly—with agonizing patience and dread—lifted the window. The alarm remained untriggered. He secured the pistol in his belt, swung one leg over the windowsill, gauged the distance to the ground, and dropped heavily. It was a longer drop than he'd expected. His depth perception must be off, he knew. How much else was off?

Picking himself up, he spilled rather than ran down the hill in back of the large brick building. His adrenaline was running high, despite the drugs still present in his system.

Several times he fell, rolling and tumbling end over end. His training caused him to roll instinctively, sheltering his head with his arms.

Somewhere behind him a Klaxon sounded, and quartz-halogen floodlights—many times more powerful than the Institute's usual floods—suddenly opened up, stabbing shafts of light into the woods down the hill.

By now, the guards had loosed the dogs from their kennels and were giving them the scent by rubbing their noses in other clothing from Dr. True's closet.

The dogs were specially bred oversized Rottweilers, silent in pursuit, trained to respond to supersonic whistles, and to kill their prey without mercy.

Each dog weighed 95 to 110 pounds and was held in check—but only with difficulty—with a stout leather lead wrapped securely around the fist of its master.

The guards had 9mm Heckler & Koch MP5 submachine guns slung from their necks, suppressors screwed to the stubby muzzles to reduce the sound of automatic fire.

The quartz-halogen lights helped illuminate the darkness somewhat, and Pretorius was grateful that he was running into fewer trees, and wearing dark clothing. He hit the bottom of the hill running, leaping at once into a fast-flowing stream, submerging himself totally as he fell. Pulling himself to the surface, he struggled to the other side and scrambled onto the bank. His breath was coming hard, and he felt a sharp chill as the wind plastered the soaking sweater and trousers to his skin.

Now he could hear the shouts of the guards as they began plunging down the hill, following as fast behind the dogs as they dared. But heavily armed men do not usually cover as much ground as the unarmed, both from fear of discharging their weapons, and from the overconfidence that too often comes from carrying shoulder firearms.

And so Pretorius knew he had a lead—one which would be aided by the dogs' confusion once they reached the stream. He ran alongside the stream in the darkness, now and then blundering into a low branch, and covered more than a thousand yards before doubling back across the stream.

The water felt less cold now that his body heat had risen with the pursuit, but it was still a penetrating, shocking sensation. The fall night was cool, about forty-five degrees, and he knew he could not last long in his weakened state, especially with wet clothing.

Shouts told him the dogs had reached the point of his first crossing and were confused. Their handlers would be pointing their Streamlites across to the other side, searching for footprints leading from the water.

He pulled himself out on the other bank at the same moment his pursuers crossed over at his first fording. He ran desperately alongside the stream, knowing the dogs—if any were let off their leashes—would easily outdistance him on the other side and alert their handlers to his presence.

His knees pumped furiously, putting as much distance between him and his hunters as possible. Stumbling, falling, he righted himself and continued through the chill darkness.

And then the trees opened up, and he could suddenly discern a clearing to the left. Far in the distance, he could see the soft rose-colored undersides of clouds that indicated some sort of city below.

He tore across the clearing in that direction, hearing shouting on the other side of the stream some 500 meters or more behind him.

And then—with the speed of a high-powered automobile—a huge blur hurtled out of the undergrowth ringing the clearing. The dog was one of those let loose without a lead, and had not been hampered by dragging along a handler behind. He had but one target, one goal, and that was the human across the clearing. At the moment the human saw him, the Rottweiler launched itself in a powerful leap across the twelve feet remaining between him and his startled prey.

Pretorius reflexively swept up the Colt in the two-handed

Weaver position, automatically laying the front sight over the dog's chest in midflight, and fired. The beast was dead within a split second, but the momentum of his leap brought him forward and on top of Pretorius, who took the weight full on his chest and was suddenly slammed backward six feet.

The breath was knocked from Pretorius' lungs, and as he rolled away and out from under the dog's inert weight, he struggled to his knees and gasped, unable to bring air back into his rasping, heaving chest. From across the clearing came the dog's handler, squinting in the near-blackness, his H&K submachine gun coming up just as he spotted Pretorius. But Pretorius' training paid off. He brought his pistol up in a smooth, fluid arc and planted three rounds within a six-inch group in the man's chest, one of the bullets speeding directly into the left ventricle of the heart. The sub gun dropped from the man's hands as he collapsed, dead before he hit the ground.

In the main building, hurriedly shrugging out of his laboratory coat, Dr. True spoke into his walkie-talkie, swearing at the guards for their failure to stop the escapee, determining the search was now to the east, dangerously near the highway.

He pulled on a windbreaker and jammed a .38 caliber Smith & Wesson Chief's Special into one pocket. Slamming open the back door, True sidestepped his way down the hill, crabwise, until he reached the bottom. There, he turned left and ran toward the distant sounds of shouting, cursing as he ran.

True took a shortcut across a field to catch up with the pursuers, speaking into the walkie-talkie as he ran, getting a better idea of their position.

The group had now recrossed the stream and were nearing their quarry. Pretorius could hear them gaining, crashing through the underbrush. Rising to his feet and gathering all his energy into a desperate sprint, he sped toward the soft light in the distance.

Dr. True could now hear the search group and spoke quickly into the walkie-talkie, urging them to terminate the escapee, to not take any chances. He was now only a few hundred feet from his guards and shouted to them. One of the men shouted a greeting in return, holding his dog back as the others suddenly wheeled toward True.

Catching up with the guards, True began ordering them to fan out more, when suddenly one of the dogs sprang directly at him—tearing its leash out of the handler's fist.

The Rottweiler, his keen nose catching the scent of True's clothing, knowing the human who wore that clothing was his target, sprang directly at him.

In sudden shrieking horror, the doctor realized the escapee had been wearing clothing stolen from his apartment, and that the guards had shown the dogs his clothing for scent.

The beast's jaws closed on the doctor's hand as he struggled to bring out the little .38 from his windbreaker pocket. True's wrist snapped under the terrible pressure, and razor-keen teeth tore at tendons, shredding them until the hand dangled useless.

By now, the other three dogs had caught the scent—not only of the quarry's clothing, but of his blood—and could not be restrained.

Two of them hurled themselves forward with enough vehemence to snap their leads instantly. The other dragged his handler helplessly along the ground as he, too, closed in on the hated prey.

The four Rottweilers savaged the doctor with such ferocity, the guards were too stunned to react instantly. Afraid to shoot for fear of hitting the doctor, afraid to dive in among the dogs in their bloodlust, the guards stood paralyzed as the beasts tore again and again at the figure writhing on the ground.

The face was torn literally to bits, one dog ripping off an entire cheek and an ear in a single swiping motion. Two worked on his neck and laid open the arteries, causing the blood to arc a full meter in the air.

A fourth drove his jaws deep into the doctor's lower torso, working through the clothing and exposing his soft white belly for an instant before ripping into it.

Finally, a guard fired his H&K into the mass on the ground, spraying the dogs and their quarry with 9mm rounds until finally the terrible carnage was over.

Playing his flashlight over the remains, one guard turned, sinking to his knees on the ground, vomiting. Pretorius, gasping for breath as he ran, heard the shots and wondered what had happened. And then suddenly, breaking through the underbrush, he flailed his way down a slight incline—directly into the path of an automobile speeding along the highway.

Inside the car, the driver—clutched suddenly by his terrified wife—swerved violently to one side and slammed his foot down on the brake simultaneously, nearly capsizing their vehicle.

The tires shrieked in unison as the rear end swung around, narrowly missing Pretorius, carried forward by his own momentum.

The driver swore at the creature in the road, obviously a drunk tumbling out from some local party, from his disheveled appearance and his lack of a jacket or coat in this weather.

As Pretorius turned and approached the car, the driver, having checked to see if his wife was all right, floored the accelerator to get them out of there. Whoever the drunk was, or whatever his problem was, he was definitely trouble.

Pretorius stood in the middle of the road as the car tore away, gasping deeply in the cold, unable to catch his breath. A vein in his temple throbbed, and he shivered as he felt the full impact of the cold penetrate his soaked clothing.

He knew at this hour of night he could expect little sympathy from most passers-by, and that, very likely, the Institute had connections with both state and county police and would have reported him as an escaped and dangerous psychopath. John Doe records would have been prepared to this effect, for precisely this eventuality.

He retreated into the woods across the highway and, paralleling it, ran once more toward the glow of lights, not knowing how far it was, only knowing he had to reach some sort of civilization and call the 703 number as instructed.

Pretorius' breath began to come more regularly as he settled into a rhythm, striding more evenly, realizing that only in this discipline could he cover the necessary ground and survive.

The gas station stood in the glare of the highway lights, its empty bays dark through the windows. A few cars and the station's lone wrecker had been parked near a shattered telephone booth, under the single bright highway light.

Pretorius stumbled against the phone booth wall, his stamina nearly gone, his eyes aching. His breath came in great rasping sobs, racking his chest. As he lifted the handset, it seemed as if he could almost *feel* the bones of his rib cage as they expanded and contracted, sweeping the cold night air into his lungs, filling them with the clean oxygen they needed so deeply.

Slowly, his mind began to clear, changing its focus from his uncertainly functioning body to the even more uncertain future ahead of it. His instructions were to dial the 703 number, listen for the high-pitched tone, then punch in a special series of numbers which would reroute the call far from the original area code and connect him with his control.

Pulling the booth's aluminum and glass door shut to cut off the chill October winds, Pretorius saw the number above the telephone punch pad: a 914 area code, so he must be close to New York.

He dialed zero, then the number with the northern Virginia area code, and finally the charge number he'd memorized at the op's beginning. He waited. After a series of clicks—which indicated the call was being rerouted from its original number and could end up nearly anywhere in the world—the sound of the other end being rung began. After three rings, a tone came on. At this point, Pretorius' instructions were to report his codename and position, along with the number from which he was calling.

Instead, Pretorius stared at the payphone dial, listening to the silence which, he knew, indicated that anything he spoke was being recorded. Something, something evil and disturbing like a small alarm circuit in the base of his brain, told him not to speak, not to let them know. Pretorius was a survivor. And survival depends not so much on the orderly thinking out and weighing of options as on listening to the small things one's brain generates on a more or less constant basis. He knew one of the reasons so many young men die in the trade lay not so much in inexperience as in consciously ignoring the small signals, in dismissing them as intrusive and trivial, irrelevant. Pretorius had seen more men killed and crippled by following the dictates of tidy logic than by listening to their own nerve-endings. And right now, his nerve-endings were telling him not to speak. But why? What was there that told him that simply dialing a telephone number—*that* number—was dangerous in the extreme. The uncanny feeling of loss and guilt was still there, was even stronger . . . and he could not relate it to anything. It was if it had invaded his body with the drugs. But as the effect of the drugs was receding, the ugly foreboding feeling advanced. He snapped out of his introspection.

And then Michael Pretorius did a curious thing. He pressed down the hook several times. And dialed 0 once more. And asked for the overseas operator.

Many miles away, the reels of a GPO Ferranti computer snapped into life, logging in one of many thousands of telephone connections. And then, having been programmed to enact certain procedures in the event this one telephone number were dialed, the computer sent data through a secure modem which patched the digitized conversation into yet another computer in London only a few blocks away, in a brightly lit room at Jubilee House, near the end of Putney Bridge. This was the "C" Department computer of the Special Branch.

A catch-all part of the Metropolitan Police which seems to specialize in the altogether impossible, Special Branch has grown in its hundred-and-some-odd years from a handful of detectives with Irish backgrounds to a highly sophisticated and technologically advanced intelligence-gathering organization. And here in SB's Jubilee House facilities, men and women anxiously monitored the various whirrings and clickings of their electronic charges, from time to time placing telephone calls and making notes.

This particular conversation satisfied the parameters of a highly secure program stored in the computer for the past month, and a tape recorder began turning, recording the telephone call originating in the United States. Two separate agencies within the world's intelligence community would ultimately dissect the contents of that call, and would place people in the field because of it.

At the conversation's end, Pretorius stood in the wind of the booth's broken glass, the cold razoring through his sodden clothing.

Then, as if in slow motion, he replaced the handset on the hook. A terrible feeling of hopelessness, of aloneness, enveloped him. The shaking from the cold became uncontrollable now.

He began to reconstruct what he knew, what seemed to have happened after being chloroformed. He'd awakened in that tiled room, knowing he had been drugged, the straps restricting his every movement, save those of his mind. His mind—what had they done? He remembered his briefing by Hornbill, and later by others, on the probable course of his interrogation. He'd been told of his programming and had even been surprised at how much of it he was able to produce on command, fully conscious. He wondered how much more had been brought to the surface by his interrogators, whoever they were. A brief, jagged image jarred its way into his reflections, like a sliver of broken mirror: There was a flash of metal, of wire spectacles, and with it an antiseptic smell. The feeling was like that of *déjà vu:* one image, similar to the first, but following in lightninglike remembrance.

For some unknown reason, it was profoundly disturbing, and he knew it must be important.

Pretorius edged out from the booth, shivering violently. Walking swiftly to the door and looking inside he could see something, a jacket hanging from a nail on one wall. He looked back over his shoulder, sweeping his eyes up and down the road. No cars in sight. Suddenly, he snapped his foot forward in a short, swift kick, and the door's striker plate parted company with the doorframe. Moving quickly, he slipped inside and closed the door.

He peeled off his sodden clothing and rubbed himself dry with paper towels from the station's one toilet. Then he pulled on the clothes—a pair of jeans and a blue woolen Eisenhower-style jacket with an oil company insignia on one shoulder and "Jim" in soiled yellow script over one breast pocket. He was grateful for their dryness and warmth.

Finally, he opened the top of the toilet and pulled out a connecting piece of stout wire that held the float in place. One end of the wire had a J-hook bent in it.

He rummaged through one of the tool kits in the service bays and emerged out front with a ball peen hammer, a large screwdriver, a pair of pliers, and an eight-inch length of insulated copper wire.

Suddenly an engine sounded in the distance and grew louder, coming closer. Quickly Pretorius dodged back into the station, pressing himself flat against an inside wall.

A car entered the station and paused for a minute in front. Someone in the car slowly played a flashlight over the service station, obviously checking for signs of forcible entry, then flicked it off.

The driver gunned the engine and the car took off down the highway. Pretorius lowly expelled his breath, grateful he hadn't shattered any glass when he'd broken in.

He switched license plates on two of the cars, then chose one, a nondescript Plymouth Gran Fury. He slipped the toilet's wire down between the driver's side window and the lower portion of the door.

In a few seconds, he found the locking mechanism with the hooked end of the wire and pulled sharply upward. The door clicked and swung open.

Once inside, he placed the screwdriver against the ignition lock, hit it a single blow with the hammer, then pried out the mangled ignition with the screwdriver's blade. Pretorius formed his insulated copper wire into a U-shape, bridging the terminals on the damaged ignition, and the engine fired up immediately.

He switched on the headlights and yanked the automobile out onto the roadway.

23
THE EASTERN
UNITED STATES

The morning of October 23 dawned dark and spattered with rain. But to the Fisherman and Hornbill, the day couldn't have begun better. It was already clear Pretorius' abduction triggered off the planned series of events, and Aurora was now rolling in high gear.

The only glitch was an COMINT-intercepted report to Moscow Center that the agent might have escaped after having yielded up his carefully seeded information. Still, he could be contained if he reported in, as would likely be the case. Every eventuality had been foreseen by the planning staff, including a possible escape. The Fisherman, in contact by scrambled telephone at his Maryland estate, reckoned the operation was going as well as could be imagined.

From this point forward, certain telephones through the U.S. were monitored more closely than ever. Under Hornbill's emergency directive, dozens of experienced officers and employees at DIA were temporarily assigned to duty on the project. Around-the-clock surveillance was set on just under 170 officers and employees of the Central Intelligence Agency, more than twice that number of KGB agents and officers in the United States, and certain U.S. citizens known to have been "sensitized" by either the KGB or the GRU (Chief Directorate of Intelligence of the Soviet General Staff).

At Fort Meade, Hornbill's people compartmentalized one entire electronic surveillance section, sealing it off from technicians of the National Security Agency itself. Their authority was a presidential directive, of a priority that denied any questioning of White House staff.

Within only twenty-four hours of Pretorius' capture and initial interrogation, things began to fall in place. A senior CIA officer was able to give his other employers far more complete details of the B(AT)-3 than they'd been able to read in *The New York Times* or *Aviation Week*. Indeed, more information than was contained in the Agency's DCID (Director of Central Intelligence Directive).

These employers, who resided at Number Two, Ulitsa Dzerzhinskogo, Moscow 101000 (telephone 221-07-62), were properly appreciative, and, as was the tradition in their trade, requested even more.

The officer responded within the week. Using a one-time gamma encoding pad, he forwarded the requested information and added his own recommendation for action. However, the officer, whose home in Alexandria had been covertly wired two weeks previously, had a series of misfortunes.

On quite another (and considerably less important) matter, he'd decided to telephone a KGB asset in Florida, a Cuban used for minor tasks. He'd called the asset from a telephone booth in downtown D.C., a secure telephone. But later, the asset had grown agitated over the matter discussed and had, against all rules, decided to call back the officer at home.

Calling information in the D.C. area, he made a list of all the people listed with the CIA man's name, and finally reached the astounded officer.

"O'Connor?"

"Yes?"

"You alone?"

"Jesus, this isn't a secure line—and you—"

"Okay, okay. Forget it. I'll get hold of you later."

The line went dead. But not before the DIA computer patched into the line in Alexandria had traced the originating call to a specific Miami number in an apartment in Undertown.

A special crew then bugged the asset's apartment, office, car, and several telephone booths within a short walk of both his apartment and his office in downtown Miami.

Their yield, even within forty-eight hours, was impressive.

In that time, the subject made five calls from one of the coin booths to New York City. DIA agents monitored and traced three of them to known KGB officers attached to the Soviet UN mission, and two others to equally interesting people of whom the DIA had no prior knowledge.

In addition, all Agency people with whom the CIA officer regularly worked or had repeated contact were placed under special surveillance.

From that point forward, every detail of the officer's daily life was examined microscopically. Within CIA were four Defense Intelligence agents planted years ago, and who were now activated by their DIA case officer at McLean.

One was in a position to pull the errant officer's file and make a copy, which went directly to Arthur Hornbill's office for analysis and action.

The other three began to do "sensitive surveillance" on the case. For the first week, the team devoted themselves to identifying the subject's behavior patterns, his routines. Then they began checking for variations, for exceptions, for anomalies.

Toward the end of the second week, they struck gold.

The officer, Franklin James O'Connor, made a weekend trip to visit his girlfriend in New York. He stayed in her apartment at 334 East 57th Street. Yet the girlfriend was nowhere to be seen. Inquiries established that the apartment, although showing the girlfriend's name on the mailbox, was actually rented by the Contacen Corporation, a small electronics parts company with an office in Brooklyn.

Contacen's office was taken apart, then put back together

188 / GUY DURHAM

again, that Saturday night. O'Connor, meanwhile, was followed over the weekend to two museums, the boathouse in Central Park, an off-Broadway theater, and a small Pakistani restaurant near Lexington Avenue and East 28th.

At the restaurant O'Connor dined alone. But he was observed to have left his newspaper on the table, where it was picked up by the middle-aged busboy who cleared the table. The DIA agent tailing O'Connor radioed for a rolling tag on the busboy, who—carrying the newspaper—was followed to a bookstore on East 19th Street specializing in socialist publications: *Struggles of the Angolan People Against Fascist Intervention*, and similar tales.

The busboy unlocked the padlock on the darkened store's front door and let himself in.

A DIA black bag team arrived at the tailing agent's urgent request and entered the store silently from a rear freight entrance. Using a small aerosol spray canister and a length of surgical PVC tubing, they released an odorless gas under the door of the small office in which the busboy had secreted himself.

After a two minute wait, the black bag team opened the door wearing gas masks and found the busboy slumped over a desk on which there was a newspaper and a microscope.

On the microscope's slide was a single microdot.

Without removing the slide, the team quickly mounted a camera on the microscope and photographed the dot, bracketing the exposures as they shot. They reset the recumbent busboy's wristwatch thirty minutes early, left the office, and turned over their trophies to a helicopter waiting near Battery Park, which then flew directly to a highly specialized lab in McLean, Virginia.

The busboy woke up shortly, thinking he had dozed off a minute or so, and resumed his inspection of the microdot.

24
DARTMOUTH
AND LONDON,
ENGLAND

The Dreaded David Lloyd George glared balefully out at a pitiless world.

Through the window, the crows roosted fearlessly in the plane tree in front of the cottage, taunting him. His reddened eyes, so sadly misplaced on that long white visage, fixed on the birds with infinite regret.

If only the Man were here, he thought, he would be let loose instantly against them. He envisioned himself, a blurred white scourge, hurtling himself into the midst of the enemy, driving them from their imperious perches, scattering their cackling blackened forms to the winds.

But the Man had been gone a very great while. And the Woman did not take DLG's duties (at least vis à vis the much-hated crows) altogether seriously. And, although the Woman was very gentle and spoke to him intelligently and soothingly, she was no replacement for the Man.

DLG longed for the solitary rambles on which the Man would take him, padding soundlessly through the old back roads where no machines dared roll with their roiling, belching black exhaust. David Lloyd George was, not to put too fine a point on it, in a state of profound desolation.

Susannah, being lonely for Pretorius as well, recognized the symptoms in the dog, and tried to compensate. But the disgruntled beast seemed to find no consolation in her feminine companionship, nor in the extra food, nor the trips into town in the Rolls-Royce, nor the strange dog toys the woman insisted on bringing home from the pet shop in the High Street, the one with the birds and snakes.

Susannah, as the Dreaded DLG sat on the windowseat regarding the enemy, was curled up in her favorite chair reading a John Dickson Carr mystery. On the tripod table next to her, a stack of postcards teetered precariously in a silver toast-holder, that British invention which allows air to chill the warmest toast within milliseconds.

The postcards were from various odd places of tourism around the United States, each with Michael's comments, and usually quite funny ones. An alligator farm in a town with an impossible name in Florida, the Chicago lakefront, an Indian reservation in South Dakota, the La Brea Tar Pits in Los Angeles, the Grand Canyon, and four or five more.

America, Susannah concluded, seemed an improbable place. When Michael had left, he'd explained his need to go back and really see his country before he settled down for good here. And knowing he'd suffered terribly as a result of the shipboard accident which had caused his early retirement from the Navy, Susannah felt Michael must have some deep-seated need to reaffirm his roots before coming to some sort of commitment here in England. She hoped that commitment would include her, for she missed Michael more than she thought she could ever miss anyone. A dozen times a day she would see something or think of something she wished she could share with him. The awful part was not knowing when—or even, at times, if—he'd return to her. It felt like a cavity within her, a hollowness that seemed unfillable.

The wind howled around the corner of the house and she looked up to see the tree branches bobbing outside. The dog, as usual, had taken up his post at the window, watching God alone knew what.

Susannah, when the phone began its soft chirring, stared at it for a moment. And knew, knew beyond any doubt, that it was Michael.

Contemplating the excellence of his shoes as they rested on his desk, Brian Fanthorpe, a twenty-seven-year-old clerk consigned to the administrative bowels of Special Branch, was about to set in motion a series of cataclysmic events.

His feet, he felt, were among his best features, and he viewed a well-shined pair of perforated wing tips as one of the marks of the Truly Well Bred. He crossed one ankle over another, discovered with some annoyance a scuff on the side of the right heel, and recrossed his ankles so the offending blemish would not be seen. Fanthorpe sighed and returned to this morning's irksome task, working his way through yet another printout sent up from Q section.

Fanthorpe, as usual, was bored with this as with all activities surrounding his job. Worse, he was still feeling the lingering effects of the previous night, which he'd spent pubcrawling with his former brother-in-law, a career boozer of Cro-Magnon intellect but limitless wallet. Fanthorpe's office was painted a particularly unpleasant yellow-green enamel, referred to by its victims as Administration Bile. The effect was worsened by a coffin-proportioned fluorescent light fixture fixed precariously to the ceiling, which beamed down several thousand more footcandles of light than absolutely necessary. All this combined to cause Fanthorpe's eyeballs to contract in pain, and shriveled forever the few scraps of good humor that today remained within his psyche.

And so it was something of a miracle that Brian Fanthorpe happened to notice the one item on the printout that would trigger off a series of potentially lethal events both in Britain and in the United States, to which Fanthorpe would remain blissfully oblivious.

Ticking off each item coded with the prefix for which he was responsible, his jaundiced eyes suddenly swiveled and focused on one number: SB7801-88. Checking the number against the memorandum thumbtacked against regulations to his wall, Fanthorpe registered a silent *Bingo*. There was no doubt. The printout indicated a call had been made at 2200 hours the previous night, with reversed charges from the United States. This number, Fanthorpe knew at once, was one of those flagged by Administration as requiring immediate attention.

The call had caused the GPO computer to trigger a special program routing the information to a second, and rather more specialized, computer in the labyrinthian mazes of Special Branch, and that computer had then produced the printout Fanthorpe now held in his moist and eager hands.

Fanthorpe's instructions were precise: Immediately upon receipt of any such information relating to SB7801–88, he was to inform the duty officer and turn over all copies of this section of the printout.

Unknown to Fanthorpe, the duty officer would then route the information to an individual whose responsibilities included certain rather awkward points of liaison work with the Cousins in the U.S. intelligence community, as part of the "special relationship." This individual, blessed with a singularly high security clearance and correspondingly low salary in the Home Office, had neglected to inform his employers that he was also in the pay of an arcane part of the United States government; specifically, a small, highly compartmentalized group within the Defense Intelligence Agency.

The process, from time of telephone call to the end of this curious routing process, took five and one half hours, by which time the Fisherman knew Pretorius had placed a call of some fifteen minutes' duration to Susannah Kenney. A recording of the call would be retrieved and played for the Fisherman. In the meantime, the originating call had been traced to somewhere in upstate New York, and the exact location would be pinpointed sometime within the next twenty-four hours.

Susannah Kenney, at the very least, would be placed under

surveillance not by Special Branch—whose usefulness was now ended in this matter—but by contract operatives directly responsible to the Fisherman, and partitioned off from the mainstream of Aurora. At worst, if the recording revealed Pretorius had divulged details of the operation, she would have to be dealt with on a more direct basis.

The Fisherman was not happy at this complication: He had frankly not expected Pretorius to survive the interrogation, let alone emerge free and operational.

25
NEW YORK CITY

Karger thought the party was going exceptionally well.

An attorney of unclear but generally positive reputation, Blake Karger danced on the periphery of politics, both city and state. And this afternoon, in his superbly chintzed Park Avenue apartment, Karger had assembled a covey of high rollers notable for their proclivity to invest in public candidates for private gain.

On this particular occasion, he was engaged in loosening purse strings on behalf of Gary Klein, state assemblyman and now candidate for the United States Senate from Manhattan's Silk-Stocking district. Klein, a thin, saturnine individual with wiry black hair graying at the temples, possessed a certain vulpine charm. And, as he desired to become Senator Klein more than anything on earth, he had spent hours in front of mirrors practicing the Art of his Charm.

As a result of this dedication coupled with inborn ability, Assemblyman Klein was able to turn on such a concentrated, focused fascination that its recipient was convinced Klein respected his opinion enormously and that—if elected—Klein would undoubtedly respond to his advice on virtually any subject.

Klein, in fact, seldom listened to any of the people he met at these affairs, except to mentally assess their probable net worth or their ability to marshal blocs of votes.

One exception was the well-known greenmailer, Harold Uhlens, who had a God-given ability to pierce even Klein's outer charm. Uhlens' guiding belief was that genius consisted largely of the ability to see the obvious and to act on it.

He resembled a taller, slightly better-looking Woody Allen. He smiled benignly on the charming Mr. Klein as the politician attempted to flatter him about a few of his deals recently reported in the press.

Uhlens had a certain amount of well-deserved pride in his work but knew Klein had only the foggiest idea of how a takeover was done, despite his obvious memorization of a few articles in *Forbes, Business Week,* and *Fortune.*

Finally, after Klein exhausted his supply of superlatives, Uhlens smiled even more kindly, and said softly, "Dear sir, kindly save the shit for the guppies here. What's the take-out? If I stick half a million in your campaign, what do I get out of it?"

Klein's smile—the pride of not just one, but two of Park Avenue's most expensive dentists—froze. He cleared his throat. "Just what do you have in mind, Harold?"

"I have in mind your being my personal mouthpiece in the Senate on certain business issues, should they come up. Nothing that would warp your fine sense of values, you understand."

"I understand. Well, we should get together and discuss the matter.

"This is the discussion, Klein. We've having it right now. Do you want the half million, or don't you?"

Klein flashed a momentary, nervous smile. "Well. Um. This is rather quick."

"It's really a very simple deal," continued Uhlens blandly. "I give, you give. Are you in or out?"

Klein's lawyerlike mind, nimble and flexible as a garden snake, slipped into its well-oiled logic track and calculated his risk. "In," he said, smiling his most engaging smile.

The two men shook hands. Uhlens wandered off to resume his earlier, far more fascinating conversation with a recently divorced redhead who appeared to be in heat.

Karger, whose sharp ears had been monitoring this exchange, grinned. Uhlens really knew how to go for the jugular.

A young man from the catering service handed Karger a wireless phone. "It's a Mr. Walton for you, Mr. Karger."

Karger's jaw muscles worked and tensed as he took the phone and walked over to a corner of the room. "Yes?" he inquired into the mouthpiece, his entire being on edge. The voice spoke in a crisp monotone. "Call me in ten minutes from a secure location." And the connection was broken.

Karger handed the telephone back to one of the catering service's hors d'oeuvre-bearing chorusboys and went over to his wife.

Beverly Karger, a former airline flight attendant he'd met on one of his innumerable flights, was a willowy blonde whose figure would've been the envy of most Ford models. Beverly was an attractive and devoted woman, totally devoid of guile. True, as a flight attendant she'd occasionally employed the stratagem of spilling liquids on attractive men she wished to engage in conversation.

But other than that singular though effective lapse, Bev Karger was as honest and true as the day was long. And Bev honestly believed in Blake Karger more than she believed in anything in her entire life. She never questioned any of his actions and built her life around him.

She was the perfect hostess as well. She had refined the art of listening to perfection and could make any of Blake's male friends feel he was, for the moment, the most attractive man on the planet. But at this moment, Bev Karger was distracted. *Why would Blake leave so abruptly, with all their guests getting on so well? So unlike Blake. Almost,* she thought with just a twinge of disloyalty, *rude of Blake.*

His clients, after all, were not criminal law clients, needing to be bailed out at odd hours. No, they were the cream of the corporate crop, engaging her husband's talents largely over turgidly drafted contracts and intercorporate litigation, the stuff of which fortunes are made. She bit her lower lip, scarcely listening as the man talking to her continued to pour out his sad tale of real estate development in midtown Manhattan.

Outside, Karger hurried over to Lexington Avenue to a phone booth. Although it was a crisp fall afternoon, a slight sheen of sweat had broken through his normally perfect composure. He punched in the number impatiently.

"I'm here," he said when the phone was picked up at the other end.

"You will activate the first team now; he'll try to make contact soon, and we'll have to reach him first and without damage, please. He's a very, very valuable source, as it turns out. We'd like you on full alert, no distracting activities. You'll be contacted later when we obtain more specific information. Are we clear?"

The skin on the back of Karger's neck prickled. "Clear."

The other end went dead. But Karger continued to hold the receiver a few moments longer, looking down Lexington Avenue at all the nice, normal people walking through their nice, normal lives.

Then he dialed another number and spoke quickly, precisely.

26
NEW YORK STATE

The wind roared through the open window, but Pretorius didn't mind. It helped keep him awake. And staying awake had suddenly become the difference between living and dying.

They would pick up his trace soon. They would have contacts in unexpected places, and he was too noticeable: a two-days' growth of beard, the service station jacket, the look in his eyes. His glance kept flicking to the mirrors, but no vehicles seemed to be covering him. Certainly none was in pursuit.

He varied his speed and sometimes took an off-ramp to see if anything followed. But so far he was clean. He kept the automatic on the seat beside him, beneath a newspaper.

Easing up to a toll booth, Pretorius ran his hand over his forehead, pushing away the unruly lock of hair. He looked at himself in the rearview mirror: The face that looked back at him was older, and oddly unfamiliar.

He readjusted the mirror and glanced down at the fuel gauge. A full tank, or near enough.

Just past the toll area, a battered black van was parked; one of six radio units covering the main highways leading away from the Institute.

In the passenger's seat, a man swept his binoculars over the cars creeping between the toll booths. It was an easy surveillance. Few cars were going through at this hour, and although most were driven by a sole male occupant, Pretorius' description had been accurate enough for him to be spotted at once.

As Pretorius went past, the van's driver radioed the Plymouth's description and plate number to his control and swerved out into traffic to intercept.

Pretorius was numb with fatigue, and the car's heater did little to dispel the chill he still felt. His alertness was down, dulled to nil. The black van advanced steadily, cutting the distance to four lengths behind its prey. Then three. Then two.

In this dark hour, no other cars were on this stretch of highway. And as the two vehicles were approaching a curve, the van made its move.

Pretorius' brain dimly registered the headlights looming up behind him, and sensed—in their sudden gaining—imminent danger.

He floored the gas pedal, but the Plymouth responded as sluggishly as a dowager attempting a sprint. The old car was no match for the van, which seemed to have enormous acceleration. It easily edged up alongside the Plymouth and the man with the mustache motioned to Pretorius to pull over.

Pretorius, looking up at the van window, measured his chances. He could not outrun the van, considering whatever it had beneath its hood versus the squirrel mill under his own. And the odds were they were armed. He was, too, but he had no idea of the competency of the others, and they might even have automatic weapons. He could afford no mistakes.

So he did the right thing.

He smiled and waved to the man, put on his indicator light, and began pulling over. The van matched his car's moves, edging off the highway onto the shoulder, and parking exactly two car lengths behind.

The men exited from either door and were confidently sauntering to their quarry. The smaller one had his pistol already out. The bigger man with the mustache had his hand deep in a jacket pocket.

Pretorius turned around in his seat, smiled a welcoming smile and waved again. Then—with the engine running—he threw the Plymouth's gears into reverse, floored his accelerator, and wrenched his steering wheel to one side.

The van's driver tried to jump out of Pretorius' way but wasn't fast enough.

His knees were shattered on impact by the Plymouth's rear bumper, instantly folding the legs backward. His body was dragged down under the big car's wheels, and he began screaming in sudden terror as sharp edges of the undercarriage tore him apart.

The other man stroked out his revolver into a two-handed hold, trying to fire through Pretorius' window. But the gunman, never having been educated in the misbehavior of projectiles launched at angles greater than thirty degrees against tempered glass, was stunned to realize his slugs had skipped along the glass, rather than penetrating it.

Pretorius now slammed the gear level into first and swung the car's hood over toward the man with the gun. He felt the car lurch ever so slightly as it hit the body and sent it rolling off to one side.

Pretorius turned off the Plymouth's ignition and investigated his attackers. Both were dead. Neither carried ID. And the van had nothing in its glove compartment nor behind its visors to indicate its registration. There was, however, a small arsenal in the van: a 9mm Uzi submachine gun, a much-modified Remington 870 police riot gun, a Winchester .308 (7.62 NATO) Marine Corps sniper's rifle, a Colt Woodsman .22 automatic pistol fitted with a Maxim-type silencer, steel containers of ammunition for each of the firearms, as well as a few surprising additional pieces of weaponry.

One by one, he placed the pieces of the miniature arsenal on the floor behind his front seat, covering them with some oily rags he found there.

Pretorius pulled the bodies off the road's shoulder, leaving them in a ditch half-filled with water. Then he climbed back in the venerable Plymouth and pulled back onto the highway.

The abandoned van was spotted only fifteen minutes after Pretorius had pulled away. The man from the Institute who looked over the scene found the bodies in the ditch and wondered what could have caused such carnage.

Pulling out one of the bodies and rolling it over, he saw no evidence of gunshot wounds. Only severe gouges and gashes made by some large and jagged metal object. Then, noticing the tire marks gouged in the grass on the roadside, he pieced the scene together. This Vojtec must have suddenly run over them as they approached his car.

Rising from his kneeling position, the man clicked off his flashlight and went back to his Chevrolet to radio for a cleanup team.

Then in seconds he was streaking down the highway, eyes sweeping the road for the escapee's car. He nailed the accelerator to the floor. If stopped for speeding, he could produce FBI identification that would survive an initial check with the Justice mainframe in D.C.

The man wondered about Vojtec. There had been only two escapees in the history of the Institute and both had been almost child's play to retrieve.

Vojtec, though, was different. Either very, very good—or very, very lucky. Lucky, certainly, in the matter of the Director's carelessness with the dogs.

Still, they'd pick him up. The only worry was if he managed to reach a telephone. Then the explanations would be more difficult, the denials less plausible.

The man in the Chevrolet chewed his lower lip thoughtfully. No further reports on the escapee came over the radio, although two additional vehicles had been dispatched to cover the Taconic nearly all the way down to Hawthorne.

Then suddenly, as he rounded a turn, he saw the escapee's Plymouth in his headlights. He wouldn't take chances as the others had.

Up ahead, Pretorius was alerted by the speed of the car swinging up suddenly behind him. He pressed his accelerator to the floor, but the car only responded with a sluggish lurch. Pretorius wished fervently for his old Jaguar with its nimble acceleration: For a big car, it had been astonishingly agile.

The needle edged up with infinite, maddening slowness to seventy, then eighty, then held, quivering, at a gut-straining eighty-six.

His pursuer came up easily, smoothly, holding his position just one car length behind and to one side, waiting for his chance. Then, coming up on Pretorius' right, a low stone wall appeared, separating the road from a steep slope down into a valley.

Suddenly the Chevrolet accelerated with incredible speed, slamming its full weight against Pretorius' vehicle. The ancient Plymouth hit the wall, showering a stream of sparks as the metal shrieked out in protest. Scraping along a forty-meter section, the Plymouth—miraculously—didn't plunge over, due to its massive weight and low center of gravity.

His attacker's car slammed into him again and again ferociously, forcing him to scrape the wall for another five or six seconds. The sound was horrific: the shrieking of tires and shearing of metal, not only on the side of Pretorius' car nearest the wall, but between both cars.

In this contest, Pretorius knew he had to seize what slim advantage he could find, which could only be in a combination of his car's weight and bulk, the narrowness of the road, and his own training.

The repeated slamming was having its effect. Pretorius' left front fender, on which his attacker was concentrating his ramming, crumpled in and began scraping against the tire.

The entire right side of Pretorius' Plymouth was a shambles, a scene from a demolition derby in Hell, the metal scraped away by the stone wall, the door bent inward sharply. His attacker continued his assault, ramming again and again. Pretorius' front bumper separated from its left support and began dragging under the car, setting up an earsplitting sound.

He remembered his instructor's words, at the special driving school outside D.C. where most of the Feds were taught: Always check your target's front wheels. They'll tell you his intentions faster than the overall movement of his car will.

And as his pursuer cocked his front wheels first slightly to the left to begin yet another ramming attempt, Pretorius literally stood on his emergency brake, yanking the wheel and sending his car into a classic Bootlegger's Turn.

The entire rear end of the massive Plymouth swung sharply around. Pretorius' car was now facing 180 degrees in the opposite direction from his attacker. And the other driver was panicked into hitting his own brake pedal and losing control of his vehicle.

Flicking a glance in the mirror as he floored his accelerator, Pretorius saw the other car smash head-on into the wall, and—as if filmed in slow motion—flip lazily, end-over-end, over the low parapet. Pretorius exhaled slowly and noticed his hands trembling slightly on the steering wheel. He did a three-point turn, and resumed his drive south.

Hornbill paced his office in Manhattan at Six World Trade Center. There were precisely eleven striding paces in the long dimension and nine in the short. His fingers were interlaced behind his back, his head bent. His pace was mechanical: two and one half lengths of each dimension, then a right-face in the center of the office, then two and one half lengths of the other dimension. This metronomelike motion often helped him think in moments of stress.

Hornbill seldom looked out the windows, never noticed anything other than what existed within his office. He was a man of almost total concentration, able to draw deeply on powerful resources of intelligence and imagination.

Pretorius, he knew, had been taken six days in the past. By that time, they should have completed their interrogation. And by now, Pretorius should have reported in. If, of course, he were still alive.

Hornbill had his doubts about the Fisherman's choice of Pretorius. There was too much of a personal element in the choice of John Pretorius' son. Besides that, there had been too little in the dossier, and what little there was seemed a bit too tidy, almost as if it had been edited, instead of being the careless bureaucratic prose found in most dossiers.

Over the Fisherman's objections, Hornbill had insisted on Pretorius going to remedial combat instruction in Arizona to increase his survivability.

Pretorius was, after all, a prize package, especially prepared for their delectation. He would, in all probability, be handled by expert hands, and under the most stringent security arrangements. And if, as was planned, they were able to peel back Pretorius' guise as Vojtec and discover they had a DIA agent assigned to protect a highly sensitive military project, then the chances of Pretorius ever regaining freedom were slim indeed. But all this had been contemplated and weighed, decided upon long ago.

Pretorius was one of the expendable ones. Although, as the Fisherman had often laconically remarked, we were all expendable. Right up to and including the President.

Even so, although both Hornbill and the Fisherman had often sent off young men to their deaths in order to accomplish a larger mission goal, this one felt different. He'd felt regretful— no, even deceitful—about being so positive about the mission to the young man. Possibly it was because he'd been so close to the father and had considered John's death a terrible waste. But more likely, it was because the younger Pretorius had been shanghaied; unwillingly taken from a comfortable, normal life for his role. He'd not volunteered.

Hornbill halted in his pacing and breathed deeply. This is part of what makes the trade so gut-wrenching, he reflected. The need for the choosing of lives in cold, simplistic terms. There are no blacks and whites in this work any more than there are in other, more traditional, forms of warfare. Everything occupies its own particular niche within a continuum of gray, and someone somewhere inevitably has to choose. This man lives, that one dies. These people here survive, those over there perish.

Hornbill sat in his chair behind the Sheraton breakfast table he used as a desk. As always, he was attired in a three-piece tweed suit and bow tie. The next twenty-four hours would, he felt, determine whether or not Aurora would be successful or not. Everything had been prepared and set in motion with as much care as possible. The preparation of Pretorius had been, the experts had assured him, as close to a masterpiece as their trade could produce.

Only time, then—in its utter, awful, ticking inflexibility— would decide.

Susannah Kenney entered Terminal Four and headed toward the British Airways check-in. She was now a priority target, and a full surveillance team had been assigned to her.

Two of the tags were a smartly dressed young American couple, plastic shopping bags emblazoned with the arms of Burberry's and Fortnum's. The third appeared to be a British businessman: balding, pudgy, and rumpled, lugging a scuffed and bulging leather portfolio. Each was equipped with a miniature short-range UHF receiver, concisely constructed in the case of a Sony AM/FM Walkman.

From several vantage points in the huge terminal, other watchers kept the three advised of Susannah Kenney's movements, transmitting to the bogus Sonys, whispered comments relayed through the headsets.

Moving into position, the three tags arranged themselves in the lounge area; the couple strategically placed near the glass doors leading to the gates, the businessman artlessly slouched on a lounge chair in front of the duty-free. The businessman watched Susannah over his half-glasses as she entered the lounge area and moved toward the newsstand. She purchased a newspaper and a paperback novel, then found a seat three or four rows away. The youngish American couple could see her from their vantage point but kept up an animated conversation, chattering on about their neighbors, the coming week, and so on.

None of the tags and the watchers had been assigned by either Special Branch or Hornbill's people at DIA. They were the Fisherman's people. They were, in their way, an elite group.

On paper, they existed as having been transferred to a dozen or more different government agencies, their trails obliterated by a mass of government paperwork. Their salaries were paid from a variety of sources and were substantially above DIA pay grades. They each carried identification papers and badges from a number of intelligence and law enforcement agencies, not one of which reflected their actual unit or employer. Yet their security status and connection was such that each, if arrested, could be almost instantly released after placing a single telephone call.

As the flight was announced, Susannah rose and walked through the door of the glass partition toward the gate. The businessman nodded to the American couple and followed Susannah to the gate from a distance of about fifty feet.

When Susannah showed her ticket to the gate agent, the businessman hung back and seemed to be looking for his ticket through his case. Then, after she'd gotten her boarding pass and was seated some distance away, the man discreetly showed the ticket agent his identification, said a few words, and was quietly let through to the gate.

Later, after the last passenger was boarded, the businessman—looking out the big window at the plane being slowly towed away from the ramp—pulled a UHF transmitter from his case and radioed his control.

As Pretorius poured his concentration into keeping the car pointed along the asphalt, the scenery slid past in half-caught frames, with his memory and imagination attempting to call up corresponding images from the past.

But staying awake had become an agony, and there was something in his mind that threatened to come forward, something menacing beyond all description.

He knew it wasn't simply the drugs; it was something else, something nameless—yet real, and evil, and infinitely threatening.

Pretorius concentrated and tried to bring the thing forward, to recall the feeling that triggered such cold apprehension, such an uncontrollable feeling of helplessness. Something about—about the glint of light on steel. His fingers clenched tighter on the steering wheel.

Christ, he knew he'd been pushing himself dangerously, well beyond his physical limits. But he had to get to cover, away from the torment, until he could put together the pieces and either call Control—or disappear altogether.

Earlier, Pretorius had driven the battered Plymouth into a shopping mall and parked it between two cars outside a movie theater. He had to switch cars: The Plymouth was attracting too much attention, looking, as it did, like a refugee from a Georgia demolition derby.

Instead of walking up to the ticket booth to check when the next feature started, or getting out and going to a phone booth to call the theater for times, he preferred the less-noticeable tack of staying precisely where he was, reading the newspaper he'd found in the Plymouth.

After nearly an hour of waiting, things began to happen. Several cars pulled up to park and people began stepping out, locking their vehicles, and walking to the theater. Soon he saw what he wanted: a late model Chevrolet Malibu, inconspicuous color, slightly dusty, not too noticeable.

The owners would be inside for an hour and a half, easily enough time to get away from the area.

He pulled his car over to the Chevy, and parked beside it. No alarm system. Perfect. Feeding the J-hook between the window and the outer door panel, he slipped the lock and it snapped up smartly.

Looking around, he saw no observers, no mall security cars. He slid inside the Chevy and inserted the screwdriver into the ignition, striking the handle with the heel of his hand and quickly prying it out as he'd done hours earlier with the gas station's Plymouth. The Chevy fired up after an agonizing moment's hesitation, and Pretorius—after wiping off the dusty windshield with some rags—was on his way.

He couldn't risk being pulled over for speeding, carrying Dr. True's driver's license which could never correspond with his own appearance, and having plates which didn't correspond with the car. Having no destination and no objective other than to elude any possible pursuit from the Institute, he needed the time to think, to decide. He chose smaller roads now, to avoid the interstate highway and the big gas stations that would be obvious targets for checking.

Pretorius' imagination was raging: There was something his mind was desperately trying to conceal from him, something so deep and terrible that when he forced his mind to the task of retrieving it, the thing, the memory—whatever it was—burrowed deeper and deeper in his subconscious. But a residue remained, and his mind could not find rest. The sensation of loneliness, of acute and aching aloneness, accented his misery as well.

Once again he thought of fulfilling his orders, of calling his control, of being able to unburden himself, to Hornbill or to anyone else. He saw a phone booth by a small service station, yet somehow he would not—could not—stop. He knew, logically, that safety lay in checking in, in reporting his escape and his location, and being picked up by DIA team members and, after cleaning up and having a rest, going to a debriefing in some air-conditioned, windowless conference room in McLean, answering a nice, logical string of questions from Hornbill or somebody else.

But that, of course, was logic, and what he had decided was just the reverse. But why? What was it, buried deep inside, that kept warning him against reporting in to control?

Without being able to articulate it, without knowing precisely why, he knew. With the instinct for self-preservation all animals possess, Pretorius knew calling would somehow result in his extinction, in being blotted out like an insect.

Pretorius chewed at the inside of his cheek. How could he know this? No logic could sustain such a radical choice. It had to do with something else, something he couldn't summon up to a conscious level—the nameless something which had burrowed into the dark and fevered depths of his brain and which refused to come forth. It had to be that, had to be related. For there was nothing else which gave any rational explanation for his decision not to call his control.

A sudden glint of sunlight, flashing off the chrome and glass of a car in the oncoming lane, blinded him for a split second. And as the light printed its image on his retina, it stabbed at something in his mind, triggering off a series of other images, reflections from within his deepest memory. Like the multiple burst of an electrical discharge, the images formed and re-formed with millisecond-frame rapidity.

Suddenly Pretorius swerved to avoid hitting a car in the oncoming lane, its horn blaring, dopplering sourly past. Pretorius' brain filled with thousands of images, and then sounds: unrecognizable voices, humming sounds, electronic noises which defied description.

Sweat began running from his pores as he fought to keep control of the car, finally wrenching the steering wheel to wrestle the car off the highway and onto the shoulder. A car in the shoulder lane hit its brakes to avoid Pretorius' car as it whipped over and finally bounced along the verge. The car was still moving at something over 60 mph as Pretorius slammed down the brake pedal, bringing it into a sudden, gut-wrenching spin, nearly slamming Pretorius against the windshield before he somehow got the car under control.

His breath came heavily, rasping up from deep in his lungs, and he slumped back. The sweat ran freely, soaking his clothes. The images were coming stronger now.

And then—in sudden terrifying focus—the first definable image came, and with it, a voice: *And the coefficient which would follow in that case? And why would no carrier be involved? Speak up, we can't hear you. Speak clearly.* Pretorius mumbled his answers as he had in the class so many years before, trying to speak his words clearly. But something was wrong—terribly, terribly wrong. Class. It wasn't a class: It had been an interrogation—the interrogation. And which answers was he giving them? A flash of light off steel-rimmed glasses again. The chillingly calm, priestly voice: *Ah, but you know you have the answers, the right ones this time. And you know we know all about you and your petty deceptions. But now the theater is closed to all but you and I, my friend. The tickets have all been collected. And it's just you . . . and I . . . and the truth.*

Pretorius sat bolt upright, stifling a scream, the sweat running in rivulets down his back, his shirt and the seatback saturated.

His eyes looked out across the hood of the Chevrolet, across to the highways and the fields of the countryside—and beheld nothing but horror—the horror of what was happening within his mind.

The family cars, the trucks, the local business vans, all came and went along the road that morning as Michael Pretorius, lately of the United States Department of Defense, Defense Intelligence Agency, choked and sobbed and screamed soundlessly into the wadded newspaper he pressed to his cracked and bleeding lips.

For Michael Pretorius was realizing he had been broken, completely, irrevocably. And that he had failed his mission— that the enemy was now, in fact, in possession of a far larger set of facts about the B(AT)-3 than when he'd begun, for he'd learned much of a classified nature about the aircraft, and his engineer's mind had absorbed it eagerly, with fascination.

And he had given it all to them, to the man with the oddly insistent, almost priestlike voice, the man whose voice was so familiar—who—ah, God! This had all happened before, had

happened near Nordhausen. This was the Soviet interrogator—
and this was the source of all the nightmares, all the nameless
fears from that day until this.

Because this same man had broken him before as well.

Pretorius' utter encompassing despair knew no limits; he was
completely engulfed, turned inside out upon himself, as devoid
of defense and volition as an animal struck by a car at high
speed.

The traffic whipped past, no one bothering to look at the man
in the Chevrolet. All sound seemed suspended, only the whipping wind created by the cars having any presence as the force of
the terror penetrated every level, every layer of consciousness.

And then, with the terrifying swiftness with which they had
come, the images disappeared. Pretorius, once again, was aware
of his surroundings, of the traffic, of the gathering storm on the
horizon. But he felt eviscerated, gutted like a fish, and knew a
pain within himself which had never been there before, and
which—he suspected—would be there forevermore.

Wiping the sweat from his eyes with a palsied hand, he looked
down the highway and knew where he must go. There was one
place which could be his refuge until he could begin to sort out
the devastation of his life. He switched on the ignition and slowly
moved the big car onto the highway. He glanced at the fuel
gauge. Good. He could make it without refueling, even moving
along the slower back roads, avoiding the bigger highways.

Random Lake, where he had gone with his parents every
summer in his childhood, would be only about an hour from
here. Pretorius hadn't seen it in the fifteen years since his mother
died. He had inherited it and still owned it, and had sent off
checks once a year to the local bank that kept it up for him.
He'd thought someday he might return to it, and although it
stood empty all those years, Pretorius didn't want to rent it out,
didn't want anyone else in the home where he'd known such
happiness and comfort with his parents. The place had no heat
or electricity for years, he knew, but it would be a refuge for

him until he could piece things together, until he could decide what to do with the shattered remnants of his life—and escape from the people who were pursuing him.

Suddenly, in his rearview mirror, Pretorius noticed a yellow and blue New York State trooper's cruiser moving in and out of lanes, coming up slowly behind him. He looked at the speedometer: 63 mph. He backed off the accelerator slightly, forcing himself to relax. Pretorius was surprised to find he was shivering slightly, the sweat, now chillingly cold on his skin, beginning to evaporate.

The cruiser kept pace with him, on his left rear quarter, just within the frame of his left door's rearview mirror. And then, after an eternity, moved up.

Pretorius forced a relaxed, easy-going, friendly expression, putting his right arm on the passenger seat top, fingers dangling just above the newspaper concealing the weapon. Although Pretorius didn't look left at the trooper's car, his peripheral vision detected the bulk of the cruiser holding even with him.

Finally, the trooper pulled ahead, his flashers now beginning to operate, accelerating after some speeder up ahead.

Pretorius passed the trooper in a few minutes, the cruiser stopped, flashers still revolving in the sunlight, behind a gleaming new Mercedes sedan.

He expelled a long, slow breath.

27
MOSCOW, UNION OF SOVIET SOCIALIST REPUBLICS

COMINTSurvRep   003625/AA/RD   (OP:AURORA,CREEK SPECTRE) Soyuz Sovietskikh Sotsialisticheskikh Respulik CCCP
   Location: Ministry of Defense, Ulitsa Kirova 37, Moscow 103160.
   Subject Surveillance (telephone): S.F. Akhromeyev, MSU; A.M. Yefimov, MASU.
   Login: 2105 GMT, 10/22/90.
   Source: Omicron 67. Monitored phone 293-07-14.
   (Note: Subject placing call is Sergei Fedorovich Akhromeyev, Marshal of the Soviet Union and First Deputy Minister, General Staff. Subject responding is Marshal of Aviation Aleksandr Mikolayevich Yefimov, Deputy Minister, Air Forces.)

SFA: Our friends of the *Komitet* have overreached their limited abilities once again . . .
   AMY: What now?
   SFA: Not altogether a disaster. But they have let the subject slip from their grasp. The Third Directorate should have handled this, from the beginning . . .
   AMY: Did they get any product first?
   SFA: Yes, that is the only redeeming feature. There is a tape on its way with Gvosdilin. It is as we suspected . . . their stealth

technology will continue to be their strategic focus. But there is a new technology . . . a new aircraft which superficially bears some resemblance to our own latest configurations, but has new technology of which we have known nothing—nothing for all the period of its development. It now appears as if our radar installations will have to be either scrapped or radically changed, our bomber strength built up far beyond anything we have now or have planned for the next thirty years . . .

AMY: Perhaps now the Politburo will listen, and release the funds.

SFA: Gvosdilin feels there is more to the subject's knowledge, that if we could recapture him we could save years of research at Dnepropetrovsk. But he has given us much, far more than he was prepared to give. We now know of the existence of their new aircraft, plus much about the formulas, the materials . . . but it will mean years of new research. I have already consulted with Zaikov, with Systsov and Finogenov. They are with us. Aleks, we have much lost ground to recover. If we had not detected this new technology . . .

AMY: To hell with it, Comrade! Terminate him now . . . cut down the chances of the Americans knowing what we got from him. Better they should never suspect what we now know, that we're going on in the same old way. We should also roll up the Institute, in case he's gotten to the phone . . .

SFA: The Chekists are ahead of you there, Marshal. The Institute is back to normal . . . no trace of anything of ours. Our people are now in Canada.

AMY: But what about the subject . . . has he been located?

SFA: No, but Bobkov has people in pursuit. By the way, it is interesting that he has caused a certain level of damage to KGB people on his way.

AMY: A simple aviation engineer?

SFA: Hardly, my friend. The man is a trained agent, specially selected for the security of this project. At first, he attempted to give us diversionary material, much of it useless. If

Gvosdilin had not been the genius he is, and not stripped the man's subconsciousness bare, we would have diverted much of our budget on obsolete technologies. But as it was, the agent knew rather a lot about the actual direction of their new stealth technologies, a radical departure from the directions of years past. It will take us years to catch up . . . but at least now we know what the bastards are really up to . . .

AMY: When will the tape arrive? We will need to analyze it immediately and to prepare our presentation to the Politburo . . .

SFA: This afternoon. Bobkov is accompanying Gvosdilin to bring it here personally.

AMY: Let me know the instant it arrives. It will also be interesting to hear the Deputy's interpretation of events. I shall have my car standing by.

SFA: Patience, Aleks. We have waited years. We can wait hours.

AMY: True, Sergei. At least until this afternoon.

(Call ends. Logout: 2113 GMT.)

28
NEARING RANDOM LAKE, NEW YORK STATE

As Pretorius poured his concentration into keeping the car pointed along the asphalt, the scenery seemed to slide past in half-caught frames from the past.

He was now on a road he'd been on many times when he and his parents had come up to the lake. The drive from Baltimore was always long, especially to an eight-year-old. But the magical prospect of the Teepee at Random Lake always kept his patience in check. His parents and his grandparents had always called it the Teepee because of its eccentric roofline which, like the top of a canvas tent, had upward-sloping sides with a pronounced concavity.

It was always the same when they'd arrive: his grandparents—his mother's parents, who'd emigrated from Europe at ages sixty-four and sixty-eight—spent their summers there. It reminded them of the lake area in Austria's *Salzkammergut*. Even before his father's car would crunch to a stop on the gravel horseshoe drive, the grandparents would be out front, and his grandmother would scoop him up in her arms and give him a bearhug and say wonderful, funny, crazy things in German and nuzzle him as if he were a puppy. His grandfather would then give him a very formal handshake and ask in a deep voice of mock gravity, "And how is the young gentleman?" to which the young Michael Pretorius would be unable to answer except in peals of delighted giggles.

And then they would all bring their suitcases and boxes into the great embracing house with its paneled walls and deep, capacious easy chairs in the library, the huge white kitchen in active, bustling contrast, the bedrooms—endless bedrooms, it seemed although there were actually six in all—with their deep, fluffy mattresses and big, thick goosedown pillows and books, books, and more books everywhere.

After settling in their rooms, they would come downstairs to the great porch which overlooked the lake, and between sips of grandmother's special lemonade-tea (guaranteed to slake the thirst of even the very thirstiest of eight-year-old journeyers), would recount their lives since their last letters and phone calls to each other.

Grandmother—called Mutti by everyone in the household—lavished affection and food on the young Pretorius, and taught him to speak German over the course of five or six summers. He'd a quick ear for it, and one day surprised everyone by conducting a long and heated argument with Mutti when she (in one of her few exasperated moments with the over-adrenalined young Michael) forbid him to go swimming because he'd broken one of her Meissen porcelain figures, a shepherdess she'd had since girlhood.

His parents listened with wide-eyed wonder at their young son explaining the accidental nature of his crime with a perfect Bavarian accent, words flowing effortlessly, logic unassailable. At the end, his grandfather simply said, "I think the young gentleman has made a good case, Mutti. Perhaps we should acquit him of this very serious offense, just this once." And then they all laughed, and Mutti gave him one of her very best big hugs, and they all went down to the lake and Michael Pretorius swam all the way across to the other side with his father. It was a good time, and they were so very happy to all be together.

But it had been only a very short time until his father had his brains blown out in the car on the Baltimore-Washington Express-way by person or persons unknown. And it seemed even shorter when his grandparents passed away, and finally his mother had died in a car accident on her way up to visit him at college.

Everything he passed now seemed more and more familiar. For this area never seemed to be hung with the tinsel of com-merce accelerating too rapidly—the real estate offices, the fast food huts, the thousand and one pieces of detritus enshrining the short-term, quick-buck values of real estate developers. He wished Susannah could someday see this, could walk with him in the woods and fields where he'd walked so many years ago, could share something of the childhood he'd known here.

He missed Susannah more than he could express. But a life with Susannah now seemed so beyond reality that the thought of it ached and weighed like a stone within him.

Reality was something else, something else entirely. Reality was his utter failure as a professional, as a man, as even an instrument of someone else's will.

Sooner or later in this business, you accepted that your func-tion was exclusively that. An instrument, fashioned and sent to accomplish a piece of something, so it fit into another piece, and so ultimately things were put together which would work to deceive, to destroy.

Things like the one he'd just failed in. Failed as he had in East Germany. Failed twice, at the same thing. The same thing? No, two different things . . . two unassociated operations, with the coincidence of the same interrogator, the same ultimate ef-fect: his failure, and the failure of the mission.

Although Pretorius was exhausted, he now began to think more clearly. Unassociated . . . but the same. The same inter-rogator. *And so you think we are not aware of all your petty deceptions, all your tiny, mewling schemes . . .*

Unassociated? Unlinked? Pretorius had been trained always to look for patterns, for linkages, testing them as you con-structed your pattern. Every major intelligence agency in the world, in fact, had readers who combed the newspapers, the magazines, the wire service reports, textbooks, anything and everything, searching for patterns, putting it all together.

Langley employed thousands of such drones, Pretorius knew, reading their brains out, entering stuff into the huge relational database the Agency was forever building and refining. Half of intelligence work, in fact—even in the field—was piecing together patterns. Coincidences were something that belonged to an alien faith, a convenience for people who didn't want to look beyond the immediate. Coincidences, in his business, could get you killed.

Once you began to think of these alleged coincidences as *related actions* instead, the pieces began to fit. And then the same agent—interrogated by the same specialist—could not be the choice of the inquisitor. It had to be the choice of the people who sent him. *They had to know he'd be broken again, as he had been before.* So what did that make them? People who would knowingly send one of their own to be turned inside out, to be gutted like a sheep in a slaughterhouse? *Why?* In the name of God, *why?*

A light turned red, interrupting his flow of thought. Pretorius was entering the limits of the village now, getting near Random Lake The signs were all familiar, the architecture and streets those of home.

He began thinking of Susannah again. With great effort on the part of his numbed brain, he forced his imagination away, and began to think of the operation again. He began to consider calling his control, even to report his failure. Somehow, it didn't seem so unthinkable now, even the admission of failure, of the total, unquestionable, absolute botch-up of the operation. Perhaps he should. Because he had to *know.* And yet—and yet the small warning bell at the base of his brain began its shrill ringing again.

The light turned green. Pretorius pressed the accelerator to the floor.

29

NEW YORK STATE

Its thick links encrusted with rust, a padlocked chain sagged between the pillars. Pretorius looked around, trying to match what he saw with the images within his memory. Everything seemed overgrown, grotesquely tangled; underbrush plundered the once-proud flower beds edging the entrance, brown tendrils blurred the borders.

He fingered the rusted hulk of the lock. An ancient, over-sized Chubb: deceptively stout looking, yet prehistorically simple.

Returning to the car, Pretorius leaned inside to retrieve a piece of steel wire with a pair of alligator-nosed pliers. Working quickly, he snipped off a short length, doubled part of it back on itself, and created a series of sharply peaked small kinks.

Inserting the crude instrument in the lock, he fished back and forth, and rotated the wire—feeling for the projections inside.

Within seconds, the old lock reluctantly swung open. Pretorius drove the Chevrolet through the gate, then put up the chain again, snapping the lock shut.

The road leading to the old house was high with yellowed grass. No signs of recent travel were evident; the inevitable strewings of empty beer cans and bottles showed only faded images of labels. Pretorius drove at an almost stalling speed, looking for familiar trees, old paths, anything to bring back the memories which had begun to fade like the labels by the road-side.

And then he saw the house.

A proud shambling old thing, the Teepee seemed at first as he remembered it. But then he saw the traces of neglect, of time, the dust of uncaring attendance. The porch swing lay partly on the old Victorian porch, suspended now by a single strand of twisted links. Leaves lay across the porch boards, now and then lifting up in soft scuttling gusts, gathering momentarily in shapeless dark brown crowds, only to be stirred by newer, stronger winds to blow away once more.

Too many memories were here, he realized. Ghosts of long-faded, slumbering summer afternoons, of his parents and grandparents, and a life that once upon a time seemed as if it would never end, as if it would simply continue happily ever after.

Every corner, every tree, every particle of the place seemed to speak. Yet Pretorius knew that even in the days he remembered as golden, his father had been dealing with the same dark world in which he himself was now mired.

Pretorius drove the automobile to the barn and took the supplies out. He slowly slid the huge door shut to conceal the car. Then, slinging the canvas duffel with the weapons over his shoulder, he picked up the two paper bags filled with groceries and began to walk back to the house. The silence seemed massive, overpowering.

Michael Pretorius had come home.

Several agents were in position at this end. A man in a U.S. Immigrations uniform watched the outpouring of flight 177, as did a woman wearing a Walkman headset, slouching like an impatient tourist near the infuriatingly slow-turning baggage carousel.

Susannah came through carrying only a small canvas bag and entered the line for non-U.S. passengers. The Immigration inspector moved in for a closer look, and after she'd gone through, verified her identity with the agent on duty.

Through the doors, a fat man dressed in the midnight blue suit and black tie of a limousine driver held up a sign that said "Mulvane," as if waiting for a passenger. He recognized Susannah instantly and keyed the transmitter in his pocket.

Outside, two plain automobiles moved into position. A black man, lounging near the entrance, spoke softly into the microphone concealed under his tie.

In one of the cars, an agent picked up a telephone handset and dialed a number which was—after special processing—routed to a secure location somewhere in Virginia. In this way, the Fisherman was advised of the subject's arrival in the United States.

Susannah got aboard one of the Carey buses scheduled for Manhattan. Pretorius had advised her not to rent a car, in case someone was monitoring the computers of the agencies.

As the long, lumbering vehicle left the airport, Susannah looked out the smudged window, her blue eyes regarding a world of concrete and elaborate unconcern for beauty of any kind. Small wonder, she reflected, that people in big cities like this seem so despairing: nothing in view indicates any care for what the individual thinks or sees.

Behind and in front of the bus, the shadowing cars took their positions.

Pretorius slipped the front door lock easily with one of True's credit cards. The door swung open upon the old front hall, now dust-encrusted. The local bank, as coexecutors of the estate, had been charged with keeping the house and grounds in good condition—and had even been given funds for the purpose. Obviously, thought Pretorius wryly, somebody had other priorities. If the house degenerated much further, the place would be an invitation to vandals.

He moved through the rooms one by one. A few pieces were

still here, including the big leather Chesterfield sofa in the library, its familiar shape outlined under a dust-laden muslin sheet.

In the dining room, the old table still stood erect beneath the Dutch brass chandelier. He imagined everyone around the table at Thanksgiving, the last weekend before they would close the house for the winter, passing the turkey, the cranberry sauce, the candied sweet potatoes under their crisp cover of baked marshmallows. Pretorius realized with a start how desperately hungry he was and went to the kitchen to prepare his first meal since escaping.

In the Port Authority bus terminal, one agent nearly blew the surveillance by getting too close. The crowds at rush hour were swarming, and the agent thought he was losing the subject. She was beautiful, all right. The blonde hair and blue eyes—and that figure. Even under the coat, she looked like a real handful.

He didn't know the purpose of the surveillance, only that it was ultrasensitive and—like most of his recent assignments—compartmentalized from the rest of the Agency. He stood in the line behind her and heard her buy a ticket to Random Lake. Christ, he thought. Maybe she's going on vacation. Still, he was ready. He'd packed a razor and a change of clothes in his vinyl locker room bag.

Out near the entrance to the drive, Pretorius was completing his arrangements. Dark green nylon fishing line was strung across several probable points of entry, set low. He'd used fine sandpaper and burnt cork to reduce the shine in case anybody used a flashlight, but anybody after him at this stage would be a pro. Not somebody who'd use a flashlight in an approach.

He'd also used a spade from the barn to dig a pit topped with a light lattice-work of small branches, covered with fall leaves. The pit was well over eight feet deep, with up-ended bases of broken glass bottles lining its bottom. It lay directly in what seemed like the only obvious path around the chained entrance, a little more than thirty yards along the way.

He'd warned Susannah not to approach the place, but instead gave her a rendezvous time and point just outside of town where he'd collect her. Using a light rake to ruffle over any signs of disturbance on the ground, Pretorius worked his way back toward the big house to sleep. Even after a nap earlier in the day, he was exhausted, and the drugs were only now beginning to be purged from his system. He would have to be sharp for what was to come, he knew. For they would ultimately find him, unless he could figure a way to either utterly disappear—or to checkmate them in some way.

Leaning on the rake and squinting up at the darkening sky, Pretorius felt the patterns of his life seeming to weave together and form larger secondary patterns, like the stark black branches of the trees, interlaced against the leaden clouds.

30
LONDON

It was one of those marrow-chilling, pervasively damp days in which Londoners take perverse pride.

Catchpole shivered under his ruined mac as he leaned through the glass doors of Special Branch HQ, hands thrust deep in pockets. He hated days such as this, and would cheerfully have traded it for the blasting heat of the Gobi.

The fact was, if Catchpole hadn't been so endowed with a profound sense of duty or guilt (he was never quite sure which), he would doubtless have taken the day off and sat in his robe by the fire, reading history, or possibly finishing up research on the new book. He'd decided to tackle the subject of William Kent's architecture, with its ebullient, rollicking forms that echoed the Italian taste. Kent, though English to the teeth, was an anomaly among English designers; where others held back with traditional reserve, Kent's mind surged forward like waters suddenly released in a millrace. His character fascinated Catchpole mightily, who hoped the book would reveal and prove the intriguing linkage between Kent's character and his architecture.

Still lost in his musings, Catchpole poked his plastic badge into the slot, and was rewarded by a most satisfactory *kerchunk* of the door lock being electrically released.

The corridor into which he stepped was unlike any other police entry in Britain, or possibly the world. The Branch has a total lack of any bulletins, notices, target criminals, or crime-related information of any sort upon the walls: to do so might reveal some of their interests. In fact, all information is passed between SB officers either verbally, or—in the case of files—by hand.

This calculated absence of the normal police decor disappoints first-time visitors to the Branch, who expect a touch of the dramatic, but find it as unrelievedly boring as the offices of a very good firm of chartered accountants.

As Catchpole lumbered along the corridor, an older man in civilian clothes, resplendent with a military-style ginger-and-gray mustache, startled the Detective Chief Superintendent out of his reverie as he barked, "Morning, Chief. Right bit of weather we're having, sir."

To which Catchpole, not yet having had the benefit of having his customary cup of Ovaltine, nor having spoken to a solitary soul this morning, nor even having had a good electric fire to warm his sodden feet, grudgingly rumbled, "Mmmrpfh."

Catchpole lurched ahead to his office down the brightly lit corridor, nodding now and again to his fellow officers. He wondered idly if the lights were so infernally bright for the convenience of the floor cleaners who materialized promptly at six each evening, or whether the blinding brightness was simply better for security purposes, in case something broke loose here in HQ.

Either way, Catchpole felt the brightness was an abomination to civilized man, and should be reduced to a less painful level for the sensibilities of all concerned.

In this foul and cantankerous mood, Catchpole entered his office. A single and much-scarred desk dominated the small room, its surface bearing testimony to many spilled cups of coffee, legions of too-firmly pressed ball point pens (carbon copies having once been the vice of all bureaucracies), and a number of markings whose origins could not even be guessed at.

Catchpole's secretary was a veritable dragon at the gates, a woman whose sole and all-encompassing mission in life was the preservation of Donald Catchpole's authority and personal tranquility. To this end this morning, knowing full well the Detective Chief Superintendent would be in an impossible funk, Miss Lillian Taggart provided him with a single steaming mug of Ovaltine, for which he favored her with a rueful smile.

Catchpole had once made an offhand remark to Taggart that, on days such as this, nothing seemed quite as restorative as Ovaltine, and that on similar days when he was quite small his mum had always dispatched him off to school with a cup of that elixir. Later, at public school, he often missed Ovaltine during damp and drizzly days and forever afterwards associated it with care and kindness.

Taggart carefully filed this fact away in the recesses of her brain with millions of other seemingly unrelated items which formed one of the unit's most valuable data banks. Taggart knew the personal habits of each of the men and women within Catchpole's command, the essential facts of most investigations occurring within the past twenty-seven years, the quirks and foibles of many of Britain's politicians who had at one time or another come under either Branch surveillance or Positive Vetting, a series of background inquiries to determine loyalty of an individual, usually done when the person concerned is given regular access to secrets.

Taggart could also, at the slightest prompting, cite chapter and verse on all official procedures within the Branch. Several officers had even speculated on the potential disaster of Taggart ever falling into enemy hands, for her brain was a thing unique, a treasure to be valued highly. It was their considered conclusion that they would rather the Head of the Branch be taken instead. Catchpole, in fact, had succeeded in more than a few investigations by consulting the redoubtable Taggart.

The brain of Taggart, coupled with her unerring instinct for making life more bearable for Catchpole, was why this small, gray, lusterless woman was considered both unique and irreplaceable.

Sipping comfortably at his Ovaltine, then, Catchpole browsed through the paperwork which had accumulated like a snowdrift through the night. The commercial attaché at the French embassy seemed to be forming some sort of liaison with a young woman who had rather obvious links to the Czech consulate; one of the newly promoted sergeants in the City of London Police (not to be confused with the Metropolitan Police) had accidentally stumbled onto what appeared to be a clandestine radio transmitter in his rooming house—noting the receiver was tuned to one of the current listening frequencies for Moscow Center folk; and a certain Labour MP was letting his homosexuality get out of hand, possibly setting himself up as a blackmail target.

All very much, as Catchpole noted riffling through the flimsies, business as usual.

He leaned back in his heavy, spring-loaded oak office chair (Government Requisition circa 1935), and, to a cacophony of the venerable chair's creakings, interleaved his fingers behind his head. The mug of Ovaltine, now down to a third, had chilled to form a skin across its surface. Catchpole scowled at it. He was in a foul and contrary mood and felt he would go mad if he sat there one additional minute.

"Taggart," he shouted into the outer office as he pulled on his cardigan, "I'm going to pay my respects." Which was Catchpolese for snooping about the office to see what was really up. By the time reports were written, filed, and circulated, they were ancient history, as nourishing as stale toast. They were generally useless and often so sanitized by their writers as to be infuriating. Far more was to be learned by needling the people actively engaged on the cases, the people too busy to write and file every damn thing going on in their professional lives.

Catchpole had an unerring, almost eerie sense for finding the right person and the right missing piece of information, to make everything slot logically into place in an investigation. Behind his back, the men referred to this ability as his "nose," and grudgingly admired their boss's ability to suss out a case in which he hadn't been remotely involved.

This morning, Catchpole—normally the most gentle-natured of all SB senior staff—was both bored and feeling edgy. His caseload was down, and nothing made him feel worse than feeling useless. He sauntered down the bile-green corridor, peering into one office after another, until he came to the one inhabited by Fanthorpe.

Fanthorpe, Catchpole felt, was a deadweight in Special Branch. A young man of limited intellect and impeccable connections, Fanthorpe occupied space without creating any compensating energy.

It was not, in Catchpole's book of ethics, a cardinal sin to be dim-witted, but it was bordering on a capital offense to be both dim-witted and a slacker whilst carrying Special Branch plastic. If any of the enemy—IRA, KGB, or whatever—ever met young Fanthorpe and judged him typical of the forces arrayed against them, Catchpole speculated, they would sleep far more easily.

"Feet off the desk, Fanthorpe," said Catchpole, irritated and wishing to be irritating in return.

"Wot? Oh—sorry, Governor," returned a sullen but suddenly alarmed Fanthorpe. "Been thinking about this case. Bit of a nuisance, this one, actually.'

"Really?" said Catchpole, with a sudden change of tone into a mock-friendly, almost unctuous utterance that old hands knew heralded the beginning of a verbal onslaught.

"Oh, yes, Gov," struggled Fanthorpe, blithely unaware of the gathering storm. "A bit much, actually. You'd think the beggars would know we were on them by now, but, well, it does rather seem . . ."

At this, Catchpole swept up the stack of papers on Fanthorpe's disordered desk. "And to precisely which case are you referring, Fanthorpe?" he continued in the same eerily friendly tone.

The young man rushed to fill the silence, craning his neck to spot a single name on one of the flimsies, "Ah, the, um, Khomiakov matter, Gov."

"Oh, really," answered Catchpole, now with open distaste

displayed in his tone, "And now what on earth would you ever know about the Khomiakov matter, Fanthorpe?"

"Well, it's just that . . . um, it's really rather a bit of a, um, bother, Governor, if you know what I mean."

Catchpole, tiring of his cat-and-mouse game, was on the verge of pouncing when a name caught his attention on one of the computer printouts. "When did this come across your desk?" he snapped out sharply.

"Oh, I should say about sixteen hundred hours yesterday," replied Fanthorpe with relief at not having to further reveal his Olympian ignorance of Comrade Khomiakov and his circle.

"And what does this designation mean," said Catchpole, pointing to a six-figure coding at the end of the printout.

"That means, well, you know what that means," replied young Fanthorpe furtively.

"No, damn it all, I do *not* jolly well know what it means," thundered Catchpole, "and I would cherish the honor of a simple and direct answer—if you can at all manage such a feat."

"Well, sir," began Fanthorpe unsteadily, "that's the special security code that means I'm to alert Mr. Evans."

"Evans? Evans? And who in the name of sweet leaping Jesus in Evans? He works here?" raged Catchpole.

"Well, yes sir, of course he does. At extension 2531. Some time back I got a special directive to alert him if ever we got a C Department Computer intercept of a US/UK conversation on that number."

"Just a minute," said Catchpole, snatching up the telephone receiver and punching several numbers vigorously. "Miles?" he asked in an impatient tone. "Who've you got holding extension 2531?" A few moments' pause. "Certain of that, are you?" A moment more. "Have any chap name of Evans on the premises?" Pause. "No, no, not that one. He was invalided out ten years ago. More, maybe. Hum. Well, thanks. And—could you send your tracing boffins around here right away? Got a bit of a puzzle."

He slammed down the receiver and glared at Fanthorpe. "No Evans anywhere in the Branch. No bleeding Evans, in fact, anywhere near the premises. And that extension, which used to belong to Technical Support, hasn't been assigned to anyone for at least eighteen months. *Now just who in the name of the Almighty have you been funneling classified government information to?*"

Fanthorpe turned pale as a mackerel, sweat beginning to bead on his pasty forehead. But Catchpole had only begun. "Tell me, you blithering twit, or I'll have you out of here and into a uniform faster than anything you've ever seen. Like to become a point man in Belfast, Fanthorpe?" stormed the Chief Superintendent, now thoroughly enraged.

"Ah, Gov, just a minute. I'll explain . . ." interjected the hapless Fanthorpe.

"Don't you bloody well *Gov* me!" shot back Catchpole, "Who the hell have you been shopping our secrets to, damnit!"

Fanthorpe's eyelids fluttered spasmodically. "Ah, sir," he murmured. "I think—I think I need a glass of water—"and slowly, ever so slowly, he slid to the floor in a faint.

Catchpole looked at the slumped, recumbent figure—all elbows, knees, and feet—and shook his large, sad head. "Not your day, old son," he said to himself. "Just not your day."

The printout, when traced, led to a reel of one-quarter inch recording tape which inexplicably had been erased. Nothing recorded on either side of it had suffered the same end; only the telephone call from the United States to Susannah Kenney. A call to a certain number in New York City yielded the information that the call had originated in Random Lake, New York, and had been of five minutes' duration.

A second call, this one to the American Embassy, produced a somewhat miffed-sounding Dick Coldwell, who'd heard something had "gone off the rails" with Pretorius, who, in any case, was not working through CIA channels but rather through other American intelligence facilities which he was not at liberty to name or discuss—and that, if there was a ringer working in Special Branch, it certainly had nothing to do with any CIA work under his purview.

Catchpole cursed and swore, but Coldwell seemed genuine in his protestations. And, indeed, the "special relationship" between Coldwell's people and the senior level of the Branch dictates that prevarications between the two services be restricted to only a very few and very large lies.

The bus was nearing Random Lake, and Susannah marveled at the gently rolling countryside. Like all British visitors, she was fascinated with the idea that Indians once had this country all to themselves, living in an Arcadian paradise, finally warring with the invading Europeans, and, in the end, vanquished more by disease and by treaties than by battle.

The sun was beginning to set as the lumbering bus approached the outskirts of town. Soon, Susannah thought. Very soon now.

Catchpole swung into action with a speed that belied his bearish appearance. Inquiries down in Somerset revealed Susannah had closed up her house and restaurant, saying she was going to the Continent for a short holiday. Yet the investigating officer (a pensioner of the Branch living in Bath), upon checking with the kennel at which she boarded her dog, found she'd said her absence might be anywhere from two weeks to a month or more, and that she seemed quite worried about something when she'd brought in the dog—hardly a woman in a holiday mood.

Airline manifests were checked both to the Continent and to the United States, and quickly yielded the name of one Susannah Louise Kenney of Ripping Beck, Somerset, booked on British Air Flight 177 to New York.

The flight had, in fact, landed and—from cross-checking with U.S. Immigration by Telex—Susannah Kenney had entered the United States at 4:50 P.M. giving her address in the United States as the Plaza Hotel in New York. The Plaza, of course, had no record of either a reservation or a check-in in the name of Susannah Kenney, so Catchpole decided to concentrate on the originating telephone number on the computer printout, the one in Random Lake, New York.

As his staff got busy speaking with the local telephone company and the local police department, Catchpole did an inter-agency check of Pretorius' service record—and *then!* a summer home address fifteen years in the past—in Random Lake, New York. In the meantime, at the suggestion of Richard Coldwell, a Mr. Arthur Hornbill called Detective Chief Superintendent Catchpole from the United States to discuss a matter of mutual concern. The call was switched to a secure scrambled line, and Catchpole listened with interest.

After finally hanging up the telephone and switching off the scrambling device, Catchpole drummed his fingers thoughtfully on the old desk's scarred and troubled surface.

After a few moments he cleared his throat. "Miss Taggart," Catchpole said, "get Travel on the blower. I'll be taking a short trip to the United States."

A few thousand miles away in New York, Arthur Hornbill leaned back in his chair, rubbing his reddened eyes. He'd not slept in forty-two hours and too many things were breaking far too fast for his taste. Pretorius had escaped and although COM-INT reports suggested the opposition had taken the bait, Hornbill felt distinctly uneasy about the operation.

For one thing, Pretorius had not logged in: a very bad sign. For another, the very fact of his escape so early was something not in the script. He'd been well-trained, but the usual routine for these interrogations involved stupendously heavy sedation for several days. How could Pretorius have gotten out from under the drugs so early? How much had they gotten from him?

For once in his career, Hornbill was worried the opposition's interrogators hadn't gotten enough—everything depended on them having opened Pretorius' subconscious to the ultimate layer. Hornbill had, in fact, even resigned himself to the possibility of Pretorius being killed during or immediately after the interrogation. It had always been a consideration, despite all the training. And Hornbill's usual defense against the possibility of operational disasters was to always assume the worst, then be surprised by the exception.

In Pretorius' case, because of his and the Fisherman's ties to his father, the emotional shock of the operative's death would be severe, but not insupportable, considering the operation's value in achieving the final objective of Aurora.

Hornbill furrowed his brow and glared at his telephone. The other puzzling thing was the unexplained trace set up with the Special Branch computer. None of his people had done it, and he would be most unpleasantly surprised if either CIA or State's INR had done it. And if the KGB had done the tap, then everything was at peril. Unpleasant alternatives, all. But not, he reminded himself, necessarily the only possible alternatives.

He reached for the secure phone again and called a number in Maryland.

31

OXON HILL, MARYLAND

The Fisherman was particularly sensitive to smells. And on this October evening at Oxon Hill, the smell of fallen leaves was mustily evocative, summoning up memories of a thousand autumns in the past. Images of a less-complicated time swirled and swarmed in his imagination: a campus, young men hurrying heads-down to their next classes; a football game in some forgotten field; driving someone's borrowed Packard convertible down a country lane in New Hampshire; smoke curling from a farmhouse chimney once seen over a golden field.

He stumped awkwardly around the grounds, pausing now and then to lean on his cane, finally forcing his still-agile mind to fence with the problem.

The call from London, from the operative known as Evans, had been something of an unpleasant surprise. And the unpleasantness had been compounded by Hornbill's call with the information that Special Branch was now interested. If anything, Hornbill had further complicated the matter by reassuring the too-inquisitive inspector that DIA had nothing to do with it. Damn, and damn again, he thought to himself. So close, and yet . . . and yet . . . Aurora had gone surprisingly well up to this point; cost-effective, and as far as operational success went, the Soviet planners seemed to have at least initially swallowed the bait.

But then the key piece had gone missing, and suddenly everything was set awry. An eventuality to which the Fisherman had assigned a minuscule probability; no one had ever escaped from Gvosdilin's people before. It was virtually unthinkable, and therefore no contingency plan had been set up. He cursed himself for this and for being the one human being who had to make what, to others, would doubtless seem a dark and soulless decision. But there was no one else who could possibly know or deal with all the variables. Not even Arthur.

The sun was slipping fast into the soft mist of the hills, and a chill began to settle in his bones. No point delaying the decision. It had to be made, and there was really only one answer. Aurora went back more than twenty-five years, and the success of the operation was the only important consideration.

He'd made hard decisions before. And, despite his advanced years, he'd make a few more after this one. And no one would understand. No one—unless they'd had to make the same kind of decisions over the decades—or had seen numbers of men needlessly killed as a result of hesitation, sympathy, or some other silliness that could have no place in this job.

What made the difference between the pros and the spate of amateurs who were often attracted to the job was a simple thing: the ability to weigh the worth of men against the objective, in a near-mathematical manner. Which was why, in the crunch, when lives were at stake, the amateurs faded or folded.

They seldom were up to the sacrifices, the carefully calculated expenditure of lives, balanced only by cold results. In this job, very few souls would be able to avoid being shriveled by the things they would have to do in the name of their country. Not like playing soldiers; not at all like the dreams of glory.

When amateurs ran an operation and it went sour, unless you had a pro who could take over fast enough, the cost in lives would be insupportable and the failure of the op a foregone conclusion.

This one was tough. But as he once again reassured himself as he stumped into the hall, closing the heavy door, there was no question about what the decision had to be. No question at all.

He envied the nice normal people who never had to make such decisions. Who indeed would find such decisions unthinkable. Because the guilt never quite left you, and each such decision seemed to erode a portion of you.

At times like this, the Fisherman often thought back to when Churchill—in possession of the Nazi Luftwaffe codes—*knew* Coventry was going to be bombed to near-obliteration.

And yet, to evacuate Coventry so soon after intercepting the code transmission would alert the Nazis that all their radio traffic was compromised. Which would, of course, require them to change their cipher instantly—and lead to even greater loss of British life.

And so the Great Man and his War Cabinet let Goering's bombers destroy the English city of Coventry. The damage was incalculable, the deaths and maimings so horrible that the Nazis were to coin a new word: "Coventryize," meaning to obliterate an entire city.

But the decision was correct. And the Nazi transmissions continued to be read by the British, alerting them to much that would save hundreds of thousands of lives—and, in the estimate of many—be one of the factors which ultimately won the war.

One could only wonder, though, at what passed through Churchill's mind when he made the decision. The knowledge that no one, not another soul on the planet, could take it off his hands. And the knowledge that, to his grave, he would carry the responsibility for the deaths of thousands of his countrymen.

Although the lights were out in the library and the last remnants of sunlight had faded through the big side window, the Fisherman's thin, almost skeletal fingers found the telephone easily.

He punched in the first eleven numbers and waited for the computer to produce the connection tone. Then, more carefully, he punched in four numbers more.

Many miles away in northern Virginia, the Fisherman's call

was routed in a complex and unusual way. Any law enforcement agency or even counterintelligence unit would, if they checked the call out, find it seemed to originate from a number in the Midwest which didn't exist. And any individual who—by accident or court order or other, less legal, means—managed to monitor the conversation would hear only a strangely pitched series of howls and screeches.

The scrambling transmission computer was applying random pulse code modulation to the information, and only a receiving computer keyed to the initial code setting (which was based on a one-time pad) could lock into the continuous PCM changes, track them in parallel, and de-scramble the call.

He waited, and finally a second, lower-pitched tone came on the line for a fraction of a second, then stopped. He spoke his message into the mouthpiece, and at the other end the recorder's reels whirred, listening, eager to capture the words.

When he spoke, he was surprised to find his lips were dry and his tone no more than a rasp. "Neutralize the subject. Exercise the highest caution, use no outsiders, but neutralize him. There must be no—repeat no—identity trace." Then, very carefully, he replaced the handset in its cradle.

At length, the Fisherman poured himself a glass of brandy and settled back in his chair facing the window. "Ah, God, John," he said aloud to no one. "Forgive me."

32

RANDOM LAKE, NEW YORK

He buried his face in the shimmering, tumbled wealth of her hair, tears coursing down his cheeks. Words wouldn't, couldn't come; thoughts tore through his mind in torrents, too many, too momentary to express. And when at last the words came, they were Susannah's, not his.

"Michael, Michael," she cried at last. "How I've missed you and loved you and wanted you so—"

He laughed through his tears and hugged her supple body closer, ever closer, and knew he would never leave this woman, not ever again. Together they walked down the road, toward the house, their arms around each other, their conversation now coming in rushes, and they were like children opening presents. The wind stirred and shifted the leaves along the edge of the road. The sound of a locomotive echoed across the lake.

Pretorius had never felt this way, even that magical first time in Ston Easton. Something hurt in his throat as he struggled to tell her all he wanted. The emotional outpouring was almost overpowering. But now he knew for all time, knew she would share his life in every conceivable, every possible way.

The wind was shifting, the chill drifting in from the north, and they shivered in the gathering dusk as they entered the old house. Pretorius had the coals of a fire glowing in the library fireplace; after fanning them into life, he began nestling several small logs in place over the velvet-and-white flames.

Susannah's smile—a sudden, surprising smile so wide and engaging it was almost shocking—was very much in evidence as Pretorius showed her through his old home. She felt close to him here, close to the boy that became a man, and to the man who lived through all these things to become her love. Her fingertips traced the hard, tough calluses of his hands; the bunched muscles that seem to never quite relax at the base of his neck; the scar that ran its jagged, crazed course down his back.

And when at last they lay in front of the fireplace, the flames playing their bodies' shadows in dancing shapes against the walls, their desire for each other was all-consuming, nearly unbearable in its intensity.

The shadowy shapes of her breasts and their now-aroused nipples were enlarged on the oak walls as she bent low over him, taking him full into her mouth, kissing and wetting him, preparing him for herself, delicious and delicate and filled with wonder. His breathing became sharp, his control began to go and his emotions were brought to a pitch that rose and still went higher, and when he thought he could not possibly bear it any longer, climbed higher still, beyond anything he had ever conceived.

And then, as she spread herself for him, her great blue-green eyes, those eyes which to Pretorius forever seemed curiously upside-down, opened wide in the wonder of their love, and she whispered urgently, without seeming to form the words in conscious thought, "Make love to me, make me pregnant, Michael. I want to have your child—our child. God, Michael, love me—"

He thrust himself powerfully and deeply into her, willing himself to give her everything, wanting—more than anything in his life—to create a child with her. He was dimly aware that never, never in his life, had he wanted to give this much of himself to anyone, for his life had been a guarded and distant existence.

Now their rhythm became a thing apart from their own volition, and his thrusts and her responses grew deeper and more urgent. Then, as if from a very great distance, he heard her begin to keen: a high, wailing cry of release as they exploded within and around each other.

And as their passion was slaked and they subsided into the warmth and tingling of afterlove, each looked into the other's eyes and knew, knew without words, that they had begun a life together.

Outside, in the chill darkness, the watcher in black faded soundlessly, invisibly into the night beyond the trees, to make his report.

33
RANDOM LAKE, NEW YORK

They came in ninja-like silence, lithe and fluid as reptiles, clad in black. Each of the three had been trained by experts at a certain government facility in Little River, Virginia, and each was a veteran of many black-bag jobs, both military and civilian.

None was even remotely interested in the reason for the operation. Only in its success, which—given their finely honed professionalism—was somewhat inevitable.

The trip-wires, of course, were spotted early and easily. The men had been given a dossier which, among other things, detailed the subject's training level, and therefore used caution in making the approach.

No lights were on in the old house. This was also expected: In the briefing, they'd been told no electricity had been supplied to the house for over five years. More to the point, as the subject was highly trained, he would not be so careless as to illuminate an unoccupied house to be noticed by people across the lake.

In the large master bedroom on the second floor, Pretorius and Susannah lay deep in sleep, wrapped in the warmth of each other's arms, each oblivious to all but the other's rhythmic breathing in the night. The embers in the bedroom's stone-mantelled fireplace had long since cooled down, and a slight chill filled the room.

At the edge of the clearing nearest the house, the team leader had no need to check possible points of entry. Everything had been memorized hours before: a court order had given them access to plans of the house in county real estate records.

The operation, to all outward appearances, was a bona fide, federally authorized raid on premises suspected to be used in drug trafficking. Anyone checking with the Treasury Department's TECS (Treasury Enforcement Computer System) this evening would find the action logged in under special authorization.

The day after the raid, however, a hidden command planted in the program controlling such authorizations would wipe the TECS reels clean of any reference: It would be as if the operation had never happened.

In their packs, the men carried line and weapons, including the flash-bang stun grenades used by Britain's SAS. They knew the value of surprise and confusion and they would capitalize on it. In case the noise of the attack caused any inconvenient telephone calls to the local police, one of their number (in normal civilian clothing) had positioned himself near the station with a portable VHF receiver, and could instantly furnish the officer on duty with a document authenticating the raid and establishing federal jurisdiction.

Pretorius rolled over, his arm seeking Susannah's waist within the enveloping softness of their sleeping bag. The scents of the night were familiar; a faint mingling of Susannah's perfume with the smells of the house itself. Pretorius could always remember those smells, even years after he'd left the house—redolent of good healthy country living, of cooking, of hickory and applewood fires in the big downstairs library fireplace, of all the people who had been born and raised and lived and died in this house. In his semiconscious state, Pretorius smiled to himself, happy to be here, in this place, with this woman.

And then something made his eyes flick open.

Everything was quiet; nothing should be wrong.

And yet something was.

He strained his ears, listening for the slightest noise, heard none, and once more closed his eyes. But then realized the very silence was strange. Crickets, tree toads, and other nightlife should be audible, but there were no such sounds. Only a chill, still silence. Pretorius had learned long ago to obey all such signals, however small.

And so now the adrenaline was coursing madly, surging almost violently through his system. Silently, ever so carefully— resisting the almost-overpowering desire to move fast—he raised himself on an elbow, rolled over, and slid noiselessly off the edge of the bed in one fluid motion.

Looking out the front window over the porch roof, Pretorius began scanning the possible field of attack. Slowly, his vision began to penetrate small areas of the darkness outside.

Below, the team was at the edge of the stand of trees that faced the old house. The leader, through a pair of large night-vision binoculars, was painstakingly examining the house's exterior—yet failed to see, at one upstairs window, a face looking directly at him.

Pretorius, of course, could not see the leader, nor either of the other two. But he caught the glint of the night glasses as they swept their objective. He pulled back slowly from the window, keeping his movement deliberate, knowing the slightest unevenness of movement would instantly attract a watcher's eyes to that particular window. And he knew their survival, small though its possibility might be, depended utterly on being far more ready for them than they would be for him.

He edged over to Susannah's sleeping form and placed his hand over her mouth slowly. Her eyes came open and she struggled for an instant. He whispered in her ear, "Darling, don't speak or move. We've got people outside—don't know how many—but they're probably pros. For God's sake, stay right here while I sort it out. Stay still. Okay?"

Susannah nodded, and he removed his hand from her mouth. He looked worriedly into her eyes. "And don't—whatever you do—come downstairs until it's over." She squeezed his arm and brushed her lips along his cheek. And he glided silently off into the blackness.

Susannah lay stock-still, scarcely daring to breathe. Who were these people who had come for them? What was Michael involved in? She could hear nothing, but sensed his movement just outside their room.

Pretorius edged open the upstairs linen-closet door and carefully pulled out the Remington 870 police riot gun. The pump-action Remington, one of this country's favorite hunting pieces, was also law enforcement's favorite "social shotgun" when specially modified.

The extended magazine held six rounds in all, not counting the one in the three-inch magnum chamber. Each round held ten pellets of triple-0 buck, each pellet weighing seventy grams, measuring very much like a .36-caliber bullet. The standard wooden stock had been removed and replaced with a special Choate Steel folding skeleton stock for close quarters work. A special reverse choke had been fitted, which spread the shot out in a slightly flared pattern. All in all, it was a weapon designed with only a single purpose: to instantly disable an attacker anywhere within a two- to fifteen-meter range.

That death would be an almost inevitable by-product was a secondary consideration: The main thing was to stop, and stop it would, far more effectively than any pistol. Men had been known to take multiple rounds from a .357 mag and keep on coming. But few lasted more than a split second after taking a charge of 000-buck in the chest or abdomen.

Naked, holding the shotgun across his chest, Pretorius came down the staircase behind the kitchen and soundlessly opened one of the cabinets. Taking out a medium-sized cloth bag, he slung it across one shoulder and drifted into the large old library.

His eyes were now fully used to the darkness, his ears attuned to the slightest noise. He glided, rather than walked, across the huge room, his feet sliding along the wide-planked floors. A slight creak from one of the boards, and Pretorius froze. Then another sound, ever so slight, this one from the porch directly outside. He quickly crossed the rest of the space and pressed himself against the wall next to the large center window. The moonlight from outside spilled onto the floor, and he watched the mullioned pattern on the boards closely.

In a few seconds, he saw what he wanted: a shadow crossing, left to right, its asymmetric shape revealing the presence of a weapon.

He waited for another shadow, another shape, but there was none. Quickly and quietly, Pretorius glided further away, into the depths of the old house. Edging toward a window, he could see a second attacker drifting from under the trees toward the house. Unwilling to fire until he knew their strength, he thought through the problem as if he were the intruders. Pretorius planned what their next move might be, where their next assault would come from. They might be getting near a door, ready to kick it down, throw in a stun grenade, and spray the room with 9mm subgun fire. Or—and this was the alternative which suddenly made his blood run cold—they could be planning an assault from above. How many were there outside? Could any have gotten on top of the porch, or crept along one of the spreading oak tree branches to get on the roof itself?

If that were so, then Susannah would now be in mortal danger. More danger than she, in her entire lifetime, could ever comprehend.

But which of the two approaches would they make? If they were good—really good, not just hired hoods—they'd put lowest priority on frontal assaults. Which meant the next attempt would likely be mounted from above.

Pretorius made his decision. Silently gliding up the great oaken staircase, keeping far to one side to minimize pressure on creaking steps, he listened intently for alien sounds: the clicking of metal parts, the quiet forcing of wood, the cutting of glass to create an opening for a hand to unlatch a window.

Moving into the bedroom, he saw with relief Susannah's dark and silent form. *"Quick,"* he whispered, *"Come with me—but don't make even the smallest sound."*

She arose, naked as he, and came toward him.

At that moment, the window shattered into a thousand splintered shards as a black-clad fiend from Hell exploded into the room, the lethal snout of a submachine gun swinging up sharply even as he landed.

Pretorius' shotgun muzzle was already in position toward the window and roared its anger at the intruder, blasting him back against the jagged splinters of the window as if he were slammed by a gigantic, unseen fist. The intruder had only time to loose off one burst as Pretorius' barrage of lead pellets tore into his flesh, wounds spurting blood at a rate that indicated a severed artery.

Pretorius grabbed Susannah by the hand, and the two of them ran in a crouch toward the center second floor hall, away from the windows.

Downstairs, already in the house, the team leader waited, listening, assessing the sounds from above. Submachine gun. Then shotgun. Who the hell *was* this guy? Whoever he was, he was good. Too good for the others.

He slid into the next room like silk drawn through a hoop. His movements were liquid; were long, lithe flowings of motion; were almost dreamlike in their smoothness.

Nobody in the States, of course, had the skill he had. If he were to compete, he would be the best-known martial artist in the western world. But of course, competition in the normal sense held no interest for him. He existed only for the fullest use of his art—the pitting of his skills against another's in a life or death contest, no rules, no restraints. Only this could ever send the electric thrill spiraling into his brain, giving it the rush he lived for, the narcotic to which he devoted his existence.

The leader had killed limitless times. Had killed with his bare hands and his feet, had killed with garrote, with knives, with pencils and rolled-up magazines and umbrellas.

He relished what would come next. The quarry seemed accomplished in his use of a firearm. But how would he do in unarmed combat, with only his brain and his training? And how would he, the leader, reduce the quarry to this—how could he remove the advantage of the shotgun?

He flowed into a dark corner of the library. In a few scant seconds he detected, with super-attuned hearing, the cat-soft tread of feet above, moving swiftly toward the stairs. He grinned in the darkness and reached for something in a small black sack slung around his waist.

In the darkness outside, the third member of the team moved in closer to the house. More cautious than the others, he'd been chosen as a rear guard. He had no idea of the damage done to the team, only that some level of retaliation had occurred. As he advanced, he pulled something from his kit—a small grenade, of a sort seldom seen in the military. Black and cylindrical, the grenade was capable of disintegrating an entire automobile, while simultaneously spraying flechettes—tiny, lethal arrows—for ten or twelve meters in every direction. The French Sûreté, having once seen the almost unbelievable damage this weapon could inflict, promptly dubbed it *Le Porcépic*—the porcupine.

As he advanced, the man pulled the pin, keeping the lever fully compressed with his fingers. In this way, the grenade would be safe until a quick toss would deliver a hail of lethal shrapnel to the enemy within a split second. Keeping the pin in could, in combat like this, cost him his life against an adversary suddenly appearing without warning, and so he crept closer to the house, keeping under the cover of low-hanging branches as he—

And then the earth opened up below to swallow him, and the fingers of his one free hand scrabbled against the edge of the pit into which he suddenly slipped and then he felt, unbelievingly, the pain, the unbearable, searing, screaming pain of unseen things cutting upward into his legs, his knee, his right arm, the arm of the hand that held the grenade safely despite the agony.

It was, he realized as he lay screaming and gasping in the pit, blood pouring from gashes slashed by the glass, a Nam-style mantrap. Only instead of Charlie's sharpened bamboo stakes, this one was all glass. The pain was coming in waves now, and he could feel his own heart pumping out his blood. He would certainly die if he stayed here, he realized. And he would just as certainly die if he released his grip on the grenade.

In the house they heard the sounds of the man crashing through the trap, and his gurgling screams of pain. The leader knew, then, it was only him against the quarry and the woman. But he discounted the woman totally. In fact, if anything, she could be used to force the man to be taken without a struggle.

But this wasn't what he wanted. No, if anything, he would eliminate the woman to be able to isolate the man and deal with him directly. He knew this one would be worthy of him, would give him a chance to sharpen the killing edge, that honed and glistening edge of the psyche that gave him a keening pleasure beyond any rational human conception.

The footsteps above had not moved since the screams outside had begun. The leader calculated the pair would be directly overhead, and so he sank to the floor and began crawling along it, silent as death itself. His thoughts were of the woman: how to neutralize her, how to remove her from the field. It must be only him and the quarry, with no distractions, nothing for the man to protect other than his own life, nothing in between.

A noise from above alerted him. He'd reached the floor area just at the edge of the downstairs front hall and he froze in place. Something was being lowered on a cord from the second floor, something . . . round, and slowly revolving on the cord . . . and he stared at the thing, too late in realizing what it was: *a magnesium foil bulb at the end of a battery cord.*

His eyes, fully accommodated for night vision, had their irises enlarged to the maximum. And as the foil was ignited, and the all-consuming brilliance of it exploded the darkness of the downstairs hall into blinding whiteness, his eyes could only register a single negative image of the staircase, caught like a still photograph of the bomb over Hiroshima at the moment of detonation.

And as he rose to his knees, grinding his fists into his eyes, he caught the full momentum of a kick directly into his solar plexus, and then, toppling forward, the edge of a toughened palm struck down toward his neck.

He felt the wind, rather than saw the edge of the palm itself, and shifted an infinitesimal fraction—just enough for it to land on muscle instead of the targeted carotid artery. Even so, the effect was stunning.

Pretorius followed up with stiffened fingers driving upward under the ribcage, as the leader—still momentarily blinded—began to respond slowly. The fingers found their target, but the bunched muscles of the man's abdomen were ready and muted the impact. Pretorius was aware of a shattering pain as the man instantly reacted with an elbow to his kidney. Then, whirling to one side, the man began a long roundhouse kick to where he thought Pretorius' head had to be. But Pretorius knew the move all too well, and with the advantage of having some vision— even in the darkened hallway—countered with a sudden snap kick to the man's testicles.

As Pretorius saw him double over and roll, he knew what the next move had to be: the man was classically trained, most likely by a Korean master. And so Pretorius was already there, anticipating by a split second the man's response. The man, he thought, was amazing. His vision had to be almost nil and he was fighting only with his sense of sound and smell. Still, he was the most formidable opponent Pretorius had ever faced— and now he had faked Pretorius into a foolish response, a sucker move.

At the millisecond in which Pretorius was just realizing it, the man had both palms coming straight down toward both of

Pretorius' collarbones, striking to snap them—and render Pretorius as helpless as a sack of flour.

But Pretorius, having been trained ceaselessly by Henry Koo for just such lethal eventualities, lifted up his arms in a sort of triangle and instantly sank to the floor, causing the man's strike to glide off Pretorius' forearms. There was some momentary paralysis to the muscle tissue in the forearms, but Pretorius was still in action and, rolling backward, he got some distance between himself and his opponent who now seemed to be regaining some vision.

With surprise and dread, Pretorius now noticed the way the man was advancing—fingertips of each hand gathered together and pointing rearward, angled wrists forward in the style known as the chicken-head. Few but the very best ever employed this style of striking, and Pretorius now knew he was facing a master, although one with momentarily reduced vision. He backed away, keeping his eyes on the opponent. The man suddenly seemed to fly through the air at him, the edges of his feet aimed directly at his throat.

Pretorius rolled, coming up on his feet and chopping and connecting with the left kidney area as the momentum carried his opponent past. Then, incredibly fast, the man recovered and launched a high snap kick at the side of Pretorius' head. It landed at a slight angle and Pretorius knew if it had landed squarely it would have almost taken his head from his shoulders. As it was, Pretorius' vision clouded over and he began to sink to his knees. The man—his vision now fully operative—tore at Pretorius with a blindingly fast series of blows, using both the sharp, incredibly painful chicken-head strikes of the wrists as well as back-blows with the elbows.

Pretorius whirled away from the torrent of the man's near-lethal strikes and delivered a back-roundhouse kick, the *ushiro-kekomi*, to his tormentor's exposed neck, and was rewarded with a gurgling gasp before the man riposted with a downward strike at Pretorius' kidney area with both hands joined. The pain was staggering—Pretorius never knew such concentrated agony and he reeled with the immensity of it, paralyzed as if he'd been struck by a cobra.

He could see the man's face clearly in the moonlight now: a cruel and wise face, smiling, the eyes glazed yet strangely alert, savoring the moment of the kill.

And then it happened. And for years ever after, Pretorius would always remember the fraction of a second which was its frame in eternity.

The face seemed to swim forward, and Pretorius—helpless in his paralysis—saw as if in slow motion the man withdraw the wire from beneath his black jersey and fit its two rings in his middle fingers, snapping the wire taut. And Pretorius knew, knew at that moment what was inevitable.

The wire was close now, looming ever so close, seeming so much larger that it could ever possibly be, moving in miasmic, awesome slowness. And the face smiled, and—as the wire slipped swiftly over Pretorius' head, dropping to the pale vulnerability of his neck—the infinitely evil, pitiless eyes stared wildly into his own and rolled backward as the man's head disintegrated like a rotten melon dropped from a great height.

There seemed, at that moment, to be no sound, no sound whatever. But then later, when it was over, his ears were ringing with the shotgun's detonation.

Pretorius lay on the floor, unable to throw off the torn corpse of the man lying across his chest. Susannah stood naked and glistening in the moonlight in the center of the hall, her bosom heaving with great racking sobs as she let the shotgun drop clattering to the floor.

Across the lake, lights had been switched on and families wondered at the gunshots echoing: deer poachers, more than likely. One man called the police and was told it would be looked into right away. A plainclothes car working a narcotics detail not too far from the scene of the reported shots picked up the call and the detective on the passenger side clamped the flasher to the roof as they sped off toward the lake.

The man in the pit was now facing his own death, either slowly from the bleeding or quickly from releasing the lever on the grenade. Curiously, the pain began to subside and he realized what was happening: The drainage of blood away from his brain had begun to dull the senses and inevitably unconsciousness would follow, and with it, death.

But oh, God, he didn't want to die, not just yet. The others would come; the others had to come. They wouldn't leave— they couldn't leave him like this—but what was going on? There was the one last gunshot, like a shotgun, from inside the house, and then nothing. Nothing at all. They had to come. They had to get him out. His head began to swim in a warm, almost pleasant flood of overall dampening of the pain. Somehow, with a great gathering of a few shreds of energy, he managed to scream. And the scream, to his own ears, sounded as if it were coming from a great distance, and not from himself.

And inside the house, clinging to each other, each shivering in the aftershock, Pretorius and Susannah heard him.

"There's still one more," Pretorius managed to stammer. "There's one more of the bastards out there—"

Susannah clung even more desperately to him in her nakedness. "I don't care, I don't care—why can't they leave us alone? Michael, who are these people?"

Pretorius drew her with him as he carefully advanced to one side of the window. "Christ, I think he's in the trap—there may be more out there."

And at that moment, the flashlights of two Random Lake detectives began to pierce the darkness through the trees. Back near the entrance, on the other side of the chain, the radio in their car carried the dispatcher's message recalling them to the station house. But they were too far away to hear it, advancing through the dark toward the reported location of the poachers.

They heard the soft whimpering in the pit as they advanced toward the clearing and the house. *"Jesus God,"* said the younger of the two. *"What the fuck's down there?"*

The older detective, his .38 Chief's Special at the ready, froze and motioned to the other man to be quiet. Then he dropped to the ground and began crawling toward the pit, keeping his weapon's muzzle well above the dirt and the leaves. The keening sound got louder as the older detective shone his Streamlite down at the black-clothed, blood-drenched figure in the pit.

"Holy Mother a God, it's a man! And he's cut up and he's got something in his hand—something like a—"

And then, with the wounded man's last remaining shreds of energy, the grenade came up out of the pit. The explosion drove a thousand tiny flechettes through the air and into the two policemen with a suddenness that preceded any possible surprise itself. Their last thoughts were of light and wind and a soft hush before dying. The older man's flashlight, still shining, rolled a little way and stopped, illuminating the porch steps.

Pretorius and Susannah watched from the house and saw the explosion. They waited, then, until they could be certain nothing was moving. And then they dressed to leave the house and the carnage in this once-peaceful place. Pretorius examined each body, looking for some identity. But no labels were in the clothing, no wallets or cards to declare the intruders' names. And then he recognized the face of one man: a face he'd seen, briefly, at Chino.

My God, Pretorius thought, *could these be his own people?* And then the questions flew through his head. Why would they be after him? Did they already know he'd broken? Why would they want to kill him? Who had cut the orders?

It was then he heard the whimpering from the pit.

The man inside was trying, unbelievably, to pull himself out. From where Pretorius and Susannah stood, they could see one hand in the near-darkness, grasping the edge. Pretorius waved Susannah to one side and picked up the Streamlite that had rolled away from the shrapnel-riddled detective. Carefully, he edged toward the pit, holding the flashlight wide away from his body, in his left hand. In his right, he held the shotgun, finger on the trigger.

The light carefully played over the man in the pit. He was unarmed and staring up at the light, still on his feet, but swaying with the pain and the numbness which was flooding his body from the loss of blood. The gashes were deep; the blood saturated his clothing.

"Help me," the man whispered in his unremitting misery, "Oh, God, please help me!"

"Who are you?" Pretorius' voice rang out. "Who the hell are you people?"

The man looked up at Pretorius, his eyes sick with fear. "Get me out—" he managed to wheeze.

"I'll get you out if you tell me who you people are," snapped Pretorius, shifting his one-handed grip on the riot gun. "Tell me, damnit. Or you'll stay there until you goddamn well bleed to death!"

"DIA—" the man managed to speak. "Defense Intelligence Agency—special group."

Pretorius involuntarily stepped back. It was true, then; his own people were trying to kill him. "Who gives you your orders?"

The man shook his head.

"*Who*, goddamnit! Is it Hornbill? Arthur Hornbill?"

"No—not Hornbill. Don't know Hornbill. Other man—"

And then Pretorius saw the man's hand slide hesitatingly down toward his belt, on the right-hand side where a holster of some sort rode high in the FBI style. "Freeze!" Pretorius shouted, "Hold it right there!"

But the hand kept creeping, and Pretorius' finger tightened on the riot gun's trigger: the explosion tore the man nearly in half.

And then all was silent at Random Lake, except for Susannah's soft crying sounds as Pretorius held her close.

34

TO NEW YORK CITY

Susannah's face was serene and untroubled in sleep, and the passing lights along the highway shone in brief flickering fragments on the tousled blonde hair that framed her face. They'd left Random Lake a little before four in the morning and were headed toward New York along secondary roads in the stolen Chevrolet.

It would be easier, Pretorius thought, to disappear in the city among several million strangers than anywhere else. Once in a secure location, they could make plans for working their way back to England, away from whatever insanity was being orchestrated by both their own side and the Soviets.

But could they really return to their lives now? Not bloody likely, Pretorius realized. Whoever and whatever was pursuing them would, he knew, never relent until they were erased from the scenario. It was something from which there could be no escape. The end of it could come only from their own destruction—or by facing and destroying the thing itself. He was now facing not only the KGB "wet" section, but some sort of unit within DIA itself. Alone. With no external resources. And here, sleeping, peacefully on the car seat beside him, one extreme liability.

From experience, Pretorius knew even this brief moment of

safety was illusory. Time was against them, and every second ticking past was being used by their pursuers to seek and destroy them.

As he knew well, the resources of the Agency were enormous. The pursuers would have the cooperation of virtually every state, county, and local police department. Hundreds of thousands of law enforcement officers in the Northeast would be looking for a couple answering Pretorius' and Susannah's description. They wouldn't have a vehicle description, at least not yet. And with Susannah sleeping, her head below visibility of any passing highway cruiser, their odds for survival were temporarily better.

But it couldn't last. Their executioners would be checking every stolen car report and would be placing high priority on any vehicle missing from the area between the Institute and Random Lake. Time was running out, and fast.

Realistically, Pretorius knew he would have to use some kind of external resource. Working as an individual alone, he had flexibility, but extreme vulnerability. He needed to tap into something big enough to give him the clout to deal with his pursuers. But what? Or who?

Catchpole was his first thought. But this wasn't a Special Branch matter, unless Susannah, as a British subject, could be reckoned to be linked to an espionage problem. And even if he could enlist Catchpole's help, the man was thousands of miles away and links between Special Branch and the U.S. Intelligence community were known to be tenuous at best. Even if Catchpole could find someone within the U.S. who would be interested, odds were that DIA would squash it and use the information for finding Pretorius even more quickly.

Coldwell, too, could be contacted. But he was new within the Company, and CIA—especially in London—was notoriously insecure these days. Even his own briefing had confirmed that.

Still, could Coldwell as an individual be trusted? Possibly.

But what Pretorius really needed was not merely another individual, but someone who could bring an organization into play to give him the survival clout he needed.

Which led, inexorably, to Hornbill.

Instinctively, Pretorius had confidence in the man, and had—even from their first encounter—felt an innate goodness within him. Second, Hornbill had known Pretorius' father, had worked with him. Blood counted for something with men like Hornbill. And third, the man in the pit had, even *in extremis,* disclaimed any knowledge of Hornbill's association with whatever unit within DIA that was hell-bent on destroying him. Pretorius bit his lower lip and considered. Hornbill was still a risk. Very few "wet squads" would have any knowledge of whoever at the executive level had cut their orders. Still, no other possibility presented itself at the moment.

He glanced away from the highway stretching in front of him to look down at Susannah, her face curiously serene, considering all she had been part of in the past twenty-four hours. His mind kept churning, turning over the occurrences, the patterns, all the odd pieces of information. Trained to analyze raw intelligence in a certain way, he now focused on his own present predicament.

What were the anomalies in the data? What were the constant threads, the consistencies? Which facts seemed the least explainable, the least rational? What were the patterns and coincidences?

He drew a deep breath and began his mental inventory.

The first anomalous and traumatic fact, as well as the least explainable, was that he'd been broken. Utterly and absolutely turned inside out.

It was now obvious he'd given them all his knowledge about the B(AT)-3. Not only the planted, diversionary information, but everything he knew of its real capabilities. And that was a sizable chunk of hard, usable intelligence: He'd been privy to the aircraft's unique defense avionics, its radar pulse storage capabilities, all the highly sensitive data on its configuration and its composite surface and structural materials. At Edwards, the engineer who had really been in charge of the aircraft had even spent days with him, explaining every cranny and crevice, every detail and device, holding back nothing. Every question had been answered fully, without hedging, without reservation.

Second anomalous and least explainable fact: He'd not only been broken this time, he'd been broken years ago in East Germany as well *and in the same way, by the same interrogator.* There could only be one conclusion. The DIA knew and in fact had chosen him because of this. Not because he'd had "experience" with this form of interrogation. But because they'd wanted the Soviets to have all the *real* information, not just the prepared chaff.

Which had to be why, in the first place, he'd been given so much information. His cover didn't require all of that.

Pretorius suddenly sat up straighter in the seat, swerving to avoid hitting an on-coming vehicle which had strayed into his lane. One thought burned in his brain: How could DIA know he'd been broken in East Germany—and still pick him for this particular operation?

Finally, a third anomaly. Not only was the KGB after him, but his own employers—the DIA—as well. Or at least a small, well-trained, elite group within DIA which may or may not have anything to do with Hornbill.

Conclusion: The Agency—or part of it—was now trying to terminate him before he could either discover something damaging, or do something against their interests.

Pretorius' fingers clenched the steering wheel tighter, while beside him, Susannah breathed deeply and regularly in her sleep.

He knew, now, everything he loved was represented in this woman. Everything he wanted in terms of peace, of sanity, of a future like other people had. And the bastards had tried to kill her as well.

But Hornbill? He didn't seem the type. On the other hand, some of the world's most implacable killers never quite seemed the type.

He decided to take the gamble.

35

NEW YORK CITY

The sun was still hesitating, hanging low on the horizon. The backlit buildings across the river stood like frosted sentinels, and traffic was already beginning to infuse Manhattan with its metallic adrenaline.

Before driving into the city, Pretorius had driven Susannah to the Scarsdale train station, instructing her to register under a different name at a certain large hotel in midtown Manhattan and wait for him there. From this point forward, he would be at greater risk than ever. And he still had no idea whether Hornbill could, in fact, be trusted.

He'd made the phone call to the 703 area code number from the train station. After the codechecks and voice recognition procedures, Pretorius finally found himself talking to Arthur Hornbill.

The conversation was guarded, hesitant. Hornbill professed no knowledge of the attackers at Random Lake. He seemed frankly astonished, even skeptical they were actually DIA.

"Impossible," he scoffed. "We've never had a single instance of a rogue team. People who claim to be DIA people turn up now and again, you should know that. For God's sake, man, we're your own people; get back to reality."

"I've just *had* a healthy shot of reality, Hornbill. Reality is having guys trying their damnedest to blow large holes in me. Don't talk to me about your goddamned *reality;* I've had all the reality I want. Those guys were DIA, no doubt about it. I'd even seen one of the bastards out at Chino!"

After ten minutes or more of heated conversation, Hornbill was able to convince a still-reluctant Pretorius to come in.

Instructions were given for contact once he entered the city, and Pretorius got in the car and was on his way. His nerves were stretched to the limit, taut with the near-certainty that DIA had planned, from the beginning, for him to divulge the real secrets behind the B(AT)-3.

Pulling off the FDR Drive at 96th Street, Pretorius put the car in a garage between Second and Third. The owner would have to be found and the car returned with some compensation, but that would have to come later, after contact with Hornbill.

He walked west from the garage along 96th Street at an easy pace, looking at the neighborhood with the detached, yet enormously focused fascination of someone recently arrived from Mars.

He'd been instructed to place a call from a particular phone booth, and a special DIA team would pick him up. Pretorius found the phone booth easily enough, glass walls glistening with graffiti, on the northwest corner of Lexington.

Pretorius surveyed the area around the phone booth, looking for signs of surveillance. Nobody in windows looking down. Nobody in late model parked cars. Clear.

Then he entered and made the call: almost immediately a professional, clipped-sounding voice answered and instructed him to begin walking west on 96th, toward Central Park. At Fifth Avenue he was to walk south on the wide sidewalk bordering the Park, and an Agency car would pick him up and bring him in for debriefing and medical attention.

Suddenly Pretorius had a prickly feeling on the back of his neck as he listened to the voice. He looked through the glass with its sprayed graffiti at the world outside, certain he was being watched. But no, nothing. *Then what? Why the feeling? A delayed reaction from the narcotics?*

He hung up the phone and began walking. Everything was normal, here in a structured world, kids scurrying to school, grownups hurrying to jobs. Yet the uneasy feeling persisted. He crossed over Park Avenue and continued toward Madison.

And then the car materialized from nowhere, the engine nearly silent. A navy blue Chevy Malibu, plain blackwall tires. Government car. Driver in front, second man in back. Both in business suits. The driver leaned over and opened the front passenger door, smiling. "Fast enough for you?" he said. Pretorius slid in, looking around at the man in the back. A pleasant looking young man in his late twenties, slightly balding.

"I'm Dill," said the driver. "He's Perry. We'll be bringing you in. Guess you must be feeling pretty wrecked."

Pretorius let out a long, weary breath. "I'm too numb to know how I feel just now." The two agents laughed dutifully.

As the car moved down Fifth Avenue, Pretorius began to relax for the first time in what seemed like weeks. Even at Edwards, he'd been on his guard, alert for whoever would be making the move. Now, looking over the stone wall into Central Park as the car moved swiftly along, he began to feel almost normal. He wondered when they'd let him call Susannah. The debriefing would take a day or so, and the medics would give him a full physical before turning him loose, but that would be it. He could be back at the cottage by the weekend.

The driver next to him was talking, but Pretorius was listening only to the tone of his voice, not to the substance. Something was off; something wasn't right. He tried to ignore it, but the feeling was too strong. And then the car entered the park at the 72nd Street entrance and drove south, passing the morning joggers. Despite the driver's easy chatter, the tension in the car was running too high. Pretorius could sense it, almost smell it, like a thing alive. He knew something would happen soon, and his adrenaline was running high.

He heard a slight movement behind him and moved just as the hypodermic stabbed at his neck. The driver flicked his eyes over to Pretorius and swerved the car suddenly off the park drive and onto the shoulder, jolting over the curb and onto an asphalt path. Pretorius' hand snapped onto the wrist of the agent behind him, twisting it suddenly. The hypodermic dropped.

The driver slammed on the brakes, pitching Pretorius forward against the dashboard. The driver swiveled around sharply, swinging up a .22 caliber Colt Woodsman with a heavy suppressor barrel toward Pretorius' face. Thousands of neural synapses clicked within milliseconds in Pretorius' brain, bringing muscles and sinews into play, snapping the organism into action. The man in the backseat was yelling and the driver's index finger tightened on the trigger as Pretorius' forearm slammed into the man's hand, diverting his aim. Two shots spat from the weapon's snout and Pretorius drove the edge of his elbow into the throat of the driver, crushing the larynx and causing immediate death.

At that precise moment Pretorius saw a movement out of the corner of his eye: The man in the backseat was bringing up a pistol, but by then, Pretorius was already gripping the man's gun hand, wrenching it suddenly inward and clockwise, reversing the weapon. The vulnerable bone of the trigger finger snapped and the man screamed a fraction of a second before Pretorius fired the man's own weapon directly into the forehead.

Pretorius took the breast pocket wallet from the driver and catapulted himself out the door, jamming the pistol into his waistband and concealing it beneath his sweatshirt. Pretorius ran out of the parking lot back toward the Park Drive. In the sweatshirt, baggy trousers, and black sneakers, he blended in with a southbound group of morning joggers.

Jesus, he thought, who the hell *were* those people? Was there a double somewhere in communications? Were they KGB? How the hell did they make the intercept? They couldn't. Couldn't possibly. His heart hammered inside his ribs as he realized the truth. *They had to be his own people.* But why? Was the project penetrated?

But he knew. Knew there was only one possible answer: He was an untidy piece of leftover business. Something to be disposed of in a perfect operation. But why? What did he know that was so dangerous to the Agency? Who in the Agency had ordered his termination?

His heart pounding, he continued running south on the Park Drive. And then he began to hear the sirens. A blue-and-white Central Park precinct car, red roofrack flashing, swept past him on its way to the parking lot.

It would be at least another ten or fifteen minutes before anybody at the scene could piece together the situation, and then another five or so before anybody could put out an all-points on him. He wondered what the story would be. Mugger? Somebody on the most-wanted list spotted by accident?

He had to make the best possible use of these few minutes and go to ground at once. The silenced Colt began to slip from his waistband, and he adjusted it through the thickness of his sweatshirt as he peeled off from the other runners.

Near the Columbus Circle exit he stopped near a large tree and, leaning against it, pulled out the driver's wallet.

The ID was good. Staring up at him was a man with dark bristling brows and an intense expression. The crisp, bold type of Washington officialdom informed Pretorius that the individual designated is—or, more correctly, was—an employee of the Department of Defense, and specifically of the Defense Intelligence Agency.

Tyrone Eustace Hadley and Calvin Jones DeHaven saw the lone jogger pause by the tree, obviously out of breath. They had been waiting for something like this for a little over an hour. Joggers often carried money in little wallets, and when they were tired, they were easy to rip off. And this one was checking his wallet for money, probably going to get some coffee soon. Hadley nodded to DeHaven and they moved over to the solitary jogger. He'd noticed them already, looking up quickly from the wallet. He was sharp, he might be trouble. Hadley smiled at him, moving to the left as DeHaven moved to the right.

The man slowly put his wallet back in his hip pocket and watched Hadley and DeHaven as they began moving in from either side. Hadley noticed something weird: *The dude wasn't looking shit-scared, the way they usually did when they caught on to what was happening. The motherfucker wasn't even looking around to see if anybody could help him—just like he didn't give a shit. Crazy fucker. Sheeeit. Takin' candy from a baby.*

Hadley and DeHaven were within three feet of the dude, one coming up on either side, the way they usually did, when life began to get complicated. A foot came out of nowhere, connecting sharply with Hadley's groin. He doubled over at the moment when DeHaven, his knife out, felt his head nearly lifted off his shoulders by the edge of the runner's stiffened hand.

Another spin by the runner brought a foot slamming into the side of Hadley's face. DeHaven, now on the ground, fumbled for his blade, felt a heel suddenly grinding into the back of his outstretched hand, just before a second heel hit the base of his skull and slammed him into unconsciousness.

Less than seven seconds after the first move, everything was over, and the runner was gone.

The phone jangled and Hornbill's hand snatched the receiver off its hook. "What in the name of God is happening?" he snapped.

The voice at the other end gave its report in a detached, almost mechanical fashion. As it continued, Hornbill's face gradually purpled with rage. At the conclusion of the report, Hornbill slammed the receiver down without a word. Then, wheeling suddenly around in his chair, he faced his assistant and, in barely controlled tones, gave comprehensive, detailed instructions. The assistant, who had heard much in his twelve years in the Agency, stiffened with surprise.

Then Hornbill got on the second phone and punched in the Fisherman's scrambled line.

36
NEW YORK CITY

After staring at the autopsy reports for what seemed like hours, Arthur Hornbill looked up and ran his hands through his hair. He'd not slept since early yesterday morning, when the call had come from Pretorius.

His appearance had degenerated into a fair imitation of Alastair Sim playing a distracted university professor. The normally perfectly knotted bow tie hung loose, untied; the tweed vest lay open, unbuttoned.

Looking out from his window, he wondered about Pretorius, and about who his attackers were. Hornbill's office faced a battery of other gray buildings, grim and assured in their cement serenity. Somewhere out there in the canyons, Pretorius was being hunted by person or persons unknown, and he, Arthur Hornbill, had been caught unaware. Totally unaware.

He had given the order for Pretorius to be picked up and brought to the safe house on East 74th Street, but the team had radioed in to report zero contact and no trace of their subject. The subject had obviously disobeyed instructions. Or had been picked up by someone else.

The car with the two bodies in Central Park had been spotted by a sharp-eyed civilian who'd seen a man run from the vehicle and join a group of runners. Thinking it odd, he'd walked over to the car, discovered its blood-spattered contents, and promptly threw up.

The NYPD Central Park Division officers had found Department of Defense identification on one man, no identification on the other. A call brought a DIA investigating unit to the scene within minutes. The DIA team had radioed in the one ID, which the computer checked as real. But its bearer was at that moment very much alive and on duty at McLean. At that point, Hornbill had got the call.

The two bodies yielded zero information. Their photographs had not checked with any known opposition agents or simple (i.e., nonpolitical) criminals, and their fingerprints had been surgically sanded some years ago. Their dental work was either American or Canadian and showed no unusual techniques nor materials which could be traced.

Their clothing and all particles found on its outer surfaces and in its pockets had also undergone examination, but had drawn blanks.

The car had been signed out from a government motor pool in the lower parking levels of the World Trade Center. The signature belonged to a U.S. Customs inspector who had, the previous week, been reassigned in Hawaii—and who had been on the job in Honolulu during the hours in question.

All in all, a professional setup. Altogether too professional, in fact. Which was why Arthur Hornbill, for the first time in years, was more than a little worried.

Whoever had pulled this knew something about Aurora, and had been sufficiently in place to put things in motion from Pretorius' first call. Otherwise, the government car couldn't have been lifted in time, and they couldn't have got in position as fast as they did. It had to be somebody inside Aurora itself. Somebody exceptionally smart, exceptionally well-placed. But who? Who could have monitored that call, let alone have been waiting for it to come in?

Hornbill had, of course, reported the killings to the Fisherman, who had offered neither comment nor advice, other than asking to be kept informed.

He stared down at the autopsy reports again. Look for the anomalies, he reminded himself, look for the anomalies. It's often in the inconsistencies that the shape reveals itself, in the negative spaces. He pressed his knuckles to the sides of his head and concentrated. There had to be something, something perhaps not too subtle, but not too obvious. But what? His eyes ached from lack of sleep, and he rubbed them slowly. The eyes, the eyes.

Suddenly, Hornbill sat bolt upright and shouted through the open door to his assistant. "See if anybody can do a retinal scan on those two bodies. If they can, compare the data with all U.S. intelligence community records. And keep a lid on it. Use an outside phone for all calls, including this one. No reports, no memos, nothing written."

In his college years, working summers in Nantucket, the Fisherman had developed a love of whaling lore.

What an incredible thing, he thought, for men to venture to the farthest reaches of the world's seas, to challenge enormous creatures in heavy seas from platforms of twisting, bobbing longboats—risking death or maiming from the flailing torment of the whale, sometimes to return home after three or more years, sometimes never.

Sitting late at night on the beach at Scionset, looking out at the blackness of the sea, he'd wondered what kind of men they had been: to risk everything constantly, unceasingly, to never know the certainty of home and hearth for more than a few warming moments.

He found more than a few parallels between the Quakers who sailed in quest of the whale and the strange, almost ascetic men he was even then beginning to know, who took posts in remote parts of the world, risking death or imprisonment, utterly without compensation of renown or wealth, living their lives under names and conditions not their own.

And now, having survived so much for so long, the Fisher-man found his collection of whaling relics satisfying. He liked to run his hand over the cool ivory smoothness of a whale's tooth, marveling at the delicate tracery of its inked carving, wondering who, on what day and month and year, sat down and crafted this small, perfect fragment of time.

The Fisherman had, over the years, collected a museum-grade assortment of whaling artifacts: whaling irons and killing lances, intricate pieces of scrimshaw carving, painstakingly written logs from the whaling ships and barks, even the vicious Greener gun—a shotshell-powered shoulder weapon which threw an iron harpoon with staggering force, and which had hastened the near-extinction of many species of whales. The Greener was kept fully loaded, as were all the guns in the house; it was a rule of the Fisherman's, one which underscored the need for regarding firearms not as playthings, but as instruments of pur-pose.

An odd collection, perhaps, here on a Maryland farm. But no more unusual than the Fisherman's memories of a life spent in the intelligence trade.

Tonight he sat before the fireside in his library, the lights out, his fingers steepled as his deepest, most secret thoughts pursued their course. Hornbill would know soon; the Fisherman re-garded that as inevitable. What was not inevitable was how Hornbill would respond, nor how he would be handled.

The telephone jangled and the Fisherman's hand snatched at it. "Yes?" he inquired. The voice on the other end, filtered through the scrambler, sounded oddly flat. The report was pro-fessional: to the point at once, facts only, no opinions, no as-sessment.

The Fisherman spoke the order crisply: "Do it at once," then replaced the receiver slowly, thoughtfully. Containment is al-ways the most difficult part of any operation, he reflected. Al-ways the most awkward. The end game would have to be played quickly, radically, or everything—all the planning and work of all the years—would be lost.

His long, bony fingers drummed softly on the arms of the chair.

The laboratory reported readable scans on the retinas of the two bodies: deterioration had already set in, but the retinas were still flat enough to produce a verifiable image. The scans were sent transmitted for an identity check. By three that afternoon, Hornbill's terminal, linked by modem to a mainframe at McLean, displayed a brief report:

SUBJECT SET ONE: AVILEZ, Ernesto William. Currently TDY(SA) from Department of Defense, DefIntel. Reference: SecDef Order 27779B-9/79. RAI.

SUBJECT SET TWO: HYMES, James Phillip. Currently TDY(SA) from Department of Defense, DefIntel. Reference: SecDef Order 27779B-9/79. RAI.

Hornbill frowned, and again passed a hand through his tousled hair. Two men, each detached for temporary duty (special assignment) in September of 1979, by order of the Secretary of Defense, with a Report All Inquiries flag on both files.

Hornbill had never heard of either man. And he had been with the DIA since its inception; in fact, he had helped MacNamara design and implement the Agency. But neither name—Hymes or Avilez—meant anything to him. Therefore, a number of possibilities:

A. Original files possibly with other names had been compromised and names altered or replaced.

B. Current transmission of files compromised and names altered/replaced, report invalid.

C. File created as a fiction to provide DIA cover for non-DIA personnel.

D. Some unknown screw up which might never be explained.

Any one of the first three possibilities would require access at a very high level, especially if the files had been created as covers originally without his knowledge. Only a direct SecDef order, indeed, could authorize them.

So, to narrow the possibilities, Hornbill placed a direct call to the Secretary of Defense at his home in Bethesda, Maryland.

The conversation was short. Within ten minutes, as a result of a direct order from the Secretary, a series of commands written in ADA flashed briefly on Hornbill's screen, and then, in plain language, the following datafile appeared:

SECDEF SPECIAL DIRECTIVE 27779B-9/79

1. As a Special Implementation Directive, this order shall remain effective unless and until revoked by the Secretary of Defense or his designated representative.

2. The purpose of this Directive shall be to provide enhanced implementation (within the terms of its charter) of Executive Order 2135 of the President of the United States dated October 13, 1963, codename AURORA. Access to this order restricted to the President, the Vice President of the United States, the Secretary of Defense, the Chairman of the National Security Council, or their designated representatives.

3. A special covert operations group shall be created to provide enhanced security for AURORA. Personnel and budget allocation shall be determined on an ad hoc *basis by the Secretary of Defense in consultation with the Chairman of the National Security Council.*

4. The head of such group may from time to time draw upon resources and facilities of the Armed Forces including, but not limited to, their intelligence organizations, as well as the resources and facilities of the Defense Intelligence Agency. Access on such basis to either or both the Central Intelligence Agency and the State Department Bureau of Research and information is specifically denied.

5. The head of such group shall report directly to the Secretary of Defense on a regular basis and shall submit budget requests annually.

6. All inquiries and investigations regarding this Directive are to be immediately reported to the office of the Secretary of Defense.

Hornbill stared at the screen, scarcely believing what he saw. He, one of the principal architects of Aurora, was now looking at evidence of a covert operations group existing within Aurora—*a group that had existed for over ten years without his knowledge.*

Hornbill leaned back from the console and clasped his hands behind his head. Only one individual could—or would—have set this up without his knowledge. And that individual had to be responsible for the attempted termination of Pretorius. Even worse, it could—in fact, would—happen again unless Pretorius could be warned or picked up fast.

He looked across the console at his assistant. "Stephen," said Hornbill evenly, "it appears the cat is among the pigeons. Would you be so kind as to call in Guinness, Lulu, and their team?"

37
NEW YORK CITY

The setting sun reflected itself from the mirrored walls of the building opposite their hotel, lightly touching their sleeping forms, burnishing their bodies with gold.

Earlier, when Pretorius had finally come into their room, Susannah welcomed him with kisses and enveloping arms and legs, collapsing them both to the floor in a giggling, tousled heap. They made love immediately and afterwards fell into a serenely deep sleep.

As Susannah lay in the huge bed, Pretorius rose soundlessly and looked out at New York's surging late afternoon crowds, the thousands thrusting forward to catch their trains and taxis and subways. He knew now that he and Susannah were utterly alone. The people sent by Hornbill were killers, no doubt about it.

And with Hornbill's federal clout, all airports, train and bus terminals, rent-a-car locations, and bridges and tunnels would be covered by men like those in the car.

Hornbill, or somebody behind Hornbill, was out to eradicate them, to obliterate the fact of their existence. Therefore, Pretorius knew he had to blow the whistle on them before they could still him for all time.

But the only person in officialdom he could utterly trust was, of course, Catchpole. Thousands of miles away. Still, with the Branch behind him, Catchpole could at least begin to pull some clandestine strings to get them out of the country. Or at least make some of this public, so whoever was running this op couldn't sweep it under the carpet.

Crossing the room in catlike quiet, Pretorius pressed the bathroom door closed and got a call through to Special Branch in London. Catchpole's personal dragon at the gates, the invaluable Taggart, recognized Pretorius' voice from other phone calls of far less consequence and gave him a number in the United States.

Barely able to believe his good luck, Pretorius punched it in, heard first a series of worrisome clicks, and then—after a pause of about ten seconds—heard the unmistakable New England twang of Arthur Hornbill. Pretorius stared at the handpiece as if he were grasping a cobra, before slamming it back into the wall unit. *Would they have been able to trace his call in that short time?* He didn't know. He didn't think so.

"Michael?" came Susannah's sleepy, butterscotch voice from the outer room. "What's the matter?"

"Nothing, darling," came his uneasy reply. "Just dropped something. Be with you in a minute."

And so he came back in and lay down beside her and slept as he hadn't slept in weeks.

On the floor of the corridor just outside their room, an electrician bent over a disassembled fluorescent wall fixture. He took care not to look at the door directly, in case it suddenly opened. He was one of the team which had used the past three hours to pinpoint Pretorius' and Susannah's location.

Despite all the technology at their command, the Fisherman's team had a tough time getting a trace on the line and were racing to silence the couple with only a half-hour lead against Hornbill's own people. But soon they had the possibilities reduced to just three telephone numbers. Each a hotel. Each within a short radius of Grand Central Station.

Checking the rooms was simple. Instead of interviewing long lines of cleaning people and waiters, the investigators started a merge-purge check of room registrations on the computer.

The first cut excluded all guests registered three days or more before the date of Pretorius' appearance in New York. The second excluded all families with children. The third, all rooms which had no telephone charges at approximately the time of the call.

Two rooms in one hotel remained after this sifting: One with a female vaguely answering Susannah Kenney's description who checked in the day before, the other booked by a male, dark hair, roughly Pretorius' height and weight, and—according to the registration clerk—*very* suspicious looking.

The doors to both rooms were placed under surveillance by agents posing as electrical workers. After three and a half hours, one of the individuals emerged from his room and was suddenly slammed to the floor by an electrician who pressed a .38-caliber snub-nosed revolver well into the man's nostrils. The unlucky guest turned out to be a Venezuelan drug trafficker just in town to do a little business. To his utter astonishment, he was released: a free though somewhat shaken man. He checked out immediately.

Naturally, he used his counterfeit card to settle the bill.

Pretorius smiled at Susannah as she brushed out her hair by the dresser. The sleep had done them good, and, with the appetite of a stranded regiment, they ordered ambitiously from the room service menu.

In fifteen minutes, the knock came. Susannah went into the bathroom, closing the door behind her. Looking out through the peephole, Pretorius saw a waiter with a service table. He opened the door and the young broad-shouldered man pushed the table by. "Good evening, sir. Where would you like this set up—facing the television?"

"That's fine, right there. Right where you have it," said Pretorius impatiently. "I'll take care of it."

"Oh, that's all right, sir," said the young man pleasantly. "Besides, I have to turn off the warmer. It's an alcohol burner, you see, and—" The waiter reached down to pull out the steak from its heating compartment beneath the table, and Pretorius noticed his hands. The edges of his palms were calloused, thickened. Like his own.

Not a waiter's hands. Not, in fact, a waiter.

As the man brought up the .45 Colt auto from the warming compartment, Pretorius was already throwing the pot of hot coffee at his face. The waiter screamed, a high-pitched wail, almost like a woman's, and dropped the pistol as Pretorius chopped at his carotid artery.

The man staggered back, beginning to black out, and Pretorius followed up with a roundhouse kick which dislocated the waiter's collarbone. Incredibly, the man tucked into a roll as an almost automatic response—amazing for someone who'd just taken several near-crippling blows—and came up scrabbling for Pretorius' eyes.

Susannah, startled by the noise, darted into the room wrapped in one of the hotel's terrycloth robes. The man's eyes shot to her, sizing her up as a threat. It was just enough of a distraction.

Pretorius deflected the man's clawlike hand by spinning around, sharply coming down on his opponent's right kidney area with an elbow blow, then finishing it up with a stiff-edged palm to the base of the skull.

The man slumped to the floor, lifeless.

Pretorius knew there'd be a backup waiting in the corridor. Motioning to Susanah to pull her clothes on, he quickly pulled off the waiter's jacket, trousers, and shirt, and changed into them. He slicked his hair back like the young man's, and, holding the pistol he'd brought with him from the ambush in the park—a specially-modified .22 Colt Woodsman with a Maxim-type suppressor barrel—beneath a small napkin-covered tray, he backed out of the room. Keeping his head down as if looking at the bill on the tray, he moved toward the service elevator.

"Everything okay?" came a voice from just to his left. "Just fine," he replied, looking up into the flat, gray eyes of a suddenly very surprised man in an *ersatz* electrician's uniform. Pretorius placed two almost simultaneous shots just under the man's chin, firing upward to reach the brain. The electrician sagged to the floor at once, and Pretorius dragged him into 1207 to join the erstwhile waiter.

Pretorius and Susannah began dressing quickly, realizing at any second the disposal team would be checked on. Leaving the room, they took the stairs up four flights, then rode separate elevators down. They would meet tomorrow morning at ten, at the Alice in Wonderland bronze sculpture in Central Park; Susannah to arrive slightly ahead of time and, if she suspected she was under surveillance, to open up a newspaper.

Downstairs, Pretorius emerged from the elevator bank with the silenced weapon now placed in his belt against his spine, concealed under a jacket. He walked in a loose, ambling gait, like somebody bored, out for an evening walk.

As he left the hotel through the 42nd Street glass doors, two men began moving quickly toward him. Going around the block, Pretorius dove into one of many entrances to Grand Central Station, attempting to blend in with the commuters.

He felt, rather than actually saw, his pursuers.

Entering the tunnel of a downstairs track with a train about to leave for its usual sequence of Westchester and Connecticut bedroom colonies, he walked swiftly toward the head of the train. Pretorius stepped on board, then moved through one car quickly. Coming out between cars, he lowered himself to the tracks on the opposite side from the platform and edged his way forward in the semidarkness.

The train started inching forward ponderously. A few businessmen gazed down distractedly through their dust-encrusted windows, surprised to see a man flattened against the tunnel walls, illuminated by flashes of light from the train's interior as it gathered momentum.

Pretorius knew he had scant seconds before the train's hulk

disappeared down the coal-black corridor. Despite his closeness to the metal sides of the train now hurtling past him, he moved as quickly as he dared. The perspiration came trickling down his back, making the presence of the silenced pistol against his spine all the more uncomfortable.

The train cars flashed by faster and faster, dazzling his eyes in the contrasting darkness. And then, so suddenly it almost took his breath away, the train and its flashing and its noise were gone, and all that remained was the blackness and—directly across from him—a gunman taking cool, deliberate aim at Pretorius in a classic Weaver stance.

Pretorius did the only logical thing in such a situation. His pistol was still pressed against his spine and he knew he could never reach it in time, so he dropped instantly to the ground, below his opponent's line of sight, rolling fast to one side and getting the pistol out.

A .22 caliber pistol is a useless weapon in many ways, best reserved for sport and plinking, and seldom for self-defense. It does work well with a suppressor, though, especially in densely populated areas where a suppressed .38 would still make a significant amount of noise. You can't do your usual act of placing three or four shots inside a six-inch spread across the abdomen, because the stopping power simply isn't there: Your assailant would die, but not before he'd be able to punch your ticket quite effectively.

Brain shots are equally difficult: The skull is surprisingly thick, and bullets, especially ones as lightweight as .22s, tend to glance off the bone even at the slightest angle.

So Pretorius quickly planted three shots in the gunman's throat, letting the slight recoil stitch the shots vertically upward about three inches.

The immediate effect was sudden shock and blinding pain; the assailant dropped his weapon and reared over backwards, grasping at his throat. The central nervous system was hit, and the man's movements began to slow spasmodically.

Quickly, Pretorius advanced across the tracks where the gun-man lay dying, staring up into God alone knew what. Pretorius kicked the gun away and knelt down swiftly. "Who the fuck *are* you people—who do you work for?" he shouted at the gun-man. But the only response was a strangled gurgling as the blood gushed forth.

From far down the tracks nearer Grand Central, Pretorius was aware of activity, of footsteps and shouts. He lowered him-self to the tracks and felt for the gun he'd kicked away from the man next to him. He'd need better armament soon, he knew. His fingers scrabbled among the rubble of wrappers, discarded cartons, bottles and other garbage, then finally closed around the reassuring cold steel. He got to his feet unsteadily and began running down the tunnel, heading north.

Far above Pretorius and his assailants, Hornbill and his team of agents discovered the bodies in room 1207. No ID was found on either, and the somewhat shaken assistant manager on duty couldn't identify them as hotel staff. Time of death appeared to have been within the past hour, and so Hornbill placed a call from the room to the 17th Precinct, four blocks away. Within five minutes, the 17th's commander had deployed virtually every man, uniformed and plainclothes, to find Pretorius.

Although he had no means of knowing it, Pretorius at this moment had six pursuers: three on the tracks, moving up qui-etly and quickly, and three more on the street in radio contact with those below.

The followers on the tracks were cautious now, having found their team member shot through the throat, his weapon miss-ing. They moved quickly, avoiding chicken-walking (the too-cautious crisscrossing that can get you killed faster than the time it takes you to say *Oh shit*), and making sure they kept close to the tunnel walls, so their shapes wouldn't separate from the blackness enough to allow a clean shot.

Fifty meters ahead, Pretorius couldn't see them, but knew they must be back there in the blackness. He kept moving as fast as he dared, knowing his destination would be coming up within the equivalent of three or four more city blocks. If he could make it before his pursuers could nail him, he had a chance. If not, well, it's been a real busy day here, folks, and nice to have known you.

Up on street level, the other three were beginning to notice unusual police activity all around them. Although they were prepared with FBI identification, none of them wanted to be stopped at this stage. They knew Pretorius' approximate location and were racing to find an entrance to the tracks ahead of him.

Then, with a jolt of realization, the team leader knew where Pretorius had to be heading: *the old Presidential train station, still intact beneath the Waldorf-Astoria.*

The Waldorf-Astoria has always had the communications and security setups necessary for heads of state. And, before the era of presidential aircraft, part of the security arrangements included the most exclusive train station in all the world: constructed directly below the Waldorf, especially for heads of state.

On the north side of the street level of the Waldorf, a single gold-colored door leads down to this station. Few people know of it, and the gold door is sufficiently intimidating to discourage most curiosity seekers. And few people who ever opened the door and peered down the gloom of the iron staircase beyond would venture any further before returning to the sunlight and safety of Park Avenue.

Pretorius' pursuers on the street flung open this door and scrambled down the stairs, startling a derelict woman who had been sleeping, wrapped in black Hefty bags, trapping the warmth against her ravaged body.

They emerged, finally, on the platform itself, where a single electric light burned for maintenance crews. The gunmen secured the area swiftly, taking positions of advantage where they couldn't be seen by anyone coming up from the tracks on the Grand Central side.

The team leader at the Presidential Station whispered into his walkie-talkie. "We're in position just ahead at the old train station just below the Waldorf. Keep moving and drive the subject closer, but don't expose yourselves unnecessarily."

Far down the tracks, in the gloom, one of the others received the brief transmission through his earphone and clicked his PTT button twice in acknowledgement.

Pretorius was neatly boxed.

The young Conrail policeman who came upon the body radioed its presence to his lieutenant, who passed the word to Hornbill and his men. Their reaction was immediate: a Conrail plan of the track area immediately north of Grand Central was unrolled. Hornbill's eyes went immediately to the old Presidential Station: "He'll come up here," he said, a stubby finger pointing out the exit, "It *has* to be here. Kindly move it, gentlemen."

Pretorius now was very aware of the men coming up fast behind him. He considered whether it would be best to frustrate pursuit by placing a few shots down one side of the tunnel—he knew they'd be hugging the walls—or to not reveal his precise position by his muzzle flash. He opted for keeping quiet and moving ahead even faster.

Up ahead, the men in position were kept aware of Pretorius' progress by their opposite numbers following him along the tracks. He would be within range in seconds, they knew, and they aligned their sights to where he would be sure to appear.

The team leader, in position near one of the doors on the platform, felt the sweat trickle as the tension increased. Unless they got this sucker, he knew, it would all be over. The bank account in the Caymans, the place in Middleburg, everything

284 / GUY DURHAM

else. His new wife knew him as a comfortably retired government employee now doing consulting for large corporations all over America. She had no idea of his real profession, nor of the money rapidly piling up in the numbered account.

He felt a muscle twitch between his shoulders and gave an involuntary shiver. The earpiece gave a minuscule crackle of static, and a voice said, *"Subject now appears to be within twenty-five, no, twenty meters of your location. I can see him against the light . . ."* And then three shots echoed down the cement confines of the tunnel, so quickly they almost sounded like the chattering stutter of a submachine gun. The earpiece crackled again, this time echoing a confident drawl. *"Man down. We got him."*

The man waiting at the station relaxed, pulling the earpiece out. He smiled and started to rise from his place of concealment. Then, incredibly, he felt the cold circle of a revolver's barrel placed ever so gently against the base of his skull.

"April Fool, motherfucker," a quiet voice said.

38
NEW YORK CITY

He came out of the dream with a sense of unreality, of blissful, evanescent ease. The sheets around him seemed at once caressing and cool, and the ceiling was high above, huge carved oaken beams intersecting.

Tentatively, he lifted his head from the pillow to look around the room. Antique furniture. Books and magazines on a chair pulled near the bed. And in the corner of the room, high up near the ceiling, all but obscured in shadow, a monitor camera, cyclops eye glinting in the gloom.

He lay his head back down and closed his eyes. *Where in God's name was he?*

His left arm felt a twinge of pain as he turned it slightly. Some damage, level unknown. But probably not too bad if the arm was all there and he could nevertheless turn it.

Then he realized, remembering: the tracks below the Waldorf. Lying there, bleeding in the blackness, amid the filth of the tracks. *But where was he now? Not a hospital. Definitely not a hospital.*

In the distance he could hear hushed voices, and he strained to catch a word, a tone of voice, anything that would give him a sense of language.

Then the voice, booming, engagingly bombastic: "God's trousers, Michael, but you do look a sight! Bit like something the cat dragged in, then decided to drag out."

Pretorius was astonished to see the bearlike shape of Donald Catchpole lumbering into the room, filling it with his sheer size and good nature. Still confused, Pretorius struggled to sit up in the big bed—a stoutly oaken Jacobean affair—as the Detective Chief Superintendent swept the magazines and books off the chair with his huge paw of a hand and sat down smiling with a great sense of occasion. Pretorius managed to speak. "Donald, what is this place? What—where is this?"

Leaning forward conspiratorially, Catchpole said "Well, it's obvious, old thing. You're in New York, in an Agency safe house, and—considering all you've been through in the past few days or so—you're in quite good nick."

"Jesus," Pretorius finally said, rubbing the bristling stubble on his face. "How long have I been out?"

"Well," reflected Catchpole, "You seem to have arrived by way of a particularly discreet train station two days ago . . ."

Pretorius made a face. The detective reconsidered. "You've slept the sleep of the just, as it were, for better than thirty-six hours. And I have it from reliable sources that you've done one hell of a job, considering your tender years."

Then Catchpole turned around in his chair as Arthur Hornbill entered the room. Peering down over the seated Catchpole's shoulder at Pretorius, Hornbill's face loomed like a beaming, bespectacled moon. Pretorius was on edge, not knowing whether this professorial figure was the architect of his doom or his benefactor. But Catchpole's presence was a good sign.

"Michael, Michael. Good God, what you've been put through!" the older man began, examining Pretorius curiously over half-glasses balanced precariously on his nose. "You've not only fulfilled the mission admirably, you've drawn out a cancer right in our own organization. We owe you a great deal, lad. A very great deal."

Pretorius tensed, the pain shooting up his arm. "Then you know it was DIA people at Random Lake—and the pickup team who almost wasted me were carrying Agency ID." He shifted position, the better to study Hornbill.

"We know about Random Lake, and the vehicle in the park. But they weren't ours. They don't appear anywhere on the DIA books. And the only way the bogus pickup team could've known your position was a telephone intercept, which we ultimately found in our cellars. The fake team picked you up first; ours got there minutes later, waited, then radioed in for new instructions. We had no idea where you were."

Pretorius' anger came boiling to the surface. "Forget about me, Hornbill! Who the fuck were those guys? Where do you get people like that? Dial-a-Spook? We were both damn near killed—and all because of you guys playing your goddamned games! Games, man! That's all you guys do, play your fucking *games*. Only you use people as the pieces and throw them away when you're done. Where's Susannah now?"

Hornbill pursed his lips. "She's safe, quite safe, and you'll be with her soon. We picked her up not long after you made your rather hasty exit. Detective Chief Superintendent Catchpole was most helpful in that regard. With any luck, if your debriefing goes well, we should get the three of you on a plane to perfidious Albion by the weekend. But first, would you tell us just a bit of what you remember?"

"An Air Force captain and a state trooper made the intercept coming out of Barstow—"

Hornbill interrupted. "Yes, very well, we know that part. You were under surveillance during your abduction until you were carried onto their plane. And we were able to trace the plane to Westchester Airport and were there, watching from the control tower, when you were loaded like a frozen pike into their ambulance and taken to the Institute."

"You don't miss a trick, do you?" said Pretorius. "*I* didn't even know how I got there."

"We endeavor to give satisfaction, as Jeeves said to Bertie," intoned Hornbill. "But tell me how the interrogation went—"

Pretorius froze, the memories beginning to flood back with a vengeance. "There's something you should know. The man who interrogated me knew me from before, from East Germany. *He knew who I was. He'd known me before—he'd done this thing to me before.*"

He paused to see the reaction on Hornbill's face. And it came: a look of disbelief, of horror. But of course Hornbill had all his life been expert at assuming such reactions, like putting on and taking off masks in a penny charade.

Hornbill leaned closer, now anxiously scanning Pretorius' face. *"How much did they get, Michael? Did they get what we prepared for them?"*

Pretorius darted a glance at Catchpole. Hornbill said, "It's all right. He's got clearance for this now." Still, Pretorius spoke guardedly, the words coming slowly, scarcely audible now. "I think they got what you wanted to give them. I think it worked."

Behind the words, Pretorius was struggling with his emotions, wondering if Hornbill was behind all this, if he were the person responsible for everything that had been done to him in the name of—national security? Isn't that what they call anything they wish to excuse, no matter how inexcusable? And he knew that if this man were his enemy, if he had in fact cold bloodedly sent him to be broken again, his survival depended utterly on not revealing how much he knew, on not revealing his realization of their scheme—at least part of it. He had to play it out, had to know who was responsible, had to *know.*

Catchpole had been saying something. "Sorry," said Pretorius, "I must have been drifting off. Don't feel quite myself. I—"

"Don't worry, lad," said Catchpole. "I just wanted to see you were safe and sound. Susannah will be in soon, after the doctor's had another dekko at you. Meantime, you take good care of yourself. We'll all get together for dinner tomorrow night, according to old Jeeves, here. Anyway, see you then. Good luck with the debriefing."

Hornbill acknowledged the British detective's departure and

leaned forward in his chair. "Got to get going myself as well, my boy," he said. "Make sure you get some rest. You've done admirably. Admirably. We'll have a briefing tomorrow, when you've had a chance to restore yourself."

Pretorius looked away. "Spare me the violins. Just let me get out of this, and back to Devon, and leave you people to play your games."

Hornbill rose from the chair to leave. "If you're up to it, we've arranged for a rather special treat for you, Catchpole, and Susannah tomorrow night. I'm told the cooking's rather special."

The thought of Susannah went through Pretorius like a spear. *He'd already placed her in so much danger—he, and he alone. If she'd been hurt or worse, killed—*

"Oh, by the way," said Hornbill at the door. "There was a small news item in the media saying that a Dr. Charles Vojtec, late of California, was killed in an automobile collision. Sad thing it was. A great man, little appreciated by his contemporaries. There was, of course, an appropriate body—supplied by our friends at the ME's office—to make it convincing for the KGB, who generally like to check up on such things."

Pretorius winced.

"Don't worry." Hornbill reassured Pretorius. "It was somebody who'd been killed earlier the same day in a real accident. We had to throw the hounds off, otherwise they'd be looking for you for years. Consider yourself fortunate to be the late Dr. Vojtec. Think of it: all the advantages of being deceased, and none of the rather disconcerting disadvantages. You should've taken out a good insurance policy."

With that, Hornbill took his leave, to be succeeded by the doctor, and finally, blissfully, by Susannah.

The next day Pretorius, fresh from his final debriefing and in a set of new clothes bought for him at J. Press, went with Susannah to a small restaurant just off lower Fifth Avenue, in the Flatiron district.

Their driver, a young DIA agent just up from Fairfax, parked the Agency car down the street and stayed with it as Pretorius, Susannah, and Catchpole entered the restaurant.

They chose a table behind one of the big Corinthian columns that gave the place its architectural beauty. Susannah and Pretorius kept staring at each other. For the first time in months, they were in a normal situation, doing what normal people do. "Come, come," boomed Catchpole, "can't a man get something to eat in this place without people making love and mooning about? Thunderation!"

Pretorius and Susannah laughed with the big detective, and the three of them chatted about this and that, about England, about Catchpole's impressions of New York, and most of all about the food in Manhattan—much of which was new to both Susannah and the Detective Chief Superintendent.

Pretorius was delighted by the menu. "This looks like a cross between K-Paul's and Galatoire's. You can't mean New York's finally caught on to New Orleans cooking."

Catchpole smiled. "Well, they tell me the proprietor happens to be one of New Orleans' top-drawer chefs, Paul Bonnier. His family's been in the restaurant business since before your Civil War."

For starters, the three of them ordered Oysters Rockefeller, a dish made famous by the New Orleans institution named Antoine's—whose chef labeled it Rockefeller because of the richness of its spinach sauce.

For entrees, the choice seemed best among several crawfish dishes, and so Pretorius chose Crawfish Etouffée, while Hornbill settled on Crawfish Gumbo, as he was partial to okra.

The young proprietor came over as they were well into their entrees and asked if everything was satisfactory.

Pretorius was enthusiastic. "I've never had Crawfish Etouffée like that," he said, enjoying the spicy yet delicate flavor.

Bonnier leaned back on his heels and laughed. "It's really simple. You just use the head, the claws, and the tops of some young spring onions for the stock, and the rest is just a bunch of fresh garden vegetables, simmered with the tails. Simple is better. Always."

"No," rejoined Pretorius, "there's something different. Something I've never tasted in an etouffée before."

Bonnier laughed again, an infectious sound that made everyone around him smile. "True, there are just two little things that are—just a little out of the ordinary. I make up a special version of bay seasoning, a recipe we've had in our family for years. And instead of Tabasco, I use Outerbridge's sherry pepper sauce. Works better, although in New Orleans it's a substitution that's considered a class-A felony."

Pretorius agreed; the combination was wonderful. The young proprietor wished them bon appétit, and disappeared into his miniature, incredibly crowded kitchen.

The restaurant was a delight. It even served Dixie Beer, a plain but honest New Orleans lager that helped mute the searing Cajun spices.

Catchpole chatted along merrily as they ate, comparing the relative merits of different national foods from the hotter climes, lamenting on the lack of evolution of Mexican food into a higher level of cuisine.

Pretorius retorted that Mexican food's charm was in its straightforwardness, and that true aficionados could find many different subtleties in it, including the difference in taste of food spiced with a jalapeño versus the narrower, somewhat shorter serano pepper.

Besides, he ventured, good honest farmers' food, which was the nature of Mexican cuisine, should be appreciated on its own terms, instead of comparing it to . . .

At that precise moment, the entire front window of the restaurant blew inward with an eardrum-splitting blast, showering them with long razor-sharp shards of glass.

Everything was plunged into stygian blackness. The tinkling of falling glass mingled with the screaming of injured and frightened men and women.

Roiling black smoke and falling debris from the ceiling made the darkness even more impenetrable, and it was a few seconds before Pretorius could see Susannah was on the floor, protected by the bearlike form of Catchpole.

Susannah was conscious, but dazed. She seemed well enough to respond to his questions. Nothing broken, no signs of internal bleeding; simply disoriented, bewildered. Catchpole, though, had been knocked cold, but seemed to have not suffered any damage. Pretorius felt for his friend's pulse and, to his great relief, was rewarded by a strong, steady beat.

The young DIA driver came running in, obviously shaken. "They—had some kind of a bomb. I couldn't really see what they were doing in that light. It happened so fast, oh, shit—"

Pretorius interrupted, shouting, "Where the *hell* are they?"

The man got himself together. "They got in a Camaro, dark blue, Jersey plates. They headed down Fifth."

"I'll drive," shouted Pretorius as he ran toward the car. "You got a shotgun in the vehicle?"

"Up front, on the passenger side, under the dash."

"Get it out. You're going to need it," Pretorius yelled, kicking the car into action. The rubber of its police steel radials shrieked as he accelerated, the siren ululating in a deafening wail, headlights and behind-the-grille flashers alternating.

Several federal agencies, including the DIA, ordered LTDs in the special 351 CID high output "police package" for pursuit use. The bumper was then sometimes strengthened for ramming purposes, and agents were taught to go for the metal just in front of the front wheels to immobilize an opposition car.

The Ford roared at eighty-five or more down Fifth Avenue, shooting across 15th, 14th, 13th in seconds. Traffic parted like the Red Sea and a block and a half ahead, Pretorius and the agent soon spotted the blue Camaro.

The Camaro had already struck a pedestrian in its way and the bloodied body was slung like a suddenly unstrung marionette into the middle of Fifth Avenue.

Pretorius dodged it, whipping the end of the Ford around as he mashed the accelerator to the floorboard.

His siren was loud in his ears as he began to close the distance. Then the Camaro hit Washington Square and, jumping the curb, tore around the arch on two wheels, going full out.

Pretorius' Ford shot through the Square after the Camaro, scattering the late-night crowd around the fountain like leaves.

The Camaro exited the south side of the Square in a blur, slipping down the next few blocks, then careening left into Houston Street, and the distance lengthened for a moment.

Once on Houston, Pretorius kicked down one gear and the big Ford Windsor engine slammed up all its reserve strength. They began closing again, and in a few moments Pretorius saw the Camaro swing down the ramp onto the FDR, slipping easily in among the late-night traffic.

He plunged the Ford down the ramp and almost sideswiped a couple in a convertible who were hypnotized by the action. Pretorius swerved at the last moment and nailed the accelerator to the metal.

Although they were whipping through late-night FDR traffic at over 90 mph, Pretorius tracked the Camaro easily by the white light spilling through a break in its left taillight. As they closed on the Camaro, Pretorius could see the man on the right front passenger seat dive over the seat and bring up some sort of weapon. He swerved the Ford back into protective cover behind a car in between.

The man in the back of the Camaro drove the butt of his weapon through the rear window, then reversed it and opened fire through the two-foot hole in the shattered glass.

From the look of the piece, Pretorius figured it was some kind of shortened AKM-47*. Not a bad choice for vehicular fire, he thought: short even to be maneuverable, and the 7.62 × 39

*Modernizirovannyi Automat Kalashnikova, improved version of the standard Soviet military automatic rifle.

mm rounds could drop a tire flat in about eight seconds, while no duty pistol round—not even a .45 ACP—had a hope in hell of causing anything more than a slow leak.

"Get the goddamn shotgun up," he shouted to the agent. But the agent was already easing the weapon's blunt snout out the window.

Pretorius pulled up two lanes to the left, keeping as many cars in between as he could. Every time part of the Ford showed, the gunman in the Camaro spewed a burst of automatic fire from the AKM.

And then Pretorius swerved the wheel, slewing the vehicle all the way over, a thirty-degree swing, and came up alongside as the agent fired his buckshot into the driver's window.

The first shot was a slug round, to open up the glass, and the next three—slamming through the aperture like rapid hammer blows—were double-O buckshot.

The young agent was good with the riot gun. With the driver taken out, the Camaro spun out of control, going around and around twice, causing Pretorius to stand on the brake to keep out of the way.

Smashing hard into the divider, the Camaro bounced back and rolled over several times, ending upside down on its roof, slowly rotating, the metal scraping against the highway cement, sparks showering. Pretorius slammed his Ford to a stop and he and the agent were out of the car in seconds. The smell of spilled gasoline was everywhere, and it would only be seconds before everything would go up in a single searing inferno.

The man in the rear of the car was trying to scramble through the window, struggling to bring the AKM out with him.

Pretorius, his hands locked around his pistol, a three-inch barrelled Smith & Wesson Model 13, shouted, "Freeze! Federal agent! Hold it right there!"

But the man, his face bloodied from shotgun pellets, swung the rifle barrel toward Pretorius, who instantly put four rounds into him, all entering within a three-inch group.

The rifleman flopped face down onto the concrete, jackknifed half in and half out of the upside-down car. Pretorius advanced warily, and then—unbelievingly—recognized the ruined face of the rifleman.

Fraker. It was Colonel Fraker.

Then—on the opposite side of the car—the driver moved slightly.

Pretorius hit the ground in a roll to get to a better position. He came up behind a mailbox a dozen feet away, in a two-handed Weaver hold sighted on the driver who was now exposed to his field of fire.

And then he realized the movement had been simply the corpse dropping down out of the restraining seat belt, its head blown into fragments by the shotgun blast.

"Oh, shit!" Pretorius whispered to himself, his hands beginning to shake around the grips of the pistol.

39
OXON HILL, MARYLAND

The Fisherman was alone in the house, Hornbill knew.

It was Saturday, and the housekeeper had driven the station wagon into town for groceries. Hornbill realized there had to be intrusion alarms throughout the property, although he hadn't been to Oxon Hill since the Fisherman's "retirement" from the Agency.

The Fisherman wished to diminish any suspicion of his continued involvement in the intelligence community. So all contact had been scrambled via telephone for well over a decade.

Hornbill elected to simply drive straight in. The entrance gates were, as they had always been, wide open. A video camera just to the left, behind the William and Mary brick wall to which the black iron gates were attached, watched and recorded everything within a 120-degree arc.

The black government Ford crunched on the gravel as it moved down the long straight drive flanked by Lombardy poplars, then around the horseshoe drive to the house's front door. *It was again as he'd remembered it,* Hornbill reflected. *A very, very long time ago.*

As the sun rose on that particular morning in 1962, the men stepped from the blind, their shotguns held high to clear the water.

There were nine in all. Each chosen because of his particular powers, and because of beliefs tested in many ways before being selected to join this very special group. Three were from the intelligence community, two from the private sector, one was an Air Force four-star general, another a government scientist, and two were cabinet-rank officials.

They walked back to the house, talking and laughing among themselves. The hunting had been good, and they would have the ducks for dinner that evening. Their adrenaline was running high.

A foxhound yelped somewhere out beyond the barns. Shadows moved among the trees.

The big brick house loomed up suddenly, backlit by the yellow sun filtering through the morning mist. Its big central pediment and the two flanking dormers on the roof gave it a formal, yet welcoming appearance. The house, built in 1723, overlooked Broad Run and had been host to many unusual groups of people over the past two centuries. Yet never had it contained as powerful and diverse a group of people as approached it through the mist this morning.

The men entered through the kitchen, laughing, shucking off their damp coats and waders, handing their shotguns and the ducks to the waiting staff.

After changing into dry clothes, they gathered in the big paneled dining room for breakfast. One seat was left empty, as its occupant would be arriving shortly after breakfast.

Breakfast consisted of Smithfield ham in red-eye gravy, breakfast fries (a mixture of baking powder, flour, sugar, and milk, dropped in dollops in a hot cast-iron pan and fried), buttermilk biscuits with honey, and the strongest coffee this side of a Texas truckstop.

The men ate enthusiastically, glad to be together. They held many things in common.

The gravel crunched suddenly outside on the driveway, and the men looked up sharply from the table. The sounds of car doors being opened and closed cracked through the still morning like pistol shots. It was an almost alien sound here in the Maryland countryside, where the centuries seemed telescoped together.

"He's here," the man called the Fisherman said. "I'll go bring him in."

Outside, under the small portico, he met their visitor, the eighth man. The Secret Service men from the cars deployed themselves around the house, but none was permitted inside.

The President came in wearing a tweed sport jacket over a thick knit sweater. His thick brown hair was ruffled, and he grinned his wide roguish grin.

"Hope I'm not dressed too formally for you guys," he said as he shook their hands. "Somebody said there's a hell of a party going on over here in the country and I thought I'd crash it."

The Fisherman, lean and professional, made all the introductions. The President liked the Fisherman, and considered him one of the few realists in intelligence. He also held great respect for the Fisherman as a man of letters, a civilized man who read Dante and wrote poetry for relaxation.

Taking the vacant seat at the head of the table, the President turned to the Fisherman. "Everything ready before we begin?"

"Yes, Mr. President. The staff has been dismissed and won't return until one and a half hours before dinner time. The rooms have all been swept and our electronic countermeasures are in place. Everything's ready."

"Good. The lord loveth a suspicious man, at least in your business," Kennedy said. The men laughed, even the Fisherman, who seldom was seen with anything more than a wry smile.

"Now, then. This is probably the most venturesome thing I'll do this year, and if it works, Mr. Khruschev and his friends will be barking up a wrong tree the size of a sequoia for some time.

"We've finally had, after along series of failures, some notable successes in space. We haven't been first, but we've laid the foundation for a far more vigorous and successful space program than anything we know the Russians have.

"Their military airpower is behind ours, but from our national intelligence estimates, they may easily overtake us, especially if Congress withholds the funds we need to maintain our advantage.

"We have a decided edge in the breadth and depth of our technology as a nation—far beyond the rest of our particular planet.

"And here I'm not talking solely of military technology, nor even of the advanced capabilities we're building in intelligence technology.

"It is a simple fact that our industrial power will be increasingly based on technology, as will our economy itself. And it is needless to point out that the base of our military power will always be our industrial power. It also should be obvious that we need to direct our military power in a manner which will give us the highest possible leverage.

"These sentiments are nothing new to you gentlemen. The fact that you yourselves possess them is precisely why you've been asked to be here this morning.

"I have some specific proposals to direct to you. They are strategic in the broadest possible sense, but there are immense tactical implications. Without you, neither strategy nor tactics will work. For you gentlemen are, at this moment, the single most valuable group in the United States.

"The commitment I shall require from you will last throughout your lives. The secrets you will carry can never be revealed to anyone. Not to your families, not to your friends, not to anyone.

"You will be asked to undertake what I believe to be one of the most important strategic missions in our history. If it is successful, your part in it will go unheralded. If it fails, your failure will be trumpeted.

"I can only tell you—before we go further—that it is critical to our national security well into the next century. I must also ask now if any of you would rather not participate in this thankless and terribly consuming task. You may certainly refuse with honor."

At this, he looked at each man in turn, his eyes questioning, measuring, analyzing. What he saw there obviously satisfied him. "Well, we're all in this together, then," he said, the schoolboy grin once again spreading.

"Our representatives of the intelligence community will tell you they have already begun a new initiative in new technologies pertinent to their efforts. For example, the National Security Agency will have, within only a few years, a technological capability far beyond the imaginations of the Eastern bloc. With our new satellites, we'll be able to see on which side somebody in the Kremlin parts his hair. We'll be able to intercept and break any clandestine communication, any code, any cryptogram. We have programs being developed at M.I.T. and at Cal Tech right now that will make it all but impossible for the enemy to communicate without our full awareness and understanding.

"In terms of tactical military technology, you all know—as does the opposition, unfortunately—that we are, and will continue to be, far superior. But in strategic weaponry, we come to something of a crossroads.

"Our Intercontinental Ballistic Missiles will undergo constant evolution, and their systems, range, and power will improve on a more or less steady basis.

"They do not need human pilots, any more than our space rockets do. As you well know, the decision to employ onboard decision-making capability in Project Mercury was a purely political one.

"Everything done within the capsule is, as we all know, capable of being done and monitored by ground control. But human pilots were frankly used for two reasons: It gave the race for space a distinctly personal, heroic flavor which would guarantee its funding through its critical years. And candidly, once we'd entered our first astronauts in the NASA training program, the publicity made them heroes. The astronauts recognized their power and capitalized on it.

"So, ultimately, it became politically impossible to send them up purely in what was their original role—that of, well, very valuable guinea pigs."

The President smiled ruefully and poured tea from the carafe into his cup. He poured carefully and slowly, using the time to gather his thoughts.

"We tend not to think of our NASA programs as part of air power. Nor, in fact, do we even think of our ICBM arsenal as part of air power. When we use the phrase air power, we conjure up visions of B-52s streaking across the skies, contrails streaming, all the rest of it. Jimmy Stewart at the controls."

The men relaxed and chuckled. The tension in the room had been almost visible, a tangible thing, and the President, with his consummate politician's skill, had known precisely when to break it, to keep them with him.

"But the fact is, air power includes all those activities, and more. It includes our work on satellites which will not merely have intelligence gathering and communications functions, but strategic weapons capability.

"In fact, it's not inconceivable that satellite-based weaponry will, by the century's end, become even more vital to our defenses than our entire ICBM arsenal. I have been advised that a totally new category of non-nuclear weaponry is possible for creating a defensive 'umbrella' over the United States, a sort of shield in space to deflect Soviet ICBMs and other offensive weapons—without poisoning the atmosphere with radioactive waste and fallout.

"Air power, by virtue of its breadth and depth in defensive capability, is the keystone of our security. It perhaps requires a new phrase, one which is more inclusive. After all, it commands not merely the air, but the seas and the land itself.

"Whatever we call it in the future, it requires new thinking, a new concept to leverage it to the utmost. And now we come to the point. Our air power can be, should be, and—with your help—*will* be based on technologies which will not require on-board human control.

"The fact is, although the Air Force believes its sworn function is to place as many pilots in the air as possible, that strategic air power will very shortly no longer require traditional aircraft, nor the traditional role of the pilot.

"It will, instead, require *counter*traditional thinking, and countertraditional technologies. And we're only now seeing the beginning. Strategic air power which leverages the new technologies to the maximum will gain us greater and greater advantage over our enemies, no matter who they may be in the future.

"But if we continue to invest in World War II concepts of strategic air power, in the bomber, in the fighter to protect the bomber, and in all the expensive hardware that supports their traditional roles, we hobble and hamper our efforts enormously.

"Yet every officer in the Air Force would have a seizure at the thought of a pilotless Air Force," said the President, smiling.

"Fortunately, so would every serving officer in the Soviet Air Ministry, as well as those of their Eastern bloc captive nations. Think of it," the President said, leaning forward intently. "A military force unlike anything in history, based totally on to-day's and tomorrow's best products of science, and not held back by the baggage of previous conflicts.

"It would be beyond the traditional three-service concept. The battleship admirals and bomber generals would be part of the same strategic service, without the squabbling, without the ceaseless battling over funding, but most of all without the draining, debilitating effects of pursuing ancient history at the risk of our nation's security.

"Gentlemen, we are currently a nation whose Congress and military spend most of their waking hours debating the relative values of crossbows and maces, or chainmail and shields.

"It is only while our enemies are engaged in similar pursuits that we can both survive and sharpen our edge in national security. Now obviously, if we were to overtly rededicate our resources to such a concept as I've outlined, the Soviets would certainly follow suit. And we would shortly lose the overwhelming advantage it could give—lose it forever.

"The dilemma, then, is how to commit our resources to the new technologies over our internal opposition, without setting off all sorts of alarm bells in the Kremlin.

"The people around this table have the capability to begin to do it. You have, within your spheres of operations, the possibility to reshape, to remake the future of American air power—while, at the same time, keeping the Kremlin lulled into a more traditional approach.'

He rose from the table and, walking around behind the seven men still seated, paused now and then to touch several of them on the shoulders as he spoke.

"Gentlemen, we can't do it through traditional means. If I called together the Joint Chiefs of Staff, they'd mutiny. If I called together more than three members of the Cabinet, it would be in *The Washington Post* the next morning. If I confided in even one congressional subcommittee, it would be in the Kremlin by nightfall."

The President stopped at his chair and sat down, looking around the table at each of the seven men in turn, assessing the impact of his words.

"I must rely on you, here today. I want your clearest and best thoughts. It may never come to be, but if you believe what I believe, then by what we plan today and do tomorrow, our children and our grandchildren will have the confidence of living in a lasting peace."

He leaned back in his chair, lacing his fingers together. "Gentlemen, I'd like the Director here to outline a vital concomitant activity to the development of our new defense technology."

The bespectacled Director of Central Intelligence rose from the table and brushed his mustache with his index finger in a characteristic gesture. Then he began to unfold, for the first time, Plan Aurora.

And as the DCI addressed this small group in Maryland, the plan he unfolded was primarily the Fisherman's—although one other individual, technically outside the intelligence community, had also been a participating architect.

No one else in the Central Intelligence Agency knew of its existence.

The DCI, in spinning out the details of the Plan, had the rapt attention of every man in the room, for what they would decide today would chart the destiny of nations for decades to come.

Outside the farmhouse, the sun rose high, and the wind softened, and clouds scudded across a timeless sky.

40
OXON HILL, MARYLAND

Hornbill snapped out of his reverie. The ghosts in this place were strong, too strong to ever be dispelled.

He wondered about the man inside who had woven an almost impenetrable web of deception. Life had been seemingly simple when he, the Fisherman, and John Pretorius had been in college so many lives ago, when the world was young. Though perhaps not simple to the mind of the Fisherman, for he was born to his calling.

The Fisherman had now become, Hornbill realized, capable of anything, no matter how unthinkable. For it was the Fisherman who had masterminded the last twist to Aurora—the termination of John Pretorius' son—as if the young man were no more than an untidy bit to be disposed of, for the sake of the Operation.

The Operation. It was the Operation for which the Fisherman lived, and nothing more. Not for human passion of any sort, nor even for patriotism—but for the Operation, always the Operation.

Hornbill drew a deep breath and swung open the car door. He felt as he were being watched as he walked up to the deeply paneled front door. It had been years since he had passed through this door, years in which the world had altered radically.

The door was, he noticed, slightly open. He lifted its heavy knocker, a brass dolphin, and let it fall on its anvil with a satisfying sound. No sound came from within, no one came to the door.

Hornbill prodded the door open with his stubby forefinger, and it swung open easily, soundlessly. The door seemed to have been counterbalanced, and its hinges carefully lubricated.

The center hall inside was dark, musty. In the gloom he could make out oil paintings of landscapes, all with rivers and streams figuring prominently, covering the walls. Hornbill remembered the Fisherman loved his English and Scottish streams, and wondered if he still fished as devotedly as ever. In the old days at the Agency, a dog-eared first edition of Izaak Walton's *The Compleat Angler* held pride of place on his desk. Hornbill knew it was not simply a prop; the Fisherman had read from it almost daily, especially evenings, when the pains and pressures of the job required a momentary distraction.

Perhaps it was the pain, accumulated over the decades, which had driven the Fisherman to become a creature of unrelenting ruthlessness, an individual possessing a passion so amoral it could not even be described as evil. Whatever it was, the Fisherman—

"Come in, Arthur," a voice rasped out from the library opening off the hallway. "I've been expecting you for some time now."

The library, too, was dark. No light illumined its recesses, except that which filtered in from the drawn curtains. The harpoons and other weapons which lined the walls were only slightly visible, dark shapes against an even darker background. Hornbill squinted in the gloom until he could pick out the skeletal figure seated in the wheelchair near the fireplace. "Please have a seat, Arthur. You must be tired from your drive." The Fisherman waved an emaciated arm toward a leather wing chair near him.

Hornbill could not believe the change that had overtaken his friend of years past. The Fisherman, although a shade over six feet in height, had shrunk to a cadaverous thinness. He could not, Hornbill realized, weigh much above one hundred pounds.

Easing himself carefully into the capacious chair, he could not take his eyes off the Fisherman. "It's been—how long?—fifteen years?" he managed to say.

"And I've changed, is your unspoken observation. Yes, I have changed. In many ways. But then our enemies require change, don't they, Arthur. You and I were good together, in the days when good was good and bad was bad, the good guys were always plainly identifiable, and we played by a definite series of rules. No more, Arthur. Sadly for everyone, no more."

Hornbill wondered why the Fisherman's head had that odd slightly weaving, side-to-side motion; he'd seen it before. It was as if the Fisherman were using that motion to take his bearings, to get a sense of placement of things around him. And then he realized:

The Fisherman was blind, totally blind.

"You're too quiet, Arthur. Not like you. You're the one who always had to fill in the silences; now it seems to be me."

"How long have you been blind?" Hornbill asked, realizing a strange tension occupied the room, unlike anything he'd ever experienced. Was it his imagination, or was something operative beyond his own senses?

"Ah. Always perceptive, as I might have known. About eight years; but I have little need of sight now. My housekeeper reads to me, and I find that soothing, even more relaxing than reading for myself. My legs have precluded me getting around easily, so I'm not terribly likely to bang into things from lack of seeing them. It's odd how being blind enables one to use the other senses better. For example, my hearing is really rather extraordinary now, especially for someone my age. One even learns to recognize the different sounds of the seasons, as well."

"I'm sorry, really I am," Hornbill ventured.

An odd smile twisted the Fisherman's face. "Oh, don't waste

your pity on me, old friend. It's the rest of the world that's to be pitied. The poor fools who will not see."

"How so?" asked Hornbill, shifting his weight in the chair.

"You know. You know as well as I, or you should," retorted the Fisherman. "How many times must you be shot down from your white charger to realize we're in a different world? The old morality is like tilting at windmills; only the strong can possibly prevail. Those who will not flinch at what must be done, no matter how repugnant to smaller minds, in order to carry the battle to the enemy.

"You and I began together in an altogether different world, Arthur. A world where differences were clear, and roles were easy to play. We all were playing our little roles, we all had our acts and entrances, our exits and applause. You helped win over a madman in Germany? Very well, kindly accept this tiny bit of ribbon as a token of our esteem. You dropped a bomb which extinguished the lives of thousands? Good show. Have this shred of parchment which we've prepared with our very own signature to show we are pleased.

"But life begins to be complicated in our trade, yours and mine. How about the lives we expend, lives of our own people, to prevent the shedding of still more lives? Churchill knew the feeling, when he could have prevented the bombing of Coventry, and knew he mustn't let the enemy know we'd broken their codes; he knew, right enough." The Fisherman slumped back in his wheelchair, painfully gathering his breath. His chest heaved with the effort, and tiny flecks of spittle trickled down from one side of his mouth.

"And what about the killing of John Pretorius' son?" Hornbill said, leaning forward from his chair. "Is he expendable too?"

A strange laughter issued from the bloodless lips of the Fisherman. "Expendable? God, what an old-fashioned term! Of course, Arthur. But it's like asking, Does he breathe? Does he consume food? Being expendable is the human *condition*, old friend. We've always—all of us—*always* been expendable. If we weren't, those of us who are in our trade, well then, we would be useless, wouldn't we?"

"And so young Pretorius must die?" Hornbill pursued.

"If he doesn't, then Aurora may be needlessly jeopardized." The Fisherman's fists pounded on the arms of his wheelchair. "Do you know how many billions of dollars, how many years of work, and how many lives could be forfeit if he is *not* terminated?" He sank back into his pillows, exhausted.

"But we don't *know* that. And at worst, the odds of that ever happening are, well, frankly minuscule," retorted Hornbill.

"Would you gamble everything on even those odds, Arthur?" spat out the Fisherman. "Would you indeed? Well, then, you haven't grown wise with age, old friend. You've grown careless. Too careless."

Hornbill, at that moment, knew the Fisherman was beyond any reasoning. He also knew that Aurora, if it were to succeed, would be at the cost of the lives of everyone associated with it, including himself. If the Fisherman had concluded that his friend's son must die for it, then why not Arthur Hornbill himself? Was he not, by the Fisherman's definition, expendable? Could the Fisherman ever rest, once Aurora was complete and had succeeded, knowing a single person could blow the entire operation? A tingling coldness flooded his body.

At that moment Hornbill knew the Fisherman had made his decision years ago. Had, in fact, overseen the education and early training of John Pretorius' son just for this operation.

Hornbill got to his feet and his hand slowly moved for the revolver snugged against his hip in its high-ride holster. "No, I wouldn't, Arthur," came the oddly disembodied voice of the Fisherman, as he pulled away a portion of his lap robe to reveal the lethal snout of a sawed-off shotgun. "Being sightless endows one with—other advantages. A heightened sense of sound, as I said. Do you know I can hear the rustle of fabric, especially the tweed of which you've always been so fond, and know not only precisely where you are in the room, but the position of your arms? Intriguing, really. So don't, please, do anything so ill-advised as reaching for your weapon. You must know it's over, anyway."

"Yes, I've figured that much out." The Fisherman relaxed his stance, being careful not to make any unusual moves. "It's over for one of us, at any rate."

"No, Arthur," the Fisherman softly laughed. A dry, rasping sound that carried no mirth. "Really only for you, and for your friend there."

Hornbill wheeled involuntarily to see Pretorius standing in the gloom by the open library door.

41

MOSCOW, UNION OF SOVIET SOCIALIST REPUBLICS

COMINTSurvRep 003678/FC/ND (OP:AURORA, SENIOR STRETCH, DSCS/ROFA
Location: Ministry of Defense, Ulitsa Kirova 37, Moscow 103160.
Subject Surveillance: S. L. Sokolov, MSU; S. F. Akhromeyev, MSU; A. M. Yefimov, MASU.
Login: 1300 GMT, 10/27/90.
Source: Omicron 67.
(Note: Subjects monitored are Sergei Leonidovich Sokolov, MSU, Minister of Defense; Sergei Fedorovich Akhromeyev, MSU, First Deputy Minister, General Staff; and Marshal of Aviation Aleksandr Mikolayevich Yefimov, Deputy Minister, Air Forces. Due to unfavorable transmission conditions, some sections are technically unreliable and are therefore deleted; still others have required computer-aided reconstruction.)

SLS: (TRANSMISSION FAULT) . . . new direction should take us far. Your people will have much to do, now that we've unearthed the Americans' intentions.
AMY: Yes, Comrade Minister. The Americans have never been proficient at chess . . . (TRANSMISSION FAULT) . . .

corruption of the system intrudes too often on the purity of logic. And logic is essential in any strategic . . . (TRANSMIS-SION FAULT) . . . one so vast as this.

SLS: The Politburo will take some convincing.

AMY: With respect, if they do not have the ability to accept the clear evidence, then we are all in the bear's mouth.

SFA: Our comrades in the *Komitet* have lost a great deal. The American Federal Bureau of Investigation has finally stopped reading their own propaganda and started working: The KGB has lost many good people there, just in the past week. I have heard they seem to feel there is a connection between this American agent and the arrests . . .

AMY: It could easily be. Possibly a retribution for our abduction of him, although . . . (TRANSMISSION FAULT) . . . not know in whose hands he had been.

SLS: Come now, Comrade Marshal . . . even the Americans would know. Who else could it have been other than KGB? Father Christmas?

AMY: Whatever it cost the KGB, at least we have the ammunition we need to go before the Politburo. It has to be counted as the single biggest intelligence coup of the last two decades.

SLS: It seems almost inconceivable that the Americans thought they could conceal their new strategic bomber initiative from us . . . they even kept their little secret from their own CIA. But that, of course, is understandable . . .

AMY: As is well known, they are children in many ways, Comrade Minister. They believe what they want to believe. They want to believe we will honor any treaty we sign with them, so they *do* believe. They want to believe we won't know about their stealth technology, so they *do* believe. Children. Big, simple, clumsy children . . . so easily seduced by a smile . . .

SLS: And yet, we *had* fallen into their little trap for years, believing they were going for laser defense networks, cruise missiles, and such, rather than the strategic stealth bomber initiative . . . (TRANSMISSION FAULT) of value . . .

SFA: It has cost us billions so far. Billions literally flung into outer space . . . we won't make the same mistake twice.

SLS: We must focus more than ever on the strategic bomber initiative and not allow them to keep this edge . . .

AMY: My people have the prototypes on the boards right now. We've only to get them funded, and the future is ours, Comrades.

SLS: We shall be depending . . . (TRANSMISSION FAULT) . . . and more in the years ahead, Comrade Marshal . . .

AMY: The Ministry shall not fail.

SFA: I know, I know. But we are talking when instead we should be doing . . . and there is much to do before next week.

SLS: Until then, Comrades.

(SOUNDS OF CHAIRS SCRAPING, THEN SOUND OF DOOR OPENING AND CLOSING. TRANSMISSION ENDS.)
(Logout: 1309 GMT)

42

OXON HILL,
MARYLAND

The Fisherman swung up the sawed-off shotgun, and both Hornbill and Pretorius inhaled sharply. Grasping the stock with one clawlike hand, a skeletal finger caressing the trigger, the ravaged figure craned forward:

"Who are you, there? One of Arthur's bodyguards?" rasped out the Fisherman's voice, knife-edged with unease.

"No. My name is Pretorius."

The Fisherman's expression never changed. But one could sense the mind behind it chirring and working, the variables being computed, the decision being made. Keeping the shotgun leveled at a point precisely between the two men, the Fisherman remained motionless for what seemed, to Pretorius and Hornbill, a minor eternity.

Finally, the lips parted, and were moistened by his tongue in a darting, lizardlike movement. "Well, young Michael, it appears we finally meet. *No, no, gentlemen. Stay exactly where you are.* I prefer no moves from that side of the room; it would—disturb my tranquility. And," he continued with the same sightless, expressionless stare, "in your case, it would disturb infinitely more.

"Now then, Arthur, you first: withdraw your revolver—I assume you still favor a revolver?—from its holster and drop it on the carpet in front of you. Then you, young Michael. I assure you my finger will pull this trigger if I hear anything, or sense anything, which seems different from that which I expect."

Hornbill complied with the order carefully, lifting his three-inch barrelled Model 13 from its shoulder holster and placing it on the floor, his unblinking eyes never leaving the man in the wheelchair. Then Pretorius followed suit.

"Thank you, gentlemen," the Fisherman continued, now easing back into his chair and lowering the weapon's snout. "I wish devoutly I could see you, young Michael. Even more, that I could spare you. That last time we met, your father brought you here when you were five or six. I've—taken an interest in your career over the years, Michael, although I've had to stay somewhat in the background. You sound remarkably like your father. You seem to be about as tall, as well."

Pretorius edged closer. But the Fisherman's voice suddenly froze him: "*No.* No closer. I think you both had best stay where you are. Arthur, please sit back down. There is something I must tell you, before we play out our—endgame."

He waited until Hornbill sat down slowly in the big creased leather chair, cracked and capacious as a gargantuan catcher's mitt. "By now, Arthur, you will have discovered there is a second team to Aurora, operating exclusively at my direction. They were recruited over the years from some of the best. I needed a cadre of men who were totally compartmentalized, completely removed from any knowledge of Aurora itself, and wholly under my control.

"You see, I'd always known you could never take Aurora to its logical conclusion, Arthur. You were always good, but too soft to deal with—a higher logic. And for Aurora to succeed, succeed utterly, no one—absolutely no one—must compromise even a fraction of it."

"What are you talking about?" interrupted Pretorius warily, moving slightly closer to the wall near the fireplace.

"*No! Stop right there!*" snapped the Fisherman, his shotgun instantly leveled at Pretorius with uncanny accuracy. From its angle, Pretorius knew a single blast would destroy most organs in his abdomen within a fraction of a second.

Hornbill, his voice kept carefully even, urged, "Michael, don't move any further. He's fully capable of killing you; we both know that."

Pretorius halted and kept his hands carefully still. "Who in God's name *are* you?" he asked of the emaciated figure in the wheelchair.

"My name is John Moses Sharpless," he began in a thin, reedlike tone that seemed to be produced from the thin chest at great effort. "The name, I trust, is not entirely unfamiliar to you, although I've been retired for some years now. Your father and I were quite close at one time. He, as you must have gathered by now, was an extremely important man to us. Not only during the War, but when he become more involved with us in the 1950s. So important, in fact, to a particular operation of ours that he was killed. By one of the KGB's best penetration agents, working inside the Agency. We think it was Bobkov himself, but we can't be sure.

At this, Pretorius drew in his breath sharply.

"Yes," continued the Fisherman, "quite a man. He somehow never seemed to take the trade as seriously as some of us. But he had a natural, almost effortless aptitude for it. Arthur here also worked with your father and me in those halcyon days, when one knew precisely who the enemy was, and could act accordingly. But those times, as all things, changed.

"And so the Agency became populated by amateurs and cretins, by bureaucrats and bunglers of the very worse sort. Its ultimate penetration, given the conditions, was inevitable. A child could have done it, let alone the largest intelligence *apparat* in the world.

"As Arthur can tell you, when I revealed how easily the Agency could be penetrated—and, in fact, *was* and *is* penetrated—I was ridiculed. When I persisted, I was dismissed. And for a while, until they finally lost interest in me, I became the butt of every cheap joke in the Washington cocktail circuit.

"No one wanted to know how badly we'd become compromised. Even those who knew were privately warned not to push it any further, if they wanted to continue with their careers in the Agency.

"But my dismissal served my purposes well. In fact, it gave me the freedom to evolve my plans further, without the bureaucratic interference the Agency had begun to accumulate as part of its working style.

"My *magnum opus*, my masterpiece—Aurora—was still in place, still intact. In fact, due to the meddling of the new DCI at the time, the few officers who were aware of parts of it were fired for various reasons, and they all, within months of their dismissals, either died of natural causes or met with accidental deaths.

"Only a handful of individuals now remain within its circle; the President, of course; the Secretary of Defense; three members of Congress; a very few individuals in private industry; two people in the Bureau of the Budget; and, of course, Arthur and I and now yourself. Even then, very few know of our recent gambit with Michael, here. And I'm quite sure not even Michael knows of his real value in Aurora."

The scream of a pheasant outside caused the Fisherman to interrupt his head's slow, side-to-side weaving for a second, but neither Pretorius nor Hornbill dared move.

The Fisherman continued, wetting the purpled crevice of his mouth. "Michael, you will be somewhat dismayed to know that under narcosis you spilled everything you knew about the new superstealth bomber, the B(AT)-3. Not just your cover story, but *all* your knowledge, as well as your true identity."

He smiled at Pretorius, who now wore an expression of unutterable horror, then continued smoothly. "But it was precisely what we intended. We had programmed you to do exactly that."

"What do you mean?" Pretorius rapped out. "You sent me in there to be turned inside out *purposely?*"

"Yes, and you succeeded admirably. Our friends are now convinced our entire defense strategy is predicated on stealth technology, and that SDI is merely an arms control pawn, something to be held out as a bargaining point. When, in fact, developing and refining the technologies of space defense has been our whole objective, ever since John Kennedy was in the White House, and MacNamara began the first stages of its implementation. NASA, in fact, was not begun as the font of civilian discovery it was ballyhooed as, but as an organization to probe the military uses of space.

"The Space Defense Initiative, even in its current crippled state, is only one result of all this. To provide SDI and other programs with the protection they need to survive until they are completely in place, we created Aurora. But Aurora evolved into something far bigger.

"You see, Michael, the real arms race has never been the mere stockpiling of ICBMs and such. It is, instead, a war of economics, of the strategic deployment of defense budgets. The objective is always economic victory. And now, with the collapse of the Soviet economy within view, the value of Aurora is incalculable."

Pretorius stared at the shrunken specter in the chair. "You mean this is all some—some bizarre form of economic warfare? There is no stealth bomber program, apart from this scheme of yours, this *Aurora?*"

The Fisherman laughed, a noise devoid of joy, empty of humanity. "No, no, my dear boy. Stealth bombers do exist. At least the Northrop B-2 and the Rockwell B-1B exist. But their real objective has been, quite simply, to keep the Soviets thinking we're still besotted by bombers and fighters and to force them into increasing their defenses against penetration bombing and other conventional forms of warfare.

"By diverting billions of the Soviet defense budget over a period of decades, we've accomplished more than entire armies or navies, at remarkably little expense.

"It might interest you, Michael, to know each new generation of our aircraft stealth technology causes a corresponding increase in Soviet radar defense spending of *five times* our investment in the new technology. How much better, then, not to even fully develop the aircraft—but rather to *seem* as if we did—for far less expenditure, and in much less time. The B(AT)-3 Superstealth bomber, sad to say, does *not* exist; what you saw was essentially a reconstructed Tupolev Blackjack, with some very real stealth modifications.

"It came into being when it became obvious even to the Soviets that both the B-1B and the B-2 had so many shortcomings, they couldn't possibly be counted as our main thrust. The B1-B had become a joke; its electronic countermeasures couldn't even handle half the threats under what was, by any standards, a test program which was generous to a fault, an instrument landing system that restricted the aircraft to localizer minimums, and materiel failures that defied the laws of probability.

"There was also the fact that the B-2's announced mission of destroying ground threats during a thermonuclear exchange couldn't be taken seriously by anyone outside of a lunatic asylum.

"We couldn't keep up the pretense on those two for much longer. Yet we needed more time. Not a lot, simply more than the B-1B and B-2 could then buy us, now that their limitations were very nearly public knowledge. Now that the Soviets are scrambling for western credits, they're especially vulnerable to economic deception.

"Our COMINT from Meade also told us the Kremlin planners were beginning to look harder at our SDI sources and at other aspects of our space technologies. We couldn't have that, of course, and so we had to infuse a simulation of new investments in our strategic bomber program. We needed just enough time to get certain pieces of hardware, including our long-term lasers, in orbit. Enter the B(AT)-3.

"It played directly to their egos by inexpensively—compared to our B-1B and B-2 investments—converting a Tupolev Blackjack to a new stealth configuration, and feeding their CI people just enough tidbits of technology. They've already begun to believe we're developing an even more formidable strategic bomber along lines they themselves had already been pursuing. Much more believable: Their own genius was confirmed. Which, of course, is where you've served so admirably. You couldn't possibly have acted it out better, *simply because you weren't acting.*

"You were, to them, a trained intelligence officer, a totally believable professional, spilling his guts out. Because of your cover, and the rather obvious programming we gave you, once they peeled away that layer you were all the more credible. And you gave us the added bonus of smoking out some of our internal enemies within CIA. We've probably identified more penetration agents through you than any five or six separate operations previously."

And the Fisherman laughed, a rasping, hacking parody of a laugh which became a cough, and the spectral figure sank back into his chair, exhausted.

Pretorius stared at Hornbill. "Is what he saying true? That the whole idea, this Aurora, is something to divert their spending away from countering our real defense efforts in space?"

Hornbill nodded. "If we can continue to convince the Soviets to spend more in countering conventional air power, we not only gain time, but we divert billions away from their efforts to counter our real technologies—SDI, among others.

"For example, our laser pointing and control technology, which the Soviets have been desperately trying to obtain up in Teterboro and other places, can identify and destroy any offensive weapon within seconds. Far more effective than conventional weaponry, stealthy or not. Indeed, gravity bombs and even most forms of cruise missiles have no place in the defenses of the future, and so aircraft to carry them are—by concept and definition—obsolete.

"But there is a larger aspect to Aurora, something which has kept it fueled all these years, waiting for this moment. We'd known, even back in the 1960s, that Soviet statistics had been cooked to disguise some genuine, and potentially disastrous, economic problems.

"Indeed, every year since then, the same "doctoring" of the statistics has given us no end of trouble in deciphering what, precisely, is going on with the Soviet economy. Until, as General Secretary Gorbachev found upon taking office, the ills were too numerous and disastrous to sweep under the carpet. Enter *glasnost*. And then his cherished *perestroika*.

"One really has to admire Gorbachev's appreciation of our naivete. Think about it. In his simulated *perestroika*, the only thing he'd really disarmed is American public opinion. No matter that in the past year, according to our own DOD reports, Russia produced twice as many fighter bombers and fighter aircraft and seventeen times as many nuclear-capable artillery pieces and rocket launchers as America. The amazing thing is, while he's doing this, *he's actually getting America's banks to help finance his war machine, his ICBMs, his everything.* You might expect the West German banks to finance him; after all, they finance Gadaffi as well. But U.S. banks? Our capacity for naivete is really staggering.

"Despite the General Secretary's guile in extracting western credits, the Soviet economy is teetering on the brink of an abyss. The true statistics from the *Gosudarstvennyy Byudzhet SSSR* reveal a hidden budget deficit of 130 billion rubles this year: *close to $208 billion U.S.* The long lines in the streets, created by shortages of basic consumer goods like bread and milk and canned goods: It's all come home to roost. A misdirected budget, the size of what it would take to counter something like a bigger, newer, more sophisticated version of stealth, could be catastrophic."

As Hornbill spoke, Pretorius watched the thin figure of the Fisherman, the head still moving in that odd side-to-side motion. "And so I seem to have been your pet guinea pig—"

Hornbill protested, "You've not been a guinea pig, Michael. You've been crucial to Aurora's success. Without you, nothing would have been possible. You've been the critical element in what will someday be recognized as America's most important intelligence scheme in decades."

The Fisherman's hacking charade of a laugh once more pierced the tranquility of the room. "I quite agree with Arthur. I wish it didn't have to be taken to its logical conclusion; you could have had an excellent career in our trade, otherwise—"

Throughout Hornbill's explanation, the Fisherman's head seemed to be weaving in a slightly more emphatic pattern. Pretorius sensed he was trying to get a more exact position on the two of them. And could only be doing so for one reason.

It would be only a split second between blasts of the shotgun as it would swivel from its first target to its second. And the Fisherman's sense of sound was easily accurate enough to give him a fix for his targets in the room. Carefully, Pretorius gauged the distance between himself and the wall.

And then, speaking slightly louder than normal, he began moving his hand toward his pocket, as if in a slow-motion film. "But why on earth should you kill us, especially now?" Pretorius began. "Surely neither one of us would ever compromise the operation."

"Ah, but there you're wrong, quite wrong," interrupted the Fisherman. "There are a thousand ways in which you could destroy it. For example, Michael, your face is now quite well known to the opposition. And the opposition would, I'm sure, like to be permitted to speak with you a bit more—which, of course, we couldn't permit. They had just enough of you for you to be convincing. More prolonged interrogation would, I think, have deleterious effects on your believability.

"Will you then live in an hermetically sealed canister for the rest of your natural life? Or will you take the risk of someday being identified by someone who will show you to Moscow Center?

"No, no, you're far too volatile an element to exist in a natural state. And you, Arthur, your usefulness is, alas, over. You don't imagine, after what you've done to my little network, I could possibly permit you to further endanger the operation. And so, for quite separate reasons, you must both have—your separate exits."

By this time, Pretorius' fingers had finally reached their goal: the keys in his pocket.

It was over in seconds.

Pretorius hurled the keys off to one side of the Fisherman and they had the desired effect: his head jerked in that direction as he swung the shotgun up. Which gave the split second of time needed for Pretorius to reach the wall as Hornbill dived to the floor with speed surprising for a man of his age and bulk.

The Fisherman fired the shotgun at the precise position in which Hornbill and Pretorius had been an instant before. But in that instant, Pretorius had jerked the Greener harpoon gun from its cradle on the wall and pulled its trigger.

With an ear-splitting explosion, the charge sent a five-and-a-half-pound steel harpoon hurtling through the air, trailing and whipping the thick nylon line, the huge arrowlike head plunging through the old man's ribcage, transfixing him to the wooden back of the wheelchair.

The Fisherman gasped soundlessly, once, twice, his mouth forming a questioning O, like some ancient landed fish.

Pretorius stood motionless a long time before slowly, ever so slowly, turning and walking out the door into the darkness, the Greener loosely dangling from his hand.

43
NEW YORK
AND VIRGINIA

Karger nodded his good mornings to Lex, the curiously named Indonesian hallman and to Mike, the doorman who never commented on anything but the weather. "Looks like another nice fall day, Mr. Karger. Might cloud up later though."

"Sure looks it, Mike," he replied automatically, stepping out into the crispness of what was, indeed, one of those perfect days in which New York seemed to be even more alive than usual.

Karger's usual practice was to walk down Park Avenue as far as 57th Street, then to walk over to Fifth, then down to his firm's offices in Rockefeller Center. And this morning, as he strode out, he felt more at ease than he had since the phone call last weekend. The air felt good, and he inhaled deeply. *God, it was good to be alive on a day like this*, he thought.

The sun was gently warming as he stepped off the curb at 72nd Street. A friend passed him in a sweat suit, jogging down Park Avenue. Karger thought of his own slowly thickening waistline and considered whether or not he should take some more formal exercise.

His wife, Bev, went to an exercise class every day, which in part accounted for her trim, lithe figure, although it also accounted for altogether too much of her conversation. Yes, he'd have to sign up for some sort of regimen at the club, something not too boring. He hated exercise for exercise's sake. Maybe Doc, the head of the club's fitness department, could concoct some sort of every-other-day plan to take off some of the weight, and give him a little more tone in his muscles.

There seemed to be something familiar about the man in front of him. Now, as he crossed 70th Street, he realized the man, dressed in a raglan shoulder tan raincoat, had been maintaining precisely the same distance since 76th Street. Had he seen the man before? Maybe yes, maybe no. He couldn't be sure. He dismissed the thought.

To the left, the new Asia House rose in red granite serenity above the people hurrying past it. Karger had been to a number of receptions there, usually fund-raising affairs for some of his candidates. Occasionally, as a steady giver to many New York cultural affairs, he was courted by various committees as a target himself.

Target. Of course. He stopped in his tracks and, as if he had suddenly remembered something he'd left at home, he looked first at his watch, and then behind him.

There, approximately forty feet away, were two men—each with hands in raincoat pockets, no attaché cases—moving toward him. He twisted back and noticed two things simultaneously: One, the presence of a plain black car now just ahead of him, moving along Park Avenue slowly, too slowly. And two, the man in the raincoat in front of him and stopped and turned, and seemed to be waiting, a patient, almost sad smile on his face. As if finally meeting a friend after a long wait.

Karger knew these men were FBI. They had the look, and the setup was traditional. He let out a slow, even breath and he walked forward to the agent in front.

"Mr. Karger?" asked the tall young man with a pleasant smile.

"Yes?" he replied as casually as he could, although his breathing seemed suddenly to be more difficult.

As the agent's left hand left his raincoat pocket and started to bring out his federal ID, Karger was suddenly aware of the black sedan pulling up to the curb alongside him, the doors opening, and agents getting out. He felt his arms being gripped as the young agent said, "Special Agent Kapelsohn, FBI. You're being placed under arrest on suspicion of espionage and treason in violation of federal statutes, title 18, section 798 and 2381. You have the right to remain silent—"

As the agent read him his rights, Karger suddenly became aware of sharp pain in his right arm and shoulder, of an unexpected shortness of breath.

The agents caught him as he crumpled, snapped on the cuffs and placed him firmly in the backseat of the sedan, one agent on either side bracketing him. The driver accelerated as the agent in the front passenger seat reached out the window and placed the magnet-based red flasher on the roof. The entire action had taken less than a minute, and few passersby were even aware of the slight ripple in the pattern of their lives.

In Alexandria, Virginia, Frank O'Connor was in his car on the way to Langley when he noticed a tag in his rearview mirror.

He was not alarmed, as it was standard practice for CIA officers to be placed under surveillance by the Agency from time to time. It was also standard practice for him to report such surveillances if noticed, in case the interest was not the Agency's.

The shadow car fell back a few lengths, then disappeared. O'Connor watched to see if a replacement vehicle would be brought forward. Scanning his mirror, he couldn't find it at first. Then he noticed a gray van with two men in front, both wearing sunglasses. *Shit*, he thought, *Won't they ever learn? They've always got to announce who they are. No wonder the Agency is so fucked up.* He grinned.

Getting on the parkway, he saw the van being replaced by a gray Ford, which seemed to be closing the distance quickly. This was no longer a covert tail; this was very open, very official. *What in hell*, he thought, as the Ford pulled alongside and one of the two men inside motioned for him to pull over.

He eased his Plymouth onto the shoulder of the road and the Ford parked in position four car lengths behind. As the agents got out, another car—which O'Connor had failed to notice before—pulled in front and the occupants stepped out, one with a riot gun leveled directly at O'Connor's head. He placed his hands in plain sight on top of the steering wheel.

One of the agents from the car behind him came alongside with drawn revolver and ID case out. "Federal Bureau of Investigation, Mr. O'Connor. Step out of the car, please."

O'Connor briefly considered driving the car straight at the agent in front with the shotgun, taking his chances on the reactions of the agent alongside with the revolver, but realized he'd have a far better chance later, once his control at the Agency got involved. Yet something told him this was part of something big, something even bigger than what he had going in the Agency.

O'Connor and Karger were only two of a total of 115 individuals arrested by agents of the Federal Bureau of Investigation that morning. The carefully coordinated net was arranged in concert with officials of the Defense Intelligence Agency as well as with the cooperation of the Central Intelligence Agency at the very highest level.

This latter cooperation consisted in the DCI and his Executive Assistant being informed by the FBI that a number of arrests within the Agency were imminent—in fact, would occur within the next hour—and that they would be shortly informed of the identities of the personnel concerned.

The people at Langley were aghast at this treatment. And when a representative of The New York Times asked an Agency spokesperson about the rumor of imminent arrests, the young woman replied with characteristic hauteur, "We don't comment on such things as a matter of policy"—when in reality she was as hopelessly at sea as the DCI himself.

Admiral Wakefield was apoplectic. With all the blustering, righteous anger he could muster, he demanded to know whose authority was behind this unprecedented intervention in Agency affairs, including the identities of those under suspicion.

A cool FBI Director's assistant replied he was not at liberty to disclose that information due to Bureau policy, and Wakefield almost strangled on his own anger.

44

WASHINGTON, D.C.,
AND MOSCOW, U.S.S.R

It had been several months since the CIA/KGB arrests, and damage to U.S. prestige abroad had been incalculable.

The British, despite all the highly placed MI5 and MI6 officers who had been moles for the KGB over the last four decades, suddenly and sharply cut their communications with the U.S. intelligence community. Although the U.S. had been forbearing in the cases of Burgess, McLean, Philby, Blake, and Blunt, the British did not see their way clear to return the courtesy.

Meanwhile, news within the intelligence community came thick and fast. Admiral Wakefield Palmer, Director of Central Intelligence, respectfully tendered his resignation. Dick Coldwell was brought in from London as acting DCI. Massive changes were taking place on both sides of the Potomac.

Rumors of a new intelligence entity were circulating among the Georgetown set. Some said an NSCID *(National Security Council Intelligence Directive)* had been handed down asking for recommendations for assimilating the civilian and military intelligence agencies into one super agency. The new agency would be created in the new year, combining NSA, CIA, DIA, INR, and the three service agencies into a single unit within the Department of Defense.

Intelligence work, the proponents of reorganization argued,

is an activity which has application only for defense purposes, and is as integral a part of defense planning and operations as any of the traditional military branches, and to now consider it a thing apart was seen as either folly or irresponsible elitism. Their corollary argument was that the line between political intelligence and military intelligence was nowadays almost wholly arbitrary.

CIA paramilitary operations were to be combined with certain specialized portions of the Army and Marine Corps, and organized into a new DOD group mobilized as a counterguerilla, counterterrorist strike force deployed at pressure points around the world.

Richard Helms, testifying at the Senate hearings on Intelligence reorganization, gave a cogent and thoroughly convincing analysis on the whole supporting reorganization.

Only a few members of both houses of Congress, including Senator Gary Klein of New York, opposed it. The recent arrests, though, had shaken almost everyone else's faith in a separate CIA integrity.

Novoye Vremya (The New Times), in contrast and not altogether unexpectedly, decried the move as "yet another example of the western imperialist war machine generating yet another spy apparatus to oppress peace-loving peoples everywhere."

Georgi Arbatov, head of the Institute for the Study of the U.S.A. and Canada, acting in his KGB-assigned role of promoting "a feast of reason and a flow of the soul," denounced the reorganization as military turf-grabbing, detrimental to the interests of Russian-American understanding.

Curiously enough, at about the same time Arbatov was posturing in his predictable way, one of his lieutenants at the Soviet Embassy in Washington, Valentin Mikhailovich Berezhkov, whose Chekist history runs forty-five years back to Stalin, was arrested by agents of the FBI in Livermore, California.

This long-time apostle of peace was allegedly attempting to talk an employee of the Department of Energy nuclear weapons lab into compromising their "Octopus" network of Cray and Control Data supercomputers.

Protest groups throughout the United States and abroad, neatly stimulated by KGB-trained organizers, held rallies against the proposed Combined Intelligence Group.

In much the same way that leftist linguists had helped Soviet propagandists by dubbing the Strategic Defense Initiative with the wholly inaccurate, reckless-sounding label "Star Wars," protesters somehow began using "Military-Spy Complex" for the new intelligence structure.

Still, after all the hearings had been held, after all the protesters had ranted and chanted, and all the press had nearly exhausted the subject, one unassailable fact remained, to Moscow Center's consternation:

The proposed Defense Intelligence Force could emerge as the single strongest, most efficient intelligence organization in the western democracies.

Internecine squabbles, which had plagued the intelligence community for decades before, would dwindle, though never quite disappear. Data collection and analysis would be less subject to inter-agency sanitizing and stonewalling.

A new counterintelligence section in the existing CIA was set up by Coldwell, with the good advice of Arthur Hornbill, who monitored the new CI unit until it was able to operate wholly on its own.

That stage was realized when it unearthed a fresh KGB attempt to burrow within, and Coldwell's CI officers turned the would-be moles into unwitting triples against Moscow Center.

In Moscow Center itself, the KGB congratulated itself on its coup in the Vojtec/Pretorius affair, through which they'd managed to unmask the United States' well-hidden strategic stealth bomber program through their skillful interrogation of a top DIA agent.

KGB Deputy Chairman Filipp Denisovich Bobkov, for his personal role in supervising the highly sensitive operation, was made a Hero of the Soviet Union. Several KGB officers in the field were given promotions and letters of recommendation. The Ministry of Defense made a highly convincing presentation to the Politburo and was rewarded by receiving permission to shift budgets and manpower away from outer space technology and into the far more urgent stealth bomber offensive and defensive measures.

Marshal of Aviation Aleksandr Mikolayevich Yefimov initiated three major programs which would see fruition sometime in the mid-1990s, including a massive early detection system to guard against the Americans' superior B(AT)-3.

These new programs diverted massive amounts of money away from other areas of Soviet defense, particularly space defense technology.

Within the Presidium, the new focus was held to be a wise redeployment of budgets: the U.S. superstealth bomber initiative was clearly the largest single threat to Soviet security in decades.

The U.S.S.R. budget deficit grew another fifteen million rubles. A cabal of U.S. banks, recently enlightened about the true state of the Soviet economy, had visions of revisiting their recent Third World debt default scenario, and began calling in loans as well as repulsing recent attempts by General Secretary Gorbachev's smiling minions to gain even more credits for the *Rodina*.

Perestroika, it seemed, was no longer fashionable.

45
NEAR DARTMOUTH, IN DEVONSHIRE

The venerable Norton, its metal contracting in the cool evening winds after its run up the old Roman road, made small crackling sounds, contrasting oddly with Pretorius' harmonica.

Sitting with his back against the hilltop's solitary oak, Pretorius played his harmonica, spinning out a tune of his own invention. At times the tune vaguely resembled a fugue, but then seemed to verge on a blues. Only Pretorius himself would have known precisely what it was he was attempting. In fact, it was merely the musical equivalent of daydreaming, and Pretorius was, serenely unaware of it.

The notes floated downhill until, somewhere in the cool still air near the edge of the trees, they disappeared altogether.

It was one of the early evenings of spring, and Pretorius had once again come here in a sort of pilgrimage, a search for his own tranquility.

The nightmares were getting less frequent now. In the first few months after Aurora, Pretorius would suddenly sit bolt upright in bed, sweat glistening from every pore, eyes wide with terror. Susannah would soothe and hush him, and afterward he would sink back to a deep, dreamless sleep, her arms encircling him protectively.

David Lloyd George, at Susannah's insistence, came to live

at the cottage with Michael. The dog became inseparable from Michael, following him everywhere, sleeping at the foot of his bed, and even doing a creditable job of deterring the rabbits from their depredations of the garden. In fact, it looked as if this spring there would be a bumper crop.

Susannah was spending more and more time with Michael (and, of course, the Dreaded DLG) at the cottage now, and had hired an assistant to run her restaurant on days she was away. She'd begun to like the idea of not being forever tied to the restaurant, and Pretorius was happy to have her with him.

Sitting now on the hill with the mists beginning to settle, Pretorius wondered at his great good fortune at being in this place and at simply being alive.

It was quiet here, and he could see lights beginning to wink on in the valley below.

It was time to go home.